DAUGHTER
OF
DARKNESS

Mandy M. Roth

NCP

Be sure to check out our website for the very best in fiction at fantastic prices!

When you visit our webpage, you can:

* Read excerpts of currently available books
* View cover art of upcoming books and current releases
* Find out more about the talented artists who capture the magic of the writer's imagination on the covers
* Order books from our backlist
* Find out the latest NCP and author news--including any upcoming book signings by your favorite NCP author
* Read author bios and reviews of our books
* Get NCP submission guidelines
* And so much more!

We offer a 20% discount on all new ebook releases!
(Sorry, but short stories are not included in this offer.)

We also have contests and sales regularly, so be sure to visit our webpage to find the best deals in ebooks and paperbacks! To find out about our new releases as soon as they are available, please be sure to sign up for our newsletter (http://www.newconceptspublishing.com/newsletter.htm) or join our reader group
(http://groups.yahoo.com/group/new_concepts_pub/join) !

The newsletter is available by double opt in only and our customer information is *never* shared!

Visit our webpage at:
www.newconceptspublishing.com

Daughter of Darkness is an original publication of NCP. This work has never before appeared in book form. This work is a novel. Any similarity to actual persons or events is purely coincidental.

New Concepts Publishing
5202 Humphreys Rd.
Lake Park, GA 31636

ISBN 1-58608-684-7
© copyright Mandy M. Roth

Cover art (c) copyright Eliza Black

NCP books are available at special quantity discounts for bulk purchases for sales promotions, premiums, fund raising, or educational use. For details, write, email, or phone New Concepts Publishing, 5202Humphreys Rd., Lake Park, GA 31636, ncp@newconceptspublishing.com, Ph. 229-257-0367, Fax 229-219-1097.

First NCP Paperback Printing: 2004

Printed in the United States of America

Other Titles from NCP by Mandy M. Roth:

Misfit in Middle America
Immortal Ops
All Hallow's Eve
The Valkyrie
Valhalla
Peace Offerings
Revelations
Last Call
The Enchantress
Gypsy Nights
Cyber Sex: Prepared to Please
Ghost Cats (Anthology, now in Trade Paperback)
The King's Choice
Christmas

DAUGHTER
OF
DARKNESS

Mandy M. Roth

Erotic Paranormal

New Concepts   Georgia

Dedication

To my family, friends, and faithful red pen:
Each of you has stood by me and never tired of listening to me
ramble on about fairies, vampires, and werewolves. The support
you have shown has been amazing. Thank you, and thank you
Andrea for taking a chance on the new kid.

Prologue

I lay in the field of flowers taking in the glorious scents. Violas were littered around me acting as a warm blanket to shield me from the cool night. The beauty of the shades of glowing purple and yellow pulled me to them. I plucked one up, put it to my lips and took in a deep breath. Their fresh scent soothed me, making me feel at one with the earth.

Small white clouds formed against the sharply contrasting royal blue sky. I traced the edges of one with my fingers. I wanted to reach out, grasp it and cuddle it to my body.

Rolling onto my stomach, I propped my chin up with my arms. My hair got caught under my elbow, and I freed it to relieve the tension on my head. From the corner of my eye I caught the fluttering of a small butterfly. It hovered above me a moment and I put my hand out towards it. Perching lightly upon my wrist, it sat motionless.

The white cottony clouds that I had been so desperate to hold turned gray. Suddenly, the sky grew dark and ominous. A crackle of thunder made the earth beneath me vibrate. Wind circled around me, pulling at the tiny blue sundress I wore.

There was a sharp pain in my wrist. I looked down--a gold snake lay in place of the butterfly. Like two tiny daggers, its fangs were firmly planted into my skin. Most people would flick the thing off, right? Well, I'm not most people. Besides, this wasn't my first go around with the dream. I'd been having the dream long enough to know what was to come. I braced myself. The ground below me gave way and I found myself spiraling into a bottomless pit. Darkness surrounded me, and I knew better than to bother to scream.

The familiar sound of a woman's voice whispered to me. "You are the balance. You will bring light to the darkness."

Chapter 1

I pulled up outside of the main gate. The blood red sign that stood high in the air read "Necro's Magik World & Supernatural Theme Park." I hated the idea of being here but you do what you have to do to make a living. Prior to working as assistant to the City's Chief Paranormal Prosecutor, I hadn't been able to keep a job to save my life. I'd tried a little bit of everything, from being a marketing director to stripping. Hey, a girl's got to make a living, right?

My friend Sharon got me the job at the Paranormal Regulators Law Offices. She'd worked with my boss and now ex-fiancé, Ken, enough to pull some strings and get me an in. He hired me as his personal assistant, sight unseen. After a year of working for him, he caught on to the fact that I had some special skills. I began showing signs of extrasensory perception, ESP, at the age of sixteen and still hadn't quite gotten the hang of using it. My ESP would manifest itself in the strangest ways.

I spent one week home from work because I couldn't stand the noise anymore. I had begun hearing others' thoughts and I couldn't block any of it out. The inside of my head had so many voices going on I thought I was schizophrenic. Ken came knocking at my door after my third day of missing work. I confessed my problem to him and he took me to see some friends of his. They helped me learn to shield myself from outside interference, so to speak. Now, I was able to gauge someone's feelings and thoughts fairly well without being privy to every sordid little detail.

Ken then asked me out for dinner. I felt like I owed him a huge thank you so I went. We made a better couple than I thought we would at first. After a few months he finally managed to get me into bed with him. We were in his posh two-story townhouse, going at each other like animals. When I climaxed, I threw my head back as a burst of energy come over me. It was like my body was being ripped into a million pieces, not pain so much as it was pressure--a pressure that I had no alternative but to release. Pictures flew off the walls, dishes crashed to the floor in the kitchen, and all of Ken's paperwork blew out of the window.

That was my first brush with psycho kinesis, and it scared the hell out of both of us. That's when I revealed the fact that I was of magical descent, most likely faerie. I'd feared it would scare him away. It did the exact opposite. He asked me to marry him.

Being a romantic fool, I believed I was truly in love. Things were good for almost a year--that should have tipped me off. Then one night he told me he was going to stay home from the office. He said that he hadn't been feeling well and was going to rest. During my lunch hour I stopped off and picked up some lunch for him. I used my key and let myself into his place. When I walked into his bedroom he was busy pushing his long hard body into some redhead. Needless to say, I broke the engagement on the spot, along with two of his bedroom windows.

Mess with a magical chick and you get some major cleanup when she's pissed, just a little motto I think all should remember.

Ken spent weeks trying to make it up to me. He claimed that he couldn't control himself, and he didn't mean for it to happen. I asked what the redhead's name was, and he didn't know. I gave him the choice of being friends or being enemies. He settled on just being friends, and that's the way we've been for the last six months.

Work's been keeping us pretty busy with the rapid rise in the number of supernatural-related homicides in the city in the last few months. I thought Ken's promotion was a curse. We'd been working sixty-five hours a week since he made Prosecutor, and there seemed to be no end in sight. We not only had the supernatural cases to deal with, we had everyday human cases to handle as well. It was the only way the city could justify having another prosecutor. Tax payers would wonder why it was they had to pay for a prosecutor who never saw the inside of a courtroom.

If they only knew.

I focused on the task at hand, taking a look around Necro's Magik World. It had only been open for business six years, but in that short time frame had managed to corner the market on ticket sales for theme parks. Someone had come up with the brilliant idea of having a theme park that revolved around the supernatural. By doing this the area had become a Mecca for the undead and magical creatures. At the park, demons didn't have to hide who they were. They were able to live among humans without fear of persecution and mass pandemonium. I'd even seen some of the "employees" walking around downtown one night. No one looked shocked to see a vampire roaming the streets--they just ran up and asked for his autograph.

Teenagers were heavy into imitating the undead, and of course, dead attire was all the rage. I wondered if creatures of the undead ever thought of sending thank-you notes to rock stars that ran around looking like death on stage. The more I thought about

Hollywood and rock stars, the more I wondered how many of the images weren't an act. I knew that there had to be a few celebrities that fell into the category of supernatural, I just didn't know which ones they were.

Necro's Magik World was huge, or so I'd been told. While the park spanned over four hundred acres, it wasn't all developed yet since they'd left room for expansion. They had picked the location wisely. They were close enough to the city to generate business, but far enough out to remain secluded and away from the watchful eye of others. People were eating up the idea of a supernatural theme park to the point that various spin-offs were popping up all around the world. There were restaurants, clothing stores, and, believe it or not, a website. But hey, who didn't have one of those, right?

A computer literate vampire, funny thought, huh!

The park only operated during nighttime for obvious reasons. I didn't know too many vampires that would be willing to sit out in the sunlight to greet guests. Here's your ticket, excuse me while I burst into flames.

I still wasn't sure about the outfit I had chosen. I'd decided on a pair of dark blue flare bottom jeans that made my legs look longer and at five foot five I took all the help I could get. I'd debated on wearing long sleeves or short because of how cool the summer nights could get, and finally settled on a red short sleeve top. I'd chosen jeans because I always felt most comfortable in them. I had also been told that red brought out my best features--my eyes and my hair.

I was ticked that I hadn't brought a brush with me. I'd left the house in such a hurry that I hadn't taken time to blow dry my hair. I fumbled around in my purse until I found a hair tie. Gathering up the front and sides of my hair, I pulled it loosely behind my head. Wrapping the tie around it several times, I did a quick check. Little black wisps fell from it and framed my face. That was just the way I liked it. I'd been thinking of cutting my hair off again. It seemed rather silly because every time I did it, my hair grew back to just above my rear end within two months. My hair liked to be that long and didn't take kindly to my attempts at doing anything else with it.

Being awakened out of dead sleep by Ken's phone call did not suit me. I looked like crap. Sure, I was grateful that he'd ended the nightmare I was having, but peeved that he'd wanted me to go out in the middle of the night to question a master vampire.

I touched my face and decided that I didn't have to fuss with much. I'd been blessed with flawless skin. It was, however, rather pale. I tried tanning beds and hitting the beach every day for a summer, but I couldn't get myself to burn, let alone tan. I did my best to make up for the lack of color by adding a touch of blush to both cheeks and some lip gloss to my lips. I was so sick of everyone asking if I had collagen implants. I wanted to get a t-shirt printed that read, "Yes, I do see the light of day, and yes the lips are real too."

Grabbing my purse from the passenger seat, I fumbled through it until I found my eyeliner. I was big on the whole lining of the top lid with black craze. Prior to its recent revival, I had been seriously out of date with the look, but did it anyway. I loved the way it brought out my eyes, and I was into retro.

Satisfied it was as good as it was going to get, I got out of the car.

When I swung the door shut I thought that the car had finally had it. It was an '84 Thunderbird and it had seen better days. The roof was dented beyond repair, and it had no floor in the back right passenger side. Every time it rained, my seat ended up soaked because the seal on the door was missing. I tried to remember to lay a towel on the seat when I got out, but every now and then I would forget. My absolute favorite thing about the car was that I had to use my best judgment to find the right gears. When you put the car in park, you were really in reverse and when you put the car in reverse, you went forward. Parking had always been a guess because the spot for it was somewhere above the letters on the dash. The only thing the car had going for it was that it was paid for and it still ran. I was worried about getting my student loans paid off before I bought a new one. I figured I'd be paying for my loans until I died at this rate, and considering the fact that I was pretty sure I had *Si* (pronounced shee) blood in me that was funny. Most *Si* were immortal, creatures of magic. The banks would just love me!

I walked towards one of the ticket booths. It was made to look like a mausoleum. Gray granite rock covered it and mythical creatures were carved into its molding. The boy sitting behind the counter resembled a zombie. The makeup slathered on his face gave him the appearance of rotting flesh, and his costume looked as though he had just crawled from the grave--just looking at him made me smile. I assumed that they had real zombies working here, but this kid was obviously not one of them.

"Ticket please."

I tried not to laugh. He sounded so ridiculous. The makeup and wardrobe were one thing--the overdone enunciation of his words was just too much.

"Gwen Stevens. I'm here to speak with Pallo." I had to bite my lip to keep from busting out laughing.

He didn't look amused as he turned to pick up the phone. He hung up and glanced back at me. "Mr. Pallo will see you shortly. Go through the red doors and downstairs, someone will meet you there."

Giving him a nod, I headed in the direction he had pointed.

A gigantic limestone building loomed before me. The gray stone exterior formed a sharp contrast to the small, landscaped flowerbeds that lined the walkway leading up to it. They were full of what looked to be lemon verbena and green sage. I thought it odd that someone would grow only herbs in a spot made for flowers. Stone gargoyles stood in the center of each bed. I really didn't like the idea of being at a place where they prided themselves on scaring the shit out of you, but Ken needed information … bad. I really hated the fact that I was his "girl Friday."

It only took me a few minutes to reach the red doors. Standing around for a bit, I waited for Sharon or Rick to show up. I'd already been at the park for half an hour so I decided to give them another fifteen minutes. Sharon was usually late. She seemed to be on a whole separate time schedule. At the office, we referred to someone who was late as running on "Sharon-time." Rick, on the other hand, had a military background and was always five minutes early. The fact that he wasn't here yet should have really bothered me, but it didn't. I was getting pretty brave in my old age, or pretty stupid, depending on how you looked at it.

My patience level was low considering I'd gotten little sleep due to my-oh-so pleasant dream. The fact that I was standing out here in the dead of night waiting for the people who should have been handling this themselves didn't help much either. I gave up and used my cell phone to try to reach Sharon. I got her voice mail, so I left her a message telling her I was going to go ahead in and I'd talk to her later. I also informed her that if I didn't call her back in an hour I was probably dead. That was my way of making light of the situation, but my gut told me that there was some truth to that comment.

I glanced up at the red door. The last thing I wanted to do tonight was go into a room full of vamps, but if I didn't go now I'd lose my nerve. I turned the knob and pulled the door open.

Instantly, I was hit with the smell of dampness. Glancing around, I tried to get the nasty taste of stale air out of my mouth as I got my bearings. I stood at the top of a stairwell, which was lit by several torches sitting in sconces along the wall. The walls were stone and looked like the inside of a castle.

No, make that the entrance to a dungeon.

I wasn't sure how anyone who owned and operated a multimillion dollar business ended up in a basement, but I trudged onward anyway. When I reached the end of the staircase I found myself in front of a large, heavy, metal door. The medieval theme was getting old, fast. I knocked on the door.

The door opened quickly and a man stood there silently, looking at me. His six foot five frame took up most of the doorway. White waves of hair spilled onto his shoulders, and large green eyes stared back at me. His face was soft, with baby fine features. The sweet smell of honey filled my head.

I'd heard that vampires smelled nice, but this was ridiculous. I wanted to lick him just to see if he tasted as good as he smelled, but I held back.

Good girl.

He was dressed like he'd just fallen out of the eighties. I half expected him to claim he was the guitarist for one of the big hair bands and not really a vamp at all. He had on black, painted-on leather pants. His white shirt hung loose from his body, gaping open to the middle of his stomach. Even in the poorly lit stairwell I could see how smooth and pale his skin was. When I glanced back at his face, he was staring at me wide-eyed. He appeared puzzled and a bit surprised. Imagine that--I put a vampire off guard.

"I'm Gwyneth Stevens. Kenneth Harpel sent me down to speak with Mr. Pallo." I extended my hand to him, but he just stared at it.

A few seconds went by in silence. I had the strongest urge to bolt back upstairs and out the door.

"Please come in," he said, stepping to the side. "We do not get many new visitors here. I apologize for my lack of manners."

I'd never met an honest to God gentleman before, so it took me a moment to respond. "Thank you. I'm sorry for coming at such a late hour, but Lydia phoned our office requesting I meet with Mr. Pallo tonight."

His green eyes widened. "Yes, Lydia, umm, come in please. I will get Pallo for you."

"So, do you have a name or is Def Leppard mega-fan all right by you?" My voice dripped with sarcasm.

"I am Caradoc." He seemed taken aback by my attempt at humor.

"Caradoc, the name doesn't sound familiar."

"Should it?" he asked as I walked past him.

"No, I guess not. I just got the feeling that I knew you from somewhere."

Caradoc led me into a room with a large stone fireplace in it. Two red sofas sat across from each other. They were trimmed with beautiful gold leafing that made your eye follow the s-curve of the feet. A massive Serapi rug covered the floor. Cherry end tables flanked each end of the red sofas. Candles sat on them and dripped wax down onto the rich wood. I had half a mind to walk up and put a coaster under them to protect the integrity of the tables. I got the feeling that no one else here cared, so I let it be.

The room had several doors in it. I had no clue where any of them went, so I kept my back near the exit. I didn't like leaving myself vulnerable, but the room didn't leave me many options.

"Please have a seat." Caradoc motioned to one of the couches. "Can I offer you anything to drink?"

I wasn't sure how to answer that. I was afraid to say yes and get a big glass of blood, and afraid to say no and come off as rude.

He winked at me. I wondered if he was flirting or just had something in his eye. My money was on hair spray--that was of course if he held true to his eighties ensemble. "Would you like a glass of iced tea?"

"Yes, thank you."

"Please make yourself at home."

I watched him exit out the door to my right and sat with my hands folded on my lap. I turned and stared at the large fireplace. Tiny pixies and faeries were embossed in it. They were all naked and each one wrapped itself around the one below it. Standing in a Master Vampire's living room alone when he obviously had a thing for naked creatures of magic, wasn't the best idea I'd ever had.

Gulping, I rubbed my palms across my jeans, trying my best to keep the nervous sweat that was building to a minimum.

The place let off a strange vibe, yet; oddly it felt more like home than the apartment I'd been living in for the last two years. I'd been in the place for less then fifteen minutes and I already felt like I could throw my feet up on the sofa and kick back awhile. I resisted the urge.

"Sorry to interrupt you Ms., but Pallo will be with you in a moment." I didn't sense anyone in the room with me so I was caught off guard. When I turned around Caradoc was standing behind me. He bowed his head slightly. "Forgive me, I did not mean to startle you."

"No, you're fine. I'm sorry." I felt a little silly with a man bowing in front of me so I put my hand out to him. If Sharon were with me, she would have shot me dead on the spot for being careless and trusting a stranger who also happened to be a vampire. I didn't feel that he posed any threat to me.

The door to my left opened and a man entered. He looked to be in his early twenties but I knew that if he was a vamp he was more likely to be in the hundreds. His hair was short and blond with pink tips. It appeared as though he used gel to spike it. He was wearing black from head to toe. He had on a t-shirt, jeans, and pair of army boots. He definitely had the James Dean look down pat. When he saw me, he froze in place. Gee, I was having that effect on a lot of people lately. He opened his mouth and stood silent for a second. As fun as it all was, I didn't want to play the game anymore.

"Pallo, I came here to speak with you regarding the hellhound homicides." My ability to be all work and no play came so easy. I expected him to start pouring his heart out about what they knew. What I got instead was his face looking even more shocked.

"Blood and sand! Caradoc, she thinks I'm Pallo. What the hell's going on here? If anyone should remember him, it's her," he said, his voice thick with a British accent as he pointed at me.

Shoot. I thought he had to be the head guy--guess I was wrong. That didn't happen too often, so I was a bit nervous. I usually just knew things that other people didn't. It had always proved to be an asset until about thirty seconds ago. Suddenly, it seemed rather useless now. I'd wanted to question him about my knowing Mr. Pallo, but changed my mind.

Caradoc stepped forward. It was clear he didn't want to touch me, and that was just fine by me. "I'm sorry, *Ms. Stevens*." He put a lot of emphasis on my name and stared hard at the James Dean-looking vamp.

"This is Jameson. Master Pallo will be with us momentarily."

Jameson, James Dean? I shrugged and laughed in my head at the irony. Jameson approached me with speed that no human possessed and extended his hand to me.

"Nice to meet you, *Ms. Stevens*." With the amount of attention they were giving my name, I was beginning to wonder if they thought it was an alias. Yes, often I run around giving bogus names--geesh. Besides, I would have come up with something more original than Gwen. "Faerie with attitude" had a nice ring to it.

"Nice to meet you too, Jameson." His hand was cool to the touch. I pulled mine away slowly.

"James. I go by James." He smiled wide at me and I saw no fangs. I'd never actually met a vampire up close before. I always assumed they walked around with these huge dog-like fangs showing. Guess I was wrong--again.

"Can either of you fine gentlemen tell me where Pallo is? I'd love to spend another hour being stared at like a circus freak, but a girl's got to get her beauty sleep you know. So, now that the pleasantries are out of the way, can someone find Pallo or Mr. Pallo for me?" I turned to face Caradoc. I could sense that between the two, he was higher up on the seniority ladder, but I wasn't sure by how much.

"He cannot help you find him, but I am sure I can." The deep exotic voice ran over the room and covered my body. It was familiar to me, soothing, sexy. I turned, expecting to see someone I knew.

A man walked out from behind James. He was around six feet tall and had a head of loose brown curls that hung almost to his shoulders. The guy leaked sexuality. Prior to this meeting, I hadn't known that was even possible. His face looked as though it was chiseled from stone. His pale skin had only the faintest hint of coloring. He had a strong chin with a small dimple in it, and his lips were full. They looked soft, kissable.

I let my gaze slowly fall down his body. He wore no shirt. His shoulders were broad, and from where I stood it appeared as though tiny freckles covered them. Muscles rippled down his stomach, forming a six pack and forcing my eyes lower. He wore a loose pair of black pants that I wished were invisible. They looked to be pajama bottoms, but I wasn't sure. I was too busy staring at the way his chest went from being completely bare to the start of tiny black hairs from his navel area down. He wore his waistband extremely low and I was positive he wasn't wearing any underwear.

I glanced down towards the floor and saw that he was barefoot. I did a quick second look at his body as I retraced my steps back to his beautiful face. The most intense pair of crisp, dark-brown, almost black eyes stared back at me. When I was finished mentally undressing him, I noticed the expression on his face. Gee, what a shocker. He looked like he'd seen a ghost.

"Would you guys please tell me if I have a huge horn sprouting from my forehead?" I was tired and I was sure it was pushing at least three in the morning.

Caradoc spoke first. "No, Ms. Stevens, you've not sprouted a horn as of yet. Why do you ask? Is this something we should watch for?" His sincerity made me burst out into laughter. James and the mysterious tall sexy vamp laughed as well.

"Everyone I've met so far has stood there staring at me like a deer caught in headlights. What gives? Where the hell is Mr. Pallo? I'm done for the night, boys. It's been fun, but I really must be going now."

"I am Mr. Pallo," the drop dead gorgeous one said. "Pallo is fine. I am sorry if we've upset you, but you remind us of someone we once knew." He tossed his hair out of his face with his hand and stepped towards me. "My apologies for looking like I just rolled out of bed, but I have been sparring in the gym. I wasn't expecting any visitors."

Sparring in the gym? The very thought of it made me drool. Was going weak-kneed and passing out an option? I hoped so, since it was exactly what I felt like doing.

When Ken told me that I was going to meet Pallo, I pictured a six hundred year old vampire who still spoke like he was in the Old World. Pallo didn't seem much into using contractions, but his English was perfect, accented slightly, but perfect nonetheless.

"I'd have thought that Lydia would've told you I was coming. She phoned and requested that someone be sent down immediately to speak with you. Two others were supposed...." I didn't finish my last sentence. I wasn't sure it was wise to spill the beans about being here completely alone with no sign of backup coming. My patience level was growing very thin. The only thing that helped me keep my grip was that I was surrounded by three of the sexiest men I'd ever had the pleasure of laying eyes on. Did I also forget to mention the fact that they could probably kill me before I knew what hit me?

Sexy and deadly, just the way I like them.

The room fell silent. Caradoc and James exchanged glances. Pallo was the first to break the silence. "I have not had a chance to speak personally with Lydia in some time now. My apologies. Please stay. I will answer whatever I can Ms…?"

"Ms. Stevens. Thank you."

"Yes, of course, Gwyneth Stevens. I have seen your name in the Nocturnal Journal recently for your office being involved in the break up of a Ghoul-fighting ring." He took a step towards me, "Most impressive indeed, Gwyneth."

This poster child for the "dead and doable" saying my name made me want to melt, and in some ways I did. I've heard that vampires could persuade members of the opposite sex to fall for them with ease. Knowing this should have prepared me for the way I was starting to feel, but it didn't.

It would be easy to get lost in Pallo's alluringly dark eyes. I wanted them to be looking down at me, staring at me while his body moved in and out of mine. I wanted to run my fingers through his wavy brown hair, to hold it while he brought my body to its climax. I wanted him now. I had to concentrate on not leaping across the room and straddling him. I pushed the desire down and for the first time felt how strong his pull was. Thankfully, I was stronger.

"Why are you fighting me?" Pallo asked.

"What do you mean?" I thought I'd play the dumb blonde routine for a minute.

"You are trying hard not to come near me, like I mean you harm."

I guess the dumb blonde routine doesn't work well, especially when you're a brunette. "Look, no offense, but you could be a homicidal maniac for all I know. After all, you are a--" I stopped short of saying vampire.

"True. But why would such a lovely young woman come alone to a maniac's house in the middle of the night?" His smile was so sexy that I had to fight with myself not to jump his bones then and there. Of course, I was willing to settle for a dry hump.

"Okay, you've got a good point. I must be crazy to come down here with a room full of vampires anyway, so why even bother with the shenanigans?"

"The 'shenanigans' you refer to were merely a test. I do not want any of my staff revealing information to someone not associated with the likes of us."

I was well beyond the point of feeling the need to be polite. "Well, I'm so happy that I passed your little Club Bloodsuckers initiation test, we can gather around and throw up gang signs later. Right now, I would really like--"

His hand came up suddenly, motioning me to stop. Surprisingly enough, I did. He must have thought my last comment was amusing because he laughed. It was quite possibly the most perfect laugh I've ever heard.

"Well I'm so happy to be your entertainment for the evening, thank you, and good-bye!" I headed towards the door. Pallo stepped in my path. Under normal circumstances a vampire standing in front of me would scare the hell out of me. This time it just pissed me off.

He stepped close enough for me to touch. He put his hand out and brushed mine. I flinched a little. Even though I'd mentally psyched myself up for meeting vampires, I couldn't bring myself to not be scared of what they could do.

I began to pull back, but his touch felt familiar to me. Sensual. Inviting. He lifted my hand to his lips and kissed it gently. Warmth flowed over my body. Suddenly, my insides felt like a thousand tiny fingers were moving throughout me, caressing me. Pallo's hands never left mine, yet I could have sworn that he'd just rubbed my most vulnerable spots. I felt it again, the feel of fingers caressing between my legs. I gasped and my body reacted to him. Damp, and breathless, I felt my hair lift up and I saw his do the same. I yanked my hand back, as if I'd been scorched.

"Nice to meet you too," he said, grinning at me. He'd planned that!

I smiled back, trying to look nonchalant, as if this sort of thing happened often. "Do you do that to all the ladies?"

He leaned in so close that I thought he would kiss my neck, or worse yet, bite it. I put my hands up and touched his chin. His skin was so smooth. Ken had always had a five o'clock shadow by ten in the morning. This guy was like touching a porcelain doll's face. His cool breath ran over my neck. I wasn't sure my legs were going to hold out if he got much closer.

Falling on my ass in front of the sexiest man I'd ever seen was not on my to-do list.

"That is reserved for the beautiful ones. And in my two hundred and seventy-five years on this earth I have only met two worthy of that show," he whispered, his sweet breath promising of endless passion between the sheets. Moisture pooled between my legs and while the idea of a hunky stranger making me cream myself was a favorite fantasy of mine, I thought it unwise to do so with a vampire.

I gave his chin a little push, and he stepped back.

"Can we just get down to business?" I asked, feigning annoyance, but wanting another hair-raising experience. Who wouldn't?

"I will get down whenever or wherever you would like, Gwyneth. You have but to ask."

My heart skipped a beat. I was so mad at myself for letting this two hundred and seventy-five-year-old corpse smooth talk me. But God, he was a good-looking corpse. I moved closer to him, filling the tiny gap between us. Two could play that game. I slid my hand across his chest. I really hoped this plan didn't backfire. If it did I would probably end up dead--so what the hell. They could write, "She couldn't beat 'em, so she caressed 'em" on my headstone. All would know I died a happy death.

I like to think of myself as being semi-attractive, and if he insisted on playing the Mr. Sexy game, I'd play along and then get the hell out of there. I knew before I touched him that he had two tiny scars under his right nipple. This didn't surprise me. I figured I could have caught a glimpse of them--he did have his shirt off after all. But I knew *how* he had gotten them.

"Been avoiding picking fights with sailors I hope? It always ended so nasty for you." Words came into my head and they fell from my lips. I was used to getting random visions of events in peoples' lives, but this was different. No vision had come to me. I just knew this to be true. I couldn't explain it. I pulled my hand away from him quickly, completely freaked out.

He looked a little shocked, and then smiled. I was beginning to really like that devilish grin, and was dangerously close to naming it his wet-panties smile.

"Yes Gwyneth, I learned my lesson."

"A punctured lung will do that to you. It's a shame that it took that to prove it to you." I grabbed my mouth. For some reason, in my head, I thought this would solve my problem. I never claimed to be smart--just semi-attractive.

Pallo leaned into me, brushing his lips over the back of my

hand. My knees grew weaker. Six months without sex had taken its toll on me. "Yes, one can learn almost any lesson if pain is involved." His deep voice moved over me, around me, through me, caressing me to my core.

Oh, he was good!

He shrugged and smiled. He definitely knew something I didn't, and he wasn't about to let on to what it was. The cocky routine was beyond annoying. I was flirtatious by nature, but this was getting on my nerves. I wanted to ask about the hellhounds and go. I wanted to leave this place and never look back. I wanted to run my hand over his chest again and pray that he decided to flex for me. Hey, cut a girl some slack--it's not very often that the poster boy for every woman's deepest sexual desire takes an interest in you. The desire won out. I felt his smooth chest one last time and stepped back.

Pallo reached out and touched my hip. I pushed his hand away lightly, unsure who I trusted less, him or me. He smelled good enough to eat and that's what I wanted to do. I wanted to swallow him up. Problem was, I knew what this guy was, and he would think of *me* as the main course.

Nevertheless, I wanted to know how it felt to have his body pressing against mine. I could feel his lust for me as well. I knew he was thinking of more than just pressing himself against me. I could see it in the way he smiled at me and in the way he moved. His movements were like ripples in water, so smooth, so sure of where they were going, so full of purpose, so making me horny.

I shook my head and cleared my naughty little schoolgirl thoughts. "I'm sorry, but I really just wanted to get some information in regards to some hellhound related incidents that we've had recently."

That a girl--keep focused on work and not on Pallo's glorious body.

He smiled, and I could tell that he wanted to pursue this newfound attraction more, but when he spoke, he'd apparently decided against it. "What is it that you want to know?"

I was shocked. He was going to give me some answers. "Well, for starters, do you know where we can find the Keeper of the Hounds? He's managed to elude us so far."

I caught James giving Pallo an odd look out of the corner of my eye, but decided to ignore it. Pallo's head fell back slightly and he began to laugh. The sound of his laugh wrapped around my body and made me tingle in places that I didn't even know I had. I shuddered and fought to maintain control. "I'm sorry, Pallo, but I really don't see how people being slaughtered by some crazy guy and his puppy slackies is amusing."

He glanced at me and grew quiet. "I am sorry. It is just that you seem very confident that the Keeper is male. Are we really that destructive that you would automatically assume it was our doing?"

"I'm lost--you mean as a vampire or as a guy?"

"I am referring to men in general, Ms. Stevens."

"Well, sorry to disappoint, but I really don't have a low opinion of men. I'm not one of those women who run around all day male-bashing. I think you're … err … they're just great. I'm just going off of the information I was given, and sources on the street are saying male, so that's what I'm sticking with." My tone was definitely harsher than I had wanted it to be, but I was exhausted and horny--never a good combination.

Pallo appeared very smug and sure of himself. He kept pushing a strand of his curly hair behind his left ear. Never in my life had I thought such a scene would be erotic. It was. "Your informants are wrong, and I would be very reluctant to listen to them further."

As great as that sounded, the reality was that informants were getting harder and harder for the PR Dept. to come by. They were disappearing left and right, never to be heard from again. The few that Ken had left would have to do, simply because there were no others to turn to. I got the sense that Pallo picked up on this, because he motioned for James and spoke to me. "Come here tomorrow at dusk and I will tell you more about the Keeper of the Hounds."

"Can't we just do it tonight?" No part of me wanted to come back to this place again. There was some sort of funky sexual vibe that seemed to cling to the air and I was afraid it was catchy.

Pallo smiled and motioned upwards. "I'm afraid that Mother Nature's rising sun will prevent me from going into further detail with you tonight. Please come by tomorrow and I will speak with you then. James will walk you to your car, Ms. Stevens." With that, he turned and walked out of the room.

Hmm, so much for good-byes. Secretly I was hoping for another handshake. Touching his skin made me feel alive. It was official--I really, really needed to get laid.

Chapter 2

James seemed to take great pride in being the one chosen to walk me to my car. I let him think he was doing me a favor, but in truth I'd managed to walk in alone just fine. As we neared the main entrance to the park, I saw Sharon arguing with the wanna-be zombie boy at the ticket window. She was hard to miss. Her cocoa-colored skin, dark-black hair, and height made her look like a supermodel in cop's clothing.

I sensed James tense up with the anticipation of trouble. As much as I disliked the idea of walking around at night with a vampire with pink tips, I liked the idea less of him attacking Sharon. "Relax, I know her," I said this as if this statement would solve all the problems in the world. I had to hope he was confident enough that I was non-violent and through guilt by association, think Sharon was too. James let out a slow breath and relaxed.

I smiled as we got closer because I could plainly hear Sharon telling zombie-boy that he was "a pathetic attempt at pulling off the dead." As entertaining as this was, I had to put an end to it, for no other reason then to save Sharon the risk of developing high blood pressure.

"Hey, are you hassling the help again?" I called out to her. She turned quickly in my direction.

"GWEN! I've been trying to get pea-brain here to tell me where you were." She shot zombie-boy him a look that made him squirm. Sharon's attention fell to James who was walking a couple of paces behind me. Her eyes narrowed. "Who's the vamp?"

Sharon's ability to pick up on the dead was uncanny. "Sharon, this is Jameson--James."

James walked up to her and extended his hand to her. Sharon stared at him a moment then met his handshake head-on. I could have sworn that I saw her gripping his hand extra hard, but James made no sign that he was in pain. She released him and turned her attention back to me. "What in the hell were you thinking, Gwen? Weren't you told to wait for me?" She closed in on me quick. If I hadn't known her for most of my life, I would have been terrified of her. "God, Gwen, I have half a mind to bite you myself for taking that kind of risk."

The thought of that made me snicker, and this, of course, infuriated her more. "Sure, laugh, but if you'd wound up dead, I would've really been pissed." That comment didn't make me want to laugh any less, but I managed to hold it in.

"Well, if I'm not needed anymore, I'm going to head off and have some fun," James said, making me jump at the sound of his voice. He'd been so quiet that I'd forgotten he was there. I almost asked what his idea of fun was, but I really didn't want to know.

"Thanks."

He nodded and strolled away towards the main way. I turned and glanced at Sharon with the biggest "I'm sorry" face that I could muster. She tipped her head a bit, allowing her dark hair to fall forward. "You know you are really hard to stay mad at, Gwen."

I smiled. That was all I needed. I'd known Sharon long enough to know she was over it. As we walked out to my car I filled her in on the night's events. She shook her head in disbelief. "You mean to tell me that a dead guy was putting the moves on you?"

"Your tactfulness always stymies me, really!" I had to laugh. She had a way about her that had always been blunt.

As we approached my car, Sharon came up with the idea of going out to breakfast together. Since it was pushing sunrise I thought it was a great plan. "There is no way that I'm getting in that death trap!" Sharon had never been big on me driving my old junker, so that news wasn't exactly earth-shattering. I laughed and agreed to ride with her in her new Taurus.

Chapter 3

After breakfast I had Sharon take me into the office with her. Our office is set up to look extremely normal to John Q. Public, but once you're through the reception area and into the other levels, you knew right away that it is anything but that. Only the strongest magic can get in undetected.

Sharon worked on the first floor. Being a detective with the PR Dept. had given her a lot of pull. She had her own office now. I loved to tease her about going corporate, only because of how much she seemed to hate the idea of selling out.

I was standing in Sharon's office doorway when someone grabbed my backside. I flung around and found Ken staring at me. His brown eyes glistened with delight at having gotten a free feel. Normally, I would have backhanded someone who did that, but Ken was Ken, and I was used to him.

He leaned in to kiss my cheek, and I turned my head away from him. "Ouch," he said, while gesturing that I'd just shot him through the heart. I had to laugh because the idea of him having feelings to hurt was amusing all unto itself. He was the hardest son of a gun I'd ever met. He was six foot two, two hundred and ten pounds. When I first met him, he'd a tight crew cut. I had finally convinced him to let his sandy blond hair grow out a little. I didn't want to add to his already overly inflated male ego, but he had great eyes. They were dark brown and the only thing that could have made them sexier was if they weren't attached to him. He was so smug and cocky that it could choke a girl if she wasn't careful.

He glanced down at my attire and grinned. "Hmm, I wasn't aware that it was casual day, Gwen."

"Well, I'm not here to work today. I haven't been to sleep yet, remember?" I had to fight the urge to stomp on his foot. He was the jackass that had called and woken me up to go with Sharon and Rick to question vampires, and I wasn't about to let him forget that. Lack of sleep really did turn me into quite the little sweetheart.

Ken's face softened. "What did you two find out?"

I looked at Sharon, who was now typing something on her keyboard, to try to catch her eye before she spoke, but I was too late. "Gwen was the only one who spoke to anyone. By the time I got there, she was already done with them. Or should I say him? Hey, if she keeps this up, she can apply for my job." She glanced up at me, smiling, caught the look of horror on my face, and immediately realized what she'd just done. "Well, I got held up on the job, and was about three hours late, so I really can't blame her--"

"You fucking went in there by yourself!" There was no questionable tone in his voice, just anger. He grabbed hold of my upper arm and ushered me further into Sharon's office to try to avoid an even bigger scene. He glared at Sharon. "Why the hell didn't you or Rick meet her down there?"

"Well, let's see … hmmm…. There was that pesky little hellhound murder that got in the way last night."

Ken and I both stopped to stare at her. I had no clue that another murder had taken place.

"What?" Ken asked in disbelief. He'd been at every one of the murder scenes from the start. He liked to oversee all the cases, and make sure they were covered up from the public.

"Well, if you would answer your Goddamn pager you would've known!" Sharon yelled at him as she stood. I wasn't sure who would win in a fight between Sharon and Ken, but my money was on Sharon, especially if it was *that* time of the month. "I paged you at least ten times, and I know that Rick tried too. I also tried your home phone and your cell … *nada!*"

Ken smacked his forehead. "Shit! My grandmother must have shut the ringers off again. But my pager should have…." Looking down at his side, he pulled his pager from its clip. He groaned and ran his hand through his sandy-blond hair. "Batteries dead." He held it up for us all to see. "That still doesn't explain why Rick didn't go down to meet Gwen."

Sharon shook her head. "Well, he was bringing in the cleanup teams and staving off the media. It was a mess."

"Where is Rick this morning? I didn't have a report on my desk. Did everything go all right?" Ken asked.

Sharon looked at him, puzzled. "What do you mean? When I left last night Rick was on his way back to the office with the crime scene photos and statements from the witnesses who called the report in."

She glanced at Ken and he looked at me. We all had the same bad feeling in the pit of our stomachs. I spoke first. "I'll go check his office. He's probably still typing the report out. You know how much he *loves* working with computers."

Ken nodded at me. "Good, yeah, you're right. Hey, Sharon, call Rick's house. I'll call the city police department."

I headed out of Sharon's office and down the hall. Rick was the Chief Investigator of the PR dept. He was pushing fifty and in perfect health. Rick's office was the big one at the end of the hall. We liked to tease him about being the "big cheese" just to get him going. I tapped lightly on his office door. No one replied. Out of habit, I tested the door handle, expecting to find it locked. It wasn't. I twisted it and opened the door. "Hey, Rick…." It took a minute for my eyes to register what I was seeing. I had been in Rick's office at least a hundred times over the last year, and now, everything was different. Everything was wrong. A sickeningly strong smell filled my nose. My eyes scanned the room. There was something all over his office. It looked as if someone had taken brownish-red paint and smeared it all over his desk, computer, chair and walls.

My gaze fell to the top of Rick's desk--a small, round, white object that looked like a ball lay there. I stared at it and was horrified when I realized that it was a human eye looking back at me. Nerve endings dangled from it, and the foul-smelling substance that I had assumed was paint was really blood. The eye was lying in a sea of red. I tried to back out of the room, but the floor was slick from the blood, and my sandals provided little traction. I slipped and fell. I could feel blood all around me, soaking through my jeans and all over my hands.

As I stood, I caught a glimpse under Rick's desk. A chunk of bloodied meat was lying under it. I stared hard at it as the smell of death began to creep towards me. It was a human torso lying there. It appeared as if it had been mauled by a lion, but I'd seen enough crime scene photos to know a hellhound murder when I saw one. Vomit rose in my throat, I tried to scramble to my feet, but ended up on all fours vomiting profusely. My long hair fell forward into the blood. I heard someone screaming and pushed myself up to get out of the room. I realized the screams were coming from me. It felt as if time stood still for a moment. Ken came around the corner into Rick's office. He had on designer dress shoes and damned near fell, too. He looked at me and around the room.

"Jesus, oh Jesus!" he muttered as I felt his strong arms moving under mine.

"What the…?" I heard Sharon's voice faintly. "Oh, my God!"

"Seal the building off! This isn't that old!" Ken was yelling as he lifted me effortlessly into his arms. I wanted to tell him I was fine, I could walk, but the truth was I didn't think I could. My legs were numb, my hands were shaking, and I was suddenly getting very cold.

"Come on, Gwen! Hold it together, hon." Ken gently laid me on the floor in the hallway. "Gwen, can you hear me?" He shook my shoulders.

"Gwen!"

I wanted to answer him, I wanted to shout "Of course I can fucking hear you!", but no words came out. The image of the blue eye on the desk hit me, and I knew that it was Rick's. I didn't need the coroner to confirm that for me. Instantly, more vomit rose up and Ken turned my head to keep me from choking on it. My body seized and my head threw itself backwards hard. Something tugged at me from inside. I could no longer see Ken around me and there was no more urge to vomit, no more pain.

Sitting up, I realized that I wasn't in the hallway anymore. I was lying in a bed of flowers. It was odd yet comforting. There was death here, no violence--just peace and flowers.

I stood, and found that I was wearing no clothing. I had never had much of a problem with nudity, but I was suddenly feeling very naked. A small gust of warm wind blew past me. My hair swept up in front of my face. I looked, expecting to see Rick's blood all over me, but there was nothing. Glancing down at my hands, I noticed they were now clean. "I'm dreaming." I heard the words come softly out of my mouth. I was intelligent enough to know that I was probably in shock. I had always had a keen ability to dream and be fully aware that I was doing it.

"Are you feeling better now?"

The sound of the voice made me jump. I turned to see Pallo standing behind me. He looked perfectly fuckable. No surprise there. The white light in the room seemed to radiate from him. His skin appeared tanner than I had remembered. But it was my dream, so I guess I was compensating for the whole pale, dead guy thing.

If I was going to dream about someone, a few-centuries-old hottie like Pallo would do just fine. He was incredible. I had made him every bit as beautiful as he'd been when I first laid eyes upon him. He wore a dark olive-colored pair of loose pajama bottoms and no top. His curly brown hair was pulled back at the base of his neck. I wanted to undo it and run my fingers through his hair. I didn't. Instead, I let my eyes trace the contours of his chiseled face, and soak in the beauty of his dark eyes.

"Why'd I let you wear clothes?" I asked, expecting him to be a fountain of wisdom in my own dream. The edges of his lips curved into a tiny smile. He took a step closer to me. His gaze raked over my body like one would look at a piece of artwork--studying it, examining it, admiring it.

"If you insist," he said waving his hand out in front of me.

I expected to find Pallo standing nude before me. I was actually a bit disappointed to find that I now wore a long, sheer, white nightgown. I didn't wait for him to touch me. It was my dream, and I was going to run it the way I saw fit, and right about now I wanted him in me. Reaching out, I let my fingers slide down his rippled chest. He shuddered slightly and clasped my wrist quickly. I could feel his pulse beating. I stared up into his eyes. That's why he appeared to be darker, and not allergic to the sunlight around us. I had made him human in my dream. He was alive.

Knowing that I had recreated him as a human made him all the more appealing. The few reservations I'd had about him being walking death, were now gone. There was nothing inhibiting my desire for him. I grew damp standing near him, and ached for his touch. It was obvious that my mind agreed with my body--Pallo, minus the vamp thing, equaled the perfect man.

"As much as I want to take you here and now, you would not be pleased with me later." His head fell forward slightly. I took my other hand and brushed it along his cheek. I couldn't understand why I was letting him fight me so hard in my own dream. Hell, I was ready to get busy, why wouldn't I want him to be too?

"Don't fight me, please." I let my hand slide around and trace his jaw. His lips met the palm of my hand and he kissed it gently. "You can have me. I want you to take me, really!" I said this so quickly that I took myself by surprise as well.

Pallo continued to kiss my hand, and moved slowly down to my wrist. He pulled my arm up and around his neck. I had to stand on my tiptoes to avoid having my arm pulled too tightly. Our lips were so close that I could feel his soft, sweet breath upon them. I made the first move, putting my lips to his and pushing my tongue into his mouth. It was every bit as warm and wonderful as I'd envisioned it to be. There were no fangs to be found in there, only his tongue caressing mine. His arms came around my body and pulled me close to him. The sensation of his warm body against mine made my knees give out. Thankfully, he was there and pulled me close. I drew in a sharp breath as I took in his fresh vanilla scent.

I felt like a schoolgirl with butterflies in my stomach. I wasn't sure if I wanted to giggle and write him a love note or take him to the ground and have mad animalistic sex with him. The latter of the two seemed more likely. I'd never had a dream of this nature with this much intensity before. I knew I'd been missing out all my life. If I could pull this off every night, I'd never need a man.

Pressing my head to Pallo's chest, I let the coolness of his skin soothe me. My fingers went to the tiny scars under his nipple and

I toyed with them, running my fingers across them softly. It was his turn to gasp as I slid my fingers up and over his erect nipple. My five foot five frame fit nicely against him, and left my mouth lined up with it. My tongue flickered out and over it as my mind pleaded to push the dream to the next level and have Pallo fuck me. "*Mmm*, you taste so good."

Pallo pulled back from me slightly, still managing to hold me in his arms. "Ahh," he said, sighing. "I must go now, you are safe."

He backed away from me. "Wait! Don't leave yet. I don't want to wake up … I…." The thought of Rick's office came to my mind. I didn't want to wake up. I didn't want to ever wake up.

"No, I must go now. We will be together again." As I heard the words come from his mouth I felt myself sinking. I glanced down as my body was pulled gently down into the bed of violas. The glowing purple and yellow flowers met me head on, swallowing my body whole. I didn't want to go. Pallo never moved. He stayed standing above me as I sank away into the abyss.

My eyes flickered open and stared up at a very familiar ceiling. I'd spent too many nights in Ken's apartment not to know what his ceiling looked like. I wanted to sit up, but the pressure in my head threatened to split it open. I grunted and noticed the smell of violas still clinging to the air.

"Now, that's the spirit!"

My lips curled into a smile. "Nana!" I turned onto my side quickly. Sure enough, I came face to face with one of the smallest women I'd ever met. Nana stood only four foot ten inches and was probably in her early eighties.

"Well there, Shorty. You managed to give us quite a scare! As soon as that no-good grandson of mine called me, I came right over here to see to your needs. You can't trust him to do anything. Men are like lemons. You can put them all in a bag, shake 'em up, pick one out, and you still have a lemon. Men!"

I laughed. When Nana had learned that I broke off the engagement with Ken, she immediately blamed him for it. I didn't correct her, because she was right. Even though Ken was her blood, she had sided with me. Ken knew better than to argue with his grandmother on the issue. He feared her wrath too much. Nana was a witch. She had been born to a witch and was one herself. She'd had only sons, and they in turn had only sons, so she was unable to bond with a daughter and share her secrets.

She'd tried to pass these things on to Ken, but he'd never much taken to it. He was more interested in hearing her stories about demons and other creatures of the night than actually practicing magic. Because of her, he'd been introduced to the seedier side of life at a very young age.

Ken's mother had never liked Nana. She, of course, had never believed that Nana was a true witch. No one could prove it, but everyone suspected that little old Nana had something to do with the fact that Ken's mother had three nervous break downs in the span of ten years. Hey, the woman was good, and I loved her dearly.

"Nana! It's so good to see yo--" My head spun slightly and I had to collect my thoughts before I could go on.

"Relax there. You shut your body down, you know. You plum shut it right down. You barely had a heartbeat. I told Ken no hospital. I told him you'd be all right. I had to convince him that shutting down is what powerful people have to do sometimes to avoid burning out."

"I really wish you'd quit telling me how powerful I am. I couldn't light a candle on demand if you asked me."

"Hey there! I've told ya plenty of times before that lighting a candle with magic takes skill and years of practice. You can't keep beating yourself up over things, Gweny. You were not raised with the guidance to control and use your gifts." Nana stood, slowly, and filled a small glass of water for me from the pitcher on the night stand. "I'm not saying that it's your parents' fault. They did right by you the best they could, but you needed to have someone with the gift workin' with you."

She handed me the glass, and since my throat felt like I'd swallowed a bag of cotton balls, I gladly accepted. I brought the glass to my lips and spilled some down the corner of my chin. I'd never mastered the art of drinking while lying down. I'd seen it done perfectly on daytime soap operas, but I had never been that suave. Nana just smiled and handed me a tissue.

"You've been blessed with more gifts than I've ever seen before. The things you can do are nothing short of amazing!"

My cheeks grew warm from embarrassment. "But Nana, everything I can do only happens at random. Whenever my emotions are running high, my 'wonderful abilities' get all out of whack and I'm lucky to escape with my life." I sighed deeply. It was no exaggeration. When I was a junior in high school I had been madly in love with Scott Mines who was the star of the basketball team and a senior. He of course had no clue that I even existed. Whenever I caught a glimpse of him in the hall, I suddenly got very flushed and nerves would get the best of me, causing me to do the most embarrassing things.

Once I had seen Scott walking with some of his fellow teammates after a practice. He turned and glanced up at me, our eyes met. For one brief moment I wanted to profess my undying love for him. Instead, my bottled up emotions manifested themselves in the form of a mini-earthquake. Energy rose forth from my body. I had no control over it. It oozed out of my skin and crept into everything around me. The lockers all fell open. Books flew out at us. The light fixtures cracked and popped before plummeting down and crashing onto the floor. I took an Algebra 101 book to the head and ended up with two stitches. Worse yet, Scot ended up bearing the brunt of a falling light fixture, and had to have his head shaved, twenty-four stitches, a tetanus shot and no chance at competing in the next three games. He missed the rest of his senior year basketball season due to the injury, and the team never made it to the finals. Officials from all over came to verify that it had indeed been an earthquake. Since I lived the Midwest, it was a scientific marvel and led to many nights worth of local broadcasting about our state being on a major fault line and numerous eyewitness accounts from the surrounding area. As it turned out, I had managed to push the quake to the adjoining county as well.

Ain't love grand?

"It won't always be that way! It takes time, and you've only been around people who understand these things for a couple of years now," Nana said in her ultra-gentle tone. I was sure that it had taken many years of practice for her to sound so incredibly calm all the time.

I was feeling much better. Nana always seemed to be able to bring out my inner peace. I let my head fall gently back onto the pillow. I had no idea how long I'd been at Ken's house. I was supposed to meet Pallo to discuss the hellhound murders at dusk. If I didn't show up, I was pretty sure that our one and only lead would not be speaking to us again. It didn't feel like I'd been out for days, but losing time is par for the course when losing consciousness.

"Nana?" I turned to look at her. "How long have I been here?"

She took a small breath as she turned her head slightly. "Hmm, well, Kenny called me around eightish. I got here as soon as I could. He had just finished getting you out of the bathtub." As soon as I heard her say that my face went slack. Ken had given me a bath? Yes, I had been intimate with him, and yes, we had been engaged, but I did not want the man giving me baths now. My shock must have showed, because Nana laughed. "Now, now, your friend Sharon handled the private moments and Ken simply supplied the muscle to lift you to and fro."

I relaxed. I had no problem with Sharon handling that for me. She was my oldest and dearest friend. I trusted her with my life, why not my body, too? "So, what day is it?"

"Oh, for goodness sakes, child, all this happened just today. I put a little extra Lemon Verbena in the juice to ward off any more destructive magic for awhile so that you could come out of your state sooner." She gave a small nod--obviously pleased with herself. "If I hadn't forced Kenny to give that to you, you'd sleep for a week straight. My friend Ida did that once. I didn't know then near what I know now, and sure enough the girl slept for one week straight. She frightened us all. We had half a mind to go looking for Prince Charming to come and kiss her on the lips. He was busy with what's her name, so it wouldn't have worked anyways."

The thought of Nana actually knowing Prince Charming should have surprised me. It didn't. Sitting up, I glanced towards Ken's bureau. His alarm clock said it was quarter after seven. I still had time to make it down to Necro World if I hurried. I swung my legs around the side of the bed and stood. The room spun for a moment, and I'm fairly sure that I did as well. Nana made remarks of disapproval. I hated to ignore her, but I had to talk with Pallo. Since my dream about him, I had an overwhelming need to be near him.

I looked around the room. It had been six months since I'd given Ken my key back. He was reluctant to take it, but in the end he did. He had been equally as reluctant to give me some of my things back. I knew that he was holding out hope for reconciliation but it wasn't going to happen. I walked quickly over to his black dresser. The top drawer had been mine to store things in for those nights when I didn't make it home before work the next day. I opened it and was pleased to see some of my personal items in there. I had no idea what I had left. I was in such a hurry to get out when I caught him with the redhead that I didn't stop to pack anything up. I just left. My black capris were folded neatly on top. I had to rummage around a little to find a top to go with them. I settled on a black spaghetti strap tank top. Even though it was summer, the lake breeze chilled the night air to the point that sweatshirts or jackets were often required. I didn't have anything remotely close to that in the drawer, so I turned and went for Ken's closet.

"Could you add some color while you're in there?" Nana asked from her chair. She had always been on Ken to get out of the habit of wearing only grays and blacks. I reached in and pulled out a white, long-sleeved dress shirt. I slid it on, cuffed the sleeves, and tied the shirt at my waistline. I searched around for my sandals, and I hesitated before I opened the door to the adjoining bathroom. Visions of bloodstains filled my head. Opening the door, I found nothing but Ken's perfectly spotless white and black bathroom.

"Kenny took your clothes with him to drop off at his cleaners. He cleaned your shoes up and put them behind the door," Nana said, startling me because I hadn't heard her get out of the chair. "I think he knows that he did wrong by you. I think he knows that he loves ya."

I grabbed my black sandals from behind the door and turned to look at Nana. I could feel how much she ached to have me as part of her family. I knew how much she longed for me to be the mother of her great-grandchildren. At one time, I wanted it as much as she did. No, I had wanted it more. Bending down, I kissed her on the cheek. Her hand slipped up and gripped my forearm. "You take care of yourself, Shorty!"

"Yes, Nana," I said as I kissed her gently again.

Chapter 4

I was forced to call a cab to pick me up. My car was still at the theme park because I'd caught a ride with Sharon. I had no clue where my purse was, so I had to grab cash out of Ken's hiding spot. I knew he wouldn't care if I took it. Nana tried to get me to stay and rest, but I couldn't.

The cab dropped me off in front of the main gate for Necro World. It was pushing eight o'clock, and the sun was beginning to set. The crowds weren't due in for another half hour or so. I passed the ticket window and waved at the zombie-boy. He had given up the dead act with me, smiled and waved back. I made my way past the flowerbeds lined with herbs, and stopped to take note that the herbs planted were those used to ward off evil magic. Interesting. I continued on through the red door and down the stone stairs. I reached the bottom and knocked softly on the metal door.

It opened and Caradoc's green eyes and white head of hair greeted me. "Welcome, Ms. Stevens."

"Are you the official door-opener?" I smiled sweetly at him.

He appeared perplexed. "No, we have no official door-opener."

"We really have to get you out more."

"Good luck with that." As I entered, I saw James standing close behind Caradoc. He was dressed in black from head to toe again. I still couldn't get over the fact that he had his tips dyed pink. He was pretty hip as far as vamps went, at least of the ones I'd met so far. "Caradoc doesn't do anything without checking with his master first. Do you?"

Caradoc's face went slack. Anger crept over it slowly. He opened his mouth to speak when Pallo walked in. Pallo turned and looked at James, his gaze hard. "Telling tales again, are we, James?" The tone in his voice spoke volumes. It was a threat, plain and simple.

James nodded and bowed his head slightly towards Pallo. "I was just yanking his chain, that's all. No harm, aye?"

Caradoc stepped to the side and stared intensely at James. There was a definite bad vibe going on in the room. I walked past them both and headed for one of the red sofas. I didn't feel like waiting for an invite. At the rate they were going they would have left me standing in the doorway all night while they played "I'm meaner than you" games.

Pallo walked towards me. "Please be seated." It was more of a command. All the same, I let it slide. He looked wonderful in his black jeans and gray muscle shirt. I could make out tiny freckles on his shoulders. The shirt enhanced his muscles. I knew he possessed inhuman strength, but even if I hadn't known he was a vampire I would have still thought he could kick some serious butt. He caught me checking him out and appeared pleased with himself.

"I'm happy that you made it. I did not think you would come after your ordeal this morning."

I looked at him as I sat. "I wasn't aware you had connections in the PR department."

"I have ways of finding things out." He did not attempt to deny it. At least he was honest.

"What can you share with me about the hellhounds?" Being around Pallo made my skin ache for his touch, so the quicker I got down to business the better.

"You certainly waste no time, do you?"

"That's me--Ms. Efficient. Now, what do you know?"

His brown eyes twinkled with delight. "I know that you are a very impatient woman and I like that about you." I rolled my eyes and wanted to interject, but he continued. "I also know this Keeper you speak of personally. I do not think the Keeper is someone you should go seeking. Leave that up to your friend."

"What friend?"

"The one who is in charge of bringing justice to the undead."

"Ken?"

"If that is *his* name." The way that he said it made me certain that he knew exactly who Ken was, but was just being a jerk.

"Yes, that's his name, thank you very much. He's my boss and my fiancé." I don't know why I said that, we hadn't been engaged for over six months now.

Pallo looked like I'd slapped him across his face. He turned his head slowly towards Caradoc. "What is it?" I thought he was talking to me at first, but Caradoc answered him.

"She is not being truthful with you, Master."

Pallo turned and arched a brow.

"How did you guys do that?" I asked.

"Do what?"

"How the hell did he know that, and how did you know he knew it?" I was starting to confuse even myself. Pallo just smiled at me and crossed his legs. I noticed how shiny his black boots were, he liked things nice and neat, you could tell that right off the bat. He was definitely a man who was used to getting what he wanted.

"I'm sure that you know, Gwyneth, vampires can sense when someone is lying to them."

"Then why did he sense it and not you?"

Pallo tensed up a little. I don't think he expected me to catch that one. "I thought it best not to exercise that gift, shall we say, with you."

"Why?" It was a legitimate question that I thought needed to be asked.

The side of his mouth curled upwards. "Would you have been angry with me if I had?"

"Yes! No, well I don't know maybe." I was hurt and still in awe of what vampires were capable of.

"My apologies, I was trying to be a gentleman." His smiled faded away. "Now, tell me why you felt the need the lie to me about this Ken."

I had a sinking feeling in the bottom of my gut. I didn't know what to say. I did the only thing I could think of, I told the truth. "Ken was my fiancé. I broke it off with him, and I guess I just thought it would be safer to tell you that I was committed to someone."

Pallo shifted on the sofa. He leaned towards me. "Do I make you feel threatened? Are you that afraid of me?"

I stared into his dark brown eyes. They swam with possibilities. My mind raced to my dream of him holding me in his arms, kissing me passionately. I didn't know how I felt about him. "I … I don't know." I felt that honesty was the best policy, especially now that I knew his sidekick Caradoc was scanning my every word. I shot a nasty look over in Caradoc's direction. I caught his eyes with mine, and I let my stare go icy. The more I thought about it, the angrier I became.

How dare he read me without my permission? How dare he violate my mind?

My hands grew cold. I was so angry with him I wanted to walk over and slap his face for that, but I sat still and just glared at him. My body tensed up and the tiny hairs on my arms rose up. Energy danced around my fingertips. Tiny wind gusts swirled close to my skin. Oh, no! I knew all too well what that meant. Something was going to happen, and I was sure it wasn't going to be good.

"Run!" I screamed at Caradoc. His green eyes widened as he looked at me. I turned and saw one of the candlesticks shaking slightly on the cherry end table. I glanced back at Caradoc, stood up, quickly mirrored by Pallo, and screamed for Caradoc to run. James crashed into him from behind, and the two of them went tumbling onto the floor. The candlestick flew into the wall with such a force that it was embedded into the stone at least three inches.

"Get off of me, James!" Caradoc said.

James pushed himself off Caradoc's back and stood slowly, staring at the candlestick. "That was chest level, Caradoc. She would've staked ya through the heart." He touched the candlestick. Smoke rose from the tips of his fingers as he let out a small yelp. He turned and glanced at me with a mixture of fright and admiration.

Pallo was standing directly in front of me. He put his hands on my arms, and I didn't push him away. I just stood there staring at the candlestick and thinking about what James had said. "I could have killed him." My voice was small and weak.

"But you warned him instead, did you not." Pallo's hands moved past my arms, and onto my waist. My focus moved down to the floor where Caradoc was getting up. He rustled his long blond hair from his face, stared at the wall then me. He said nothing, he didn't look angry with me--he looked alarmed.

"I did not mean to upset you. I only did as I was ordered to do," he said, softly.

I glanced at Pallo. He'd told Caradoc to tell him if I lied to him? He acted like he didn't want to upset me by doing it himself, yet he had no problem having someone else do it. Then it hit me, I would have unleashed my anger at him if he had read me. Oh, God! Pallo had been sitting on the sofa right across from me, so I would have had less time to warn him. James would have never made it in time to push him out of the way. I would have killed him. I would have killed Pallo with my anger.

My breathing grew shallow.

I almost murdered someone--all right technically vampires were already dead, but still ... I couldn't explain it, and there was no sense denying it, he meant a great deal to me. I felt light-headed. My breathing was so irregular that it drew the attention of the others.

Pallo pulled me close to him. I could feel his cool skin against my cheek. He wrapped his large arms easily around my small frame. "*Shhhh*, Gwyneth. He is fine." Pallo held me tight, rocking me gently in his arms. If he hadn't been there I would've been lying flat on the floor. I definitely wasn't equipped to deal with the fact that I had the ability to kill.

"He is fine. He is fine," Pallo repeated softly. "Do not be alarmed. We are all safe. It is done. Let us move on now, shall we?" His voice was shaky as he planted tiny kisses on my head that were caring and nurturing.

After a few minutes of being held by Pallo's strong arms, and being soothed with his gentleness, I finally calmed down. Caradoc still appeared a little uneasy to me. He seemed all too willing to head out of the room at Pallo's request. James, however, seemed disappointed. The way he and Caradoc fought when I first arrived led me to believe that he got some sort of sick pleasure out of the night's festivities.

I sat back down on the red sofa and expected Pallo to return to his spot, but he didn't. He sat next to me. The only way he could've gotten any closer to me would have been to sit directly on my lap. After the day I was having, I wouldn't have been too opposed to that idea. He put his arm around me and pulled me close to him. Any other man I would have punched in the gut and left, but Pallo was different. He was special.

"Join me on a tour of the Park," Pallo said out of the blue.

I wanted to just sit right where I was at and continue to feel safe, but he was right to assume that I needed to get my mind off things for a while. I nodded. Pallo's hand curled around mine. Brining it to his lips, he kissed it slowly, and sent tingles of sensation radiating up my arm. Instantly, my breasts felt heavy and my body seemed ultra sensitive. I rubbed my finger gently over his chin, hoping to encourage him to kiss a little further up my body.

Pallo mouthed something faintly that sounded like, "I have missed you so." He let go of my hand and rose to his feet. Without a word, he walked out of the room, disappearing behind one of the doors. I didn't go after him. I didn't even care where he was going. I knew he would be back. I could feel a mystical connection between the two of us. I'd read all of the literature in Ken's office pertaining to vampires and their powers. I knew they had skills that ran the gamut. I knew seduction was one of them, but Pallo didn't have to bother. I was already attracted to him on a level his powers could never reach.

Chapter 5

When Pallo returned, he tried to take my hand. With only the tiniest bit of reservation on my part, I let him have it. He led me out of his underground lair. As we walked out of the big red doors, I felt the cool night air hit my warm skin. Having a sexy vamp holding my hand had elevated my body temperature.

No surprise there.

I glanced back over my shoulder at the huge stone building. I hadn't really noticed how big the place was before. It looked like a mansion. I counted at least four flours, not including the basement. It must be sad to live for over two hundred years confined to a basement during daylight hours. The building could no longer hold my attention, not with Pallo so near me. I stared at the side of his chiseled face as we walked. The moonlight cast small shadows under his nose and lips. The paleness of his skin was rivaled only by the soft night light. The darkness suited him. I wondered if that had always been the case. I'd never know. If I ever did see him in the light of day, it would be brief and final. He would die. I pushed that thought from my mind.

This was insane! I was worried about the well-being of some vampire I'd only just met. This was beyond insane--it was ludicrous.

"Why do you look so sad?" His voice was so sweet and smooth.

"No reason," I lied.

"If you would prefer, I could read your thoughts."

"That is not funny! To tell you the truth, it's just plain ol' creepy." I didn't bother to tell him that I had that gift as well. I'd made every effort to push that ability down deep. It had never been something I could come to terms with. It also was something that didn't appear to help me much when I was surrounded by vampires. They seemed immune to my probing powers. I wish I was to theirs.

"I do not need my power to know what you are thinking. You wear your feelings on your sleeve." He smiled at me, and I saw little dimples near the corners of his mouth. Instantly, I wanted to kiss them, kiss him.

Just my luck--sarcastic and adorable.

We didn't have a whole lot of time before the sun would come up. For some reason, I wanted to make the most of it. I didn't care what information he had about the Keeper of the Hounds. All I cared about was how good my body felt near him.

Pallo took my arm in his and walked me towards the entrance of his theme park. The people buying tickets all gawked at him like he was a movie star. I knew he was hot, but this was ridiculous. I half expected paparazzi to leap out of the bushes at us. My luck, the flash from the camera would cause Pallo to burst into flames.

He led me through a set of large iron gates set up to what looked like the entrance to a cemetery. Once inside, I was hit with the sights and sounds of the amusement park. The smell of cotton candy was around me. I took a deep breath, and could hear music coming from all directions. The buzzing of the rides was like white noise.

In the center of the midway there was a large carousel. In the place of wooden horses were carved Boobries. These were giant water birds that were on the verge of extinction. They looked like a strange cross between a dragon and a bird. Huge talons sprung forth from the carved wood. Scales covered the creature's legs. The breasts of the Boobries were covered in feathers. Thick necks pointed the way to a bird-like head. A shiny glass red eye stared out at me from each one. The carousel was full of children laughing as they went up and down. The children held tight to the pole, perched on the backs of the black creatures. Each one had been carved with such love and patience that it looked almost lifelike. Boobries had been numerous across the lands at one time, but now their numbers had dwindled to the low twenties. People had feared them when they stopped being satisfied with snatching farm animals and began snatching the farmers instead. Who could blame them? It had been a nightmare to keep out of the news. The tabloids had picked up the story. It made the front page twice, then some pop star's newest love interest sold more issues, so they quit running it.

We walked further into the crowd of people. Visitors to the park were huddling around to get their pictures taken with the employees that worked there. A few vampire employees were really playing the part. They had on long black capes with red inner lining. Tiny lines of blood ran down their chins. People were waiting to have a chance to stand next to one and have it pretend to be sinking its fangs into them. Flocks of girls in their late teens and early twenties clustered around the vamps. They couldn't have had more than a yard of fabric between them covering their bodies.

"You guys have groupies?"

"It is not easy to keep all of my vampires happy with blood stored in coolers from blood banks. They do enjoy something a bit *fresher* from time to time."

I was shocked. "You mean you kill people here?"

He laughed and stopped walking. "Death is not a prerequisite to a vampire's feeding. It can be a side effect if one is not careful, but, no, we do not kill anyone here. They volunteer to let us feed off them. That is all."

"You mean you've been feeding off of them too?"

"Would you rather I did not? I would die if I stopped feeding from the living." He bent and kissed my forehead. "It is not as if they get nothing from it."

His words hit me hard, and squeezed at my chest. "You have sex with all of these girls?"

"Some, yes, but not all. Even I could not have sex with all of them." His tone told me he was mocking me, and I didn't care for it one bit.

"Get away from me." I pushed him back from me. "God, you're a pig." I was so angry with myself. Here I was, supposed to be doing my job, and instead I was acting like arm candy for a womanizing dead guy. I was ticked. More than that, I was jealous. I had no reason to be. He didn't owe me an explanation. I wasn't married to the guy. I wasn't even his girlfriend. I was acting like a fool.

"Why the hell did you want to give me the tour? Were you hoping to lure me into a dark corner and get a little blood from me? I'm only here tonight because someone I care about asked me to come. I didn't want to be here, and I don't want to be around you or your funky vamp mojo either."

I put my head down and walked as fast as I could. A vision flashed in my head. It wasn't a time or place that I recognized, but I knew the man in it. Pallo was bent down on one knee holding a woman's hand in his. Her back was to me, her hair was black and long, the ends curled up slightly. A slight breeze was blowing it enough for me to see her tiny, slightly curved ears. She wore a flowing white gown. It was made from so much material that it hid the shape of her body. Instead of looking plain and frumpy, it made me want to see what was underneath. It made me want to touch her--to feel if she was as real and as beautiful as she looked

My essence floated behind her while Pallo sat on bended knee before her. His skin was bronzed. His hair was longer than now. The sunlight had bleached bits and pieces of his dark brown hair to blond. He was beautiful. He appeared sun kissed and alive. My essence moved around to see the woman he was looking at so intently. My eyes met hers, and I felt myself being pulled into them. No longer a spectator--I blinked. There before me was Pallo, on his knee holding my hand.

"Say yes. Say you will spend the rest of my life with me, *cara mia*," he said desperately.

I walked into what felt like a brick wall, and the vision left me. I tried to pull it back, but it was gone. I glanced up and stared at the center of Pallo's chest. I hadn't realized he had moved. The vision had sucked me in, it felt so real. It felt like it was my own. I'd never had a vision spontaneously hit me. They only hit me when I came into contact with a person. I had not been touching Pallo when that flashed before me, but it had felt so real. I'd just met the man, and already I was seriously hoping for marriage. God, I needed to get laid! Pallo caught hold of my arm and pulled me to him.

"How do you do that?" I wanted to know how he seemed to know when it was okay to touch me, and that I wouldn't strike him.

"What?" he asked, grinning down at me. "I was not always the monster you see before you." I was going to apologize, but he kept going. "I was once just a man. I had a different life before this. I had a good life."

I didn't see a monster standing before me now. I saw a gorgeous, tall man with penetrating dark brown eyes that seemed interested only in me.

"Tell me about your life before you became one of the undead?"

"Well, I do prefer the word immortal, but...."

This time I interrupted him. "Yeah, and I prefer Gwen, but you keep calling me Gwyneth."

"Ah, *touché*!" He looked happy as he stood with me, the summer breeze blowing warm air at our backs. I could tell it had been a long time since he'd been happy, but I didn't know why. I took his hand in mine, and this pleased him.

"Answer one question for me, and I want the truth. Can you do that?" I asked.

"Can I do what--tell the truth, or answer your question?" He was making an attempt at a joke and I knew it.

"Pallo."

"I'm sorry. What is it you would like to ask me?" His fingers curled around mine--they were so cold that I brought my other hand around to try to warm him.

"Why do I feel like I've known you forever?"

"I must admit, I do tend to have that effect on the opposite sex."

"Please, Pallo."

He gave me a small smirk and turned to continue our tour of

the park. He was not going to answer my question, even though I was betting that he knew what was going on. Hell, he was probably the reason for it. His weird vamp mojo was probably leaking all over, making me want him.

Stopping, he turned his head to me. "No vampire tricks here, Gwyneth." He bent and pressed his lips to mine. I yanked back as fast as I could, watching his face go from stunned to hurt.

"Am I truly that horrible?"

My jaw dropped. Who the hell was this guy? He'd already gotten me to hold his hand and I'd known him less than forty-eight hours. Normally, it took three dates and some sweet-talking to get that much out of me. He was good, I'd give him that.

"I'm sorry, but I have to go!" I said and headed back the way we had come. "Thank you for the tour, Mr. Pallo." Overwhelmed by his presence, I wanted to push him away from me as fast as I could.

Wasting no time, I jogged away, searching for the park exit. I could feel Pallo staring at me from behind, looking through my soul. I kept wishing he would stop and just let me go. After running this through my head several hundred times, I no longer felt his penetrating gaze on me any more. I didn't dare turn to see if he was still standing there.

I kept heading in the direction I thought the exit would be, but couldn't find one. I was getting further and further away from the midway. The crowds were lighter. I hadn't remembered walking this far with Pallo during my tour, but then again my concentration had been more on his firm butt than the walk itself. The hairs on the back of my neck stood on end. That couldn't be a good sign. Glancing around, I tried to spot the carousel at the entrance to the park. There was nothing that looked even remotely similar to that anywhere around me. I saw an entrance to what was labeled the Enchanted Forest and one to House of Hell. Shrugging, I went towards the Enchanted Forest entrance, but as I neared it, I stopped. A small sign that I hadn't noticed read "temporarily closed for maintenance." I could have sworn that that hadn't been there just seconds before, but I was having one of those nights.

Since my options seemed rather limited, I headed towards the House of Hell. Moving into the turnstile, I heard the call of my name. I turned and found Pallo standing close. He was the stealthiest s.o.b. I'd ever met, but I was suddenly happy to see him.

"You are smiling," he said softly.

I hadn't realized I was. "Yes, you caught me, I'm happy to see you." This seemed to bring him nothing but delight, because he glided up to me quickly and wrapped me in his arms.

"Not nearly as glad as I am to see you."

My heart melted. I guess two hundred plus years will give a guy the ability to smooth talk with the best of them. "Come," he said, setting me down and pulling me towards the Enchanted Forest. The gates creaked loudly as he pushed them open. Ignoring the sign, he gently pulled me through the gates, and led me down a tree-lined, stone pathway. The dark closed in, making me nervous.

"You're not afraid of the dark, are you?" he asked in a teasing tone.

"Maybe, but in truth, I'm walking with one the darkness' scariest creatures, am I not?" The moment I said it I regretted it. He let go of my hand and turned away from me.

"I am a fool."

"No, Pallo. No, I am. I shouldn't have said that. It was insensitive of me. I thought we were joking around … I'm sorry … I...."

He faced me. "I am still a monster to you, am I not?" He looked like an angel standing before me, but I knew better. I knew what he really was, and I was sure he was as deadly as the Devil himself, when need be. That should have made me run from him, but I didn't. I stood my ground.

"What do you want me to say? What will make it all right? You are what you are, Pallo. I can't change that, can I?"

He glanced at the ground. "No, you cannot change that. Nothing can change what I am."

I took a step towards him, but he backed away. "You have some nerve, you know!" He looked up, a little shocked by my tone. "You get defensive for me stating the obvious, and immediately assume that I can't see past it. Hey, thanks for thinking the best of me!" I poked his chest. "You used your little vampire tricks on me and got me to fall head over heels in lo--" I stopped just short of the word love.

He perked up. "I have used no tricks on you, Gwyneth."

I could tell that he was being honest with me. "So, what does that mean?"

"It means that you do not see me as I see myself." He bent and stopped just short of brushing his lips past me.

My desire to be close to him intensified. I vividly pictured the kiss we had shared in my dream. I didn't want to miss out on what could be the greatest thing in my life. I bent forward and planted my full lips onto his. He stumbled backwards and lost his footing. My hand came to my mouth as a little "Oh" escaped my lips. I looked down at him in amazement.

He laughed deeply, and I couldn't help but laugh too. "Only you ... only you!" he said, rising in an effortless motion.

My eyes widened. I couldn't believe my kissing him caught him so off guard that I knocked him flat on his ass. I giggled again. Pallo laughed as well, and the sound of his voice made me melt. This time he pulled me close to him, and brought his lips down onto mine. His tongue made its way into my mouth. It was cool and tasted sweet. I let my tongue circle his for a moment, drawing small sounds of pleasure from him as he wrapped his arms tighter around my body. Our heads dipped back and forth as our tongues dove in and out of each other's mouths, each exploring the other. I could find no traces of fangs anywhere. His mouth was as kissable as the next guy's--probably more so.

Pallo pulled slowly away. A tiny sound of disappointment escaped from my lips and he chuckled. "Come, Gwyneth, I have something for you."

I looked at him as he took hold of my hand. He was so gentle with me. I knew that he had to be making every effort to be that way. From all the reading I'd done on vamps, they possessed enormous strength. He could have crushed my hand in an instant if he had wanted to. Instead, he pulled me down the twisting stone path, deeper into the Enchanted Forest.

"What do you have for me?"

"Ah, I will show you, but first you must tell me what the one thing you want most in the world is."

It was such a strange request that it caught me by surprise. I shrugged and said, "A repeat performance of that kiss?"

He laughed and pulled me into his body, lifted me from the ground, and spun me in a circle. It was exhilarating. "You may have as many of those as you would like, but try to be serious for a moment. What is the one wish that you have always had?"

I thought about what he had asked. My mind raced, and then it hit me. "To meet others like me."

Pallo's eyes lit up. He extended his hand and brushed back a large tree limb to expose another sign. "Welcome to the land of Faerie" was spelled out in gold lettering. I froze. He touched my arm, sliding behind me slowly, and moved my hair aside to expose my neck to him. Kissing it softly, he whispered, "This is for you."

"But how?"

"Shhh. Do not question it, Gwyneth, just trust in me when I tell you that I created this for you."

I believed him. Damn it, I believed every word he said, and I knew why. It was because I had fallen for him. I didn't question how he created this before he even knew me--I didn't question anything. He had me now, and I'm sure he knew it. He eased my body forward and we crossed the threshold to Faerie Land. The sun beat down on us. I screamed and tried to push Pallo back out. He only laughed and stood his ground. He didn't burst into flames. That was a huge relief.

"It is not earthly sunlight. It will not harm me."

I let out a breath I hadn't realized I'd been holding. "I thought, I thought…."

"I was slightly concerned that you would want to see me turn to ashes."

I gave him a stern look. "That isn't funny and you know it."

His laugh bellowed forth at me and was contagious. I laughed along with him until my ribs hurt. "Oh, my *silly* Pallo, whatever shall I do with you?"

Pallo stopped laughing and looked at me. I didn't think a vampire could get any paler, but he managed it somehow. His eyes widened. "What did you just say?"

I shrugged. "What?"

He circled me slowly, like a tiger stalking its prey, and stared at me from every angle. I turned to follow his gaze. "Okay, this is just creepy."

"Yes, Gwyneth, even I will agree with you on that one."

"Pallo?"

He shook his head and reached for my hand. "Some habits cannot be broken by even the worst of circumstances."

I took his hand and stared at him, puzzled. I wanted to ask him about that statement but he directed us down a small path. Little cottages lined a cobblestone walkway. Each cottage's chimney had smoke bellowing out of it, giving it that cozy appearance. Along the pathway, older faerie men and women were in the process of conducting their daily lives. All of the faeries I saw looked nothing like me. The tallest was maybe four feet high. Some women were sitting together working on a quilt, and others were knitting. Two older faerie men passed us riding in a wagon being pulled by two brown Kelpies. I had only ever seen Kelpies in a book before, so I reached my hand out to touch one. They appeared to be very similar to a domestic horse, and probably could have passed for one unless someone noticed their eyes. Their eyes were bright green and had a wondrous glow-in-the-dark quality to them. When I brushed the soft coat of the Kelpie, its color went from brown to gray. I drew my hand back quickly, unsure if I had caused that. The smaller of the two men on the wagon chuckled.

If a bunch of little people started popping out from behind bushes telling me to find a wizard at the end of a yellow brick road, I was going to have my head examined.

"Don't you worry none 'bout him, he does that when he likes someone." The man's voice was lower than I would have expected from someone his size. I saw that he had a small amount of facial hair. Looking to Pallo, I let my mind ponder the fact that I had always been told that faeries were tall, slim, had long hair, and no facial hair. Pallo, being the champ-vamp that he was, answered me before I could ask the question.

"There are many forms of faeries here." He looked so pleased with himself for bringing me here. He knew that I would enjoy this, and he was right. He took my hand and led me further down the path. We came upon a small stone bridge with a small stream running   below   it.

"I suppose you even managed to hire a few trolls to jump out from under the bridge at park guests?" Glancing up, I noticed the wind moving his brown semi-curls from his chiseled face. Man, how I wanted to be the wind.

He gave me a mischievous grin. "Not all the creatures in the park are employees." I could hear the truth to his words, but couldn't make sense of them.

"My dear Gwyneth, for reasons of my own I created a portal here to the faerie realm. I offer them safe passage, and in return they allow guests to walk among them." He held my hand tighter as he told me this.

The cool touch of his skin comforted me. I stared at him a minute and knew that this place was as close to daylight as he would ever be able to get with me. I wanted this moment to last forever--an eternity. As silly as it sounds, I envisioned the two of us growing old and raising a family together. Nothing like just meeting a guy, and instantly hooking a ball and chain around his leg. Great, now I was clingy and desperate for a husband.

Instantly, I was hit with another vision. This one didn't feel like it had ever taken place. It felt like I was bearing witness to someone's deepest desire. Not just any someone, but me. I pictured Pallo placing his hand on my lower stomach. It was big and round with child. My shirt was pulled high, exposing it to him. He slid his face down and rubbed his cheek against my swollen belly. He kissed it, and I knew that this life in me was ours. I was so in love with him and with the idea of starting our family. I was giddy, so much so that the vision was forced to ease its hold on me.

Shaking my head slightly, I rose up on my tiptoes, and gave Pallo a surprise peck on the cheek. The vision slid from my head and into his. I tried mentally blocking it from going, but it was too late. He jerked back from me quickly. A look of shock ripped through his devilish good looks. Before he was able to respond to me, Caradoc appeared out of thin air beside us.

I didn't scream or die of fright from a vamp materializing. Good job for me.

"Master, your services are needed immediately."

Pallo nodded. "Thank you. And Caradoc, there is no need to call me master."

"Sorry," he said, stepping back, giving Pallo and me more privacy.

I was so embarrassed I wanted to crawl under a rock and die. "I'm sorry. That was too much, I know. I bet you're going to find this hard to believe, but I'm not trying to snag a husband and--"

He put a finger to my lips, silencing me. "You've done nothing wrong. I must see to this minor detail. Would you like me to have Caradoc stay with you?" He motioned to Caradoc and he stepped forward. Caradoc looked a little uneasy about being volunteered to baby-sit me. Who could blame the guy? I had already damn near staked him once tonight.

"No, I'm fine. Go ahead. I can find my way back to the main house, and I'd like to look around here." Something sank in the pit of my stomach, as he took my hand to his lips.

"I shall be thinking of you, Gwyneth."

And I you.

The words were there, but I did not say them. Instead, I watched them head towards the entrance of the Faerie Land. The irony of two studs walking in a place called Faerie Land did not escape me. I let out a laugh. It echoed and came back to me louder, except it no longer sounded the same. I turned around. Bushes lined the stone path on the other side of the bridge. I was almost positive that laughter was coming from there. I stopped and listened hard for a moment. Then I heard it again. It was similar to my voice, yet not as it should be. That piqued by curiosity, so I headed across the bridge to investigate.

Something seized my right ankle, caught me off guard, and pulled me off my feet. My shoulders hit the ground first, then the back of my head. Something big and hairy closed in on me. My eyes widened as I made out the faint shape of pointy green ears under the piles upon piles of ratty long hair that covered the beast like a sheepdog. The dark greenish creature reeked of stagnant water and pulled me towards it. I caught a glimpse of its beady yellow eyes under a veil of hair and realized I was staring into the face of a troll. It snarled at me and snatched at my neck. I did what any normal girl would do. I kicked that thing as hard as I could. My foot struck its upper arm, bounding off as if I'd kicked a steel wall. Pain shot up my leg. I was pretty sure I'd just broken my toes, but at that moment I had bigger issues to worry about, like keeping the leg.

I screamed as loud as I could, hoping that one of the faeries that Pallo and I had passed on my way in would hear. I was beyond scared, I was pissed and in pain. Power surged inside me, rushing through my veins. I let it loose, and lashed out at the troll. It flew backwards and landed in the stream.

Rolling over to try to stand, I came nose to nose with an even uglier troll. I frankly had never seen a troll face to face before and didn't think it could have gotten much worse than the last one. Guess I was wrong. Before I could defend myself, he clamped his nasty jaw down on my shoulder, tearing into my skin. Unbearable pain inundated me, and I cried out. It shrieked and lurched back, receding from my line of sight.

"Are you all right?" a soft male voice asked from over my head.

I glanced up behind me and saw a tall man standing there holding a bow and arrow. From where I lay he looked upside down, but I don't think it mattered what way you turned him--he was beautiful. Turning onto my stomach, I looked up at him. He was angelic, but before I had a chance to fully take him in, he knelt beside me and lifted me to my feet with one hand.

"Follow me, quickly," he said. When he let go, the weight of my body came down onto my throbbing foot, and I cried out. The bow and arrow man grabbed me around my waist and lifted me with one arm. He carried me over the bridge effortlessly. He kept turning us round and round, checking for more trolls. He carried me through the large green bushes and into a clearing. It took my breath away to see the field of flowers from my dreams right before my eyes. He stopped in the center of it and set me down onto the ground. I managed to stay standing, but I had to lean on him for support. He was around six four and was thin, but well defined. When I said he was angelic, I wasn't kidding. The man was so gorgeous that he bordered on androgynous. If he hadn't been wearing a pair of tight blue jeans that cupped his groin, I wouldn't have known if he was male or female.

His hair was as long as mine and was so blond it was almost white. He had the front half of his hair tied up and away from his face. The rest lay behind his shoulders, hanging straight down his back. His skin was identical to mine--pale and flawless. He didn't look to be a day over the age of twenty, but neither did I, so who was I to judge? I glanced up to find him staring off in the distance with wide dark green eyes that seemed to glow.

"Your eyes."

He bent down on one knee before me. "I'm Caleb." He kept his head bent, and his hair trailed onto the flowers. "I'm at your service, my lady."

"What are you doing? Get up. I don't think he pays you enough to do all of this."

He rose but didn't look at me. "Who doesn't pay me enough for what?"

I smiled. This was so good. I had to admit, having the troll bite me was a little over the top, but the rest was truly authentic. "Pallo ... the troll thing was a nice touch."

"I know Pallo, and he does not pay me for my services. I answer to no one. And the trolls you refer to were not staged. They tried to kill you." His gaze finally met mine, and suddenly, he too looked like he was staring at a ghost.

I was tired of getting the look-how-spooky-you-are treatment and wanted desperately to have the nasty troll bite cleaned out before it got infected. "Cut the shit, Caleb. What's going on? Why are you running around here with a bow and arrow? Where's your band of merry men?"

"Listen. I tracked the trolls into this realm. I didn't know why they were headed in this direction. But now I do."

"Please, just come to the point. Why did they attack me?"

"Trolls are creatures of the Demon World. Someone must want you pretty bad to recruit those things to do their dirty work." He came closer and touched my wound. "We need to clean this before the poisons go through your system."

"Poisons? What? What's the Demon World? Why would someone want to get me?" I had many more questions, but only managed to get those few out before he picked me up in his arms like I weighed nothing and walked through the flowers. They parted for him as they did in my dreams so many times before. I knew this place. My sleep had introduced it to me long ago.

You are the balance….

Caleb headed for the river running through the center of the field. We came to the bank of the river, and he didn't hesitate, he just stepped onto it. When I say onto it, I mean onto it. This was too much--a hot babe who walked on water. From where we stood, it looked as though we were crossing over to an endless field of flowers, but we didn't end up there. We ended up stepping into a large white courtyard.

"What was that?"

"Glamour," was his only response. I had done enough reading on faeries to know that Glamour was the term used for faerie magic. I didn't question him any further. What had been a dull pain in my shoulder was quickly getting worse. Stomach bile rose into my mouth, and I was suddenly glad that I hadn't yet eaten.

"Caleb…," I said, just before my body went into shock and I began convulsing.

Chapter 6

I woke to the sound of birds chirping in the background. I was lying on a bed of green leaves. I was not in a room, but rather a garden of sorts. Grass covered the ground, and pink and yellow flowers wove their way in and out of the trellis-like walls. Sitting up, I saw that my shoulder was bandaged and I was still wearing all of my own clothes. I twisted my body and let my arms touch the soft grass. My sandals were lying next to me, and two tiny butterflies were sitting very still atop them.

Slowly, I pulled myself up. A wicked pain shot through my shoulder. I made a mental note about avoiding troll bites in the future and walked toward a small opening in the flowers. Beyond the trellis lay a thick mist so dense I couldn't make out if there was ground there or not, so I didn't test my luck. I turned around to examine my surroundings.

Wherever I was, it definitely smelled of peace and tranquility. A tiny iron table sat in the center of the garden and atop it sat a tray of fruits in an array of colors so vivid I thought they were wax. Starving and hopeful, I picked up a bright yellow pear and bit into it, enjoying the sweet, smooth taste unlike anything I'd ever purchased at a supermarket. The juice ran down my chin and neck, and I wiped it away, walking around the garden, looking at the flowers.

"How are you feeling, Gwyneth?" Caleb's voice came from behind me, startling me.

"How did you know my name?" I raised an eyebrow, meeting his gaze.

"That's easy. You talk in your sleep." He smiled, setting my mind at ease.

"I'm assuming by my surroundings that you're a good faerie, and that I'm not in the Demon World."

He looked surprised. "You assume too much. You are right about this not being the Dark Realm, but we aren't in the Realm of the Light either. To assume that I'm good would be foolish." He walked towards me. I noticed that he had changed his clothes and was now looking a little more comfortable in a pair of loose blue jeans and a white, long sleeved shirt. His hair flowed loose around his face, spilling past his shoulders down to his waist. Under normal circumstances, it would have looked good only on a girl, but he pulled it off somehow.

"If I'm not in either place, then where am I?"

"You are on neutral ground."

"Of both Realms?"

"Yes." He was almost close enough to touch. "This is a safe haven."

"You didn't answer my question about where you're from."

He laughed and said, "You are safe now, and alive, what does it matter?" He had a good point, so I left it alone. "Are you hungry? We could go grab an early breakfast. I know a great little diner that serves the best pancakes."

"They have a diner here?"

He laughed. "No, but I don't spend all of my time here. This is just a magical safe haven, if you will. Contrary to popular belief we faerie are not confined to this little area. We've even been spotted at fast food restaurants before." His eyes twinkled with mischief.

"Oh, as tempting as that sounds I'll have to get a rain check. I've had a snack, and I'm under a lot stress right now, with the whole troll trying to eat me thing, so I don't think I'd be very good company." I looked into his green eyes, and I wanted to be near him. I wanted to touch him, not run like a coward.

"What do you mean, you've had a snack?" He stepped closer to me and noticed the fruit on the table. "I didn't put that there."

I walked to him and let my hand brush up against his soft, white shirt. A small bit of his chest peeked out the top of the shirt, and I let my hand slide up to his bare skin. His heart beat fast. Without thought, I ripped his shirt open. He grabbed my wrist tightly, frowning at me.

"The fruit was tainted." He tried gently forcing me back from his personal space, but I didn't budge. I snuggled my body closer to his and pulled on him. I knew he was stronger than me, but he allowed himself to be pulled towards the ground anyway.

Always good to take one for the team.

"Stop, Gwyneth! It's a lust spell." Caleb looked down at me, as he pleaded with me to fight this.

"Lust spells only work on willing parties," I said as I planted my lips firmly on his. I forced my tongue into his mouth and felt him welcome me. My fingers ran up and twisted themselves in his hair. Juice from the pear had still been on my lips and now I could taste it on his. He tried to pull away from me for a moment before giving in to his desire. I tugged his bottom lip gently with my teeth. Gruffly, he pushed me back.

"This can't happen."

"Name one good reason why."

"Because we've been down this road before," he said, his voice low, haunted.

I had no idea what he was talking about. My body didn't care. "Then what's stopping us now?" I tore off Caleb's white shirt and threw it aside.

Caleb didn't answer, but lifted my black tank top over my head and cupped my breasts in his hands. He slid his fingers down my sides, making me jump. His entire chest lay exposed to me now, and somehow, I had ended up completely on top of him. I slid my head down his body, kissing his tight chest all the way. Reaching the button of his jeans, I stopped and worked little circles on his skin there with my tongue. He made a small noise, and I took that as a sign to go on. Working his pants off him, I kissed his body more letting my tongue run along his inner thigh. He wore no underwear, so it was plain to me by the size of his erection that he wanted me, as I wanted him. The very sight of his hard shaft, sent moisture to my inner thighs as visions of my riding him played in my head. Licking the head of his cock, I moaned as the slight bit of pre-come leaked out of him. It tasted salty. It tasted wonderful. I wanted to take him in my mouth and suck him off until he found release, but my body needed attention, and now. Quickly, I stood and removed my capris.

Caleb pulled himself away before I could trap him beneath me. He got to his knees, his ruddy cock bobbing, and I dug my fingernails into his arm, trying to hold onto him. Reaching down, he picked up our clothes. I let out a small cry as he put his pants on, and began on mine. I didn't want to be dressed. I wanted to be used by him, fucked by him. I wanted to have Caleb touch me and do things to me that no other man had ever done. I whimpered as he lifted my foot to put it in each pant leg, and pulled up, sliding his hands over my thighs. He spent a little too much time near my hairline. He still wanted me, I could feel it. He snapped my black capris and began to rise. His face brushed past my naked breast on the way up and I let out a cry. I could see him straining from touching me, as he continued to dress me like a baby doll.

"Whoever did this used powerful magic, and you are still under its spell. I am over four hundred years old and should not have been so easily affected by it." He was pushing out on my good shoulder, trying to keep me at arm's length. "I'd love to spend eternity with you, as it was once promised, but I can't do that to you."

As it was once promised?

I couldn't think clearly. Our bodies were close enough that I could tell he really did want me. I could feel how hard he still was, even with two pairs of jeans between us. I tried pulling his face towards mine but he kept it from me.

"I need to get you to Pallo. He will need to know about this," Caleb said, attempting to pull me towards the white mist.

"Pallo who?"

He shook his head slightly and told me he was sorry before he lifted his hand and used his magic to knock me out cold.

Chapter 7

"Why in the Hell did you take her with you? You should have called me." Pallo's voice boomed so loudly that it echoed through the entire house. He stood in front of Caleb with his fists balled tightly.

I sat very still on the edge of the bed in Pallo's room, trying to keep the focus off me as much as possible. I looked around at the décor. It was done very contemporary. The walls were a charcoal gray. The room had an amazingly grand fireplace in it, and a large zebra print area rug covering the floor. Pallo had to have spent a fortune on that--the room was massive. Spotlights ran from floor to ceiling on what resembled metal ladders. Some funky spiral iron sculpture sat near a black door. It was not the door we had come in, so I didn't know where it went. There were two identical black dressers on both sides of the bed--which was unbelievably enormous. If you took two king-sized beds and placed them side by side, and extended it at least two feet further, you'd be in the ballpark of this thing. Red satin bedcovers ran across it. There was no headboard, only a mound of white and red pillows of all shapes and sizes. Sheer, charcoal black curtains hung on rods that went all the way around the perimeter of the bed. The curtains were pulled to one side, exposing the bed to all prying eyes. The guy had taste. I was impressed.

Caleb spoke, and I glanced up at him.

"She was attacked. I cleaned her wounds. You have nothing in this fortress of yours to cleanse troll bites, I'm sure of that. Would you rather I brought her to you to die? Isn't that getting a little old?" he asked in a bitter voice. He stood near the entrance to the room with his back to me. His long blond hair seemed to soak up the lighting in the room and cast it back out. He was still a sight that took my breath away, and I was beginning to wonder if it was because he was a faerie or if it was just the lust spell.

Caleb wasn't the first faerie I'd encountered. There had been one other, a man. He would appear to me often throughout my childhood, always watching me, never speaking. I'd been struck by a car once, a drunk driver, and the mysterious man with the long black hair and navy eyes had come to my aide. He healed me and repaired my bike. I was not sexually attracted to him at all. Caleb, on the other hand, I was drawn to in a carnal way and I had no idea why.

This was all too much. I wanted to go back to my apartment, clean up, and try to forget that any of this had happened. I wasn't loose Lucy and making out with strangers wasn't something I did. I felt humiliated and angry with myself for succumbing to the effects of a damn fruit. Sharon would die when I told her about this, and Ken would go mad.

Ken would also be mad when he found out that I scored a big fat zero in the information department. My rankings were moving up considerably in the falling head over heels for strange guys area. At least something was headed in a northerly direction.

Pallo's body language shifted, turning aggressive--scary. Lightning-fast, he advanced on Caleb with his eyes burning black and fangs extended. I sucked in a breath as he brushed toward Caleb. Caleb simply put his hand up and shot his power out to hold Pallo back from him. I could feel Caleb's power moving through the air in the room.

He was old, and he was powerful.

Pallo's body pressed against an invisible force. His eyes seemed to grow even darker. I was scared of him.

"I'm sorry, old friend. She was to be mine, remember that. It was my bed she ran to, and I failed to protect her. I have lived with that guilt long enough to not want to go through it again. I will not stop her next time. I love her and will not refuse her. She is the gift that was promised to us. This time around I will not stand by and do nothing as she chooses you." And with those parting words, he walked out of the room.

They couldn't have been talking about me. I'd just met them-- we had no history. Whoever they were talking about was definitely a source of contention between them.

Glad it wasn't me.

Pallo's gaze still burned black when he turned to me. I gasped and scooted further onto the bed. He stormed across the room and put his face between my legs. "Clean up--I can smell him on you."

I sat there, frozen, terrified. He snatched hold of my upper arms, and I winced as pain shot through my troll bite.

"I said CLEAN UP!"

I tried to cover my face with my hands, but he wouldn't let go of my arms. I looked at his black eyes and watched his face changing before me. Fangs showed as he snarled. Turing my face from him, I screamed. He was upon me before I knew it, his teeth sinking deep into my neck. It should have hurt, but it didn't.

Instantly, my mind was thrust elsewhere, into a dreamlike state. I tried to hold onto my thin grasp of the here and now, but I failed. A dark room rose around me, formed of stone. I knew that the walls were stone because I was chained to one. My naked back was rubbed raw from hanging there so long. It was so dark I could only see a few feet in front of me. Rats scurried about. A furry shape brushed against my foot, but I didn't care. I was more concerned with what else was in the room with me. Others were near me. They were evil--I was terrified.

A vampire with long shiny black hair came from out of the darkness. I couldn't make his face out. Something was running over my eyes and blurring my vision. It reached my lips and from the coppery taste, I knew it was blood--my blood.

Through my blurred vision I saw the man turn and gesture to three other males. They were also covered in blood. I knew that it was my blood that covered their bodies, and I knew without a doubt that they were going to kill me. They were going to take turns biting me and sucking on me until I hadn't a drop of blood left to drink. Thoughts of Pallo filled my head as they began to feed off me. I cried out for him, wanting his strong hands to pull the shackles from my wrists. I wanted to have him hold me in his arms. He didn't come.

The vision left me and my body wilted with Pallo still clamped on my neck. He jerked his head off me and I saw that his eyes were brown again and he no longer looked grotesquely disfigured. He now looked horrified.

"Gwyneth." He was still holding my arms tightly. I noticed little droplets of blood falling onto my lap from the bite on my neck. Pallo glanced down at his arms and released me. My body limp, I fell back on the bed like a rag doll.

"I lost control. The smell of his body on you was more than I could stand." His voice was small now--weak. He leaned over me, stroked my hair, trying to brush the wrong away.

A shiver ran through me as my body grew cold. I didn't care that he had fed off me. I didn't care that my body was going numb. I didn't care about anything.

"I have taken too much of your blood." He took my sandals off and undid my pants. When he had pulled them almost to my ankles, the vision of being chained to the wall flooded back to me. I screamed and kicked out at him. He held tight and pulled my pants the rest of the way off. I fought him so hard that he had to put me in a type of headlock to get my shirt off. He lifted my still flailing body off the bed and carried me to the bathroom.

Pallo laid me down on the cool floor. I lay there, unmoving. I wanted to curl up but didn't have the energy to bother. I heard water running in the tub, and noticed him shedding his clothing. I couldn't pull my gaze away from his body. It was even more sculpted than I'd first thought it would be. His thighs were thick, muscular, and the sight of them drew my eyes to his nether region. I was impressed with the size of his member, right up until I realized that he wasn't even hard yet and was huge. From that point on, I was slightly scared of it.

Steam rose, filling the room like a blanket of fog. It touched my cool face. It was so warm and welcoming. Pallo moved to me and slid his hands under my legs and arms. Scooping me up, he carried me to the tub, and submerged me in the steaming water. It was so hot--too hot. The feeling of wanting to get away rushed back into me. I punched at Pallo's chest and scratched at his face. I hated him at that moment. I hated him so much. He didn't come for me. He left me there.

He pinned me down, cradling me tight to his body, and looked at me. "Forgive me." Unshed tears filled his eyes. I hit him one last time across the face and caught my nail on his cheek, tearing it open. Seeing blood dripping down his cheek brought me back from the edge of my madness. He grabbed hold of me as I sobbed.

"You never came." I had no idea why I said what I did, but felt relieved for having gotten it out in the open.

Pallo rocked me gently. My body began to warm again, and I noticed that he was no longer immune to the state we were in. Naked, wet and pressed against one another, I felt his cock growing against my leg. I fought hard not to notice it.

"It was just a dream," he said. I knew he was lying. It was too real, too vivid not to have happened.

"What's happening to me?"

"I do not know."

His large arms wrapped around me, comforting me, soothing me. I was having a hell of a night. I'd seen the remains of a coworker had gotten attacked by trolls, almost slept with a faerie

and was naked in the tub with a vampire. Yeah, that pretty much
summed it up. I was screwed.

A shudder ran through my body and I rose to my feet. I found
myself standing before him, still in the tub, with beads of water
dripping down my body. His face never changed, he just sat
there looking at me with the most beautiful brown eyes. I
stepped out of the tub onto the tiny carpet. Stepping off the
bathmat, I headed for the door. My wet foot touched the marble
floor and went out from under me. Pallo grabbed me. I hadn't
heard him get out of the tub, he just appeared behind me. I turned
to him, and ran my hand over his erect nipples. The same
uncontrollable desire that had seized hold of me with Caleb
came flooding back. His body was sculpted, it was beautiful, and
it was standing before me. I was naked and ready for him. I
pulled myself closer to him, allowing my body to brush his.
Rubbing my breasts against his chest, I let a throaty growl escape
me.

"No," he said.

I could sense his desire for me and it drove me to continue
onward. Running my hands down his side, I eased them over his
hips, and made a trail straight to his erect shaft. He jerked, and
pulled away from me.

"We have forever, *delizia*, forever." The words flowed from
his mouth sweetly but stung my ears.

"I can smell your desire for me." I could feel my power
building up. My body was getting warmer and warmer. Desire
threatened to eat me alive. I wanted to have his body touching
mine, caressing mine, buried in mine and knew he wanted it, too.
He backed further away from me, and closed his eyes tightly.

"I will not take you when you are still under the influence of
the spell."

"You don't want me?" I asked, hurt and confused. I'd thought
that Pallo had felt the same for me. I thought that he wanted to
touch me as badly as I wanted to touch him.

The energy ran through my veins like a drug. If he didn't want
me then fine, I'd find somebody else. Spinning around, I
stormed out of the bathroom. When I entered the bedroom,
Caleb was standing in there. A knowing smile crept over my
face.

Next victim.

"I have more information about the troll attack on you," he
said. His gaze fell upon my wet naked body, and he stood very

still. He looked to the slightly ajar bathroom door.

"I'm guessing Pallo's in there," he said, bitterly.

Heat rose through my body, spilling out from me to him. I lifted my hand and thought of him standing before me nude. My power poured forth from my fingertips and onto him. I was now emitting a slight buzz, and didn't recognize the power that flowed within me. It wasn't mine, and it was attacking Caleb.

Caleb shrieked as his clothes began to rip from his body. A look of shock crossed his face as he tried to hang onto his pants but lost the battle. A smile formed on my lips, and I didn't know why. I had never in my life been as aggressive as this. I wanted to have sex and it didn't matter who I had it with. I met Caleb's eyes and saw that they harbored desire for me as well. He stood before me, cupping his groin like I hadn't seen it before. I could tell that he was completely erect and wanted nothing more than to be inside me.

He focused on something behind me. I turned and found Pallo standing in the room with us, wearing a pair of his infamous silk pajama bottoms. Anger flashed on his face. And his eyes no longer looked brown to me, now they were black, pooling pits of rage.

"GET OUT!" he screamed at Caleb.

I could not let that happen. I couldn't let Caleb leave, or more correctly, the power that now owned me could not let him go. I wanted someone touching me now, fucking me now, I needed it. Caleb made a sudden movement towards the door. Throwing my hand up, I used the power that ran through me to call upon the wind and force the door shut. He grabbed the handle but couldn't get it to budge. A strange laugh came from my mouth. I knew that this magic would be stronger than even his faerie strength.

"Please, Gwen … open the door." He was afraid of Pallo, or was it me? A flash came from behind me and I knew it was Pallo going after Caleb. I put my hand up and forced the energy out at him. He staggered backwards and fell to the floor. I was scared that I had killed him. I tried to fight the powerful spell that gripped me. It was stronger than my magical abilities--hell, it was stronger than Caleb's.

Desire swarmed over me, calling me, making my inner thighs burn for Caleb's touch, and my quim flood with cream. I wanted his body close to mine and knew I could make him want me too.

God, what was I doing?

Something else was taking me over, something sinister. I was compelled by lust, by need. Raw, sexual desire held control of me. Crying out in pain, I dropped to my knees. I tried to focus on containing the energy, but I couldn't. I looked at Pallo's body on the floor near me. Reaching my hand out, I tried to touch him. He was my lifeline and I knew that if I could just graze his skin, that he could help me fight it.

Pallo opened his eyes, and he stared at me. His eyes held no sign of anger. They looked sad and lost.

"Help me!" My voice was small as the words came out of my mouth.

Something ripped at my insides and drew my attention back to Caleb. The magical spell seemed drawn to him. He'd been with me when I ate the fruit, and he was who the spell wanted. Yes, my mind and body craved to have Pallo's pale hand caressing me, but the magic in me wanted faerie. It wanted Caleb, and I think a small part of me did, too.

"Caleb." I heard the words come from my mouth, but it didn't sound like me at all. "Come here." He turned slowly and headed toward me.

Inside my head I was screaming at him to stop helping our little problem, but he kept walking towards me. The black magic ran through me. It beat in my head, over and over, pounding like drums until I lost track of my own protests. It consumed me with its fierceness and left me in pain, disoriented. Pressure was building in my head and I was losing my ability to think clearly. I had a feeling of fire shooting from my chest and knew it was the power spilling outwards. As hard as I tried to contain it, it didn't work. It grabbed hold of Caleb and gave him the same need I had--for sex.

Caleb was on me in an instant, his body curved around mine. He lifted me off the floor and threw me onto the bed. I couldn't hide my excitement and opened my legs wide to welcome him. He kissed my neck and worked his way slowly down to my breasts. I arched my back when he took an erect nipple into his mouth. His warm tongue inched around it, plucking, sucking until a knot of need had formed in my womb.

The power running in me propelled outward and seemed to encircle Caleb. It enclosed him in my web of need, of lust, making him want to be in me as badly as I wanted him there. I may have been motivated by a lust spell, but I knew that they only worked on willing parties, and I was obviously very willing.

Moving my body out from under Caleb, I pushed him down on his back on the bed. The power that was circling him encompassed me as well. It lifted me up gently, allowing me to position myself just right above him. I found myself standing on the bed over Caleb's naked body, looking down at his eager cock. He was hard and ready for me. I lowered myself onto him, crying out as he spread my vagina to the brink and I had only just begun. My channel was tight but wet, allowing me to fully impale myself on him. He filled me completely.

I let my weight rest fully on his hips as I tried to adjust to having his cock buried in me. Unable to move from the shock of something that size in me, I laid motionless for a bit. My body ached to ride him furiously, but I held back. His cock flexed within me and I cried out in pleasure. The sensation of his warmth filling me was too much to resist. My body responded to him, and I began to make tiny figure eights with my hips on him. Riding him, caressing him, fucking him with no inhibitions.

He reached up, cupped my breasts, and pulled me towards him. I leaned forward and lifted my hips up and down on him, driving his cock deeper into me. I varied my speed fast, slow--fast, slow. Tiny grunting noises came from me, and Caleb echoed them. It was sea of bliss, of sex, of primal needs.

My breasts bounced near his mouth. He leaned his face up and sucked sweetly on one nipple--pulling it tight, taut, and erect. My abdomen grew warm, before heading straight to feverish. I'd never experienced anything like this before. Sure, I'd had orgasms before. Ken had seen to that, but this was different, this was so much more. It was a blending of magiks, souls, and bodies. Caleb's power rode through me, marking me, claiming me, making me his.

He reached around my back and grabbed my ass, pulling me down harder onto him. He was so hot and so hard. "Ahh ... that's it ... there," he muttered as I continued to ride him.

"Tell me how you ... ohh ... like ... that," I panted. My frankness surprised me, then again I was in the process of having sex with a man I'd only just met.

I wanted all that Caleb had to offer. The heat within me grew and my face flushed. As I sat on the cusp of an orgasm I gave into it and lost control, pushing my body onto his with a speed I hadn't known I'd possessed. My channel fisted his cock with involuntary motions, prompting me to ride him harder.

Looking into Caleb's beautiful glowing green eyes, I saw my

reflection in them. I had a fraction of a second to wonder why I had thought they were glowing again before seeing my reflection in them. I was a stranger to myself, and I found that oddly liberating. I went wild with frantic pushes. I wanted him to fill me with his hot juices--I wanted to bathe in it. "Caleb, yes … yes."

"Off," he panted.

I fell to his side, my leg touching him while he released himself. His seed splattered up my leg and I felt his warmth running down my thigh. I had an uncontrollable urge to get back on him and catch any leftovers.

Waste not, want not, right?

Caleb pulled me to him. He pressed his mouth to mine, and his tongue went in search of mine. He found it, and I let my body rest as we kissed. My legs were wet and slick with the juice of our lovemaking, and I could feel him flexing his cock under me--teasing me, taunting me. My body grew hot again, in answer to him. I ran my fingers down and wrapped them around his shaft. He was slick, wet, and ready to go again. I let my slippery lower half rub against him, caressing, encouraging him to enter me. He moved, and eased his body over mine, supporting his weight on his strong arms.

Waves of silky blond hair fell around our faces. Caleb moved a hand through his hair, pushing it over one shoulder, letting me see into his eyes. His eyes held something I hadn't seen before, pure unadulterated need. He looked hungry for me, even though he should have been sated. I should have been sated as well. I wasn't. I wanted more of him. One taste would never be enough.

Something rustled on the floor near the bed. I was too fixated on Caleb's shimmering eyes to bother with it. He kissed my lips gently, and eased his cock back into me, slowly. Still wet from before, he slid in easier now, filling me fuller, filling me faster.

"Yes! Oh, yes! Just like that, Caleb." I clutched onto his shoulders as he pumped himself into me.

Caleb pulled out, and I felt every inch of him exiting my tight entrance. Our bodies made strange sounds from all the fluids smeared on us. I wanted more. I begged him for it. He kept himself propped above me and brought his cock back into me, even slower than the last time. I felt him growing harder inside of me, and was shocked because I had thought he was already at full length. My vaginal muscles clenched him, their need barely outweighing my own. He moaned and thrust into me harder, faster--chanting my name over and over, slamming into me. My toes went numb first, then my thighs, butt, and groin. Clawing at him, I couldn't find where I stopped and he began. We were one. One body, one mind, one magic.

"I'm coming … now … uhh, now." My words sounded so foreign to me, but oddly liberating. I could never again go back to being a silent bed partner.

Caleb's ass tightened as he rammed himself into me, burying deep. He stayed there, filling me with his sweet, magical juices before collapsing on me.

I held onto his shoulders for dear life, feeling that if I let go, he would leave me, and take with him the magic we shared. The need for him was both scary and exhilarating. For a brief moment, I wondered if I'd be able to breathe without Caleb near me. This outrageous fear helped to lift the fog that had become my mind. Struggling, I managed to push back the black magic curtain that had been placed over me.

Turning my head, I saw Pallo on the floor pinned by the magic I'd shot at him. He stared at the two of us, his cheeks glistening with tears. The pain etched on his face broke my heart. I was not so far gone that I didn't understand what I'd done--the pain I had caused him. Making a two hundred year old master vampire weep wasn't easy. Tears came to my eyes as well. When Pallo saw this, he closed his eyes tight. Obviously, unable to watch anymore.

Caleb lifted his head to look at me and saw my tears. Something registered in his eyes, and he leapt off me. All the heat drained out of my body, and the dark spell faded away. It had gotten what it had come for, and had no need to linger, or to see the devastation it left behind.

Caleb was suddenly off the bed, looking dazed and confused. "Gwen, I couldn't stop. I'm…." He turned and smashed his fist into the wall, screaming in rage.

Pallo appeared behind him. My gut twisted, and I feared he would kill Caleb for something he had no control over. Pallo reached out and touched Caleb's shoulder. I gasped. Instantly, Caleb stopped punching the wall. His shoulders stiffened, and he looked as though he was preparing himself for battle. I prayed that it wouldn't come to that. Though I had only known these men for short while, I cared for them in ways that I'd never cared for anyone else. At the moment, their safety and happiness was my only concern.

I didn't know if a vampire was stronger than a faerie, but I was betting Pallo's rage would be a help, not a hindrance. I couldn't let this happen. I sat up on the bed. My body dripped with the leftovers of the evening's festivities. I searched for a towel, for anything to wipe the reminder of what I'd just done from my body.

Pallo tightened his grip on Caleb's shoulder, and my stomach curled into a tight knot. "No…." My voice came out, barely above a whisper, and was completely unnoticed by them.

"I'm sorry. I should have been able to control myself. I should have…," Caleb said. His fists slid down the wall, leaving a bloodied trail from his barrage of blows against it.

"No, *va bene*--it is all right. I should not have taken her there tonight. I should have known that they would be waiting. I am too old to have been so foolish. I let my need to see her joy when she saw others like her, cloud my better judgment and it cost us all dearly," Pallo said, his Italian accent the thickest I'd heard it yet. "I have you to thank for bringing her back to me safely, *il mio amico*--my friend."

I pulled the top red sheet from the bed, and covered myself with it. Suddenly ashamed of myself, I wanted to disappear, to sink into oblivion and never have to look them in eye again.

How had I managed to make such a mess in such a short time? And how had I managed to care for two men so deeply that I was willing to do anything?

Pallo looked at me and lowered his eyes. "We have failed her again, *il mio amico*. We have failed her again."

I glanced at the two of them. They were so different, yet the same. Both were tall, but one was made like an Adonis, and the other an angel. Was I the devil between them? The temptress? The Eve in their garden of normalcy? Had I ruined the fragile friendship they seemed to have?

I waited with bated breath for a fight to begin. None did. When I was sure they weren't going to rip each other's heads off, I headed back into the bathroom. I went straight for the tub again. It was still full of water. I put my hand in to test the temperature of the water. It was still warm. How the hell hot had Pallo made the first bath? Was he trying to save me or burn me alive? At this stage of the game I didn't care. I just wanted to get cleaned up, go home, and pin a great big red letter to my chest.

Chapter 8

After I finished scrubbing away the day's festivities, I cracked the bathroom door open and peered into the bedroom. The bedding had been changed to all black. I had to marvel at the speed and efficiency of Pallo's housekeeping staff. I had yet to see a one of them, and everything was always spotless. I wasn't sure if I was impressed or spooked. Either way it was clean and tidy again. There was no trace of what had occurred.

I had no clean clothes with me, so I wrapped up in a red towel that covered all of me, not that it mattered--I had just given the performance of a lifetime. Perhaps, I could sign autographs on my way out. I felt sick to my stomach thinking about it again. I felt cheap. I hated that piece of me that wasn't strong enough to fight the spell. I was grateful that it was Caleb to whom the spell had directed my lust. I would have preferred Pallo, but I was happy that it wasn't something like one of those disgusting trolls that had attacked me. I shuddered at the thought of having sex with them, and stepped out into the room.

"Feeling better?" Pallo's voice came from my right. I jumped, startled by his presence.

He was leaning against the wall, on the other side of the bathroom door. If I didn't know any better I would say he was hiding there. He had changed his clothes and was practically camouflaged with the bedroom décor. I smiled at the thought of needing a search party to locate a vamp in his own room. Calling that in would be hilarious—"help, I've lost a two-hundred plus year old vamp … I don't know where he is, check behind the track lighting. Ohmygod, officer his monochromatic-ness has done him in." I laughed and shook the thought from my head.

Pallo's hair was pulled back tightly from his face. The loss of his soft brown curls framing his face made him look hard--made him look villainous. I had half a mind to run back into the bathroom and lock the door. I knew he could break it down without really trying, so it seemed silly to bother. I edged out of the doorway, making sure I moved away from him. His gaze dropped to the floor.

"I have no plans to harm you," he said softly.

I let out a small snort. The phrase "could have fooled me" came to my head. I took another step back from him. "I just want to go home." My voice sounded mousy.

Great, now I'm a tramp and a wimp.

Pallo kept his eyes lowered. I knew he was trying not to stare at me only wearing a towel. I was happy to know he was trying to be polite, but I didn't really see the point. He had just watched me do another guy on his bed. Short of charging admission, I wasn't sure how much more of a show I could have put on in front of him. Thankfully, I had no intention of putting on an encore presentation. Mortified didn't even come close to describing how I felt.

"I will see to it you get home safely," he said. I heard a but coming on. "I would like to offer you one thing first."

There it was, that always present string attached to an offer. Why was it the men in my life seemed very fond of bargaining that way? I watched him skeptically, wanting to ask what the condition was, but I wasn't sure I really wanted to know. He didn't wait for a response.

"I would like to offer you my friendship," he said, raising his eyes to meet mine.

I couldn't believe my ears. This guy was offering me his friendship. Was he just waiting to see how I'd react? Letting my jaw drop seemed too obvious of a response. Asking if he was fucking insane seemed way more appropriate. Surprisingly, I held back.

"Why?" I asked, waiting for the loophole.

"*Chi trova un amico trova un tesoro,*" he said, his voice wrapping around me, forcing to me to concentrate on breathing again.

I shook my head, knowing I had to look as puzzled as I felt.

"I said, he who finds a friend, finds a treasure."

I thought I'd been on the verge of melting before I knew what he was talking about. Now, I was sure I'd faint if he kept it up. Passing out by way of sexy talk wasn't how I wanted to go down. I smiled and tried to compose myself. "Pallo, I don't think this is such a good idea."

"Gwyneth, I would rather have you as a friend than not at all."

My mind raced to the various visions of the two of us I had been having. I got the feeling that there was more to the story than Pallo was letting on. I also got the feeling that his offering to be friends was a big deal. It gave me the impression that he didn't offer his friendship to anyone, and that I should take him up on it.

"Strictly friends?" I asked, secretly hoping he'd say no. I didn't want to be just friends with him. I wanted to erase the last few hours and start over.

"If the only thing you wish from me is friendship, then yes. Is that all you wish from me?"

I took a step towards him. "Yes." I was lying through my teeth, and I think he picked up on it.

Damn the vamp mojo.

A devilish grin swept over his face. He looked like a kid in candy store--lacking the innocence, of course. His dark brown eyes twinkled, and his mouth pulled into a strong, wide smile. That alone was enough to make a gal go weak in the knees. Problem was--he knew it. I rolled my eyes and began to walk away.

"Here," he said, holding out an arm full of clothes to me.

"What are those for?"

"Are you planning on wearing my towel home?"

I blushed. "No, I'm not. But where did you get all of those?"

I counted at least three different dresses. He gave me a wicked little grin. I smacked myself on the forehead lightly. "Don't tell me you keep women's clothing lying around the place." I had to laugh. The thought of him buying women's clothes was just too funny. I got a clear picture in my mind of how that would play out.

Attention shoppers, we have a vampire in aisle fourteen, women's lingerie, please exercise caution and do not leave your children unattended.

Sure, it bordered on the weird, but what with Pallo didn't?

His mood was warming--it was good. "One can never be too prepared," he said, with the slightest hint of humor in his voice.

I took the clothes and walked to the bed, laying them out on it. There were actually five dresses there. Why wasn't I surprised that there wasn't much to them? Three of them were black, one was red, and one was white. They looked like they were all made of spandex. I grabbed the red one. It had the most material to it … and that wasn't saying much. I turned and glanced at Pallo. He just stood there grinning at me, almost innocent looking--too innocent.

"Umm, Pallo, are you going to watch me get dressed? Friends don't really do that."

He released a small sigh. "It appears that we travel in very different circles. Very different indeed."

"Pallo," I said, making my voice sound stern. All I really wanted to do was bust out laughing. Encouraging his bad boy behavior seemed unwise, so I didn't.

He nodded. I waited for him to leave before snatching up the dress. It looked three sizes smaller than what I normally wore, probably a size four.

I let the towel fall to the floor as I pulled the dress over my head. Something brushed over my breast lightly as I yanked the dress down. I let out a small gasp and tried to hide the fact that it had excited me.

Pallo was standing beside me holding a little red piece of material close to my body. I glared at him.

"I thought you said just friends? Do we have to go over the ground rules?" I was mad mostly because I liked it, and I shouldn't have. I'd made a mess of things and lusting after a sexy vamp right after I'd given into a black magic spell was hardly appropriate.

He leaned close to me, his breath brushed along my skin, making me bite my lower lip in yearning. "If you would rather not have this, I will go." He pushed the material at me.

I took the scrap of material and stared at it. It was a thong. "You've got to be kidding me!"

He went to take it back. "If you would rather go without?"

I snatched it back. "NO!"

Pallo laughed, turned, and vanished from the room. I was getting sick of the whole popping in and out routine. I hoped I'd get used to it, doubted it though. Grown men materializing from thin air might be one of those things that one can never actually prepare for.

Oh, maybe I could convince them to have a call sign to alert me of their arrival. Marco--Pallo would work. My lame joke embarrassed even me.

Putting the thong on, I walked back into the bathroom to look in the mirror. I saw my reflection and was shocked. I looked like a hooker. I had no bra on, so my nipples were visible beneath the skintight material. The dress barely covered my butt. If I bent over I knew I'd flash anyone around me. With as thin as the thong was there was no way my well maintained thatch of lower region hair would stay covered. Short of going with a Brazilin wax, I was left in the position to simply not bend over.

My hair was almost as long as the damn dress. Going

'Godiva' would have covered more than the dress did. I had to laugh. I had never in a million years thought I'd wear anything like this--maybe for Halloween. No, probably not even then.

I did my best to adjust myself, and headed out of the room. Pallo stood in the doorway with Caleb. I stopped and waited for the fireworks to begin.

"I told you I would see to it that you made it home safely," Pallo said, looking at me but gesturing to Caleb.

My gut clenched. I wasn't ready to be locked in a car with Caleb. I didn't think I could control myself around him. "Thanks, but no way! I've had enough excitement for one night. Besides, I brought my own car," I added, hoping this would free me in some way.

Pallo looked to Caleb and, as if on cue, Caleb spoke. "I've already told Pallo that I'd follow you home."

"Why do I need an escort?" They were leaving something out, I could tell. They glanced at each other and then me. Fabulous, coconspirators!

Pallo spoke. "I do not wish to alarm you. However, the attack on your life was intentional. I...." He looked to Caleb. "We feel it would be in your best interest to have someone with you until we know more details."

"Listen, I don't know what the hell's going on around here. My life was fine until I came here, until I met you, and I don't need anyone to be concerned with my best interests."

Caleb stepped closer. He looked at my outfit and smiled. His lip quivered, as he bit back a laugh. "It looks like you can take care of yourself. Nice dress."

"Very funny."

"Gwen, I know you aren't going to like hearing the fact that you have to trust us, but it's the truth, and you really don't have much choice," Caleb said.

Caleb didn't look at all intimidating. Pallo, on the other hand, looked very powerful with his hair pulled back tightly from his face, and his gray shirt showing off his muscles. The two of them couldn't have been more polar opposites if they tried, yet I felt like they knew something I didn't. I felt like they shared a bond that was deeper than anything I could possibly fathom. Besides, if they wanted me dead, I would be already. Right?

"Uncle, you win. Are you ready?" I asked Caleb, anxious to get home.

"Yes."

Pallo took my hand in his. "I am sorry that I could not personally take you. The sun has already risen. I am sure you understand." He kissed my hand gently. The back of my legs began to buckle.

Keep it together, Gwen, keep it together.

"Sure, I understand." I pulled my hand free and walked towards the door. I turned back long enough to thank Pallo, but he was gone. I glanced at Caleb. He didn't seem surprised or even impressed for that matter.

"Does he do that often?"

"Yeah, he's a bit of show-off."

We left Pallo's and headed for the parking lot. It wasn't hard to find my car. It was one of only a handful sitting there. Caleb headed off to get his while I walked to mine. It was only around nine in the morning, but already it was sticky and humid. The spandex dress was making me sweat in places I didn't even know I had.

I opened my creaky car door and climbed in. I reached under the seat to fish my purse out and get my keys. That's when I noticed the car smelled funnier than normal. It smelled different. I turned to look in the back seat and my hand slid through something slimy. I jerked it back.

"What the hell?" I asked aloud, as if anyone was going to answer. Nothing seemed out of place. It was the same old dilapidated piece of junk I left parked there the other night. My nostrils curled from the odd smell. I knew that scent. It was the smell of a dog, a wet dog to be exact. I didn't own a dog, nor had I ever owned one. I looked back to the slimly pile of goop on the passenger seat headrest. It had to be dog slobber, but how?

I jumped when something rapped on my window. It was Caleb. I cranked the window down with half a mind to yell at him for scaring the crap out me.

"Hey," he said. "I just wanted to let you know I'm all set." He pointed back at a new red Ford Explorer with its door standing open.

"Thanks," I said, putting the key in the ignition. The smell of dog was so overpowering, I shook my head to try to get rid of it.

"What's the matter?" Caleb asked, leaning into my window.

"Do you smell that?"

"Smell what?" He bent his head in and his hand touched my steering wheel. His eyes closed tightly, and his head tipped to the side. I went to turn the key and he grabbed my shoulder hard. It was the one with the almost healed troll bite. I winced and went to shout at him, but he cut me off.

"Get out! Get out now!" he screamed, yanking my door open and pulling me away from the car.

He dragged me towards the red Explorer, and practically shoved me in. He climbed in behind me, threw the car into gear and made a huge loop that left us sitting about a hundred feet from the side of my car.

"What the hell was that all about?" I asked, trying to rub the dull ache from my shoulder.

Caleb lifted his hand. I flinched, expecting to be nailed. What I felt was his energy--his power brush past me in the direction of my car. I heard the engine trying to click over. He was starting my car! I was shocked and a wee bit impressed. I was about to ask him why he was starting my car when he hit the accelerator, propelling me back against the seat, sending even more pain through my shoulder. I heard a huge boom and turned. The whole area seemed to shake, vibrate, as my ears rang, and my heart leapt to my throat. My car or what was left of it was engulfed in a huge ball of fire. I turned back to Caleb slowly, my eyes wide.

"How did you know?"

"When I touched the wheel I saw it."

"You had a vision of someone doing this?"

"No," he said, clutching the steering wheel tightly. "I didn't have a vision of what had happened. I had a vision of what was to come."

I gulped. Did he mean he saw me getting blown to bits when he touched the wheel? I glanced at him. His eyes were wide and looking at me, but past me. I knew then that he had, and I didn't want any more details. I'd been on the receiving end of those visions before and I knew how vivid they were. I shook slightly, suddenly very uneasy.

He touched my knee. "Let's get you out of here, okay?"

"What about my car?"

"What about it? It's not really drivable, now is it?"

"Shouldn't we call the police or something?" I asked, looking back at the inferno.

He patted my leg. "Some things are better left unsaid. Pallo will see to it that it's taken care of. He's *good* at cleaning up messes." There was a hint of sarcasm in his voice at the end.

I knew from the way his house looked that Pallo had money,

but I never expected he had that much clout. Part of me didn't want to know what kind of people I had managed to get myself mixed up with. They were shaping up to be the supernatural Mafia. And of course, I picked "Don Pallo" out of the vamps I could have chosen from.

My week had started out pretty run of the mill. Now look at it. I had led an ordinary existence right up until I met Pallo. I went to work every day, did my job, and went home. Every now and then I had the occasional change of routine. I would take a class in self-defense, painting, or cooking. I didn't waver off the path of normal too often. I liked my little routines. I was a creature of habit, and I liked knowing what was going to happen next--it was safe. This was not.

"Can you take me home, please?" I asked, staring out the front window.

"Gwyneth...."

"Gwen," I corrected him.

"Right, Gwen, I don't think that's such a good idea. If they found you here, they know where you live. Do you have anywhere else to go?"

I thought about my options--they were Ken and Sharon. Not too many options, huh! I really didn't want to barge in on Ken porking the redhead again, and Sharon was headed out of town. Besides, she was staying with family until her apartment was done being painted. No help there.

I wanted to say that I had nowhere to go but my apartment when I thought about my parents, Paul and Sarah. They had both passed away in the last year and a half. I lost my mom to a stroke and my dad to a broken heart. It had been hard. Ken had helped me get through it. He had been my rock, the strong, steady being I needed to hold myself together. I had cried the night he proposed to me, not because I was so happy, even though I was, but because my dad would not be there to walk me down the aisle.

After they passed, Ken tried to convince me to sell their houses. They had a main house and a vacation home. Saying that made them seem so much grander than they really were, but that's okay, they deserved it. The main house was where we lived the majority of the year. The vacation home was more of a country farmhouse. It sat on about two hundred acres of land, the majority of it wooded. The closest neighbors were at least fifteen minutes away in either direction. It sat about a mile off the road.

A huge river ran through the center of the property.

Ken had managed to talk me into selling the main house, but I hadn't been able to bring myself to sell the other.

When I made my decision to move away from home and head to college, I thought I would run as far and fast as I could to get away from the small town I grew up in. All I wanted to do now was run back to it. I wanted to leave the hustle and the bustle of the big city behind.

"Caleb, I hate to ask you to do this. You can say no if you want." I paused. He glanced at me.

"Gwen, I'll do anything you want me to."

"Could you take me to my family's country home? It's about a half hour away from here."

He smiled at me, and his green eyes lit up. "The way you were acting, I thought you were going to ask me to take you to Mexico or something. I would have agreed to that, just so you know."

That made me smile.

Chapter 9

We turned onto the tiny one lane road that the house sat off of. I hadn't been there in a year, but nothing had changed. Weeds and tall grass still bordered the road. We passed two drives on the road before I had Caleb turn right into the driveway. My mom had wanted my dad to pave the driveway, but he didn't see any point in spending money trying to pave a mile's worth of driveway. We only used the place for about twelve weeks a year.

Pine trees lined the drive for the first half of the lane, extending high into the air, blocking most of the sunlight. They opened to a large grassy area. I could still remember the smell of freshly cut grass and the sound of the riding lawnmower buzzing. I missed Paul and Sarah. They were the only family I had ever known. It never once mattered to them that I was adopted, or that I had extra gifts. They loved me for me.

The corner of the house poked out at us from behind another large pine tree. I smiled when I saw the huge white wraparound porch.

Caleb parked the car around the end of the circular driveway.

He opened his door as I sat there, looking at the front of the house. It was still as breathtaking as it had always been to me. It wasn't so much that it was extravagant--it wasn't--it was how simple, yet perfect it was. All white with hunter green shutters and front door. It was perfect.

"Gwen, are you okay?"

The sound of his voice brought me back. I opened my door and got out. He followed suit. I stepped onto the small stone walkway. Grass had grown up through the cracks. It looked like it belonged there. I liked it. I led Caleb up the four wooden steps and onto the front portion of the porch.

"I don't suppose you have a spare key roaming around that dress, do you? I mean, it doesn't look like you could be hiding much in that," he said, smirking.

"It was the best choice, trust me."

"Yeah, I've seen some of Pallo's women. I don't doubt that for a minute."

The thought of Pallo having other women made my chest tight. He wasn't mine, and I had been the one to agree on being just friends. What he did was none of my business, so why did it still bother me?

I walked to the left of the front door. I bent down and moved the welcome mat. My fingers slid along the smooth stained boards. I felt the loose one and pulled it up. It was still there. My dad had made a little cubbyhole there for a spare key. He used to say, "You never know when you could be stuck on the outside looking in, best to be prepared." He had no idea how true his words had been.

I yanked the key out, straightened, and pulled open the screen and unlocked the front door. The smell of stale air hit me hard as the door swung open. I stepped in, Caleb following closely at my heels.

I put the key down on the table next to the door. It was dark inside with the curtains pulled shut to block the daylight. I flipped the light switch. I was happy I'd decided to leave the utilities on. Actually, it was more like I had forgotten to get them shut off. Ken had told me to call the utility companies and handle it. I forgot. Right then and there, I was happy I was absent-minded.

I looked around. Nothing had changed. I hadn't realized that I expected it to. The floors were still hardwood. The walls were still cream textured wallpaper everywhere, and the place still felt like home.

I gave Caleb the condensed version of the grand tour, pointing to each room as we went past it, then I headed upstairs to get changed. I walked down the hall to my room. I had still spent most of my summers here when I was in college.

I turned in and was overwhelmed with the feeling of being home. My queen-sized bed was sitting in the center of the room. A yellow and white quilt covered it. My mother had made the quilt to match the yellow walls of the room. I had insisted that my bedroom be yellow. She'd tried to talk me into pink and even white, but I wouldn't budge. I loved being surrounded by the warmth of the yellow. I had a large, old maple-colored dresser near my closet door. I'd gotten into the bad habit of buying clothes and leaving them there. I loved to shop thrift stores and bargain shops, so it only made sense to go ahead and pick a few extra items up and leave them, a just-in-case kind of thing. This was just in case.

I opened the drawer and found an old pair of cut-off jean shorts, a blue tank top, and a white, long sleeve, cotton button-down top. I had always kept undergarments here, so I wasn't worried about that. However, my underwear fashion had matured over the years, and I hadn't worn a pair of white cotton briefs in a while. Oh well, anything was better than the red string that had been giving me a wedgie since we left Necro World.

I put everything on, tying the white shirt at the bottom instead of tucking it in. I cuffed the sleeves until they were just under my elbows and went to the closet. I threw the door open and saw a few pairs of shoes I'd left behind. Brown work boots, white running shoes, and a pair of slip-on black loafers. I snatched the boots up, grabbed a pair of white socks, and put them on. When I looked at myself in the mirror over my dresser, I smiled. I looked like I was going hiking.

I searched through my top dresser drawer and found a hair band and brush. I worked the brush through my hair and braided it.

I trotted back downstairs and headed into the kitchen. Caleb was standing over the stove, cooking something. He looked so at home in my family's kitchen, I was speechless.

"Hey!" he said, turning and noticing me. "You look more comfortable."

"What are you doing?"

He smiled. "I was hungry, so I figured you would be too."

I walked over and stood next to him. I saw a box of pancake mix and syrup sitting out. Impressive. He had rummaged around that old kitchen and come up with enough stuff to make a meal. God bless instant pancake mix and hot guys.

"I wouldn't have guessed that you were a cook," I said, taking in the smell of the warm pancakes.

"Yeah, it's kind of hard to live four hundred years and not pick up a thing or two."

"You are full of surprises, aren't you?" I mused, going to the cupboard and getting out two plates.

He flipped the pancakes over. "What is that supposed to mean?"

I set the plates down on the old table and turned to get glasses. "Nothing, it just means that you're not what I pictured a four hundred year old faerie to be." He turned as I said this and gave me a puzzled look. "I would have thought you would be a little more proper, a little more refined." That's not what I wanted to say. What I wanted to say was, hey, you're so normal and gorgeous!

"Ouch!" he said, pretending to stab his gut. "I'm hurt. Really, I am. You want to know why I'm not like Pallo, Mr. Suave, right."

That thought hadn't entered my mind, but okay. "Yeah."

Caleb turned and lifted the pan, bringing it over our plates. He slid the pancakes down onto them. "I don't have to live my life in dark places, and I don't have people falling over themselves to impress me." He put the pan in the sink, turned and sat. "I don't have people falling at my feet, answering my every need. I had it once, and it wasn't all it was cracked up to be."

"Once?"

"It's not important. Anyway, I lead a pretty normal life--work, home, extracurricular activities…."

I ignored that last remark. "Okay, so where do you work?"

He smiled. "I hunt down supernatural creatures for my clients. I guess you could say I'm a bounty hunter for the things people don't want to talk about."

"Do you hunt vampires?" I was shocked.

"Only if they're wanted by the law--guy's got to have his standards, right?" We laughed and ate.

"I have a favor to ask before you go. Could you run me into town long enough to get some groceries?"

"That's not a problem. Besides, I'm not going anywhere."

"What?"

"I called Pallo as soon as we got here. He was worried sick about you. The car is being taken care of as we speak, but he was very clear on not leaving you alone here. And for once, I agree with him."

I was dumbfounded and more than a little ticked. "I don't need a babysitter. What is he paying you? I get the feeling that you're on retainer with him. Am I the new pet project for the old elf?"

Caleb looked like I'd just slapped him. His voice lowered. "Listen, I'm not going to take any shit from you. I don't think you can take care of yourself, and NO, Pallo's not paying me to do this. Don't think he didn't try, though."

I felt like such a heel. He was a nice guy, and I was questioning his motives. "So why are you being so helpful?" I asked. Old habits die hard.

"Gee, as if our little romp between the sheets wasn't enough?" I smacked his arm and glared at him. "I have my reasons for caring about you, Gwen."

We finished eating in silence, and then headed into town. We approached the main intersection of town and I had Caleb turn into Smart Food's parking lot.

We parked and headed inside. A boy, around the age of sixteen, came out of the back storage room as a little chime rang.

"Hello, ma'am, how can I help you?"

"Hi, just picking up some stuff, thanks," I said, picking up two baskets, and handing one to Caleb.

"Gweny Wheny ?" The squeaky voice said.

I glanced at him. Gweny Wheny? The only person who had ever called me that had been little Mitchell Smart, and I hadn't seen him in years. I had babysat Mitchell over the summers during college. He was around nine or ten the last time I saw him, and that would have put him about … oh, my God, little Mitchell Smart was all grown up. Well, not ALL grown up, but a hell of a lot bigger than the last time I saw him.

"Mitchell?"

He flashed me a goofy, teenage smile. "Yep. How have you been?"

"What are you doing working here?" I asked, before it dawned on me that his grandfather was Joe Smart, the owner of the store.

"Grandpa needed some extra help in the summer, so I volunteered." He blushed. "Who's that with you?" he asked, looking to Caleb.

Shoot, I hadn't really thought of running into anyone I knew.

"This is my husband, Caleb," I said quickly. When I realized what I'd said I just about fell over onto the floor. My husband? What the hell had made me say that? I tried to think of something to say to take it back. I came up empty.

"I didn't know you got married. Congratulations," Mitchell said, walking towards Caleb. "Nice to meet' ya, Caleb. Gweny Wheny's real nice."

Caleb extended his hand to Mitchell. "Oh, yeah, Gweny Wheny's real nice, real nice indeed. Darn good wife, too. She'll be good for breedin' if ya know what I mean."

Shaking my head, I walked away and picked out things we needed for the next day or two. Caleb came up behind me and put his arm around my waist. I tried to pull away.

"Now honey, don't go making a scene," he said loud enough for people on the street to hear. I wanted to stomp on his foot, hard. I figured he wouldn't feel it through his steel-toed boots, so I didn't bother.

We picked out everything we needed and I pulled money out of my pocket to pay. Caleb put his hand on mine, pulling out his wallet. Mitchell gave us an odd look, and Caleb just smiled.

"City girls are so independent," he said wryly.

Mitchell nodded and smiled like he totally understood what Caleb meant. I wondered how many relationships a boy of sixteen could have had, then I thought I didn't really want to know. We headed out, our arms full of bags. Caleb opened the back end of the Explorer and loaded everything in.

As we were climbing inside his truck, Mitchell walked out onto the store's porch, and waved goodbye. I waved back politely. Caleb turned and pressed his lips to mine. His tongue pushed into my mouth and for a moment, I forgot where I was and what was going on. Nothing but Caleb existed. His eyes closed as though to savor every second. I pulled back, and Caleb opened his eyes slowly. The shimmering I had seen in his eyes a moment ago was gone, they now were green, but deep, rich, and beautiful.

He smiled.

"Your eyes. They were on fire, glowing and green, now they're not," I said, his face still close to mine.

He pulled from me. "Well, little wife of mine, you really don't know that much about us, do you?"

"Us?"

"Faeries--you really don't know that much about faeries, do you?"

"I've only ever seen two in my life. That includes you."

He started the truck and pulled out. "Who was the other one?"

"I don't know. Just some guy that came around a bunch when I was younger."

Caleb slowed the truck and pulled off to the side of the road. "What do you mean, came around when you were younger?"

I shrugged. "He never hurt me."

"Pallo and I are the only two who knew you even existed, or at least we knew about you, not really that it was you."

They knew I existed, what the heck was that supposed to mean? Why did he look so freaked out by the fact that I'd seen another faerie? I was frankly surprised I hadn't seen more. From what I had heard, faeries were not uncommon. The only thing that was uncommon was finding a faerie under the age of two hundred.

"Can you describe him?" Caleb asked, putting the car in park.

"What is there to describe? Tall, dark hair, handsome, pretty average?"

Caleb shook his head. I was annoying him, obviously. "That's not really all that helpful. Do you think you could recognize him if you saw a picture of him?"

A picture? They kept pictures on file of all the faeries? News to me! I didn't have any doubt that I could pick him out if I saw him. I'd seen him at least a half dozen times before I turned ten.

"Sure, I'd know him if I saw him."

Caleb opened his door. "Come on."

"Where are you going?"

"To the library."

I got out and followed him across the street. I looked back and noticed that we had the truck sitting half in someone's yard and half on the road. Great! We really needed more attention drawn to ourselves. Maybe, for shits and giggles, we could erect a billboard for the whole world to know that something was going on.

Caleb walked up to the tiny red house with the small library sign and opened the brown door. I had always felt so drawn to the old library. I felt like I needed to be there, but I was too creeped out by the sensation to want to go in.

We walked in and found ourselves in a small room with books from floor to ceiling. It didn't look like the place was used much.

I glanced down at the new release section and only two books sat there. Either they were hopping with business or they didn't bother getting too many things in at a time.

Caleb stood very still, listening something. I heard nothing.

"What are we doing here?" I asked in a hushed tone, afraid of breaking his concentration.

He walked forward and went through a doorway.

"Hey!" I called after him. "Don't you think you should wait for someone to come and help us?"

"There's nobody here."

That didn't make any sense, the door was unlocked. Why would someone leave the library unattended? Caleb seemed to be thinking the same thing, because he let out a small laugh.

"I don't think they get a whole lot of people coming in here. The librarian probably went to lunch or something. Who knows?" he said, moving into the next room.

Even though we had entered another room of the house, it appeared to be identical to the last one. Rows upon rows of books covered the walls. If all the rooms in the house looked this way, we were going to be here a while. I didn't notice a computer or even a card catalogue when we came in. This was going to be the equivalent of finding a needle in a haystack the size of California.

Caleb stopped in the center of the room and whispered softly to himself. I made out only a few words. It sounded like he was repeating, "If I were a book on faeries, I would be...." I had to laugh. He turned and gave me a serious look. I shut up.

"Try mythology."

He gave me a strange look. "Its not like people know you're real. I highly doubt you'll find an autobiography by a faerie," I said. He nodded.

I saw another small doorway and walked to it. It was a smaller room set up similarly to the ones we had already been in. This one, however, had a small table and chairs, probably for studying. I felt drawn to the back corner of the room. Walking over to it, I felt like a hand had reached in, grasped my navel and was using it to yank me towards the back wall. I found myself standing before a row of books. Nothing was what we needed. They were self-help books. Although I did feel like a good inspirational speech was in order, we didn't really have the time for it. I turned to find Caleb and the pulling in my gut became painful, like someone was ramming a knife into my stomach.

Crying out in pain, I fell down on one knee.

"Gwen! Gwen, what's wrong?"

I put my hand on the bookcase to try to pull myself to my feet. I slipped back down and the book I was touching fell with me, landing open on the floor. The pain in my stomach stopped. In an instant, Caleb was next to me with his hand around my arm, bending down.

"What the hell happened?"

"I … I don't know. I just…." I stopped speaking, looking down at the open book. There, before my very eyes, was a picture of the man I had seen all of my life. He was sitting in a large golden chair. He wore black robes similar to the ones I had seen him in. His hair was long and black, like mine, but in the photo he was wearing a crown.

"That's him," I said, pushing the book towards Caleb.

He looked at it. "I thought you said you would recognize him if you saw him?"

I pointed at the picture. "That is him, Caleb, that's the man I saw."

He shook his head no and shut the book. "It can't be the same man, that's the king of the Dark Realm, or used to be at least."

"What do you mean, used to be?"

"I don't know. I had been living among humans a very long time when I got the news that King Kerrigan had disappeared."

"How does a king just disappear?"

He pulled me to my feet. "That's just it Gwen, kings do not disappear. He has to be dead. He would have regained his throne by now if he wasn't. Kerrigan wasn't a weak man."

"You sound like you knew him. Did you?"

Caleb bent and picked up the book. "Yeah, I knew him. I know his successor more though."

"Who replaced him?"

Caleb put his hand on my shoulder. "Let's hope you never meet her, she's an evil woman."

"Caleb," I said, reaching out and touching his face. "That is the man that came to me, I know it. Look." I closed my eyes and allowed him to share my memories of when I was hit by the drunk driver while riding my bike. I thrust the images of the man who came to help me into his head. He jerked away.

"Impossible!" I don't think he believed that what he had seen *hadn't* taken place, he was just surprised.

Chapter 10

I was exhausted by the time we got back to the house. Caleb said he had to make a few phone calls, and I headed up to bed. I undressed and climbed under the covers. I was just on the edge of sleep when I felt a cool breeze tickle my neck. I twisted my head into my pillow lightly.

"Gwyneth," I heard my name, but didn't recognize the voice. It was heavy accented, more so than Pallo and sounded Italian as well. *"Bella mia."* I jerked my eyes open and screamed out. It was mid-afternoon, and the drapes to my room were blowing gently from the slight breeze outside. I relaxed. It was only my imagination. The door to my room burst open.

I sat up. Caleb was standing there. He scanned the room and then glanced at me.

"I heard you scream," he said frantically.

"It's nothing. I just let my imagination get the best of me," I said, looking at him in the doorway. He had taken his shirt off and had the top of his jeans unbuttoned. My gaze slid down his smooth, hard body. He was so tall he had to duck down a bit to keep from hitting his head on the doorframe. I smiled at him and put my hand out.

Slowly he came close to me. I tried to keep looking into his dark green eyes, but my gaze kept falling lower. I remembered how it felt having him in me. It was good. It was safe, it was right. A tiny burning sensation began deep in my body. I shifted my legs and felt the moisture building. I blushed. Caleb came and stood next to my bed. I reached my fingers up to touch him near his opened jean button. He caught my hand.

"You don't have to do this, Gwen, you don't owe me anything." He sounded so forlorn.

I put my fingers into his jeans. No underwear, just like I thought. God, he was gorgeous, and my body yearned for his. Something was so right about him being near me, almost naked. I pulled his zipper down, exposing his tiny blond hairs to me. Sliding my hand in, I wrapped my fingers around his shaft. Instantly, he hardened, as I knew he would.

I leaned forward on the bed and bent my head down, planting tiny kisses on his lower stomach. I pulled on his jeans. They slid down his legs slowly, freeing him, leaving his cock bobbing near my face. I cupped his sac, kissed the tip of his penis, before taking him partially into my mouth.

"Ah … Gwen."

Licking the purple end of his shaft, I moaned and nibbled gently on it before brining him into my mouth. His hips began to move back and forth slightly. I moved my head up and down, cupping his sac in one hand and his shaft in the other. I felt him tightening in my mouth. He pulled my head back from him, and pushed on my shoulders, guiding me down on my back, sliding his hands over me.

"Ahh … you're killing me, Gwen. You know that, right?"

He got to my white cotton underwear. He laughed softy. I grinned and shrugged. They were more comfortable than the red string I'd been wearing. Caleb bit the top of them with his teeth and moved them down my body. When I was naked from the waist down, he moved back up the bed, kissing my legs. When his kisses reached my inner thighs, I cried out. He slid his finger touching me between my legs, parting my velvety folds, exposing me to him. He slid one into my core, and I clutched the bed. His lips touched me, and his tongue sliding over my swollen nub, the spot that every woman wants to have touched, yearns to have caressed, and folds once toyed with. My legs twitched as he artfully plucked my bud. He pushed another finger into me as his tongue continued to work tirelessly. I knew that the hood of my clit had retracted and that I was now engorged, swollen with the promise of pleasure.

"Ohh … yes … uhhh."

He increased his speed, and brought my orgasm with a fierceness I'd never seen. I gripped the sheets on the bed so tightly that they pulled loose from the ends.

I was lightheaded, and sated. I smiled lazily up, as Caleb moved his body over me on all fours. He was hard and waiting to enter me. His hair spilled down around us, enclosing us in a wall of shining blond beauty. I stared into his eyes. They were starting to change. The dark green color began to recede and a green glow flooded in.

I leaned up to him, kissing whatever part of him I could get my mouth on. Our lips met, and he slid his cock into me slowly. The smallest grunt came from my mouth, which was still on his. Our tongues caressed one another, groping, swirling, and mating.

Caleb eased himself in and out very slowly, savoring every

stroke. I pulled at the back of his head, encouraging him to be aggressive. He stopped moving altogether and fell on me, smothering me with his kisses. He went at my mouth as if it would be the last time he'd ever be allowed the pleasures of it. If I had any say in the matter, he'd have free access to it indefinitely.

He sat back on his knees in front of me on the bed, and pulled my body down to him, moving my hips up and onto his thighs. The sight of him gripping his shaft in one hand while his licked the fingers on his other hand was almost too much. Our gazes locked and I watched as he took the long, moistened fingers from his mouth and stroked my slit with them, working them in, making sure I was good and ready to take him again.

Biting my lower lip, I panted softly and he continued to finger me, while still stroking himself. "Do you like that, Gwen?"

"*Mmmhmm*," I murmured, too consumed by desire to form a sentence.

"Do you want more?"

"God yes!"

A slow smile crept over his face as he leaned forward. He thrust himself back into me, with a force that caused me to jerk up and off the bed a bit. Instantly, he was rubbing my tender, swollen nub with his fingertips, while simultaneously fucking me from his seated position.

"Yes, Caleb, yes!"

The pressure of him inside of me increased, as did his thrusts. He was pushing so hard that I was moving up the bed. I loved it, I wanted more of it. I tilted my head up. I closed my eyes tightly--they felt strange, different. My groin and thighs tightened. "Oh, yes … *mmm*!"

He slammed into me, and our bodies becoming one as our magics latched on to one another. We stared into each other's eyes. He yanked away from me quickly, finishing partly in me and partly on me. I grabbed at his body. He fell next to me, and embraced me.

I didn't know why he had pulled out before he was completely done. We were both magical, so sexually transmitted diseases didn't apply to us. As far as getting me pregnant, there was a fat chance of that. I'd gone and seen my witch-doctor, when Ken and I had been engaged, because I though it would be wise to get on some sort of birth control. Her office waiting room was littered with pamphlets about conception--how to achieve it, how to avoid it. I picked up the one regarding *Si* pregnancies. It was bleak. It basically said that intercourse between a human and a fey almost never ended with a pregnancy. It had something to do with a tiny difference in female *Si* reproductive systems. We rejected human male sperm. There were costly medications and treatments that one could try in an attempt to conceive, but that in itself was no guarantee. I took the pamphlet in and discussed it with the doctor. I told her I was actually three hundred and ten years old, what a lie. She said that was good, because my chances of conceiving prior to the age of one hundred were zero without medical assistance. I asked about my chances of conceiving with a faerie partner instead of a human one. She had told me that the odds of that were even slimmer than getting pregnant by a human. She never said why.

Needless to say, birth control was not necessary with Ken. I told him all about what the doctor had told me, and he said when we were ready to have a family we would do it, cost was not an issue. That had made me feel better. I really did want to have a family someday. Not today, but someday.

"Why did you stop?" I asked Caleb, holding him close to me.

He smiled and kissed the top of my head gently. "You were ripe."

I pulled back from him slightly. I was ripe? Did he think I smelled funny? I was about to ask him what exactly he meant by that when I heard the phone ringing. I kissed him on the cheek and pulled away from him. I walked out into the hall and picked up the phone.

"Hello?"

No one answered me. I heard something on the line but no voice, just a low throaty growl. I repeated myself, but only the growling noise remained. I hung up the phone and turned around. Caleb was standing in my bedroom door completely nude. Oh, was he a sight to behold. Just looking at him made me want to run my hands all over him, and have his body deep within me again.

"Who was on the phone?" he asked running his fingers along the woodwork.

"Wrong number," I said as I walked up to him, putting my arms around him, hugging him tight. He picked me up and carried me back to bed. We made love several more times throughout the night, and each time he withdrew from me prior to his release. Finally, we lay in each other's arms exhausted as sleep came.

Chapter 11

When I woke, Caleb wasn't in bed with me. I sat up. My room was dark. Had I really slept until nightfall? Wow, I must have been wiped out. Having marathon sex with the world's hottest faerie will do that to you. Grabbing a robe from my closet, I put it on, and headed downstairs to look for Caleb. The smell of food hit me when I reached top of the stairs.

Before I'd even reached the kitchen, I saw Caleb standing near the stove, frying something that smelled delicious.

"Smells good, but I'd rather eat you again. Why did you get up?" I asked, heading towards him.

He stopped cooking and stood very still, his gaze fixed on the wall behind the stove. I wanted to ask what his problem was, but when I entered the kitchen, I saw the problem. Pallo was sitting at the end of the kitchen table with his arms folded across his massive chest. His dark eyes locked on me. Pissed was an understatement.

Pallo's gaze raked over my body, stopping slowly at my waist. I felt uncomfortable and reached down to make sure my robe was closed.

"Well, you have certainly made the most of your day off, haven't you," he said bitterly.

Caleb turned from the stove slowly and walked up behind me, bending to kiss my cheek. I think it was more for show than anything else. I didn't want to play their little game. I'd had enough.

"What the hell are you doing here, Pallo?" I asked.

The wooden chair scraped against the floor and I saw a flash but it was too late. By the time I had registered what had just happened, Pallo was about an inch from my face, and glaring down at me.

"It is nice to see you too, Gwyneth, or should I say *donnaccia*?" Each word was clipped.

Caleb pulled me back from Pallo and stepped between us. "Enough, Pallo, you'll not call her that. Enough." His voice held a warning that even the densest of men could hear. I wondered what *donnaccia* meant, but thought it best not to ask

Pallo tilted his head and looked back at me. "I would have thought your earlier spectacle would have been enough. I guess I was mistaken."

Caleb lifted his hand, and I felt his power rising. I was sick of this macho crap. I turned, walked out of the room, and stormed upstairs to my bedroom to get dressed. While I was lacing up my boots, I heard the two of them shouting at each other.

"She's a grown woman, and if you ever call her a slut again…." Caleb yelled. The rest was muffled and hard to make out. I didn't care anymore what they said. I needed some fresh air--I needed away from their bickering.

I headed downstairs and walked quietly out the front door. They were too busy screaming at each other to notice that I had left, and that was perfectly fine by me. I walked down the lane, but in my haste to leave the house, I hadn't brought a flashlight with me. Hopefully, I wouldn't to fall and break my neck.

I drew in a breath of fresh air. It was cool, damp, and smelled of pine. I walked at a fast pace, feeling the stones crunching beneath my feet. The faster I walked, the more Pallo and Caleb's arguing faded. It was wonderful.

I couldn't remember how I had let my life get so chaotic. I knew it had been going pretty well up until Ken's phone call requesting me to go to Pallo's theme park. I was trying to remember why Ken had wanted me to go when I heard a faint howling. I slowed, listening. It sounded far off in the distance, whatever it was.

For a split second, I thought about heading back to the house. The idea of spending the rest of the night listening to Caleb and Pallo argue made me think better of it. The road spiraled down a small hill just past the entrance to the farmhouse lane. At the base of the hill was a bridge that ran across the river. I hadn't been down there for at least five years. It had always been so beautiful at nighttime. The stars would reflect off the water, and the faerie man had appeared to me often there.

I jogged down and reached the bottom, slowing as I hit the bridge. The view was everything I remembered and so much more. Leaning onto one of the steel beams, I looked out at the winding river. It was flowing fast tonight, but was not too high. The sound of the water splashing past the rocks, combined with the crickets, sounded like a lullaby.

I climbed onto the beam and sat. I'd always loved doing that when I was younger. I pulled my knees up to my chest and laid my head down on them. It was such a perfect night. Such a glorious--

Something hard struck my body. I kicked my feet out instinctively, trying to catch my balance but failing. My stomach leapt into my throat as I went over the edge. I hit the river with such force that it knocked the wind out of me. Water was all around me. It was pitch black, and I couldn't tell up from down. I kicked wildly about for a moment and screamed. Water filled my mouth, as bubbles floated from my lips. Bubbles--that was it--air would go up. Follow the bubbles and go up. I did, and my face broke the surface of the water. I sucked in the cold night air and was caught in a fit of coughing. The water tasted fishy and burned my throat as I attempted to go for the shore.

Something splashed into the water behind me. Terror gripped me. Whatever had knocked me off the bridge was now in here with me. Hysterical, I fought against the rush of the water to get to the side. I scraped my knee on a sharp rock. I was close, I knew it. The smell of stagnant water came up from behind me, and I heard a growl. I looked up to the bank of the river. Two small red flames seemed to be hovering in mid air. I focused. They weren't flames--they were eyes! Something was waiting for me to crawl out. I slowed down and felt the weight of the water shift behind me.

The smell of something wet and rotting hit me again. I knew that smell--it was the smell of trolls. I screamed. My foot hit something slimy, and I made sure it counted. I kicked with all of my strength. It grabbed my leg, began pulling me under the surface of the water. I tried to summon my power. It couldn't fail me now, not when I needed it the most. My lungs tightened--no power came. I kicked and pulled to free myself. The troll grabbed my waist and pulled me under. I lashed out at it and wrapped my fingers around a handful of wet hair that felt like seaweed, yanking it out. Its hold loosened, and I pushed to the top. I gasped, sucking in air, scrambling to get my footing. The river's current swept my feet out from under me.

The troll sprang from the depths beside me and knocked me down. My body slammed into the rocks, and water rushed over my face. I tried to push off the rocks, but had no strength left in me.

I let my head lay in the water and two thoughts came to my mind--Pallo and Caleb. I wanted to see them again, needed to see them. My life had changed dramatically in the last two days, but I knew they would forever be a part of it. I didn't want to die face down in a river with a troll about to tear me limb from limb. I would not go that way.

Infuriated, I felt my power creeping up. It was weak, but then again, so was I. I took what little I could muster and used it to give me enough energy to move. It was enough, it stood me up. The water pushed at me. Staggering to the edge, I fell to my knees. Red eyes sped towards me. I put my hands up in a defensive position, and braced myself for impact. Nothing came. I glanced around. They were gone. No troll, no red eyes, nothing. Exhausted, I fell against the rocky ground.

Something swooshed down next to my head. I closed my eyes and prepared for round two.

"Gwyneth." Pallo's voice was soft. "Gwyneth." He leaned over me. I tried to pick myself up but couldn't.

"Gwen? Gwen?" Caleb called.

"She is here!" Pallo called out to him. He scooped me up in his arms quickly. "What has happened to you?"

"Put me down," I said, coughing out more water. I thought about the troll and the mysterious red eyes. Pallo tensed.

"Which way did they go?" he asked.

I still hadn't been used to his mind reading tricks. I wasn't. I shook my head. "I don't know … they just vanished."

"Pallo, is she okay?" Caleb was on top of the bridge. A warm rush of power flowed through me, and something moving behind Caleb. I was far away, but somehow I just knew. Caleb and I were linked now, and he was too worried about me to sense the danger near him. My chest tightened.

"Caleb!" I screamed.

Growling came from the direction of the bridge. There was a loud splash, then nothing. I looked at Pallo.

"Help him, please, don't let him die." I was crying now and my words were mumbled between the sobs.

"I cannot leave you alone."

I could feel the battle waging inside of him. He was torn between helping his friend and staying with the one he loved. Loved? Yes, I felt his love for me. I shook my head. No time for that now.

My mind raced. I thought of Caleb, my beautiful new lover. A lover I felt I'd known for a lifetime. I thought of him making the odd comment about me being ripe. I wouldn't let them have him. I tried in vain to wiggle free of Pallo's hold.

Pallo touched my arm and I knew he shared my thoughts of Caleb. "Come … I cannot leave you." I kicked at him to put me down.

"Caleb! Help Caleb! We can't just leave him!" I screamed at the top of my lungs. What in the world was going on with him? Was he on drugs or something?

Suddenly, it felt like we had risen off the ground. I looked down to discover we had. We were moving over the top of the bridge. It was empty--no Caleb.

"CALEB!"

Pallo held me tight, and I slapped at his face. I didn't want to hurt him, I just wanted down. I needed to help Caleb. Pallo didn't loosen his hold on me. "I have to make sure you are safe." His words were concise.

He took me into the front room of the house and laid me on the living room couch. I jumped to my feet and ran for the door. He was on me in a flash, pinning me to the wall.

"I have to help Caleb! Let go of me!" I pushed at his face. His brown eyes locked on me. They held no anger for me, only sadness.

"I cannot let you go out there, and I cannot leave you by yourself. I do not know how many of them there are."

"I'm fine. I can take care of myself," I yelled at him.

"I cannot allow you to do that."

"Why?"

"*Cara mia, ti amo*--my beloved, I love you," he whispered, easing his grip on my body. I stopped fighting him for a minute. He had just told me he loved me. Did vampires really fall in love? I didn't have time to analyze it. I couldn't let anyone die at the hands of those things. Especially Caleb.

"Let me go!"

"Do you feel love for Caleb?" Pallo asked. I found that to be a strange question especially coming from him. I would have thought he'd ask if I loved him too, not Caleb.

I searched my soul for the answer because I'd learned how pointless it was to try covering up the truth from him. "Yes."

"If you had never met him, would you have loved me instead?" I couldn't believe he was doing this now. Caleb was out there, alone, and he needed us. Now wasn't the time to play twenty questions. I turned and headed towards the back door. Pallo gripped my waist.

"Pallo, let me go!"

"Then your answer is no?"

I stopped struggling with him. "No…." He tensed "No, meeting Caleb can't undo what was already done. Is that what you want?"

"I do not understand what you are telling me."

"God, Pallo, are you really that thick? I love you. I've been in love with you since the moment I met you. I can't explain it. We've only just met, yet I'm connected to you on a level I can't explain. I've had dreams about you, I longed for you. My heart bled when I knew that I had hurt you, but I can't help the way I feel about Caleb. I love you both. Now LET ME GO!"

He turned me in his arms and held me tight to him. "I still cannot allow you to go out there tonight."

"Why?"

"Because, there is a possibility that you may be with child."

He tried to avoid my gaze. He was hurt, I could tell. "What do you mean? I can't get pregnant. The doctor said it was next to impossible."

"Then the doctor was wrong," Pallo said, still not looking at me.

I stopped fighting him. "How do you know this?"

"When you thought of Caleb, by the river, telling you that you were ripe … he meant you were fertile, you were ready to accept his seed."

I thought about how Caleb had pulled out mid-way through being finished and didn't come again in me. "But I thought that the odds of pairing up with someone who is a mate for you were one in a billion."

"I suppose this one was predetermined." He stepped away from me and looked at the closed front door.

I didn't know what that comment meant, and I didn't care. I slid down the wall and sat on the floor. I covered my face with my hands. Caleb was out there somewhere and he needed our help.

"Pallo?"

"Yes?"

"You're telling me that I'm pregnant with Caleb's baby?" I shook my head. It didn't feel wrong to be saying this--it felt wrong to be leaving Caleb alone out there.

Pallo's cool hand touched mine. "No, what I am saying is that there is a chance that you may be with child. We will know for sure by the end of next week."

I moved my hands down and glanced up at him. "How will we know then?"

He forced himself to smile. "You will start to show signs."

"What?" I had heard that *Si* pregnancies were not like a human gestation cycle. I didn't realize they were that different. It would take human females months to start to show. It was going to take me only a few days. I would carry the child for close to a year, but it would grow to full size in half that time, the other half would be spent soaking up my magic.

"Oh, my God!" I said, pulling myself to my feet.

"What is wrong?"

I looked at him. "If I am with child, then I have to find its father."

Pallo stopped me at the door. I wanted to hate him, I wanted to strike him down with my power and run to the river and look for Caleb. I wanted to have him hold me. The latter desire won out, and I pulled myself close to him. He embraced me.

"I can't leave him out there, I can't." I cried against his chest.

He lifted my chin. "I have summoned for Caradoc and James. They will be here soon to help search for him. Do not worry, Gwyneth, we will do our best to find Caleb. I promise."

Pallo kissed my forehead, the vision of him bending down and touching my swelling belly came back to me. I felt like we'd been through this before, it felt like a bad case of déjà vu. I closed my eyes and let him hold me tightly as I cried. I sobbed with every ounce of my body. I cried for Caleb, I cried for myself, most of all I cried for Pallo. I could feel his sadness and I knew it would last for an eternity. I let my body go limp. He caught me and carried me upstairs to my bed. He laid me down on it and kissed my head gently as I cried. I saw him sitting on the edge of the bed as my eyes grew heavier. Sleep welcomed me quickly. Seemed like the harder I fought it, the more it won.

Chapter 12

I sat up in bed. It was still dark out. Glancing at myself, I saw I was clean and changed. Someone had cleaned me up. I had a feeling it was Pallo, and I hoped I wasn't wrong.

I slid my hands down my stomach and touched my abdomen. Nothing. It was flat and smooth. One night down, a few more to go. I don't know how I felt about possibly being pregnant. Caleb didn't feel like a stranger to me. It felt as though we'd known each other forever. I felt the same way around Pallo. I couldn't explain it. I just felt it deep inside of me. If it was meant to be, then it was meant to be. I could support a baby if I had to. It wasn't what I wanted to be doing with my life right now, but I would do what needed to be done. I had made love to Caleb, and I would deal with whatever came from that union. I wasn't sorry for what had happened.

"Caleb?" I couldn't feel his power around me anymore. I couldn't feel him at all. I did, however, feel like someone had placed a lead weight on my chest. I wanted to cry, and I had to blink away tears. Falling to pieces every two minutes would not help the situation at all.

Climbing out of bed, I headed downstairs to the living room. Pallo sat on the couch with his head bent. The moment I saw him I knew he had bad news. My stomach twisted into a knot, bile threatened to rise.

Pallo looked up, his eyes full of pity--pity for me. I knew by his look that Caleb was gone. I felt hot, flushed, and nauseated. I took off out the front door and fell down the front porch steps, landing hard on my knees in the grass. I vomited until I didn't have anything left.

Pulling myself up, I stared into the darkness. I had done this to Caleb. I had gone for the walk, I had gotten into trouble--he had come looking for me. I killed Caleb. *Me.* I staggered backwards and caught myself on the side of the steps.

"Do not blame yourself for this. Someone sent the creatures after you. You didn't do this to him. He loved you very much. Wherever he is, I am sure he is happy to know that you are safe." My mind soaked up Pallo's words and used them as an emotional crutch.

"Pallo."

He tried to help me off the ground, but I pushed his hand away. "I want to find the person who did this."

"Why?" he asked. I could tell he knew the answer but wanted to hear me say it.

"I want to kill them," I said coldly.

He touched my shoulder. "You have changed much, Gwyneth."

I had no idea what he was talking about, but that was becoming the norm, so I ignored it. Slowly, I got to my feet and went into the house. Pallo followed close behind me. He didn't make any sound when he moved, and that was creepy. He smiled at me. He knew his stealth mode routine was getting to me, so he quit.

I poured myself a glass of ice water and sat at the table. Pallo joined me. He told me that shortly after I had fallen asleep, Caradoc and James came. He and James went looking for Caleb. Caradoc cleaned me up. I looked at him sternly, but he ignored me. They had searched all along the river's edge for Caleb, but found nothing. They decided to split up, and each one took a side of the river and searched the woods. Pallo found blood in the woods but nothing else. He put his head down as he told me that it was rare for trolls to leave much of their victim behind. I winced. I didn't want to think about Caleb dying that way. I couldn't.

Pallo informed me I'd slept for almost two full days. He stayed here during the day and slept. Caradoc and James had headed back to the city shortly before I woke.

I looked at Pallo, soaking in the information he'd given me. I ran a hand over my stomach. If I had slept for two straight days and my belly was completely flat, then that meant that there was a good chance that I was not with child.

Pallo's gaze rested on my stomach. "How are you feeling?"

I nodded, but as I went to answer him, a wave of nausea hit me. I ran to the sink and began to dry heave. Pallo placed a cool hand on my forehead.

"Try to relax, Gwen." He never called me Gwen. He was trying too hard now.

I cried. "They said that I would never have children of my own. I've always wanted children. Now I may get my wish, but the child will never know its father."

"You miss him?" he asked, sitting once more.

"Yes."

I glanced at him leaning back in the chair. I had to do a double take. He was wearing a red plaid shirt and a pair of dark blue jeans that appeared to be a bit big on him.

"You're wearing my father's clothes?" I chuckled. He looked so out of place in plaid.

He propped his elbows on the table. "I did not expect to be staying. My clothes are being laundered. I hope you do not mind that I borrowed these." He put his hand up to unbutton the shirt.

"No, Pallo, its fine. You can have them. I was going to give them away. I just hadn't gotten around to it yet."

He gave me that wicked little grin of his again and I melted.

"Thanks," I said.

"For what?"

"For being my friend." I reached out and patted his hand.

We cleaned up the house as best we could. I packed a few articles of clothing and we loaded them into Caleb's red truck. Pallo and I drove back to the city together, and I dropped him off at Necro World, swearing I'd be back shortly. I headed off to get some information.

I stopped at my apartment first. I had promised Pallo that I wouldn't, but I was pretty sure he could tell I was lying so I didn't know how much that counted. I went in, changed and threw a few things in an overnight bag. I was learning that it was definitely better to be prepared. When I was done, I headed off in search of answers.

I pulled Caleb's SUV up outside of Ken's firm and went to the sixth floor, heading for my office. When I got inside, I saw that my phone was blinking. I had voice mail. I was guessing that missing work for a few days meant that I had a ton of phone calls to return. I glanced at my computer. My inbox was probably full too. Oh, well, they would have to wait. I grabbed my Rolodex and skimmed through the names. I needed to find someone who could help me find out who was sending these creatures after me. I wanted to meet them face to face, they would answer for Caleb. I had numbers for almost every sort of paranormal or supernormal contact in the area. I flipped past Lyle Martin's name and stopped. Martin was a self-appointed expert on the behavioral patterns of supernatural and mythological creatures. I had personally never put much stock into what he said, but I was willing to give him a try. The last time I had seen the guy he was appearing on a local talk show.

I phoned the number on the card, but got his answering machine. I began to leave him a brief message concerning a close friend of mine being attacked by trolls on two different occasions and was about to hang up. The phone clicked.

"Hello?"

"Mr. Martin?" I asked surprised to have gotten through to him.

"Yes, Gwyneth, it is I." The fact that he knew my name should have creeped me out. It wasn't like the damn phone was in my name. If anyone it would be Ken. "You mentioned something about hellhounds, and trolls?"

"Yes." I told him everything I could, leaving out the parts about me having sex with Caleb.

Martin was silent for a minute. "I see, this is most interesting … I would like very much to speak with you about this face-to-face."

"Yes, I understand, but I won't be able to meet with you anytime soon, and as I'm sure you can tell … time is of the essence." Truth was, I probably could have met with him, but he was creeping me out.

"Yes," he said, long and drawn out. "I shall offer you this one bit of advice."

"Yes?"

"Your past is never far behind."

The line went dead. I looked at the receiver and back at my Rolodex. I scratched the words nut job on Lyle Martin's card and thrust it back in place.

I recognized Ken coming down the hall by the sound of his voice. I didn't want to deal with him right now. I picked up my phone and dialed his office and was relieved to hear him race down the hall to grab his phone. Good old Ken, he was one of those people who just couldn't stand to let the phone ring. I gave it a second to ring some more and heard his door opening. I bolted out of my office, raced down the hall, and waved at Judy, the receptionist. She was trying to tell me that Ken was looking for me. I nodded and pushed the door open to the stairwell. Running down six flights of stairs in August will take it out of just about anyone.

I hit the lobby and headed for Caleb's truck. It was a lot later than I thought it was. Hadn't the sun only just come up a little while ago? It seemed that way, but it had taken me a lot longer at my apartment and driving around than I'd thought. Mid-afternoon approached. Pallo would be waking soon, and I had promised to go back and stay at his place for the night.

Getting in the truck, I headed towards Necro World, flipping on the radio. Caleb had a CD in--Less Than Jake. I sat there in awe for a moment. The guy lived for four hundred years and listened to punk cover bands? I don't think I could have been more surprised. I switched to the radio. I had no problem with the band. In fact, they were one of my favorites, but I was in the mood for something a little softer. I hit the scan button and concentrated on the road. The stereo ran through the various channels over and over again. It all started to sound the same to me. It faded into background noise as my thoughts drifted to Caleb.

My legs tightened thinking about the touch of his body. His dark green eyes would forever stick with me. The sound of his voice, so soft compared to Pallo's and Ken's. So … coming from the radio?

I slammed on the brakes. Thank goodness no one was behind me. I looked at the radio, half expecting to see Caleb fall out of it. I heard his voice again. He was speaking with someone I didn't recognize. The other voice was male--deep, and strong. I heard him, but what he said made no sense to me. It was gibberish. It was like listening to a foreign language for the first time. I was lost, but I knew that was Caleb's voice, I was positive.

The channel changed. I had forgotten that I was scanning through the channels. I hit the radio to try to retrieve the sound of Caleb. I pushed the seek button and heard nothing but music. Had I imagined the whole thing? Had I been so wrapped up in my thoughts of Caleb that I just invented it? I didn't know. I didn't know much anymore, except that Pallo was right. I needed to stick close to him until things blew over. I glanced in the rearview mirror and saw that I had amassed a small procession behind me. I pushed on the accelerator and went to Pallo's.

Chapter 13

Walking around Pallo's room, I tried to find something to do. The guy didn't have anything to entertain himself with in here. Looking at the enormous bed, I laughed to myself when I thought about what kind of entertaining the room was set up for--none of which consisted watching a movie, or maybe it did. Spying his dressers, curiosity got the best of me and I cracked open a drawer. It was full of sex toys of all shapes and colors. My mouth dropped open, and I blushed.

I really had to get out more.

"See anything you like?" Pallo asked, suddenly right behind me.

I hadn't heard him come in--no shocker there. I could have slammed the drawer shut and made up some silly story to cover my butt. I didn't. I put my hand in it and touched something shiny and clear. It was a long glass rod rippled with irregular bumps. I jerked my hand away. I hoped that wasn't what I thought it was.

"You are one sick puppy!"

"Thank you," he said and licked the back of my ear.

I turned to face him. He was wearing a black, silky pair of pajama bottoms, similar to the ones he wore the night I met him. They were just as low on his hips as the other ones, and I caught myself snatching glimpses of his bare, rippling chest. I forced my gaze back to his face and found him giving me a wolfish grin.

His fangs were showing. I backed away. I thought his fangs retracted when he was in a decent, normal mood and was surprised to see them out.

"Why?" It was all I could think of to say.

"I just finished--" He was interrupted when the door to the room opened and a skinny, leggy blonde wrapped in a sheet walked in.

"Pallo, are you coming back to bed?" she asked in a low, sultry voice.

Oh, gag me!

Looking her over, I caught sight of two holes on her neck. Disgust rolled over me. I couldn't believe he'd been banging another chick practically under my nose.

Pallo leaned close, letting his face almost touch mine. His breath was cool and smelled like peppermint. "Gwyneth, this is...." He looked over at the blonde, waiting for help with her name.

She appeared to be a little hurt but kept her chin up. "Sandra."

"Ah, yes, of course, Sandra." He stared at me so intently, I began to feel uncomfortable. I didn't know what he wanted me to say. Was I supposed to run over and hug the girl? Was I supposed to get mad at him for sleeping with someone else?

"Looks like you've been keeping yourself busy all day," I said with so much sincerity I almost gagged.

He licked the tip of one fang, turning his attention to Sandra. He held his hand out to her. She walked to him, never once taking her eyes off him. When she reached him, he took her hand and pulled her close, in a snuggling manner. It was as if I wasn't even in the room anymore. He put his hand up near her face but didn't touch. She tipped her neck to the side, exposing her smooth tanned skin to me. He leaned over her, his mouth wide, and pressed his fangs into her. She moaned, making noises that one only does during sex.

I wondered if getting sucked on by a vamp who's not trying to kill you was really that erotic. I shook my head. I didn't care--I was out of there. Pallo grabbed my shoulder before I could go. He watched me while he fed off her. He was enjoying this. He wanted me to see him doing this to her. He wanted to hurt me, punish me. I had hurt him, and turnabout was fair play.

I pulled free and smiled. If he wanted to suck on some blonde, more power to him. I headed towards the door. Sandra screamed. I turned, expecting to see Pallo biting her head off or something. Instead, I saw her naked body pressed to him as he feed from her. She swayed her hips, undulating against him. Pallo thrust his fingers inside her.

Jealously came upon me in a flash. I remembered Pallo on bended knee. The vision was so clear, so real. I glanced back at him fingering Sandra, and I wanted to walk over, punch her and kill him. I had no right to feel this way. He had told me that he loved me and I had admitted to loving him, but I had also admitted to loving another. Besides, I understood that emotions had been running high during our mini-confessional.

No biggie.

Who was I kidding? I crammed down the urge to lash power out at them. I concentrated on being somewhere peaceful, quiet, and relaxing. I did this until I felt myself calming down. Turning, I walked out of the room, and left the door standing open. It was clear by his willingness to finger fuck her in front of me, that he wanted an audience.

I walked to the living room, sat on one of the sofas, and leaned my head back. James entered, dressed in unrelieved black. He plopped down on the sofa in front of me. He didn't try to be all suave and debonair. He just was who he was.

He tipped his head back as well. The two of us sat, staring at the high stone ceiling. I broke the silence first.

"Does he do this often?"

"No."

"So, what's the deal?"

James snorted. Did vampires snort? James was definitely breaking down my preconceived notions of what they did and didn't do. "Gwen, you can't really be that thick. I mean, sure you're a looker, but I really thought you had bit a sense in ya."

I kept my head back and concentrated on staying calm. I was shocked to find that I didn't want to hit him. "Well, how about you help me be a little less thick and just tell me what's going on."

"I can't," he said evenly.

"Why not?"

"Because, he made me swear not to." I could hear the shame in his voice. I had the feeling that Pallo was his master, all vampires have one. Having this finally confirmed by James' reluctance to go against Pallo, I was saddened. I didn't feel like they should have to answer to anyone. They were older than humans and seemed to demand more respect, but there had always been a way among them. That way would never change. As long as there were vampires, there would be masters. I wondered who the grand master was, who ran the entire show. Did Pallo have a master too?

"James, tell me about Pallo."

"What do you want to know?" he asked.

"I can tell he's a good man. How did he get to where he is now?" I was trying to think of a good way to let him know that I was aware how ruthless one had to be to achieve Pallo's status.

James sat up. "Gwen, he's lived a long time."

I sat up too. "Yeah, but he isn't really that old, and to be where he's at, he must have been pretty...." The right word escaped me.

"Evil," James said it for me. I could tell by the look on his face that, in Pallo's case, this was true.

"But he doesn't seem that way now," I said, propping my elbows on my knees. James came closer. His blue eyes focused on mine, looking so serious. I waited for him to volunteer information, but he didn't. A look of remembrance came over him and he sat there looking at me, but past me. I touched his knee and felt his power flowing slowly up my arm. The past was the past and James knew that, so he didn't fear reliving it in his mind. I admired his strength.

It crept over me. I closed my eyes, allowing myself to receive James' memories. I saw James dressed in a pair of dark brown pants. They tied up the sides of his legs. His shirt had been light brown with puffy sleeves, now it was streaked with blood. He was searching for something, frantically storming around an old village. He walked past several horses that were all lying on their sides, not moving. He bent down next to one and touched it with his hand. His head dropped as if he was in deep thought, and then he sprang to his feet and ran down a dirt path. A modest cabin came into focus. James lightly touched the door, and it opened. He hesitated a moment before walking inside. A table lay on its side. Chairs were smashed to pieces. A fire still burned in the fireplace. Soup spread across the floor from an overturned pot.

He hurried through the house, moving into another room. A small bed was smashed on one end and covered with blood. James pushed through the mess of toppled furniture and saw a boot sticking out from the other side of the bed. He grabbed the bed with one hand and lifted it effortlessly, revealing a corpse. The man's right arm had been torn from his body, and he had died with horror stamped in his now glossy eyes. James turned and ran out of the tiny cabin, looking in both directions before heading left down a grassy slope toward a small stream. Something was moving there. It was moving with such speed that only James' vampire eyes could see it.

As James neared the figure, it began to take shape. It was covered in blood from head to toe. Long blood-soaked strands of hair lay against its bare back. James rushed it, knocking it over. It stood and stared at him with eyes of black, hideous, its face twisted and distorted to the point that no trace of humanity existed in it. It snarled and grabbed at his throat with its dagger-like fingernails. James smashed his fist into it and sent it to the ground. He looked down at what the creature had been hovering over. The half-naked remains of a woman's body were all that was left. The beast had torn the woman's throat out, exposing her spine.

The bloody body of the creature lying by James' foot began to stir. It lifted itself slowly off the ground. James made no attempt to keep the beast down. He stood very still, waiting for it to rise. It leaned over the woman's body, reached down and removed something from her dead hand. It clutched it to its face and its body began to move up and down. It was sobbing--I couldn't hear anything, but I knew what sobbing looks like. It lifted its hand in the air and gave James what it had been holding. James' hand slid around the bloody mass and let it drop to the ground. As it fell in what seemed like slow motion, I could make out the tiny animal shapes stitched into it. It was a baby's quilt, and it was smothered in blood.

The creature turned its head to look at James. It was Pallo, the creature was Pallo. His dark brown eyes stared wildly at James, as if he were lost. He looked down at his bloodied body and collapsed on the ground. James bent and picked him up.

I pulled my hand off James' knee slowly, in shock. Pallo had been a murderer. He had been evil, he had been ruthless. Was he still? I didn't feel like he was, yet I had just shared James' memory and saw it with my own eyes.

James stood and tried to walk out of the room. I reached up and took his hand in mine. It was not as cool as Pallo's always felt to me, but it was not warm either.

"What changed him?" I asked.

James stood very still and thought for a moment before answering me. "Do you want to know what turned him into the monster or what brought him back?"

"Both," I said, sliding my hand around his wrist. His pulse sped--the memory had gotten to him after all.

"You," he said, and planted a kiss on the top of my head. He cared for me, that much was clear. It was odd--he seemed like a close friend, like we'd known each a long time.

Giggles came from behind us. James stood up and we both turned to see Sandra and Pallo standing at the end of the sofas. She rubbed her hands all over Pallo's bare chest. He glared at us.

"What the hell's your problem?" I shot at him.

James tapped my shoulder, trying to tell me to let it go. Pallo could be dangerous. I was too mad to care.

"Why would I have a problem?" he asked with a hint of sarcasm in his voice.

Sandra looked like a lost puppy. It was sickening. At least she was dressed, if you could call it that. She had on a tiny white halter top and short, matching skirt. It was so short that I could see bruises on her inner thighs. Had Pallo done that to her? Was he that rough in bed that he bruised her? She was only a human, so they did tend to bruise easier, but still. She didn't look too hurt to me. She looked like she wanted him to fuck her right then and there.

She looked like a two-dollar whore, and I was talking Canadian currency, not American. The sight of her made me smile. That made Pallo mad. I think he had hoped that the sight of Sandra would send me into a jealous rampage. It almost had, but I maintained my control. I kept smiling at her and thought I would go for the smart-mouth-of-the-night award.

Hey, I'd been known to win it before, why not now?

"Sandy, we should get together sometime and go shopping. I'll be hanging out here at Pallo's for the next couple of days. You should stop by. We could have some girl time. Only if you're not too busy supplying his next meal. I wouldn't want to run you ragged before he gets a chance to."

Her eyes lit up. "Does this mean I can come back?" She sounded like she was about fifteen. From the looks of her, she was older than me. The phrase being rode hard came to mind. I now knew who it was coined after.

Pallo shot Sandra a nasty look and said no. That made me smile even harder. He didn't have any feelings for her at all. She'd been used as food, and to try to get under my skin. It had almost worked.

Almost.

Pallo had James show Sandra out, and came to stand by me. I could feel the anger stirring around him.

"What, are you going to attack me again? Should I be prepared myself?" I know that provoking an already mad vampire probably wasn't the best idea, but what else was new? He clenched his hands. Little drops of blood fell from them. I was on a roll now, why stop? "So what? You want to hit me so bad you have to inflict pain on yourself to avoid it. Oh, please don't do that on my account, really. Take a swing at me. You've already proved you're a real man by biting me. Why stop now?"

He released an ear-piercing yell. I stood quickly, to stand toe to toe with him. He was going to have to deal with me or kill me, whatever it took. I placed my hand on his chest and gave him a hard shove.

"So, big guy, are you going to bite me again, or better yet, tear my throat out? I don't have a baby in my arms, and I'm not standing in the middle of some medieval village so that may take some of the fun out it for you! But hey, there could be a baby in my belly, and that is what's got you so pissed off, isn't it? It's the fact that you got left with a possibly knocked up … what the word you used?" I tried to remember the Italian word for slut that he called me in my kitchen. I came up blank. "Right, a whore! Ha, but this whore never did you!" I was on the verge of screaming--okay, maybe I was screaming, just a little. It was taking everything I had to keep control of my volume level.

Pallo's eyes flashed to black, and he grabbed my wrist. I didn't try to pull away. I stood on my tiptoes and put my face near his. "Go ahead, kill me. You've been dying to do it since the moment you laid eyes on me. You acted like you cared so much about me in the beginning. You know, I almost bought the idea that maybe there was more to the story than meets the eye with us. I almost believed you were a nice guy." I touched his chest to push him away. "You took me to Caleb! You took me to the Enchanted Forest and left me to be attacked by friggin' trolls. I'm thankful Caleb came along. He saved my life. Don't get pissed off with me for having feelings for him. I met him because of you. This park is more important to you than me. I can't help that...." I let my hand slide over his bare chest and touched the tiny scars under his right nipple. "I love you. Him ... I love Caleb."

The blackness in his eyes seemed to spill forth brown. He was calming down. He pulled my wrist and wrapped my arm around his waist, leaving my body pressed to his. Kissing my forehead, he held his soft lips there a moment.

"You disgust me! I'm not sorry that any of this has happened. If I am going to be a mother, then you, as my 'friend', should be a little bit happier for me. You shouldn't be pissed off that--"

"That I am not the one who fathered your child? That I am not the one who was able create life with you, share that moment, and know that for all eternity a piece of us existed in someone else? Or that, if you are with child, how I would want them to know about Caleb because he was a good man. Or, knowing that regardless how hard I try, I cannot atone for the sins of my past and be the man Caleb was."

I stared at him. I had never in a million years expected him to be upset about that. I thought he was angry about Caleb, not about not being able to father a child with me.

"Pallo?"

"No, Gwyneth, I have loved you since the moment I laid eyes on you, and that has been longer than you know--longer than you can remember. I see that you are young, and have a desire to start out on the new path life has in store for you. I saw you and I wanted to be the one that gave you all of your heart's desires. I wanted to be the one who made you happy. I have not wanted to be normal for a very long time, and you make me crave it. When you are a vampire, feeling alive is the greatest gift anyone can offer you. And you make me feel alive, Gwyneth."

Pallo held me tight and I let him. My cheek was pressed to his cool chest and I didn't want him to ever let go. A cool breeze tickled the back of my shoulder. Reluctantly, I pulled back from him, still letting him hold my hand.

Wind whistled and circled around us like a small tornado. We were standing in a room that was underground so I knew it was impossible for this to be happening. Pallo's grip tightened on my hand. The wind picked up. Our feet stood firm, yet everything else moved. The room spun. I wasn't sure if that was his doing or mine. Caradoc and James came running into the room.

Pallo closed his arms around me so quickly I had no time to protest. Not that I would have anyway. I buried my face in his hard chest. He smelled like a mixture of vanilla and Hugo Boss.

Way to go, Gwen, think about how sexy he smells instead the friggin' tornado-like whirlwind.

Caradoc and James tried to reach us, but the swirling wind kept them at bay. I tried to push away from Pallo, but he held tight.

"What's happening?" I shouted.

It sounded as if a large train headed straight for us. The force of the wind made us sway.

"I thought this was your doing," he said.

I shook my head no. I was known for earthquakes, not tornadoes. The noise and pounding of the wind stopped abruptly. I lifted my head. Pallo's arms tightened. I glanced around the living room. Nothing was the same, and Caradoc and James were gone.

We stood in a pale yellow bedroom with a large, four poster bed in the center of it. The ceilings were high and white crown molding ran around the room. Thick, navy drapes hung to the floor on each side of a white fireplace. Picture frames were toppled over on the mantle, making it impossible to see who was in them from were we stood.

"Where are we?" I asked.

He loosened his grip on me and looked around the room. "In my bedroom."

"How the hell many bedrooms do you…?"

He cut me off. "No, not my room as it is today. This is my room as it once was."

I stepped away. Looking down, I noticed that I now wore a long white gown that reached the floor. I closed my eyes, wishing hard to be back in my own bed. Some part of me had secretly hoped that would work, and was disappointed when I opened them to see Pallo still standing there. I never thought in a million years that I would be bummed out to be standing in the arms of a gorgeous guy.

"When you say room as it once was, what exactly do you mean?"

"This is a place from my past."

"How far in the past?"

"Roughly two hundred and fifty years, give or take."

"Over two hundred years in the past?" Panic swept through my voice.

"That is correct."

"Does this sort of thing happen to you often? I mean, time travel, falling for girls you've known less than a week … getting them to fall for you too…?"

"No, this has never happened to me before." He ran his fingers through his hair in a nervous manner.

I walked to the bed and knelt by the side table. A folded note card sat there with our names on it. I opened it, but could not read the writing inside. It was like no language I had ever seen before.

"Pallo?"

He came to me, and I handed him the card. A wide smile spread across his face.

"Well, what does it say?"

"It is from Lydia. She wishes us well."

"Lydia? Who, exactly, is Lydia?"

"Someone who cares very much for your well-being." He looked around the room in amazement as he spoke to me.

"I don't know anyone named Lydia, so why would she care about me? And what language is that?"

"I suppose she has her reasons. Do you mean to tell me you cannot read this?" he asked, holding the card up to me.

"No, why should I?"

"It is Faerie, they have a dialect all their own."

"Well, obviously I'm not up on my Faerie. So, let's go find this Lydia and tell her that putting me in a bedroom with you is not really looking out for me, now is it? It's rather like tossing me to the sharks."

He frowned. "Do you really feel that way?"

"Yes … no, I'm not sure."

He was close enough to touch me. I backed away, scared that if he did make contact with me, I'd not be able to stop myself from loving him. "Why do you pull away from me? You have already confessed your love for me?"

"I don't know what the hell you're talking about." I took another step back and tripped over the back of my long white nightgown. The bed broke my fall.

"May I join you?" he asked with a slight chuckle. The look on my face must have told him exactly what I thought he meant. "I would like to rest next to you. Daylight nears and I grow tired."

I glanced at my wrist to check the time. "That can't be right."

"What is the problem?"

"My watch is gone," I shoved my wrist toward him. He took hold of it, his touch gentle. A man with his power and strength could have torn my arm from my body. He must have had spent centuries learning to control himself. I wondered what else he had amazing control over.

"Your entire outfit is gone."

"Again … you with the obvious." I rolled my eyes and laughed slightly.

The top of his thighs brushed my knees. I had to fight the urge to reach up and grab hold of his waist band. It was already dangerously close to exposing him as it was. I could clearly see his hip bones, and make out the tiny line of black hairs that ran from his navel downwards.

"Pull up your pants," I said, covering my eyes in sexual frustration.

"Why? Does the sight of my body bother you?" He was clearly amused.

I kept my eyes covered and relaxed on the bed. My legs were still bent at the knees. Pallo's legs pushed against mine while he stood over me.

"I didn't sign up for a vampire peep show tonight, okay?"

"It is your loss." He plopped down beside me on the bed. I sat up on my elbows and looked at him.

"What do you think you're doing?" I was not going to be shacking up with a vampire tonight, at least not if I had anything to say about it. I had agreed to stay in his home, not in his bed. We had enough issues between as it was, adding more would have been ludicrous.

Pallo lay on his side, watching me. His arm was bent, propping his head up, and long, loose curls spilled over his bare shoulder and touched the bed. "I am merely getting comfortable. Is that a problem?"

"Well, yeah, I think it is. Can we, like, call someone or

something? Because, I am not going to lie in this bed with you."

"How would you have me phone someone? Should I close my eyes and make a wish?"

I groaned. "I don't know. Click your heels together or something."

"Oh," he mused. "I can see how thought might work."

"Are you always this big of an asshole, or do you save it up to impress the ladies?" I asked, glaring at him.

"Is your mood always this sour, or do you reserve it just for me?" He gave me a grin that screamed mischief.

I wanted to have a snappy comeback, but nothing came to mind, so I just grunted. That was me, always taking the mature approach.

"My sweet Gwyneth, I am only trying to get to know you. That is what friends do, is it not?"

"I am not your sweet anything, and I think I know enough about you to hold us both over for awhile. Sharing session is over."

"And what is it you think you know about me?" Pallo asked, as he lifted his hand to touch me.

I smacked his hand away. "I know what you are, and I can only guess what you've done. There is no way in hell that you got to the position you have by being Mister Nice Guy. How many innocent people have you tortured, or worse, murdered to get your little place in the sun? Or should I say darkness? I know of at least two. I think I know exactly what you are."

"What exactly am I?" He sighed. "I am curious to hear your perspective."

I couldn't believe this guy. "You are a vampire."

"Now who is stating the obvious?"

"God, forget it. There is no dealing with you, get away from me!"

"I am sorry. Forgive me." He smiled. I knew the apology was fake, but I accepted it all the same.

"Pallo?"

"Yes."

"Why do we hurt each other so much?" It was a completely legitimate question. We had been dancing in circles since the moment I laid eyes on him. He moved himself closer to me, and exhaled deeply.

"I am sorry for the Brenda situation. I lost my temper. You were correct in assuming that my goal was to make you jealous."

I looked at him. What Brenda situation? Then it hit me. "You mean the blonde, Sandra?"

He shrugged one shoulder. "Very well, Sandra."

Well, she must have left some impression on the guy. He'd already forgotten her name. Seeing him with her had bothered me. He was mine, and I didn't want to share. Kind of ironic, considering what I'd done with Caleb, and how I expected him to share me.

Thinking of Caleb again made my stomach tighten. I couldn't believe how far I had let things go. Most of all, I just couldn't believe how much I missed him. Pallo slid his hand down my arm and brought my thoughts back to him. I smiled, and he took this as a green light.

In a flash, he slid a leg over my thighs. The thin material of his pants couldn't hide how turned on he was. I'd caught a glimpse of his cock when it wasn't erect and had been thoroughly impressed. The bulge under the silk material made my breath catch and my nipples harden. He moved his entire body over mine, pressing his erection against me, as he swayed his hips gently. I sucked in as his lips skimmed mine.

"Pallo…," I whispered his name, unsure why. He had some sort of hold over me, some sort of power.

He pressed his mouth to my ear, and his breathing deepened. It was a sound that afforded me a brief glimpse into his seductive powers. Powers that I hoped he wasn't using on me. "What do you wish of me, Gwyneth?" Rubbing his hips against me, he drove his hard bulge against me, somehow managing to stimulate my clit through two layers of material.

"Uhh … please … stop."

He let out a throaty laugh and licked the edge of my ear. "Are you sure you want me stop?"

"No … yes."

"Which is it?" He increased the speed at which he was dry humping me and my body grew hot. Wrapping my legs around his waist, I silently cursed how restrictive my nightgown was. I wanted it off, and I wanted him in me, now. My legs tightened as pleasure built in my body. It threatened to burst at any moment, and I wanted Pallo in me while that happened.

"Do … you … wish … me … to … stop?" he asked, each word terse, deep, strained as he pressed himself against me.

Turning my face, I kissed his jaw line. He lifted his head from my neck and seized hold of my lips with his mouth. Fire shot through my loins and I was powerless to stop the orgasm that swept through me. Pallo continued to kiss my mouth, and caress me with his clothed member. The prolonged stimulation that he was providing opened the door to a flood of mini-orgasms, each one making me cream more and more.

My inner thighs now soaked, I could think of nothing more than wanting him buried within me. The raw need I felt scared me. Something was off, different. A soft buzzing noise filled my head, and began to clear my mind. I knew I had been angry with Pallo, but I could not remember why. The only thing I was sure of was that I wanted him to want me, but there was something else. Someone that I should being remembering. Green eyes--for some reason green eyes seemed very important to me. I focused, doing my best to block out the erotic sensations that Pallo's body was causing me.

Green eyes … green eyes … Caleb!

That was it! I pushed on Pallo's chest. As much as I did desire him, this was wrong. I'd already made a big enough mess. Having sex with Pallo would increase that tenfold. "Off, now!"

"Ahhh," he sighed, sounding a bit frustrated. Judging by the size of his erection, he had every reason to be vexed.

"You tried to use your vamp mojo on me!"

Reaching down, he grabbed the bulge in the front of his pants and rolled off me. "Apparently, I did not do a very good job. Care to tell me why you made me stop, or shall I save you the time because I know you were thinking of Caleb."

I couldn't respond. The very mention of Caleb's name cut me to quick. I had yet to have a relationship work out. I needed to know if it was just me. Was I destined to bring down every guy I let close to me, or was there still hope? I knew that Pallo would have sex with me, that was clear by the amount of moisture I still had pooling between my legs, but I didn't want that. I wanted to be loved, the same way anyone else would want it, unconditionally. In few days that we'd been together, I'd felt that from Caleb, and I knew that he was not able to give me that anymore.

I faced the fireplace, freeing myself from the drape of his body. Pallo was on top of the covers and I didn't want to turn and ask him to move. I didn't trust what I would say or do if I looked into his brown eyes, and if he flashed that wickedly sexy smile, I'd be a goner.

Something hard bumped the back of my head. I turned to find

Pallo laying flat on his back with his hands folded behind his head. His elbow had been what hit me.

"Excuse you," I said sardonically.

"No, it is not I with the problem. It is you."

"I don't have a problem. Oh, wait that's right--I am only stuck in some godforsaken two hundred plus year old version of your love nest. Gee, why is it that I would have a problem? Hmm, I wonder?"

"Gwyneth, why do you fight your feelings for me? It is clear that you desire me, and I you." He continued to stare at the ceiling.

"Whatever!" I wanted to push him off the bed. "You are so full of yourself. I'm going to sleep, don't come near me or I'll…." I couldn't really think of what I'd do.

"You will what? Be honest with yourself?" He sounded so sure of himself, so smug. He made my blood boil, and that was the problem. Any man that could make me come multiple times without ever actually touching me was dangerous indeed.

"Pallo?"

"Yes."

"I miss Caleb."

"As do I," Pallo said softly to me.

Chapter 14

I had to fight to fall asleep. I visualized the white light of peace moving up from my toes, over my legs, past my hips, up and over my breast, sliding over my face, and moving out the top of my head. My body felt completely relaxed. I'd released the tension from the day and felt sleep finally come on me. It was glorious. I made a mental note to thank Nana for the tip.

My peaceful rest was interrupted, as my subconscious mind wandered. It was digging in deep crevices that often go unnoticed. It came up with something, and shared it with me in the form of a nightmare. I was running down a long corridor from something. I could hear it moving quickly behind me, but I couldn't see it. I didn't want to see it. I wore no shoes, and I could tell my feet were bleeding. I could feel the presence behind me closing in. I wanted to move faster, but I felt like I was wading through an invisible fog of molasses. I put my arms into it and pushed against the force slowing me down. There was a door ahead of me. I knew that was the way out. I knew that behind that door lay safety. When I reached it, I pulled on the knob. My hand was slick with sweat and it slipped off. I wiped it on the bottom of the long blue dress I wore. I pulled the trailing end of the sleeves into my hand and tried the knob again. It turned, and I pulled it open a few inches when something suddenly slammed into me from behind. My body was pressed to the door--my fingers were closed in it. I knew they were broken. I could feel the throbbing pain shoot up my arm and into my neck.

Hot breath blew against the back of my head. Something snarled and drew air into its lungs.

"Look at me." The voice was very low and barely human.

"Don't," I pleaded, leaning against the door. "Please, don't do this." Hot tears streamed down my checks.

"You smell of him," the demonic voice said. "I said look at me." An ice cold hand gripped my shoulder, pulling me free from the door. The hand ran across my very swollen stomach. "I am gone from you only a few months, and you cannot even wait for me. Instead, you lie with *him* and you betray me with *this*." He pressed hard against my stomach. Something moved inside me, I could feel the tiny life growing within. Two hands gripped my shoulders and pushed my back to the door.

I drew in a sharp breath. "No, you have changed, you're not the same, and you are a...."

"Go ahead." I fought with all my might not to open my eyes and look at him. "I am a monster now. And you thought that you had freed yourself of demons."

I tried to slide away from him, but he was too strong. I swallowed hard. "Please don't hurt the baby and me."

"Oh, that is good. Begging like a dog for your life and the bastard child that grows within you." He wrapped his long fingers tightly around my arms, and I cried. "Now you weep. Now you show that you have emotions. Tell me, did you weep so for me when you believed me gone? Did you miss me?" I knew that on some level I was appealing to whatever humanity it had left in it. "I do not think you mourned long. By the looks of you," he pushed at my stomach again, "you didn't hesitate to seek the arms of another. Look at me when I speak to you, Gwyneth."

"I can't." My voice was small. I could feel his face close to mine, too close. He pushed his mouth onto mine, forcing his tongue inside. Fangs nicked my tongue, and my mouth filled with blood.

I kicked awake in the bed, my heart pounding in my chest. Lifting my hand to my mouth, I came away with blood. I had bitten through my bottom lip during the nightmare. Something touched my cheek, and I drew in a sharp breath.

"Gwyneth, it is I," Pallo whispered. "What is wrong?"

He stared at me sleepily, and I tried to relax. I wanted to wrap myself around him and let him hold me until I fell back asleep. I wanted a lot of things in my life, but the fact remained that he was a vampire, and the last thing I needed in my life was more problems, so I sat still.

"I had a bad dream." I sounded like a child. "I…."

"You do not have to explain to me. Come, let me hold you." He slid his arm around my back. "You are safe now, you are safe."

I leaned back in his arm and wanted to thank him for being so kind, even though I had treated him so badly.

"You're warm," I said. Okay, it wasn't 'I'm sorry for being a jerk', but it was the best I could come up with.

"So I am," he said, propping his head up with his hand. From the look on his face it surprised him too. "You bring out the best in me, what can I say?" He kissed me on the cheek, and when he pulled back, his face was flushed. I caressed his cheek, and he pressed a kiss to my wrist. A shiver ran down my spine. I didn't want to have such a vulnerable spot near his mouth. I knew that he hadn't fed since we'd been here, and I wasn't planning on being breakfast.

"There is no need to fear me," he whispered between tiny kisses on my skin.

I wasn't sure I wanted to take his word on that. It took every ounce of my willpower to turn away from him and climb out of the bed. His hands brushed along my back as I stood.

"What time do you think it is?" I asked, trying to keep myself from climbing back into the bed and straddling him.

"I would say it is probably close to six."

"Great. I can still make it into the office before Ken gets in. How do we get out of here?"

He looked up at me. "Six p.m."

"We slept all day long? I've got to go."

"We go nowhere until we are both ready."

"Great, I'm hungry. Where's your kitchen? Or don't you have one of those then? Eww, I hope the food isn't as old as you."

He chuckled. "Go out the door and down the staircase. You shall find it on the lower level. Third door on the right, although I am not sure what Lydia will have provided for us. I would assume that it is a bit younger than me."

He was still lying on top of the covers, and looked incredibly fuckable.

"What, no personal tour?" I asked, smiling.

"Forgive me, Gwyneth, but I am not feeling like myself."

"You need blood, don't you?"

He closed his eyes a moment and then looked to me. "Yes."

I headed towards him. I really had no idea what I planned to do when I got there, but at that point I didn't care.

Pallo stopped me. "No, you go and attend to your needs. I will be fine."

"But," I muttered softly, figuring a two hundred and seventy-five year old vampire ought to know what's best for him. "Don't fall asleep."

I headed out the door in the direction he had pointed me, and walked out into the hall. It was grand. On the left side was a row of three doors. The right was open to the floor below. A large rounded banister ran along the side and curved to follow the staircase. I headed downstairs and stopped dead in my tracks. A large oil painting hung on the wall above the landing. There was a woman and a man standing near the edge of a river. The woman wore a long white dress similar to the one I was wearing now, and the man wore a loose, silky white shirt and a pair of brown pants. They were standing face to face, holding hands. The man's wavy brown hair was pulled back at the base of his neck. I looked at the profile harder and knew that I was staring at Pallo. I knew this was, or had been, his home at one time, so I wasn't shocked. What did shock me, however, was the face of the woman he was holding hands with. It was me. Well, almost me. The woman's face was identical to mine, except for the fact that she had the most beautiful violet-colored eyes. She stared up at Pallo's face with so much love in her violet eyes that I could almost feel it sweep over me. I clutched the cold, hard railing to keep my footing, swallowing hard to keep from being sick.

"Gwyneth." Pallo's voice came from the top of the staircase.

"Who did this?"

"Who did what?" He stood behind me, but I didn't turn around.

"Did you do this? Is this your idea of a joke?"

He touched my shoulder. "I do not know what you are taking about."

"You planned this, didn't you? You said you'd seen my name in the Nocturnal Journal. Did you see a picture, too? There's no Lydia. This isn't some house from your past. Mystical portal, my ass! What I want to know is how you managed to find someone to paint a picture of the two of us." I was so angry I could feel my jaw tightening. "I hope they didn't charge you too much, because my eyes are blue."

"Please, allow me to explain. Come back to the room."

"God, you just don't quit. You'll do just about anything to get me in there with you." I stepped down another step to get his hand off me.

"Gwyneth, that painting has been here for centuries. I commissioned an artist for it before I became what I am now." He sighed and continued, "I had a life before I became a monster, and that is one of the few things left to remind me of it."

My mind raced. If what Pallo said was true, how was it that I was in the picture with him? It was impossible. It was painted at least two hundred years before I was born.

"Gwyneth, I should have told you. When I saw you standing in my home, I could not think. There you stood, in the flesh, before me, alive … he told us we would be rewarded, but neither of us expected you to return. We never expected a second chance at…."

Pallo placed his hand on my shoulder and I cringed. Pulling away, I ran down the stairs, and had to keep grabbing the material on my nightgown to keep from tripping. I hit the bottom with such speed that I slid toward the front door. My shoulder took most of the hit. My right hand went numb and I had to use my left hand to open the door.

"No!" Pallo screamed from the staircase. He had trouble keeping up with me because he hadn't fed yet.

I glanced back at him coming downstairs. His eyes flashed wildly at me. I stepped out the door, and felt the ground give way under my feet. My stomach rose to my throat. The ground came upon me with such force it knocked the wind out of me. My hair spilled over my face like a curtain. Something crashed onto the floor next to me. My breathing went ragged, and I felt like a caged animal.

"Are you all right?"

I pulled my hair back and looked wildly at Pallo crouched on the floor next to me. He looked sick. He was bent over, holding his abdomen. He was ghastly white, so much so that I thought he might glow in the dark.

"Are you hurt?"

"No, I need to.…" He looked to me and could not bring himself to say the word feed.

"We need to get you back to the park. Come on." I stood, and it hit me that we were not sitting in front of a house, but rather what looked to be a dungeon. All the joking I had done about his lifestyle, and he really did have one.

"This is not mine."

I was getting pretty damn sick and tired of his little mind reading tricks but didn't have the energy to fight with him. When I looked at him and saw his body hunched over like a tiger about to strike, I put my hand on his back. His skin was no longer warm. It was cold and clammy. "You're dying." I bent and wrapped my body around his. In my mind, I thought that my body heat would warm his, but it didn't work.

"No. I am already dead." No trace of the strong and sure Pallo remained in his voice.

"Well, great, since you've already been there and done that we can skip it and go home."

"Home?" He turned his face to me. All of the glory had faded from his brown eyes, only gray ones remained.

"Yes, home. We can fight more after we get there." I helped him to his feet. When I was sure he wasn't going to pass out, I turned to examine the room.

"So, where are we? And don't state the obvious again."

"Hell."

"Figuratively or literally?"

"Does it matter?"

He had a point. I wanted to ask him how to get out of here, but he put a finger to his lips to shush me. I listened, hearing only silence.

Pallo gestured to a metal door at the end of the room. He whispered in an unfamiliar language. I had no idea what he was saying, but if I had to take a crack at it, I'd have guessed he spoke in Latin.

"What are you doing?"

"Praying," he said softly.

"Vampires do that?" I couldn't hide the shock in my voice.

Howling pierced the silence like a knife. Pallo pulled me behind him in a protective manner and stood tall.

The door burst open. Two hellhounds leapt inside. They stopped at Pallo's feet, growling. Red eyes blazed at us, almost glowing. They were at least the size of full grown Great Danes. Pallo pushed me back slowly.

"I see you've met the boys," a woman's voice said.

I looked to see her standing in the open doorway. She was about my height, average. Okay, short, and had long red hair and yellow eyes. She looked like she had been dunked in leather. A leather top squeezed her large breasts together, and her pants fit her body so tightly I was positive she couldn't sit down.

She was familiar to me, but I couldn't place her. Yeah, you would think that a pair of beady yellow eyes and a chick dressed like a biker-whore-from-hell would be easy to recall.

She spared me a glance then concentrated on Pallo.

"Pallo, Pallo. I didn't expect a visit from you today." She pulled a sheathed knife from her back pocket. "You should have called. I could have prepared the room, just the way you like it."

"Talia, it has been a long time."

"You know her?" I couldn't keep my mouth shut any longer.

She took a step closer and caressed the neck of one hound.

"Who is your little friend? Do not tell me you've taken to bedding virgins again? I thought you were done with that. They break so easily, don't they?" She smiled and fangs showed. I was happy at least one vamp I'd met was holding true to a Hollywood image. Now, if I only had some holy water, a crucifix, and or a stake, I'd be in good shape.

"He's not *bedding* me, and I'm not a virgin."

"Oh, I see why you like her. You always did have a thing for opinionated girls. Is she good with her mouth in other places as well?"

"Talia, to what do we owe the honor of this visit?" Pallo asked. The muscles in his arms flexed.

"I was running an errand for the Queen, but since I found you, let us just say it is for old time's sake." She pulled her knife free and licked the blade. I could feel Pallo's fear. He was opening himself up to me, and feared this tiny little redhead.

"I do not recognize these two," he said, looking at the hellhounds.

"They are new. They just completed the initiation process a few days ago. They no longer have ties to the human world. They 'severed' them. I have had to make so many new little ones as of late. I have lost many of my children. The humans hunt us like we are animals."

"That's a shocker." I bit my lip, but it was too late the words were already out.

Talia gave me wry a look. "Show her you are not animals, boys."

The two hounds' backs curved abnormally backwards as they howled. I lifted my hands to cover my ears. The decibel level was almost deafening in the chamber.

Bones crunched and blood spilled from them as their features became human. A muzzle receded into one's face. I thought I was going to be sick or possibly wet myself. At that stage of the game neither one would have bothered me in the least.

Two naked men stood before us when the transformation was finally over. They were identical in almost every way. One had a little bit longer coal black hair than the other. They looked to be only five foot seven or so in human form, a sharp contrast to their beast body. I couldn't help but notice how gifted they both were in certain areas. They could have made a fortune in a twin strip show, but their eyes gave them away. Fiery red eyes still stared out from their well-crafted bodies. The night by the river ran through my head. Those were the same type of eyes that had come rushing towards me.

"Jacob and Jonathan Wilson, say hello."

"Hello," they said in unison. This was too much. I almost burst out laughing. I stopped and thought about what she had just said. Wilson? Jacob and Jonathan--those were Rick's boys' names. A horrible thought came to my head. They had murdered their own father. That is what Talia had meant by them "severing" their ties to the human world. Oh my God! The room felt suddenly hot, making me sick to my stomach.

Talia stepped between them and ran her hand along Jacob's body. She turned and did the same to Jonathan. Both their cocks stood at attention.

"As much as we would love to stay and play with you, we really must be going," Pallo said. I was amazed at how calm he kept his voice, even though I could feel his fear as if it was my own.

"You never used to run off before the festivities began. Are you softening with old age?"

She was really starting to get to me. I wanted to walk up to her and slap her right across the face. Pallo sensed my urge to hit her and shook his head.

"Don't tell me you do not miss the days of old." She held her knife out threateningly.

He stiffened. "No, Talia. I have left the days of torturing others behind me now, you know this."

She looked pleased. "Yes, I had heard that you gave up your naughty ways. Why is that?"

"I had no reason to hate anymore."

"You harbored much hate for two hundred years, what would change you so? Did you finally get over your little loss?" She talked with her hands, the knife skimming past Pallo's chest. "I found your circumstances very unique. Tell me--how long after you were made did you have your heart broken? Less than half a year, if I'm not mistaken. To be made immortal and to lose your love ... tell me, was she worth it? Did she fuck good enough to warrant leading you to the Devil himself?"

"I do not wish to discuss this with you," he said, restrained violence in his voice.

"Answer me, Pallo. I asked you a question." She lashed out and cut his chest. Blood pooled onto the floor, nearing my feet. Jason and Jonathan began to look restless. I could tell the smell of blood was exciting them, and it made me sick.

Talia struck Pallo again, catching his face.

"Stop!" I yelled, taking a step out from behind him.

"No!" he shouted, trying to pull me back.

Talia glared at me, her yellow eyes flaring. "The virgin speaks."

"Leave him alone."

"Would you beg for your lover's life?" Her voice had gotten soft, and that scared me.

It was hard to find the courage to step in front of Pallo, but I did. That put Talia and I eye to eye. Her breath was hot on my face. I made a point of looking directly into her eyes. I wasn't going to let her see me back down. She was pissing off the wrong girl. I growled low in my throat.

Talia's eyes flickered and turned green, and then it hit me. I knew where I'd seen her before. She looked different with clothes on, if you could even call them that. She was the woman I walked in and found Ken with.

"I know you! You're the whore who slept with my fiancé." The words flew out of my mouth with such force I spit on her.

She smiled. "You will have to be more specific if you want to get a rise out of me."

"Kenneth Harpel."

Yellow flooded back into her eyes. "Harpel? The Law." The name slid off her tongue like a snake. The supernatural papers had been referring to Ken as 'The Law.' He had gotten the nickname from successfully prosecuting more than a hundred supernatural felons.

"You … you are the one who interrupted me. He was not easy to seduce, but I did. No mortal man can resist me."

"You've got to be kidding me." I rolled my eyes.

Talia touched her nose to mine. She licked the corner of my mouth. "I was going to kill him after I fucked him, but you came in and spoiled all the fun. I couldn't bring him back to me. His *love* for you was too strong. That took the fun out of it." She said love like it was a dirty word.

"Ha! You don't know Ken very well. He only loves himself." I laughed in her face. I don't think she appreciated that much. Her knee came up and caught me in the gut. I fell forward and came within inches of running my face into the knife in her hand. Pallo grabbed my body and eased me to the floor.

Talia reached over me and slashed at Pallo again. He must have been expecting that because he dodged it. Her other hand flew up and struck him with such a force he went airborne.

I screamed for him. He was weak enough as it was without this bitch throwing him around. I tried to kick her in her kneecap, but came up short and got her ankle instead. "Leave him alone!" She didn't flinch.

"Aren't you the brave little one?" She spit the words at me. "He is good, but is he good enough to risk your life for?" She nodded towards Pallo, who was slumped on the ground behind me. He was losing too much blood. He was dying.

"Pallo." I didn't turn to look at him. I was afraid to take my eyes off Talia. I got to my feet and tried to focus on calling an element. Some *Sí*, witches, and other creatures of magic have the ability to call upon the elements of earth, air, fire, water, and spirit. At that particular time I didn't care which I got, I just wanted one. A tingle began in my chest.

"Come, Pallo, let us spark the flame of hate in you once again." She put her finger on my breast and pushed. It felt like a truck had just plowed into me. My feet left the ground, and I flew across the room. My upper back hit the ground first. I was thankful it wasn't my head, or I would have been knocked out. Being unconscious with she-vamp in the room wasn't high on my to-do list.

Talia crossed the room and bent over Pallo with her knife. She licked the blood from the end of it and leaned into him. Lifting his arm, she turned his wrist and made a long slice down the center of it. He winced in pain. Blood didn't pour from it as it should have, and I knew that meant he was close to death, or whatever it was that happened to an already dead guy.

I pulled my aching body off the ground. "Get the fuck away from him, now!"

My power built inside me. I hadn't learned to control it yet, but I didn't really care how it manifested itself, just so long as it did. I thought back to Nana's teachings. She had spent months working with me on this. The most important thing I needed was a target. Talia's little lap dogs appeared as if on command before me.

"My pets will teach you some manners, young one."

Jacob hurled his body into mine, and we crashed onto the floor. The room faded in and out for minute. I blinked. Jacob's red eyes burned brighter. He smiled. His body weight had me pinned to the floor. Slobber fell from his mouth onto my forehead. I tried to wriggle free from under him, but he was too strong.

I kneed him in the groin. Pleasure blossomed on his face.

"More," he said, his voice raspy and low.

I struggled to free my arms from under his body and dug my nails into his face. Jonathan seized hold of my wrists from above my head. Jacob's hands moved down my body as he raised my nightgown. I kicked out at him. My foot came in contact with his jaw but it didn't faze him. He slid the nightgown over my waist, grabbing at my thighs. I kicked him again. Jonathan pulled on my arms harder. The way they were yanking on me, I'd be torn in two in no time.

I heard someone screaming and realized it was me. I looked around the room for Pallo. I was more concerned for his safety than my own. I caught sight of him. Talia dragged his limp body toward me. She had her fingers twisted in the top of his hair, pulling him. She was a vampire, so she made dragging a two hundred pound man look easy.

"Look," she said pulling his head up. "We wouldn't want you

to miss the show."

"Talia, kill me instead. Leave her be," Pallo said, looking at me. I pleaded with my eyes for him to stop. I didn't want him to sacrifice himself for me.

She pulled his head back further. "I have seen you do worse than this. Why the change of heart, Pallo?"

"Take me and leave her, I beg you."

She let go of his head and laughed. "Pallo, you do not beg. You are holding out on me." She pressed the knife to his throat. "If you are willing to die for her she must be some fuck. Let us all see. Shall we?"

Pallo screamed and lunged towards me, but he was too weak to reach me. I could see the determination in his eyes. He wanted to save me.

Talia stepped over the back of him. "It seems that I have found the match to light your fire of hate again, Pallo."

She left him lying there and headed towards the door. "Make Mommy proud, boys," she said and walked out. This woman was too much. If I managed to get out of this alive, I was going to kick her ass--or kill her, I couldn't decide. Right now I was leaning towards the felony.

Jacob lifted my gown higher, exposing my breasts to him. He grabbed them with his hands, cupping me tightly, his claws digging deep.

"Get off me!" I screamed in his face and tried to bash him with my head.

He raked his claws down my stomach, and I felt my skin rip open. I screamed in pain. "Screw you! You are nothing but father-murdering little pricks! Rick should have drowned you at birth, you, you…."

Pallo lay motionless on the floor near me. I closed my eyes and concentrated on him. I visualized a white light between the two of us, connecting our thoughts.

"Pallo," I called his name in my head. "Pallo, please don't give up." I was pushing this thought at him as Jacob's hands kneaded my breasts harder and harder. I brought my focus back to trying to connect with the element of fire. I pictured it in my head. I thought of the ingredients used to conjure fire. The smell of nutmeg, lemon, and cinnamon came to me. I absorbed the scents, let them dance about my head until I felt a tightening in my chest. Heat rose to my face and up my arms, wanting somewhere to go.

Jacob had moved from my breasts and was pressing himself against my abdomen. I could feel the rounded tip of his penis through my thin panties. I screamed for Pallo in my head, screamed and called for my power.

Jacob pried my legs open. I brought my foot up to kick him again, but he caught hold of it. This put my body in the perfect position to accept him into me. He smiled and began to push himself closer to me.

Jonathan pulled harder on my arms. He was trying to tear me apart. I closed my eyes. I let the power flow up my body and spill out towards him. Jonathan let go of me and screamed in pain. I could smell burning flesh, but I didn't open my eyes. I hoped the bastard burst into flames.

I grabbed Jacob's member before he could enter. I let the heat pour from me onto him. He tried to free himself from my grip. I held fast until there was nothing left to hold onto. Something dripped onto my stomach. I opened my eyes and saw a burnt, melted hunk of flesh laying on me. I screamed and let him fall away from me.

I scrambled to my feet and glanced down at him. He was holding his hands between his legs. It took a moment for my head to register what it was I was looking at. He was holding himself, and trying to fight to keep from being disemboweled. There was no skin or muscle left to hold him together. There was no evidence at all that he was male. He looked at me with eyes of fire and fell onto the floor at my feet. I felt a wave of nausea hit me. I dropped to my knees on the floor and brought my hand to my lips. I could still feel the hot energy running through me.

"Bitch!" was all I heard before I was knocked over. Jonathan tackled me to the ground, slashing at me with claws that had sprung from his burnt fingers. I lifted my hands to protect my face and his claws ripped into the under side of my arms.

Movement caught my attention, blurred above me as Jonathan's body flew off and slammed into the wall. Pallo stood above me and dropped beside me, reaching for my arms. I didn't want him to touch me. I was afraid I wouldn't be able to control the power in me. I could feel it still beating in me, strong and ready to lash out. He grabbed my hands and pulled me to him.

"No!" I screamed.

Lightning flashed through the room. A thunderous crash came from above us as the room went black.

Chapter 15

We found ourselves sitting on the floor in the yellow bedroom. Pallo was still clutching my body to his, and I screamed. I no longer felt my power rising through me. I pushed him away.

"Did I hurt you?" I asked, trying to catch my breath, my heart beating so hard, I could feel my neck pulsating.

"No, I am fine." He sat next to me on the wood floor.

I looked at his face and saw no trace of color left in his skin. I watched as he started to rot before my eyes.

"You're hurt," I said to him, reaching out to touch his ripped-open face.

He slid his hand up to meet mine and turned my arms upwards. Jonathan had managed to slice most of the skin away, leaving bone exposed in places. I could see Pallo struggling with his demon when he saw all of the blood dripping from me. He took my bloody gown from my shoulder and pulled it down. My breasts spilled out, but he didn't seem to notice. He stared at the marks on my stomach. He laid his hand gently on one and I cried out.

"I will get something to cleanse your wounds." He tried to stand, but came crashing down on the floor. I grabbed his shoulders and pulled him toward me. I began to lose feeling in my hands as my body slowly shut down. I knew that if I died Pallo would, too, and I couldn't allow that to happen. I would not lose another man I loved.

"Pallo! Pallo!"

My mind fogged for a moment, and I knew I was losing blood too fast, making it hard for me to concentrate. Then it hit me. Lifting my arms over his mouth, I let the blood drip near his mouth. I thought he would magically spring to life, but he just lay there.

"Pallo! Don't you dare leave me now … *ti amo*." I didn't know why I said that, and I wasn't even sure what it meant.

Slowly, his chalky white skin began to show signs of color.

A ringing began in my ears. Dizzy, I laid my head on the floor--Pallo's face blurred before me. I was so tired now, and I wanted to rest. I just needed to sleep for a little bit and then I'd check on him again.

Darkness swept in around me. It was so quiet, so peaceful. Something soft and warm brushed across my stomach, arms, and up to my lips. Lifting my heavy lids, I found Pallo kissing me. His eyes were closed, and his brown hair fell around my face. Every sane part of my body yelled for me to push him off me. Every other part pulled him closer. I grabbed hold of the back of his head and forced his mouth onto me harder.

His eyes sprung open as he tried to back away from me. I held tight to his hair, and pulled him closer to me. He moved until his body was on top of mine, pinning me to floor, kissing me. Power flared up around us. It wasn't mine, but it was faerie.

"*Ti amo*--I love you."

I opened my eyes. Pallo kissed my neck and whispered in my ear. I don't know if he'd told me he loved me again or if I'd just imagined it. When he looked at me, I noticed the cut on his cheek had healed.

Reaching up, I touched his chest. It was perfect, not a mark on it. He lifted his hand, grabbed hold of my arm, and looked it. I expected to see a cut, anything, but my arms were healed. I was the one who pulled the gown down further this time. My stomach was smooth, firm, and in one piece. I looked up at Pallo, confused.

"What happened?"

"Magic," he said, matter-of-factly.

Pallo bent his head down to kiss me again, and I welcomed him. We couldn't get enough of the taste of each other. I rubbed my naked breasts against his chiseled chest and could feel myself moistening, longing for the feel of him.

Pallo ground his body against mine. I could feel his cock through his pants, hard, and ready to take me. I pulled at his back and tried to get my hands down far enough to touch his waistband. Guided by raw need, I wanted to feel him in my hand, to wrap my fingers around his member and hear him cry out in ecstasy. I wanted to stroke him, please him.

He slid down and kissed my neck as he moved slowly to my collarbone. A moan escaped from me, and he laughed against my skin. He brushed my left breast with his hand, and I lifted slightly towards him. His mouth moved over my breast and he drew my erect nipple in between his teeth, tugging at it, eliciting tiny moans from me. Each slow draw of his mouth, each flicker of his tongue, made my core thick with cream and need.

"Pallo … *ohhh*."

My thoughts jumbled, and I fought to keep hold of myself--to maintain control. He was out of my league, a sexual guru so to speak. The man's dry humping skills were already rated among my top three sexual experiences--ever! I could only imagine what actual sex with him would be like. Could I take it? Was I really ready to handle all that he had to offer?

He was gentle, too gentle. I wanted him to be rough. I wanted him to pin me down and ravish me. I knew he harbored a demon within him and wanted him to channel some of its wickedness. I'd never wanted a man to use me to satisfy his own needs more than I wanted Pallo to. Pleasing him was my only priority.

Pallo ran his fingers down my stomach. He stopped at my navel and planted tiny wet kisses along it, rimming it. He teased me for a moment before moving down, trailing a line of kisses over my patch of black curls, and settling his face firmly between my legs. Cool fingers parted my velvety folds, gently caressing my ready nub as they went. I waited for a finger to slip into my hot channel and was surprised when his tongue plunged into me instead.

"Mmm," he murmured.

"Pallo…."

My body savored every second of his oral assault. His long, expert tongue eased in and out, as he tweaked my nub. Signs of a pending orgasm hit me, and my legs pulled up, catching Pallo's head in a vice-like grip. He chuckled with his face still buried between my legs, creating a vibrating sensation that sent me over the edge.

"Oh, Pallo … there, uhh…." I came hard and fast.

Pallo moaned softly and began taking long, slow lick across me, lapping my cream up as he went. Sated, yet still aroused, I reached for him, wanting to give him pleasure too.

Wrapping my fingers in his loose curls, I tugged gently on his head. He shook his head no, pushing his face against me, and inserting his tongue back into me.

It felt so good, so relaxing, that I was powerless to stop my mind from drifting elsewhere. I seemed to leave my body, yet go nowhere. The horrible visions of death came flooding back to me. I fought to stay, mentally, with Pallo, but I wasn't strong enough. Whatever had prompted the vision was determined I see it.

Images flashed before me, until I became one with them. No longer a mere spectator in my own dream, I found myself submerged in it. I stood in the familiar corridor again--my eyes still closed and my head tipped back. Fear gripped my body, leaving me paralyzed, stuck to the door while something slid over my body. It traced its way down me, scratching me with its dagger-like nails. Welts formed, and knew if it applied any more pressure it would draw blood.

When it reached my swollen belly, it began inching my dress up. I pleaded with it. "Please, don't do this. I'm sorry, I didn't mean for this to happen ... I never would've left if I'd known you were still ... I thought that you were dead."

"I am." The creature's voice was deep, raspy and somewhat familiar. "I am dead, yet I am not, caught between. I am immortal. Now, I will have forever to remind you of your betrayal."

"No, I gave up everything to be with you. Everything to be a family--" A sob caught in my throat, and tears ran freely down my cheeks. I took a deep breath in, trying to calm myself. I needed to know, I needed to find out what terrorized me. Opening my eyes a tiny bit, I peeked out. Pallo knelt before me in the hallway, naked and covered in blood. He looked up at me. His face twisted and pulled, contorting in different directions.

"Pallo, NO!"

Where was my Pallo? Gone was the man who had stolen my heart. A monster remained in his place. His forehead had thickened and his eyes were black, hollow pits that seemed to see through me. Curling his lips, he licked his large fangs.

"Pallo?" I couldn't accept that he was gone. I wouldn't accept it. I extended my hand out and touched his demonic face. For a split second, his eyes flickered back to brown, and his face softened. The monster within him took hold once more, but not before I'd spotted my love, my heart, my Pallo. He was in there, somewhere, and I was determined to reach him. I loved him too much to lose him to the darkness. "Oh, my sweet Pallo, what has he done to you?"

He threw his head back and growled out, sending shivers down my body. He clutched at my stomach and bowed his head. "I ... love you."

I gasped. "I love you too, Pallo."

Something changed, his body stiffened and when he looked up, I bore witness to his humanity slipping away. "Run, Gwyneth! Run, now! I cannot fight ... the demon within ... any longer. Run!" He thrust my body away from him.

"Pallo, no, please let me help you."

"RUN!"

I wanted to stay with him, but there was no longer only me to think about. Another life depended on my survival. Kissing my fingers, I place them on his cheek before running off into the night.

The vision receded and I found myself lying on the floor with Pallo on top of me. His tongue still flickered in and out of my core, causing even more cream to flow from me. As good as he felt, I couldn't do this. The vision was too fresh, too real for me to ignore. He rubbed my clit with his thumb, making my legs jerk involuntarily.

"Uhh ... no, Pallo."

He ignored my plea, stimulating my swollen nub repeatedly, leaving me bucking against him, caught in a state of immense pleasure and fear. I scrambled to pull myself away from him. No part of him looked demonic, no black eyes, no twisted face, but I didn't want him near me. The terrifying feeling from the dream still clung to me.

I scurried backwards, trying to put distance between us, and was stopped only by the bed. Inching my way up, I climbed onto it, and continued to back away from him. He followed me up, slinking over me, and settling next to me. Pallo glanced lazily at me, with a feral smile on his glistening face. "Don't," was all that came out of my mouth. There was no trace of anger in his face. He was just Pallo, the man--okay, the vamp that had swept me off my feet.

"I can't explain it, but…." I tried to think of the best way to tell him how I felt. He'd just spent so much time giving me pleasure that I couldn't just pull away and not explain it to him. "Sometimes, I get these random visions about you and me ... they seem real, but not from this time. Kind of like a past life thing." Great, just great! I sounded like a loon.

If I only had my own nine-hundred number, I could be physic-faerie to all, girlfriend of none. If I started speaking in tongues, or claiming to be Napoleon, we were screwed.

Pallo tipped his head to the side, his chin still wet with my juices. "What are these random visions of?"

Oh well, the damage was already done, why hide it?

"They're of you and me. In some of them, you appear human to me. I see you with golden tips in your hair, and bronzed skin. Others, you're anything but human." I'd passed the stopping point now. "They're more like a memory than anything else. It's really weird, because I could swear that I was there, with you, when you weren't a vampire yet." As I said this, he stiffened.

"Go on."

Yeah, I was on a roll. Why stop now? It's not like the straight jacket wouldn't fit in an hour. "Don't laugh, but I can totally see you asking me to marry you, and no, I'm not trying to snag a husband. I see this like it already happened, and like … it's like you're trying to get me to go away with you in a hurry, but I know I can't leave. For some reason, I'm deathly afraid for you if I go. I know that he'll kill you, but I don't know who *he* is." I glanced at Pallo, wondering how long it would be before he tied me to the bed for my own safety. His face was void of any emotion. He just lay there looking at me with blank eyes. "Pallo, I know it's crazy."

"No, no it is not crazy. Are there any other memories?"

I shook my head slowly, not sure he really wanted to hear the rest. "Please, don't take this wrong, it's just … no, never mind, it's silly."

With one hand, he lifted me quickly and laid me the right way on the bed, before moving next to me. It was a raw display of power that reminded me how powerful he truly was. "Gwyneth, nothing you have to say to me is silly. Please tell me more of this. I am very interested to hear more about these visions."

I didn't really think he wanted to hear about me seeing him as a demonic creature about to kill me and my unborn child so I let it go. "I think I might be coming down with something. I should probably rest for a bit."

He gave me a knowing look, wiped his chin, and licked his fingers clean. When he pressed his body against mine, I pulled his arm around me. Regardless of how badly the vision had scared me, he was still *my sweet* Pallo.

Closing my eyes, I concentrated hard on the dreams I'd been having about Pallo. I wanted to get to the root of them. There had to be a reason for them, and I intended to find out what that was. Slowly, I eased into a light sleep. Pallo shifted slightly, pulling me closer to him. Having him hold me tight allowed me the courage I needed to go searching for answers. Relaxing, I gradually slipped back into one.

This time I wasn't in the hallway with the vampire demon Pallo. Now, I lay in a large four poster bed. I couldn't make out the other furnishings in the room. It took everything I had to make out the door to the room through the darkness. A familiar voice spoke to me and I turned my head. There, beside me in the bed, was Caleb. He was stunning, his blond hair spilling all over the covers. I sank down next to him.

"What troubles you?"

"I thought I heard something."

"Gwyneth, you are safe. You are both safe." He stroked my swollen belly, gently, tenderly. The touch of his hand made my body warm. I wanted to be near him, I wanted to have him run his hands all over me. I snuggled in next to him and kissed his neck. He chuckled. "You are never satisfied these days, are you?"

"No, I think it has something to do with expecting. I can't get enough of you, of this," I kissed his lips, and put my hand firmly between his legs.

Caleb laughed and pulled himself close to me. He moved his hands around my body, and slid his leg up mine slowly. Moving his mouth over my breast, he planted tiny kisses on it, proving to be more than I could stand.

He came away smacking his lips together. "Mmm, it leaked. Hmm, I'll have to have another taste to…."

"Please, Caleb … don't tease. I need you in me, now. Make love to me."

He artfully moved his body over mine, careful not to lean on my stomach. He bent down and kissed my rather large belly. "Soon, we will be a family."

"Caleb."

He looked at me with his beautiful green eyes, and put his finger to his lips. "*Shhh*, Gwyneth, do not remind me that I'm not the one who put this life in you. I am not angry, for this is something I could never give you. As much as I want to be a match for you, I am not." He kissed my belly again. "This is a joyous time for me. I have you, and soon a little one will join us. I shall … *I do* … love it as if it were my own, and there is nothing you can say to change that. He is gone, and you are here with me, with child." His lips found mine. "I love you, Gwyneth."

My thoughts raced to Pallo. I knew that the child I carried was his, and my heart ached because he was dead. It'd been months since I had known his touch, and since I'd gotten the news of his demise. I'd ended up in Caleb's arms seeking comfort after Pallo's disappearance, and I had never left. Soon we would be married and we'd be welcoming the baby into the world.

Caleb's kisses brought me back to him. I arched my back, begging him to enter me. His erect shaft nudged at my entrance. I knew I was wet. I was always wet for him. Being with child only made my sexual urges stronger, wilder and I'd burst if he didn't join me soon. "Please." In one fluid motion, he slid his cock into me, sheathing himself in my silken depths, filling me completely. "Uhhhh … ahhhh," I cried out in sinful pleasure.

He rode my body, careful not to put his full weight on me, and I felt him everywhere. He pumped and swiveled his hips, hitting a spot deep within me that left me feeling as though I was on the brink of coming each time the head of his cock rubbed it. Instantly, his magic moved through me, through the baby. My magic rose to embrace his and they merged, bringing me quickly to culmination.

"Caleb," I panted.

His arms tightened as he supported himself above me, straining to maintain control as my body clenched around his. Our gazes locked, and I witnessed the look of complete abandonment as he released himself deep within my womb. "I love you."

"And I, you, Caleb."

"That is strange, last I knew, I was the one you opened your legs for, and no other." The sound of Pallo's voice made me freeze.

How?

Caleb looked down at me with a look of dread, but he didn't move. Something rushed past me. Caleb was suddenly propelled off me and into the air. I screamed. In a flash Pallo was before me, but it wasn't my Pallo, it was not the Pallo I had loved. This thing before me was a monster--a vampire. I'd come to know vampires in my lifetime, and one in particular was pure evil. I knew full well what they were capable of, and the destruction they could cause. My eyes fell upon my stomach.

The baby.

I had to protect the baby. I yanked my blue nightgown on to cover my body. He laughed. The sound of the Devil's voice fell from his lips.

"You hide your shame from me. Why? I know what you are now, *donnaccia*. I watched you allowing another to take pleasures within you."

He had just called me a whore, and I knew it was the demon talking, and not my sweet Pallo. I reached my hand up to touch him and he struck me across the face. I fell off the bed and scrambled to my feet. My cheek burned, and my body ached. I was too far along in the pregnancy to move quickly, but I knew I had to get away from him, from it.

Caleb stirred on the floor, and I feared Pallo would destroy him if he noticed. His hate was, at least for the moment, focused on me, not Caleb. If I could give Caleb enough time to come to, he could fight the demon off. I couldn't use my magic against him even if I wanted to, I carried his child, and I was powerless to cause him harm.

"Here," I said, coaxing him towards me. "No, I have no shame. I would change nothing!" With that, I ran towards the door and out into the hallway. I could feel him closing in on me. I had lied to him just then, and I didn't know if he could tell or not. Some vampires could sense a lie, others could not. I had been told it took years to develop strong vampire powers. I didn't have time to figure it out. I had to save our baby. The Pallo I knew and loved had created this life with me, and I would not let the demon side of him destroy it. I screamed and ran from the room.

Something shook me, and I woke with a start. Pallo was over me in the bed. "You, you murderer, you killed me…." As I said it, I realized how insane I sounded.

Pallo looked at me and shook his head. "I did not mean for you … I was upset … I…."

Turning, I climbed across the bed, and pulled at the blanket on the bed. With my body weight on it, I couldn't get it to wrap completely around me. I turned to keep my eye on Pallo, but he was gone. Frantic, I clutched at the blanket and pulled a corner of it over me and turned on all fours to climb off the bed.

Pallo caught hold of my arms and fell on top of me. He rolled me onto my back and pinned my body to the bed. I kicked and bit at him. He didn't fight me, he merely held me tight.

"ENOUGH!" he yelled, so loud that I thought my eardrums had burst. I stopped fighting and lay motionless beneath him.

Pallo looked down at me with tears in his eyes. "I did not murder you. I swear it, I loved you. I still love you. I will always love you."

"You walked in on her, on me … with Caleb. You cornered me in the hallway." I wasn't sure how to talk about the past. I only had bits and pieces to go off of.

"I did not mean to harm you. I was newly made, and had little control over my demon." He looked as though he was reflecting on the past, trying to make sense of what was obviously senseless. "What you did not see was me falling to floor and telling you to go, because I did not want to hurt you."

"So, you admit that this all happened? But how? What the hell is going on?" My thoughts were so jumbled my head hurt. I wasn't sure if I should run or take a nap.

"Gwyneth, you do not understand. Yes, it was you, but in another lifetime." He loosened his grip on me slightly. I thought about hitting him, but I didn't. "When we found Lydia with child, we had no idea what that would mean for us."

"What does Lydia have to do with this?"

"It does not matter. The only thing that matters is that you understand that you are removed from that life. You have a new life now, a fresh start."

"Did you kill me?" I asked dryly.

"I have already told you, no--but I did frighten you, and drove you to your death." He closed his eyes. "I drove you away ... I could not leash the monster in me."

"I wouldn't leave you for being what you are, not if I loved you."

He let go of me and slid next to me on the bed, covering my body with the blanket. "You were not the same person then. Circumstances were different." Pallo put his head back and his hair spilled out next to mine. Loose brown curls laced into my black waves and for a moment I couldn't tell where one ended and the other began.

"Circumstances?" I mulled over what he had said. "Caleb and the baby." It made sense now. I knew why I had fallen head over heels for both Caleb and Pallo in such a short time. I knew them, and had loved them--both.

"Yes, you knew Caleb. You knew Caleb for almost a hundred years before you ever even met me," Pallo said, sounding sad. I decided against yelling at him for reading me again. I wasn't even sure he was aware he did it.

"How the hell old was I?"

"Over one hundred when you died. The faerie blood in you was strong, so you would have lived well over a thousand years."

"How did I die?" The words fell out so easily, as if I talked about past lives everyday.

"I do not know exactly how it happened, but I know it was not pleasant."

"How do you know that?" I turned to face him on the bed. We were lying on the quilt and there was not enough of it to cover my whole body. I tried to ignore it and stared at his profile.

"Faeries are not easy to kill, and it took us many days before we found you." Pallo's eyes were closed again and I could tell he didn't want to talk about this with me.

"It took days to find my body? Couldn't somebody smell a rotting corpse?"

Stomach bile churned and twisted in me as the thought of this sunk in. It's not everyday you find out you were murdered in a past life.

"I did not say rotting body. I said body." Pallo turned and looked at me. It was as though he saw inside of me--looked through me, to my core. He moved close to me and instead of answering my question he kissed me on the lips.

"The baby?"

He let out a sigh. "You were no longer with child when we found you."

"Was the baby all right then?"

His hand touched mine and squeezed. "No. I knew the people behind your death, and they are not the type to keep a child around. If I could have saved *your* baby, I would have." He put much emphasis on the word your.

The reality of the situation set in and I shuddered. He grabbed my hand, and held it tight, making me feel safe when it should have been impossible to feel safe.

"You are here now. Let us hope we never know what really happened." His mouth pressed over mine, but I didn't reciprocate the kiss. Pallo's entire body enveloped me. He brought his lips to my cheek. I stiffened, and he stopped trying to kiss me. He just lay there holding me tightly.

"Tell me your thoughts," he whispered.

I didn't know what to say. My mind had been racing over the hundreds of ways I could have died and my face flushed. I was on the verge of a panic attack. My breathing was shallow and my pulse quickened. I clutched onto to him and he held me tight.

"I want to go home," I said, softly.

"Then it shall be." Wind whirled around us on the bed, as he kissed the top of my head. "I am sorry."

Chapter 16

With a loud thud, my body hit my bathroom floor. The blue tile felt ice cold on my naked body. Pallo was not with me. The thought of being rid of him should have made me happy. Instead, I was terrified. I had a vision of him being stuck in the past, unable to leave the house and starving to death.

I ran into the kitchen and grabbed the cordless phone. I dialed information. The operator gave me the number for Necro World. It took me three times dialing to get it right. I was so nervous that my fingers were hitting the wrong buttons. It rang and rang. I tried to swallow the lump in my throat. An automated answering service picked up. I listened to the endless choices of buttons to push and selected one.

"Hello, Necro's Magik World & Supernatural Theme Park. Jennifer speaking. How I may help you?"

"Pallo! I need to speak to Pallo, please."

"Who's calling?"

"Just put Pallo on please."

"Yes, Miss, I'm afraid that--"

I interrupted. "If Mr. Pallo is there, you have exactly two seconds to put him on this phone or I will hunt you down, Jenny. It is Jenny, right?" I enunciated each word to its fullest, so she would hear how real my threat was. "I want to make sure I come after the right person."

"I'll connect you now, please hold." Soft music came over the ear piece. I wasn't sure when vampires began listening to soft rock, but I figured it was one mainstream way to handle the changing technologies. If they could tolerate Kenny G, then so could I.

The phone buzzed, and someone picked it up. "Pallo's office," James said.

"Is Pallo there?"

"Ms. Stevens?"

"Yeah, James, it's me, Gwen. Is Pallo there?"

"You two gave us a hell of a scare. One minute you were there and then poof, you were gone. We searched everywhere for you guys." I got the feeling he tended to ramble, and I wasn't in the mood for it.

"Jameson! IS PALLO THERE?" I screamed it at the top of my lungs into the phone.

"Well, okay, don't get your knickers in a twist. Hang on, I'll grab him."

I exhaled. I hadn't realized I'd been holding my breath. Someone came to the phone.

"Gwyneth, James tells me you are upset. Are you all right?" Pallo's sweet strong voice filled my ear. I was so relieved. He was fine.

"I was--" I began to say worried and stopped myself. "I thought you might not have made it back. You weren't with me, and I was just...."

"I was worried about you, as well." He sounded pleased. "I could not go with you to your home. I had not been invited."

I smacked my forehead. I knew vampires couldn't enter a person's home without an invitation. If I had taken time to think, I would have figured it out.

"How did I get home?" It dawned on me that he might have had the power to bring us back from the get-go.

"We both desired to return. Together, we were strong enough to break the illusion."

"Illusion?"

"Yes. We didn't travel back in time. We merely entered another realm. A place of fantasy and dreams," he said this like it was oh so normal.

"Seemed like hell to me."

"Not all of it."

"Fine, not all of it … happy?" I was so happy he was all right that it was hard to be mad at him.

"Very." That one word penetrated through me. "Am I welcome in your home?"

"Yes, always I want you here." That came out too fast and sounded too desperate. I was at a loss as to what to say, so I did the mature thing. I hung up on him.

I stood with my back to the wall in my kitchen and relaxed. It took a minute for me to collect myself. I decided to take a shower.

I turned the water on and let it blast my body. It felt good running down my back. I bent down and picked up a bottle of shampoo. It was vanilla bean scent. I smiled, thinking of Pallo.

I moved my soapy hands over my stomach. The time frame to know if I was with child had come and gone, my belly was flatter now than when I had possibly conceived. Having a hellhound rip at it will do that to you. I wasn't sure how I felt about not being pregnant.

I checked the time and date on the weather channel. Shit! I was supposed to meet Sharon for my birthday tonight. It was the last thing I wanted to do. I mean, I had been rather busy lately having sex with faeries, getting attacked by hellhounds, saving a vampire who impregnated me some two hundred years ago, and oh, yeah, thinking I might have been pregnant by the faerie guy. Yeah, that pretty much summed it up.

Great, it was settled--I was going out.

I knew leaving my troubles behind would be the best thing for me to do. I let the water soothe me, wash away the day's grief. When I was done, I wrapped my hair in a towel and another around my body, and walked to my bedroom.

"It's about time," a voice said. I nearly jumped out of my skin.

Ken sprawled across my bed, his long, naked body reflecting the moonlight through the window.

"What the hell are you doing?"

He smiled. I loved the way he smiled, it showed off his dark brown eyes. "You never called me back. You didn't show up for work. Nana hadn't heard from you, Sharon didn't have a clue where you were. I got worried and came over. I let myself in while you were in the shower. I didn't think you'd mind." He put his hand on his hip, drawing attention to his pelvic area. He was long and hard. He always was.

I bit my lip and looked away. Ken was the second man I'd ever slept with. The first had been in college and was nothing to write home about. I'm not even sure it counted. There should be some sort of minimum time requirement to count it as sex. It was Ken who I spent my first full night in bed with and Ken who turned sex into something I wanted to do, not something I felt I had to do.

"Put your clothes on," I said, looking out the window.

"Why can't you look at me?"

"Because the last time I saw you naked was when you were cramming yourself in that psychotic slut." I faced him. "That reminds me. I ran into your little girlfriend. She's a real winner. I wish you two the best. Maybe you've been asking the wrong people about the Keeper. Maybe you should ask your girlfriend."

Ken sat up and looked at me. "You ran into her?"

"Yeah, little Miss Fangs and her pets tried to have a little fun with us."

"Us? What pets? Fangs?" His brow furrowed.

"What? Don't pretend like you don't know. You're the one fucking her." I crossed my arms over my chest.

"I've already told you, Gwen. I don't know her. She just showed up at the door, and--"

"And you fucked her in our bed," I finished the last part for him.

Someone knocked on the front door. I glanced at the clock, saw that it was almost eight, and figured it was Sharon. I thought she had told me to meet her there, but I could have been wrong. Cut a girl some slack, I'd had a rough day.

"Leave it. Come on, I have a birthday present for you." Ken stroked his shaft suggestively. I rolled my eyes, and stormed out of the room. Marching across the living room, I went to the door. I threw caution to the wind and opened it. I knew Sharon would help me throw Ken out.

Pallo stood in the hallway. He had a handful of white lilies in one hand and what appeared to be my cell phone in the other.

"Hello." He smiled wide. "This was on the floor. I thought you might need it." He lifted the cell phone in his hand.

I stared at him a minute, soaking in his beauty. The sight of him took my breath away. He looked like he was about to jump on a runway at any moment and was merely on break between photo shoots.

Mmm, my own personal Italian male model. Yummy.

"Tell whoever it is that we're busy," Ken called. I'd *almost* forgotten he was here. I closed my eyes and prayed Ken was dressed. When I looked at Pallo's face, I could tell that he wasn't.

"I am sorry to drop by unannounced. You are busy," Pallo said. He looked hurt and turned to leave.

"Don't go!" The words came out too quick. "It's not what it looks like."

I moved aside and held the door open for him. He just stood there looking at me. His gorgeous eyes widened as he tipped his head slightly to the side. It hit me that he couldn't enter without my permission.

"Please come in. You're always welcome here."

I took a deep breath, sucking in the sweet smell of vanilla mixed with a hint of expensive cologne, as he walked past me. I closed the door and turned around. Ken stood there with one of my towels wrapped around his waist. He glared at Pallo. I was happy that Ken was next to naked. If he'd had his clothes on, then he most certainly would have been armed. He was the type that never left home without a gun. With the temper he had, he would have shot Pallo right where he stood and not thought twice about it. I don't think the bullet would have killed Pallo, but I didn't really want to test that theory, nor did I want to spend the rest of the night scrubbing blood out of my carpeting.

The tension in the small room was thick. "Pallo, this is Ken. Ken, Pallo."

Neither man moved to shake the other's hand.

"Christ, Gwen, he's the vampire I sent you to talk to." Ken's body tightened as he gripped the corner of the towel. "I send you down to just talk to someone, then this guy, excuse me, corpse, shows up at your door with flowers?"

Pallo took a step towards Ken, his anger palpable.

"No," I said to Pallo. He stopped in his tracks, keeping his eyes on Ken.

Ken laughed and looked at Pallo. "You fucked her, didn't you? She threw her legs in the air, and put you on a leash in the process. She's good, I'll give her that, but come on, you're a freaking corpse." He looked at me. "That's low, even for you, Gwen!"

Ken pulled his hand across his chest leaving scratch marks on his tanned skin. He directed his anger at me. "It took me months to get down your pants, and then you just throw yourself at the first fucking vamp you meet?" He slammed his fist back and hit my living room wall. "Hell, if I had known that, I'd have let you go to all the crime scenes with me. After all, dead people make you *horny*." The last word came out of him quietly.

Instantly, Pallo was on him. He had his hand pressed against Ken's throat, pinning him to the wall. The two of them stood silent. Pallo's pale hand clutched at Ken's tanned throat tighter and I ran to him.

I put my hand on Pallo's arm. "It's okay."

Pallo turned and glanced at me. His eyes were on the verge of turning black. I'd seen this in my vision of him in the corridor, and I knew that when his eyes were black he was at his worst--maybe unstoppable.

I ran my fingers over his bare skin lightly. "Let him go, Pallo."

He loosened his grip on Ken's neck. I shot Ken a 'don't even think about it' look. Easing Pallo's arm down, I let my hand slip into his.

"He's hurt, he didn't mean it," I whispered softly.

"Like hell I didn't." Ken's voice was raspy from being choked.

I had to pull on Pallo's arm with my entire body weight to keep him from lashing out at Ken. I slid my body between the two of them. My towel came loose and I had to reach up to tighten it.

"Enough, boys," I said, and put a hand on each of their chests. Pallo's was smooth and felt like a statue, Ken's was fuzzy and warm beneath my fingers. I pushed them both back slightly, and my towel gave way. I snatched it up and wrapped it around me.

"Go!" I said to Ken, and pointed to my bedroom. He went, grinning at Pallo all the way.

I looked to Pallo. "I need to get dressed. Are you okay now?"

His eyes widened. "You are going in there with him?"

"Relax! I'm a big girl and can handle myself."

"That is not what I am worried about. I can sense your feelings for him." He hunched his shoulders slightly. "He is the one you were to marry, is he not?"

"Pallo, what do you want me to say? Do you want me to lie and say I feel nothing for the man? Do you want me to confess some undying love for you, and run off into the sunset? I can't do that. It's not that easy." I pushed my body into his. "Real life doesn't work that way."

He backed up slightly and handed the flowers to me. "No, I suppose not."

I felt like such a bully. He defended my honor, and I verbally abused him. I took the flowers to the kitchen, put them in water, and went straight to my room. When I opened the door, Ken was already wearing his navy Dockers and had pulled a white polo shirt over his body. I shut the door behind me and walked right up to him. I struck his cheek. I went to hit him once more for good measure, but he grabbed my wrist.

"You son of a bitch! You come in here and accuse me of being a slut? You're a fine one to talk." I tried to keep my voice low, so Pallo wouldn't hear.

"I didn't know you were that easy, Gwen, or I wouldn't have bothered dating you. I'd have just asked for a quickie." He leaned down into my face.

I had to hand it to him. He wasn't one to back down from a fight. I gave up. "What does it matter to you who I sleep with?"

"You mean what you sleep with, don't you?" The prosecutor in him showed through.

"What, are you mad at the fact that I slept with someone else? Or are you mad that he's a vampire?"

Ken moved closer to me. His lips were almost touching mine, now. "Both."

"Why, if I remember correctly, you were the one who started fucking vampires first, not me," I turned my face to the left to keep him from pressing his lips to mine. "Turnabout is fair play."

"Don't do this to us. Please, Gwen." His voice was soft now.

The anger receded in me. "You did this to us, Ken, not me."

"Why the hell did you go fuck the first thing that showed you some attention? How could you let some dead piece of shit demon touch you?"

I slapped him across the face hard. "Don't! Don't you ever talk about them that way again, ever!"

"Them?" he asked, shock in his voice. "You fucked more than one?"

"Ken, it's none of your damned business who I choose to share my bed with!" I spat the words at him.

"You're right."

I pulled myself away from him and walked to over to my dresser.

"I don't want to fight with you anymore, Ken."

"I don't want to fight either," he said, following me. I put my hand up to stop him.

"That doesn't mean I want you back." I turned and opened my top drawer to get out a pair of underwear. "Go, I'll be out in a minute."

"Did you really fuck him?"

"No, I didn't have sex with him." I wasn't lying. I hadn't had actual sex with Pallo. I'd had sex with Caleb. It was so very Clintonesque of me.

"Are you going to? I mean, he's, you know...?"

"I know what he is. And I know who he is." I was still whispering to keep Pallo from overhearing us.

"Could you let something that should be rotting in the ground stick its dick in you? Could you honestly spend your life with that? There's no future with him."

"Ken, you lost the right to plan my future six months ago, remember?" I tried to stay calm, but was having a hard time.

"You told me once that you wanted children someday. Is that still true?" His voice was getting louder.

"Quiet down." What Ken said made me think of Pallo's wish to give me what I wanted in life--a family, a husband, and a damn house with a white picket fence. I was a sucker for the

American dream.

"Do you still want a family?" Ken asked, smiling as he lowered his voice.

"Yes." My thoughts went to Caleb and being ripe for him. My chance at a family was dead now. I pushed the painful thoughts away. I couldn't cry now. I wanted to start getting dressed, but didn't want to give Ken the satisfaction of watching me.

Ken's chocolate brown eyes held no hate for me. He appeared concerned. "Can you settle for something that can't ever give you that?"

"He's not a something, he's a someone!" I shouted in a low, hushed voice. It wasn't easy, but I think Ken got my point. "What do you want from me, Ken? Do you want me to take you back? Forget it! Do you want me to say that I'm going to chain myself to someone who can offer me nothing but blood and death? Pallo's not like that, he's different. I have strong feelings for him. I'm infatuated with him. Oh hell, let's face it--I'm in love with him. I don't know if I can spend the rest of my life with him … I never thought I would end up with a monster. Is that what you wanted to hear?" I just glared at him.

"No, I want you to admit that you miss me. Admit that you miss us." He tucked his shirt in as he talked to me. "I know that you miss the way we were, too. I can see it in your eyes. Admit it!"

"It doesn't matter anymore. Get out, I need to get dressed."

He came up behind me. "I've seen it all before."

"I know. Go!" I pointed towards the door. I pulled a pair of black lace undies out of the drawer.

"Those were always my favorite," he said walking towards the door.

I turned and flashed him a dirty look. "Hey, Ken," I called to him before he left. He turned. "Play nice out there. You're in enough trouble with me as it is."

He flashed me one of his 'Who, me?' smiles and walked out.

I grabbed a matching black bra and put it on. I took a step over and opened my closet door. I picked out a short black leather skirt and matching top. I pulled the skirt on. The material was silky and smooth and fit me like a glove. I reached into my closet and pulled out a pair of black leather mule shoes with chunky heels. When I put them on, they made me at least two inches taller.

I pulled the shirt over my head and adjusted it. It was

sleeveless but had wide straps to hold it up. It was a scoop neck, so it wasn't too revealing. I had always had a problem finding tops that kept my breasts in without making them look huge.

When I stepped out into the living room, I saw Pallo sitting in my big comfy chair. I loved sitting in that chair and curling up with a good book. It had always seemed so perfect for me. It was covered in large flowers that were done in shades of yellow. Seeing Pallo in it made me laugh. He looked so out of place. He looked like a bad ass that had to sit in a girl's chair. Wait, that's exactly what he was!

Pallo dug his fingers into his knees, and glared at Ken who sat on my yellow couch. I had always liked the idea of arranging my furniture for conversation, but seeing them sitting that close to each other made me question my decision.

Ken glanced up at me and threw his feet up on my coffee table. That was a huge no-no. I had found an old chest at an antique store and picked it up. I brought it home and had been using it for a table ever since. I glared at him, and he smiled.

"Pallo and I were just discussing the various positions you enjoy." He looked up at me and grinned from ear to ear. "I'm shocked, Gwen. I don't think our good friend here knew you were a three input girl."

My face reddened. Raising my hand, I lashed energy out at Ken. It knocked his feet off my table. Ken looked shocked. I think I saw Pallo smile.

"Get out now, Ken." The rage growing inside me belied the calmness of my voice.

He gave me a mischievous grin but didn't budge. "Hey, Pallo, is it true that vampires have excellent hearing?"

Pallo's gaze met mine as he answered, "Yes."

I thought back to the argument with Ken in my bedroom. I called him a monster. Pallo had sat out here and listened to the entire thing. My stomach tightened into a knot. I wanted to knock that cocky smirk off Ken's face. He knew Pallo could hear every word we'd said, and he'd baited me.

The sound of Pallo's voice broke my anger. "You look exquisite, Gwyneth."

"Thanks! I'm going out to get some dinner and drinks."

"With who?" Ken asked.

They both looked at me now.

"It's Friday night, right? I'm supposed to be meeting Sharon at The Raven. You know, celebrate the whole turning twenty-five thing. We had to postpone it a bit, remember? It *was* your idea Ken."

The Raven was a huge dance club that catered to the supernatural. Sharon had thought it would be fun to take me there for my birthday. She told me to meet her there at nine thirty. I wanted to go. I wanted to forget about all of the messed up events that had taken place in my life recently. I needed a break from reality. I needed a night off.

"Shit, I forgot to tell you," Ken said, rising to his feet. Pallo mirrored him. "Sharon had to go out of town for a few days. She got a lead on one of her cases. She should be back by Monday."

"Why didn't she call?" I asked.

"She did. Have you checked your messages?" Ken was being nice and I knew how much energy that took for him. I appreciated it. Sharon was the closest thing to family I had around here. I hadn't realized how much I had been looking forward to celebrating my birthday. Guess it still did mean something to me.

"Well then, looks like I'm not going anywhere. I'm not spending the night dancing with you," I said looking at Ken.

He gave me that cocky grin again. "Gwen, I'm hurt."

"I would love to take you to The Raven. It would be my pleasure," Pallo said. He stepped right past Ken and headed towards me.

"If he's going, I'm going," Ken said, and followed behind him. I laughed.

"A smile," Pallo said, seeming pleased.

I went to get my keys and purse. I couldn't find either one of them.

"What's wrong?" Ken asked.

"I almost forgot. I don't have a car to drive anymore," I said, remembering the little burning inferno incident. "I, uh, left it at the theme park." I didn't want to alert Ken to all of the trouble I'd been having lately.

Ken laughed. "Maybe you'll get lucky and someone will steal it. I've been trying to get you to buy a new one."

"When I get comfortable with something, I stick with it," I said.

Ken winked at me. "Does that apply to more than cars?"

"Come, we shall take my car." Pallo waved his hand in the air and put it out to me. I put my arm in his and glanced at Ken. I could tell he was angry.

I leaned over to Pallo and whispered, "We can't just leave him."

"I would never dream of such a thing, Gwyneth." The twinkle in his brown eyes told me that's exactly what he'd been thinking of doing. "Are you coming?" he asked, looking back to Ken.

"Wouldn't miss it for the world," Ken said as he followed us out the door.

Chapter 17

We arrived at The Raven almost an hour later. Traffic was terrible, but the ride over was worse. I had assumed that when Pallo said we'd take his car, it would be a car. I was wrong. We ended up riding in the back of a long black limo. The three of us sat there, staring at each other, afraid to say a word. The only time the silence was broken was when the window came down between the driver and us. He wanted to let Pallo know that an important call had come in for him.

The ride took forever. I had never been so happy to get out of a car in my life. The Raven was a huge warehouse that had been converted into a dance club that catered to the supernatural element. I had never actually been there, but I'd heard plenty about it. Apparently everyone else in the city had, too. There was a line that stretched down the block and around the corner. I stood there with my mouth open. Most of the people in line appeared to be in their mid-twenties. Some looked like circus freaks. One man had his hair sprayed green and it stood at least three feet off his head. Around his neck was a dog collar and a chain ran from it to his nose. Yes, he had a chain hooked to his nose. He nodded at me when I looked in his direction. I nodded back.

Ken stepped out of the limo and came to stand behind me. He bent down and whispered to me, "I'll be seeing most of these people in the courtroom soon."

I knew he made a joke, but I didn't particularly like the fact that there was truth behind what he said.

Pallo had walked ahead of us to the main door. He talked to a large man guarding the entrance. He motioned for us to come over. I looked at Ken and he shrugged.

"Looks like the dead have good connections," he said.

"Shut up."

We walked to meet Pallo. He took my arm when I got next to him, and I didn't fight it. The man standing at the door was at least three hundred pounds. I wouldn't have been surprised if he stood seven feet tall. His skin was rich, dark, beautiful. He was mammoth. He wore a black tee shirt that had a picture of a raven on it, and a pair of blue jeans that barely contained his stomach. I noticed that he wore sunglasses. It was almost pitch black out-- the glasses were overkill.

"Master Pallo, your table is ready," he said. His voice rocked my body from the bass in it.

"Thank you, Makonnen," Pallo said as he walked through the open doors.

"Thanks." I smiled at him when we went past. I thought he smiled back, but I wasn't sure.

Ken followed close behind us. The place was awesome. Strobe lights flashed all around us. Blue, red, and yellow light beams swirled before my eyes. They seemed to correspond to the music, which pumped through the sound system so loudly it shook my body. A long, black bar ran along the left side. Shirtless men wearing leather pants were busy pouring people drinks. Every barstool was occupied, and the open spaces for the waitresses were crowded with people, too.

One girl pushed to get through the mob. She had a round tray in her hand. She was average height and weight, but had an enormous pair of breasts. They were a little hard to miss, since all she had on them was two tiny pasties with tassels on the ends. She wore a pair of boy-cut silver shorts that let the corner of her butt hang out, and a pair of matching silver go-go boots. Pink frizzy hair puffed out from her head in all directions. Pallo pulled on my arm, and we continued onward.

In the center of the old warehouse was a dance floor. The thing was at least three times the size of my apartment, and looked like it needed to be bigger. People were herded together, bumping and grinding to the music. A large DJ booth was set up directly behind the dance floor. A cage stood on either side of it. Girls in leather string bikinis were dancing in each cage, rubbing themselves against the bars. I shook my head and kept walking.

We reached the back of the club and Pallo guided me into the booth in the far, back right corner. It was L-shaped, and looked like it could seat at least ten people comfortably. I didn't realize until I sat that the tables weren't actually black, they were dark glowing and green, like the booth seat. I found myself sitting between Ken and Pallo. They still hadn't spoken a word to each other since we left my apartment, and I was pretty tired of them acting like babies. Before I could say anything, the waitress with the frizzy pink hair came to our table.

"Pallo." She said his name like she wanted to have sex with it. I stared at him and wondered if he was a regular here. The guy had his own table, for crying out loud.

"Good evening, Angela," Pallo said to her.

Ken looked like he would burst if he didn't say something snide, so I kicked him under the table.

Angela leaned forward and her breasts rubbed on the table next to Pallo. I got a good look at her and was shocked. She had long, fake pink eyelashes on both her top and bottom eyelids. She had big silver eyes. I wasn't sure if they were contacts or her real eye color. From the way she acted around Pallo, I bet he knew.

I tried my best to ignore her, but she was having none of that.

"Pallo, you haven't introduced me to your friends," she said, tracing a finger around her lips as she spoke.

Pallo took a deep breath and said, "This is my Gwyneth, and her friend Ken." I noticed the emphasis he put on the word 'my'.

Ken quirked a brow. "His Gwyneth?"

I rolled my eyes. Angela took this opportunity to lean in closer to Pallo. One of her tassels touched his face. Her little scene made me nauseous.

"Gee, Pallo, I hate to interrupt the two of you, but do you think we could eat now?" I let my annoyance show.

"No, really, it's fine. I kind of like the show," Ken said. I kicked his leg again and he let out a grunt.

"Yes, by all means." Pallo looked at me to order. It took Angela a minute to give up the menu, but she finally did. I decided on a cheeseburger, fries and a soda, and Ken ordered a salad and a glass of water. He was always watching what he ate. When we were engaged he had gotten all preachy on me about my bad food choices. He would go on and on about clogged arteries and high blood pressure.

"Why didn't you get anything?" I asked, looking at Pallo.

He smiled. "My Gwyneth, some things I cannot explain without looking like a monster."

"Oh, I'm sorry, I forgot." The fact that the man survived off human blood had totally left my mind. I reached out to touch his arm.

His other hand came and rested on mine. "It is good to know you can see past some things."

"Couldn't we just order you a raw steak or something? We could all sit around and watch you suck it dry," Ken said. I wanted to crawl under the table. He did everything in his power to be the biggest jerk possible.

To my surprise, Pallo seemed amused with him. He smiled and tipped his head. The annoying waitress headed back in our direction, carrying a tray of drinks. She bent over, laid her body on the table, and gave Ken his water. She just about dropped my soda in my lap. I caught it before it toppled off the table. She turned and handed Pallo a large wine goblet. It was full to the brim with the thickest red wine I'd ever seen.

"I brought a little something special for you too, my love," Angela said, handing him his drink.

Pallo actually looked uncomfortable. He shifted uncomfortably in his seat and took the drink from her hands. She made sure to let her fingers slide over his a little too long. She turned and walked slowly away, sashaying the entire way.

Ken leaned over me and looked at Pallo. "When the hell did they start serving blood in here?"

"When they received their liquor license, the state considered their 'special' circumstance and included that, as well," Pallo shot back at him.

"Well, I'm going to have to look into that." He acted like a child who just had to have the last word.

After the day I'd been having, I thought I should have ordered a rum and Coke, but I wasn't sure I could hold my liquor tonight. Angela finally came with our food and more drinks. I hadn't had a full meal in days and was starved. Ken and Pallo both sat and watched me eat.

"What?" I asked, suddenly feeling very self-conscious.

"That stuff's going to kill you," Ken said, his voice loud.

"I doubt that I will go by way of cheeseburger, but concern duly noted," I said, finishing up the last few bites of my meal.

Pallo gave me an odd look. "Do you always eat like this?"

I turned as I wiped the corners of my mouth with my napkin. "I eat when I'm hungry, and I eat what I want. Why?"

"I was just wondering where you put it all. There is nothing to you."

I smiled, and heard Ken cough.

Angela kept popping in with refills for us all. During one of her little passes, she conveniently dropped a napkin into Pallo's lap and reached down to pick it up. Her hand rubbed against his pants between his legs. She had enough nerve to cup her hand around him on the way up. I had had enough of their little petting show. I stood up.

"Move, Ken, I'm going to go dance."

Ken looked at me for a minute, then slid out of the booth. I walked out and felt a little light headed. I put my hand on Ken's for support.

"Hey, you better sit down," he said, and eased me back around him.

"I'm fine, just stood up too fast."

"Gwyneth, wait, I will join you," Pallo said.

Angela practically threw herself on him. His face was buried in her big fake chest. Ken sprayed water out of his nose laughing.

I searched for the snippiest voice I could muster and said, "Well, Pallo, you look a little busy. No, really, don't bother to get up."

That's me, always to the point and forever the sweetheart.

As I walked away, I could feel Angela glaring at me. I didn't care. I pushed my way to the center of the dance floor. It had taken me almost five minutes due to the crowd. I knew Ken wouldn't come out and join me--he couldn't dance. I figured that Pallo was still busy getting felt up by little Miss Pink, so I went it alone.

I moved with the music. It was techno, and I wasn't used to dancing to it, but I managed to get by. Closing my eyes, I let the rhythm dictate how I moved my hips and body. I let myself become one with the music.

Sharon asked me to teach her to dance when we were younger. Whenever we went out to clubs, she would pull me off the floor when I really got into it. She said that I pulled the men out of the woodwork.

After a few minutes, I was lost in music. My mind raced. The music beat so fast I began feeling disoriented. I thought of Pallo's body. I wanted it next to mine. I was actually jealous of the pink frizz getting all of his attention. I wanted him to myself-- she could find her own vampire. I called to him in my mind.

Cool hands slid onto my waist from behind. He had come out after all. I'd secretly hoped that he would. He moved his large hands around me so that the front of his body rubbed the back of mine. We moved together with the music. The rhythm got faster and faster and his hips rocked with mine.

His large hands slid up and under my shirt. I shifted my arms and he moved his hands around to my stomach and slid upwards. Reaching around, I grabbed a handful of leather pants and pulled him tighter against my body. I could feel something long and hard hiding in those pants, rubbing against my lower back. Funny, I didn't remember Pallo wearing leather. It didn't matter what he had on, I wanted him. As the music got faster so did we.

My breathing sounded more like panting now, and my face grew hot. He slid his hands up and around my neck. Pulling my hair aside, he kissed me with his cool lips. I felt the tiniest bit of pressure and his teeth sink into my skin. There was no pain. He was so gentle.

When I opened my eyes, I tried to focus. Men and women were dancing all around me. They hung on each other. Some were going at each other's mouths with fury. Tongues were caressing tongues. I thought I saw a man sliding himself into the back of a woman, fucking her not more than four feet from us, but my head was cloudy. I couldn't be sure.

Lips ran over my neck again. I moaned, pulled at the back of his pants. I wanted Pallo now. I wanted our bodies to become one. I needed to have him. My head felt light, airy and my heart beat wildly as he unzipped the back of my skirt, and slid his hand down it. The dance floor was so crowded I was sure that no one would notice the two of us.

"Pallo," I whispered, softly.

He said nothing. He only moved his body with mine. He let his hands continue to feel around and explore my body. My eyes opened and closed as I kept my back pushed tightly against the front of his body. His rigid cock dug into my lower back and wondered what it would feel like to have it in me. He groaned in my ear. My thighs tightened with an anticipated orgasm. My God, the guy was going to bring me by just dancing with me. He was a rare find indeed.

"Pallo," I whispered again, lightheaded. He gripped me tighter, kissing my neck. I looked sleepily ahead of me. The sea of dancing bodies had parted, and I saw Pallo coming for me.

"Pallo?" I tried to keep my head up. He pulled something behind him. I steadied myself and looked harder. A man clung tight to Pallo as he walked, bear-hugging him, trying to keep him from coming to me.

I turned around quickly, and the room spun. I managed to catch a glimpse of a pair of dark, almost black eyes and straight, long, silky black hair. I staggered in an attempt to be free, but the man held me tight to him.

"*Grazie, bella mia.*" I heard the sweet words as I drifted in and out.

"Pallo!" I wasn't sure if I yelled aloud or just in my head. My eyes opened to a room full of ravenous vampires crouched around us, fangs flaring, snarling in my direction. I screamed and tried to lift my head to find Pallo, but it suddenly seemed too heavy.

"They are my children, and this is my establishment. They will not harm you, *bella,*" the man said, his accent thick--thicker than Pallo's. I'd heard that voice before, in the farmhouse, after I'd awoken.

"Who are you?" My eyes closed briefly. When I opened them, some of the circling vampires were being tossed into the air. The dull sensation of a powerful energy came towards me. Pallo's energy hit me with such a force that I felt sick to my stomach. I pushed a thought out to him. I didn't ask for his help, I asked for his forgiveness.

Be still now, Pallo said softly in my head. I let my body go limp in the man's arms.

"It is pointless. She is mine!" The man holding me shouted out into the room. "Oh, Pallo, you should've known I would sense her presence once she was near you."

A gunshot went off. People screamed and ran in all directions. Pallo stood a few feet from me now. I couldn't get my body to move. I wanted to raise my head and look at him. I wanted to reach out my hand to him, but I couldn't.

"Giovanni!" Pallo's voice boomed. "Give her to me."

"Ah, it has been awhile," the man holding me said. He slid his hand over my throat and let it come to a rest.

"Do not come any closer, Pallo. I would hate to have to put a mark on such a beautiful face," he said, caressing my neck and chin slowly. "She is just as beautiful the second time around, wouldn't you agree?"

Pallo took a step towards us and Giovanni squeezed my chin. I raised my face up enough to look at his. He was amazing. He looked like he had just walked off the cover of GQ. His jaw was not too wide and not too narrow. His lips were a pale cherry color. He wore a dark, short sleeved mesh top that showed off his upper body. He was not as muscular as Pallo, but he was toned.

Giovanni met my gaze. Fear gripped me and I began to sweat. I wanted to get away from him. I knew he was evil, but his eyes, they called to me, pulled me.

He didn't want to hurt me. I sensed the struggle within him. I could feel how much he cared for me, and his desperation not to let me go. He glanced down at me, and I begged him to stop with my eyes, tears running down my cheeks.

Two more gunshots rang out. The remainder of the crowd opened wide, and I could see Ken pointing his gun at the ceiling. He held his right arm close to his body.

Pallo moved closer to me. Fingers squeezed my throat, and I moaned in pain. Giovanni bent and kissed my lips before letting go. "I shall see you soon, *bella mia*," he said, and threw me high into the air.

My body was limp and I couldn't get it to respond to my commands. I tumbled down, and prepared to crash into the floor. Two strong arms caught me and pulled me close. I smelled vanilla and Hugo Boss and knew it was Pallo. I concentrated on his face and pushed my thoughts into his head. I wanted him to know that I was sorry, that I thought it was him, and that I knew that was no excuse for my behavior. I wanted him to know so much. I pushed it all at him as he carried me past the remaining vampires.

I heard Angela's voice next to me. "Now you are back where you belong."

Pallo growled at her and she backed away, smiling at me. I knew she had something to do with this. I also knew I wanted her dead.

Ken came beside me. He clutched his arm to his body. Blood soaked the front of his shirt.

Pallo and Ken loaded me into the back of the limo. Pallo sat and lifted my head onto his lap. Ken sat on the seat facing us, still holding his arm. I wanted to ask if he was okay, but I couldn't seem to speak.

"She wants to know if you are all right," Pallo said, watching Ken and stroking the hair from my face.

Ken's eyes widened. "She hasn't said a word. Look at her, she's practically catatonic."

I knew Pallo had read my mind, and for once I was okay with

it. He said nothing, but continued to pull my hair back from my face, away from my neck. He gasped.

Ken looked up. "Shit, he bit her. We need to get her to the hospital."

"No!" Pallo interjected. "No, she will not be safe at a hospital."

"I'll get her police protection. She needs to go. Look at her, something's wrong with her."

"The police cannot protect her from Giovanni and his people. He will come for her, and when he does humans will learn firsthand that vampires and demons exist among them. And I think we both know that there is not a cleanup crew in the world big enough to hide a massive supernatural strike." Pallo continued to run his fingers through my hair.

"Then we'll take her somewhere far away from here. Somewhere this Giovanni prick can't find her." Ken leaned towards me and I thought I saw tears in his big brown eyes.

"He has put his teeth into her skin during passion. He can find her anywhere. He will be able to pull her to him. She will not be able to stop herself."

"Bullshit! I can't accept that," Ken said.

"It took her many years to break his hold on her. I do not know if she is strong enough to do it twice."

Ken looked at Pallo. "What the hell are you talking about? Gwen doesn't know that guy."

"Yes, she does. Her mind may not remember him, but her body does." There was a bitter sound to Pallo's voice.

"In English, please."

"Do you love her?"

Ken sat there and looked at him. The thought of Ken loving anyone was so funny. He glanced at Pallo and answered him. "Yes, I love her."

"I will do my best to protect her from him, but you will have to trust my judgment. Do you understand?"

"Do you go out of your way to not make sense?" Ken asked. "When you told me to get Gwen, how did you know something was wrong?"

"When I realized that our drinks contained something a little extra special," Pallo said.

"How'd you know?"

He chuckled, lightly. "Angela looked attractive to me," Pallo said. "I have known her for over a hundred years and in that time she has never once appealed to me."

"I don't think they could have sneaked anything into my water." Ken leaned back against the seat, taking this all in.

"Do you normally go about the city shooting yourself in the arm?" Pallo asked, voice barely above a whisper.

I couldn't believe what I'd heard. Ken shot himself in the arm? Impossible. The man went to the shooting range twice a week and was an expert marksman as far I knew. He lived and breathed guns.

"No. No, I don't." Ken sighed. "You're right. When will hers wear off?"

"I do not know."

A cool breeze tickled the tiny hairs on the back of my neck.

"You may rest now. I will come soon." Giovanni's voice filled my head. *Tonight marks a new beginning for us, bella.*

Pallo slipped his arm around me tightly and I passed out.

Chapter 18

"Come, my child," a voice said.

I knew this voice. It was the one that came to me in my dreams, the one that always talked about me being the balance between lightness and dark. I made my way towards the light. Hey, after having recurring dreams for about twenty years, curiosity gets the best of you. I pushed my way through the darkness to the light, and pulled at it. It broke open. I stood before the field of flowers from my dreams, only now a river ran through the center of it. I walked towards the water. The flowers moved out of my way on their own to prevent me from trampling them. I approached the edge of the river and glanced around. Ripples formed in the water before me.

The woman's voice was soft and breathy. "Trust them, they will help you."

"Help me with what? Trust who?" I was so lost it wasn't even funny.

"Caleb and Pallo," she said.

Caleb? Caleb was gone, he was dead. How could I trust him?

"Their love for you is great." Her voice got further away, and I screamed out to her.

I was desperate. "Wait, wait! Tell me more."

"If you need me, come here." I screamed for her to return but she didn't.

Something pulled me back from the river's edge. It was cool and comforting against my bare arms. I opened my eyes and found myself lying in bed with an arm wrapped around my waist. I stayed very still and tried get a bearing on where I was. I looked down at my waist and saw a well-defined arm with tiny freckles on the shoulder blade. The smell of vanilla filled the air again.

"Pallo!" I licked my lips to moisten my dry mouth.

"You're awake," a tender voice whispered in my ear. I turned my head to see him.

"Just rest."

He held me tight. His heart beat against my back. His breath was cool on my neck. He pulled himself up and leaned over me. I still couldn't get used to his vampire speed. I looked into his face. His hair hung carelessly over his face like a curtain, and he pushed it back. Our gazes locked.

"Sleep, my precious one, sleep," Pallo whispered.

I sat up and looked around. We were in the yellow bedroom again and I was naked. My hair was damp. I pulled the covers up to cover my breasts.

"Why are we here?" I asked him. I left out the real question I had, which was, 'Why the hell am I naked?'

"It was the safest place to bring you."

"It looks so real."

"It is as real as we make it." He eased me towards him. I let myself be lowered back into the safety of the large, soft bed. I looked into his eyes. Sadness was hidden in them. I knew that he had feelings for me, and I knew I had strong feelings for him. I didn't understand how Giovanni had come between us.

"Saying I'm sorry isn't enough, is it?" My voice quivered.

"You have nothing to be sorry for."

I let the tears come. I was hurt, angry, and embarrassed. I couldn't look at his face anymore. I couldn't stand to see the pain in his eyes. I'd hurt him twice. I wanted to die.

"Gwyneth," he said, placing his hand over mine. "Please do not think such terrible thoughts." Pallo's hand slid up my arm. "Giovanni is very powerful. You knew him many years before you met me. He has only grown stronger these past few centuries."

I didn't want Pallo saying his name. I hated this Giovanni, and

I hated myself for what had happened. I let a stranger take a bite out of me. I put his hands on my body, I pulled him towards me, encouraging him. Some part of me saw the signs that it wasn't Pallo, but I didn't care. I was drawn to Giovanni's body. I did this to myself.

"Stop punishing yourself, there was nothing you could have done differently. I should have been with you. I should not have allowed myself to be tempted by Angela." He caressed my shoulder and neck, his fingers dancing over the bite mark Giovanni left on me. "I let this happen to you once. I should not have been so careless to let it happen again. Can you forgive me?"

I laughed. "You want me to forgive you? I was the one who let a stranger feel me up and bite me. That wasn't your fault."

I caressed his cheek, and he slid his hand down my arm, slowly. My heart fluttered from his touch.

"Giovanni is not a stranger to you. He caught your interest long ago. You cared for him for many years. You tried to love his demon, but it grew too evil for you, and it is because of him that we met."

I had no clue what the hell Pallo talked about. If he thought this would jog my memory, he was mistaken. I stayed still and listened to him tell the story of how we met. He talked of seeing me come to his village when he was a young man of twenty-seven. Pallo told me how his father had tried to convince him to take a wife. His father felt that a man his age should already have a family. He told me how he helped his father run their family's vineyard, and of his two younger sisters who had blonde hair, and his same chestnut brown eyes. The joy on his face when he told me about chasing them around the yard and caring for them was overwhelming.

One day he had headed to town to discuss the purchase of more land and saw me walking in the streets. He could still remember the red dress I wore. "I had never seen any such dress before on a woman. I thought you were an angel with your long hair and skin that shimmered in the sunlight. I thought that a goddess had graced my presence. I was not wrong."

He followed me home, to a large house on the edge of town. He had heard that a rich, powerful man had just recently moved to that house. But no mention had been made of the rich man's mistress. He watched me from afar for many days, thinking I didn't see him. "I had never been so attracted to anyone as I was to you. You were captivating. I needed to know more about you."

One day, while he watched me pick flowers in a field, he dozed off in the summer sun. When he awoke, I stood over him, laughing at him. I had apparently known he had been following me all along. We spent every day together after that. He said that I never took him to my home, and I only met with him during daylight hours. We were in love.

When he finally confronted me about Giovanni, I didn't deny it. I merely told him that the Giovanni I cared about no longer existed. He asked me to run away with him. He wanted to make me his wife. He had dreams of me being the mother of his children. I was too afraid of Giovanni to go with him. We stayed and tried to hide our affair. Pallo said I disappeared for several days without notice.

Pallo just stopped, mid story. He looked like a lost child.

"Pallo, what happened after I disappeared?" I was on the edge of my seat. I had removed myself from his story and viewed it more as having happened to someone else.

He looked up at me. His brown eyes seemed to be losing some of there luster. "I went looking for you."

"And then what?"

"I believe this is where your memories of events come into play."

I thought about being pregnant with his baby, but in Caleb's bed. I had believed that he was dead and gone, but he wasn't. He turned into a creature of the night. He was becoming a vampire.

Pallo kissed my forehead. "I am tired now. I must rest." I knew a blow-off when I heard one. He looked drained.

"When was the last time you had any…?" I didn't know the right word to use.

He answered me without waiting for me to figure out the politically correct way. "No, I have not fed recently."

I wasn't sure what to say. I didn't know if I should offer myself to him or not. I wasn't sure what would happen then. I changed the subject.

"Why is my hair damp, and where are my clothes?"

He smiled. "Are you worried?"

"No," I said, smiling back. "Just curious."

"I bathed you," he said, and looked to be preparing for me to strike.

I surprised us both by just asking him "Why?"

"You are not angry with me?"

He rubbed his thumb over my forehead and down towards my temple. When Pallo's hand came near my mouth I turned my head quickly and sucked on his thumb, running my tongue between his fingers. His jaw dropped slightly and I could see his eyes cloud with desire. He shifted closer to me, our bodies pressed firmly against each other. I hadn't known he wore pants until then. I had assumed that he was naked, too. I stopped putting his fingers in my mouth and looked at him.

"No, I'm not mad. I'm sure you had a good reason," I said, my voice low and breathy.

I leaned into him and kissed his lips. He kissed me back. I could feel my body tightening with the anticipation of being touched by him. I put my hands on the sides of his face and slid my wrist near his mouth.

"Do it," I said.

He pulled back from me, looking shocked. "I will not do what you ask."

"I've already given you my blood willingly once, its okay. Go ahead."

"Gwyneth, you do not understand what you are asking of me. I will not feed off of you."

"But, Pallo, you've already done it. You need it. Here." I pushed my wrist up to him.

He shook his head. "If I remember correctly, you pushed it down my throat while I was unconscious." He sat up. "You almost killed yourself to give me life. I will not have that."

"But it helped you. You healed quickly, didn't you?"

He nodded. "Being a sidhe makes your blood powerful. It takes only a small amount to sustain me. You had given me more than I needed. When my body took your blood in, it changed in me, allowing me use of your magic, thus allowing me to save your life in return."

I smiled at him. I hadn't heard the word sidhe used in place of faerie for a very long time. The new term was *Sí,* but I liked the sound of sidhe better. "So, let me get this straight. You won't take my blood unless you can give me something of equal value in return?"

Pallo looked very serious when he answered me. "Yes, that is correct."

I sat up next to him on the bed. "I know. We could make a trade."

"What would you have us trade?"

I pulled myself onto my knees, letting the covers fall from my body. Leaning into his ear, I whispered, "I give you what you need to survive, and you give me what I need."

I blew on his ear gently, and he moaned softly. "What do you need to survive, Gwyneth?" He slid his arm around me and held me firm.

"You," I said, traveling up his spine with my finger.

"Do not give yourself over to me out of pity." He let his hand hover near my breast. I pulled it to me, rubbing his fingers around my areola, making me thirst for more. Lifting his hand from my nipple, I pulled his fingers to my lips and drew them into my mouth, one by one.

Pallo growled. He twisted quickly and slid his hands down my torso. I put my wrist up to his lips, and he planted tiny kisses on it. I braced myself for pain, but felt nothing but the sweetest of kisses upon it. Shifting slightly, he worked his way down to my elbow before heading back up towards my neck, leaving me in a state of longing.

"Pallo," I scolded him, short of breath, wanting him to stop teasing me. I needed to feel his body pressed to mine.

"Gwyneth, you are still as impatient as ever."

Lifting my arm, he kissed the back of it, moving down, tasting my body with his flickering tongue. Still on our knees, facing each other, the sight of his sculpted bare upper chest made my breath catch in my throat. I wanted him, needed, now. I pushed my hand down, trying to feel for the tiny hairs that stuck out from the top of his dark blue silk pajama bottoms. Pallo caught hold of my wrist, and pressed his weight against mine causing me to lean back.

His cold chest was a sharp contrast to my hot breasts. I was still on my knees before him, and had to sit on my butt or risk being snapped in half. Not that I would have complained. Now, as he bent me back, I wrapped my legs around his waist and my body tightened with need for him. My head touched the bed. I exposed my neck to him. Bending his head down, he caressed my breast with his lips. My nipple hardened as he sampled it. His tongue traced long circles around my now rock hard nipples.

"So sweet, Gwyneth, like berries … so sweet, *delizia*." His voice was even deeper than normal. He covered my nipple with his mouth again, and something sharp nicked me.

I gasped, as a titillating heat wave washed over me.

Pallo pulled his mouth from me quickly. His gaze met mine, then fell down to the two tiny fang marks near my nipple. He appeared shocked with himself. He obviously never meant to harm me. I glanced down lazily, dreamily. Blood seeped slowly from the tiny bite marks, and I watched in awe as it ran over my pale skin. Wanting Pallo's lips on me, I reached my hand up and pulled his loose brown curls to move his head above my breast. Blood continued to trickle from it, trailing down my stomach towards my navel.

Something primitive passed through Pallo's eyes. I watched him struggle with his demon to maintain control, and secretly hoped he'd lose the battle. I wanted him to be uninhibited and to ravish me, allowing himself to be free while bringing me satisfaction. I slid my hands down the sides of his face, pulling him to me.

"Pallo," I let his name fall from my lips with almost no sound at all.

He moved his mouth over my navel where the blood had pooled, and sucked gently on it. I pulled his hair up so I could watch his face. The thick muscles in his neck worked as he drank me down. His eyes rolled back into his head as he continued to swallow the sweet liquid from my body. His mouth traced the bloody route up to my breast. His lips grew warmer on my body. When he reached the bite mark on my breast, he gave it a gentle kiss, and it stopped bleeding.

Tiny, desperate moans came from me. I needed more. I needed fucked. I needed him. "Pallo, please…."

He pulled my body back up to him. The top of my head fit snugly under his chin as he held me in his arms. I felt so safe with him. He let his desire for me beat through his body like an accelerated pulse. Mine sped to match his. I ran my hands down his stomach. It warmed to my touch. I let my fingers frolic in the tiny curls that began on his low abdomen.

He gasped. "Gwyneth."

Smiling slightly, I pushed my hand down further, past his waistband, and was instantly greeted by his erect member. Wrapping my hand around his cock, as best I could, I grasped him tight, stroking him ever so slightly. He was silky smooth, thick and ready for me. I brought my other hand down and pulled at the navy blue pajama bottoms. They came down quickly, easily. I worked them down to his knees and touched one leg lightly to get him to lift it. He did and I pushed the bottoms off him. I repositioned myself and ended up crouched down before him on the bed. I took in the glorious sight of him. He was everything I had ever dreamed a man could be and more. Long, thick, and nestled in a thatch of black curls, his shaft beckoned me and stole my breath. He was stunning.

I put my lips on the base of his cock. The rest of his shaft lay against the side of my face, and came to a rest on my neck behind my ear. He was enormous, and all mine, the very thought of it left my folds drenched and hungry. Pressing my face into his sac, I gently pulled a portion of it into my mouth and splayed my hands over his bare hips. The smell of Pallo's sex drove me mad with lust, with need. Releasing his sac slowly, I flickered my tongue out and over the base of his cock. He twitched and I felt the muscles in his legs straining.

"Ah ... *Toccami qui*--touch me here," he said softly, grabbing my hand and moving it the base of his shaft.

Pinching the loose skin, I pulled it taut and struggled for breath, as he seemed to grow even larger. He was impressive not erect. Now, he was just plain intimidating. That would never fit in me.

He laughed softly, and used my hand to stroke himself. It was erotic and exciting to have him teaching me what he liked. I traced his member with my lips, imprinting every color change, every vein, as I took him in my mouth. Before I knew it, he hit the back of my throat, still not all the way in. Moving my hand up, I wrapped my fingers around him as I worked my head up and down leisurely.

"*Ah sì ... più forte.*" Pallo grabbed handfuls of my hair and forced my mouth to take him more, how I managed was beyond me. Pre-come leaked onto my tongue and I let out a sultry moan as I sucked harder. He tightened his grip on my hair, to just this side of too much. His shaft tightened in my mouth, and I prepared for him to end. He didn't. Instead, he arched back and pressed gently against the back of my head, bringing me with him. I increased my speed, and savored every second of his taste.

"Ahh ... Gwyneth." He pulled my head back from his body. Licking my lips, I stared up at him. The look on his face was just short of ecstasy. I imagine that my face looked relatively the same.

He looked down at me and spoke softly. "I am good, but not that good. I am afraid that you can still 'bring' me with the slightest of touches. I have shared the company of many women since you left, but you are still the only one who excites my body so."

I really didn't want to hear him talking about fucking other woman right at this moment, but fair was fair. I'd been with Caleb only a week before. I was in no position to throw stones. My glass house was cracked enough already.

Hell, who was I kidding? It had shattered into a million pieces the moment I pinned Pallo to the floor and made him watch me do Caleb.

Pallo's cock was still hard and velvety smooth in my hand. He hadn't come yet, and I knew he was waiting to seek his release in me. Moving my hands up his chest, I stopped over his heart, and pushed him backwards onto the bed. He still had hold of my hair, so I fell with him, on him. My legs wrapped around his waist, instinctively. I lay down on him gently and felt his member, still erect, against my abdomen. I kissed his neck, tasting him, loving him. He had grown so warm. He felt human to me now.

I searched his eyes for approval to continue onward. The head of his cock pressed against my saturated channel, waiting to enter. I took that as a yes, and slid down onto him carefully. He was too big, spreading me past the point of acceptance, causing white-hot pain to tear through my pussy. "Too much … uhh … too big."

Pallo caught my lips with his own and drove his tongue into my mouth, as he worked his cock deeper into me. He filled me up, and gradually my tight-fisted channel eased somewhat, allowing me to rotate my hips. My swollen clit rubbed against his lower abdomen, driving tiny animal noises from me. He encircled me with his arms, and pulled at my hips, directing my movement. Now, he lay beneath me, the director of our lovemaking, with a look of raw need etched over his chiseled face.

"Pallo … oh my…." I let out a tiny scream, and clutched his arms. I eased myself down further, driving him higher, deeper inside me. I moved my hips up and down slowly. He whispered something to me, but I didn't hear what it was. He was so large that I felt as though I would break in two if I rode him much longer.

My epitaph could read, "She died a happy death."

I put my hands on his chest and sat up on him. My eyes widened as he went even deeper into me. I didn't know how much more my body could take, but I was willing to give it a try.

His beautifully dark, crisp brown eyes took me in as he reached down and rubbed my swollen nub. That one touch brought my body. Pressure built within me, and knew that my magic had been awakened. My legs tightened and a rush of power swept over me. I cried out as I pushed it outwards, trying my best to control it. I hoped it worked. Pallo tightened below me, still trying to maintain control. I rode him so hard and fast that my breathing grew irregular. My power flowed through me without restraint. By the look in his eyes, he felt it, too. Quickly, he seized hold of me, flipping me over.

I found myself lying on my back. Pallo was still buried inside me and instantly, I climaxed. "Ohh ... uhh ... I'm coming."

Pallo thrust himself into me harder. "You feel so good ... so tight ... so warm ... so alive." He pulled himself almost out of me. I grabbed at his ass, yanking him back into me. His upper body tightened as he held himself up on his arms, in a semi-push up. Glancing down, I saw his glistening rod slipping back into me slowly. The sight of him going into me was too much. I made tiny noises, combinations between moans and grunts. He pushed into me slowly and pulled out. Grabbing at his body, I tried to pull him to me. He was stronger than I ever hoped to be, so he didn't budge. I looked up into his loving face. He looked like he held back. He was afraid he would hurt me. I remembered the bruises on Sandra's thighs. He was used to hurting women and he didn't want to do that to me.

As endearing as that was, I didn't want him to hold back. "Fuck me, harder ... oh, yes Pallo ... harder."

Pallo let his body fall down onto mine, driving his cock into me hard. I dug my fingernails into the backs of his arms and couldn't help myself as I bit down on his shoulder. His thrusts came faster now, each one felt like he drove my body into the bed, through the bed. I cried out, as power gushed over my body again. My channel tightened around him--contracting him, milking his every thrust.

Pallo threw his head back as he arched his spine. Slamming against me, he brought my orgasm out full force. He went rigid, and locked himself against me, depositing his seed into me. Warmth spilled from him and into me with every shot of come he released into me. I shuddered. "Gwyneth...," he said, breathlessly.

My eyes felt different now, they felt warm and odd.

Something dark appeared behind Pallo. His face went slack as

Mandy M. Roth

he finished releasing himself in me. Something snarled and I dug my fingers into his arm. He looked at me with disbelief in his eyes. I knew that sound, I had heard it before--hellhounds.

"What a show, what a show!" Talia's voice echoed off the high ceiling.

Pallo froze, still pressed inside of me.

"Oh, please do continue. I have not seen such a display of raw sexuality in quite some time."

Pallo didn't move from me as he spoke to her. "How did you get in here?"

Wicked, high-pitched laughter filled the room. "You should pick your bed mates more carefully if you want to stay locked away in a mystical portal."

Talia moved closer to us. Growls came at us from the foot of the bed. "Really Pallo, if you are going to fuck little *Si* girls, you should at least make sure they can control themselves when they come. She opened the portal door wide for us."

I looked up at Pallo's face. I didn't realize that was what I'd been doing. I didn't know what to do with all of the power I felt, so I had released it blindly. Pallo leaned down to me, kissed my mouth long and hard. Withdrawing from me slowly, he turned to face Talia.

"Oh, Pallo, please do not stop on account of us." She was dressed in a pair of red leather shorts that left nothing to the imagination, and a tiny red spaghetti strap leather bra. The red of her outfit was identical to the color of her hair. She looked like a homicidal stripper.

She was surrounded by a pack of hellhounds. I lost track of counting at around twenty. I figured that it didn't really matter after that. We were screwed.

Pallo moved off the bed and stood. Several of the hounds growled at him and came closer. He didn't flinch. He bent down slowly, and reached under the side of the bed. A large hellhound crouched low to the floor, ready to strike.

"Talia, could you tell your children to back down? I would like to cover myself," Pallo said, bringing something back up with him when he stood.

"But you are such a work of art, Pallo, why must you cover yourself?" She held a black whip in her hand.

Great--crazy, horny, and armed.

One of the hellhounds sniffed at the other side of the bed. It put its face near the side of my leg, and made strange noises. I thought it would push its face right into my crotch. I felt so naked, so exposed, so scared.

My gaze went to Pallo who stood next to the bed. He tossed something silky and black onto my thigh, and stepped into his pants. I picked it up the object he'd tossed at me and saw that it was a long black nightgown. This was not anything that I owned, but at this point I didn't care whose it was, I just wanted to cover up. I lifted it over my head slowly. I could feel the red, glowing eyes of the hellhounds watching my every move. I put my arms through the tiny straps and pulled it over my breasts.

"Pity, I am disappointed, but I will get over it." Talia walked around the edge of the large bed. She wore long, leather boots with four-inch spiked heels. I had to admire a woman who could walk steady on those, even if she was a little off in the head.

Pallo stood tall in front of me, looking at her. "What do you want?"

Talia raised her finger in the air, wagging it back and forth. "Shame on you, Pallo. You know what I want. She killed one of my pets. I want revenge."

I thought back to Jacob's body lying on the floor spread wide open from the touch of my hand, and cringed. One of the hellhounds rubbed close to Talia's leg. Its front paws looked burned. I knew that was Jonathan, staring at me with eyes of fire. I could feel his rage, his hatred. He wanted me dead for killing his brother. I swallowed hard, knowing that he'd get his wish soon enough.

"So, what do have in store for us?" Pallo asked. "Killing us here would not be exciting enough for you."

Talia smiled wide, exposing her fangs. "You know me well." She bent down and rubbed the top of Jonathan's head. "Soon," she said to him. "Soon."

My body tightened. She looked at Pallo and spoke again. "Come, follow me."

Pallo reached back and took my hand. He was still warm to the touch. He didn't feel like a vampire, and right now, that is exactly what we needed him to be.

Talia's "pets" ran out the door in front of her. Pallo pulled on my hand and followed her out.

"Pallo, no." I tried to make him stay in the room.

He turned and looked at me. His eyes were full of sadness. "Call Giovanni," he said to me softly.

I stared at him, horrified. "Giovanni?"

As soon as the name fell from my mouth, the hairs on the back of my neck rose. Something blew past my back. I turned and saw nothing. We headed down the staircase, passing the picture of the two of us near the river. I noted how happy we looked together. I wanted to have that moment back.

Talia stood near the front door. "Come."

I braced myself for a fall as we stepped out of the door.

Chapter 19

We didn't fall into any dungeon. We stepped into an entirely white bedroom with a large platform bed sitting in the center of it. I knew this room. I had spent many nights here. It was Ken's.

"I thought this would be fitting. This is the first place you and I met," Talia said, tossing her long red hair to one side, looking at me.

My mind raced. I never thought Ken would turn on me. I never pictured him making deals with the enemy. He had made it his mission in life to bring evil-doers to justice. This was not like him. Something was wrong.

"What did you do with Ken?" I asked her. Pallo gripped my hand so tightly that the blood stopped flowing through it.

Talia took a step towards me. She smiled and brought her whip to the side of her face, rubbing it along her cheek. "What concern is he to you? You have Pallo, and you yourself even told me this Ken loves only himself. Besides, my pets tell me that you have a blond man as well, or should I say *had*."

Pallo squeezed my hand. I knew that was his way of begging me not to say anything, but I had to know.

"You bitch! I knew you had something to do with that." I shook. I thought about Caleb, then my thoughts went to Ken, and losing him too. "Oh, my God, he's dead!" My knees weakened.

Talia let out a laugh that chilled me to the bone. "No, he's not dead yet. Soon he will be begging for me to kill him. I am surprised that he has held out this long. He is tough, for a human."

The bedroom door opened, and Jonathan stepped through, dragging something behind him. I looked at the bloody mass he threw on the floor before us. It took me a minute to understand what it was. My heart rose into my throat. It was Ken's body. He lay on his stomach, his naked body covered in blood. Large, long gashes covered his back, butt, and legs.

The whip--she had torn him open with the whip.

"Oh, my God." I headed towards him. Pallo grabbed my arm and tried to hold me back. I stared at him, terrified. "Let go of me!" Pulling myself free of him, I fell on the floor next to Ken's body.

Ken was so still. I thought he might be dead. I tried to find a spot on his body that wasn't cut open. When I finally found a tiny area, I touched him lightly. He made a small moan. He was alive! I was so happy I almost hugged him. I didn't want to cause him more pain, so I settled on leaning over him. I could see his face now. She hadn't cut him with the whip there. His once handsome face looked bloodied and bruised, like a side of beef in a butcher's shop. I choked back my tears.

"I'm here Ken, I'm here," I whispered to him.

I caught sight of Talia's spiked boot coming at me and ducked out of the way. She ended up straddled over Ken's naked body, glaring at me. I could tell she was surprised that I had been able to dodge her vampire speed. She looked pissed.

"Touching. Now get away," she ordered, lifting her whip in the air and bringing it down to strike Ken's body.

I threw myself at her feet and used my body to shield his. The leather strap of the whip ripped into my back. At first, there was no pain, only heat. Blood ran down my back. I heard screams. First Pallo's, then mine, but didn't lift my body off Ken's. If she wanted to beat someone, it would have to be me. For some reason I didn't think she'd have a problem with that.

"Pallo, the little faerie makes my head hurt. You should really teach her some manners." Talia stepped over my still hunched body. I held my arms close around Ken, and tried to keep my body from touching his. He was in enough pain. I didn't want to add to it.

Pallo's energy pushed against my skin. It trickled down my back and touched my open wound. Pushing at me hard, it almost knocked me over. I heard Pallo's voice. It sounded low and barely human. Closing my eyes, I remembered my vision of him attacking me in the hall. I knew what I would see if I turned around, so I didn't.

"She is not *my* little faerie. I took what I wanted from her, I am done," Pallo said, coldly.

I froze. He couldn't mean what he just said. He couldn't.

"Pallo, you don't really expect me to believe she means nothing to you," Talia said. "I watched you beg for her life, remember?"

The air in the room grew heavy and hot. I heard Pallo's raspy voice again. "That was before she let Giovanni touch her--mark her," he snarled.

"But Pallo, you hid her away from everyone. Do not forget that it was I who walked in on your little mystical love making session."

A demonic laugh rose from Pallo's throat. "I did not make love to that *donnaccia*. I fucked her."

His words hurt worse than Talia's whip. I tried to fight back my tears. It didn't work. Something grabbed me by my hair. I kept my crying eyes closed, as I was pulled to my feet. Someone licked my cheek.

"She weeps." Talia's breath was hot on my face.

"Shall we see if she bleeds as well?" Pallo asked, his voice coming closer. I fought to keep my eyes closed. I didn't want my last vision on this earth to be his black eyes and twisted face before he killed me.

Talia licked my salty tears again. "Either you have grown powerful enough to hide your lies from me since we were lovers, or you truly feel nothing for her." She pressed her tongue onto my cheek. "Have you found your anger again, Pallo? Have you embraced your demon?"

"Yes." The way he said it made me shiver. He betrayed me. My knees shook hard. I had to concentrate on standing. I smelled Pallo's flesh near me. He was close enough for our faces to touch. "She cannot even bear to look at me." He felt foreign as his hand rubbed my cheek.

He moved his other hand and touched me between my thighs. "You looked at me while I pleasured you, but now I am not good enough?"

Talia yanked my hair back and my face touched Pallo's. I cried out, and my eyes opened. Pallo leaned his head down to me. He was monstrous. There was no trace of his sweet brown eyes, only black holes remained. I screamed. He pulled his hand away from my face quickly, and brought it back down hard, striking me. Talia let go of my hair and I fell to my knees, clutching my face.

"Come, Pallo, we have had our fun here. Let us go enjoy ourselves." I watched as he followed Talia out of the room. The door shut. Something made a low, growling noise. I didn't have to look--I knew it was Jonathan. I didn't care if he attacked me, I didn't care what happened to me. Pallo's betrayal hurt worse than anything Jonathan could do to me.

I crouched on the floor next to Ken's lifeless body. I wanted to reach out to him, but I didn't dare move. Something tickled the hairs on the back of my neck, and a strong breeze blew in from Ken's bedroom window. Jonathan let out an ear piercing howl and leapt upon my back. His momentum sent us both rolling across the room. His paw tore through the black nightgown, pushing deep into me. I looked down in horror as his claws broke out the other side of my stomach. I cried out in pain.

The rest of him shifted to human form. He pushed his clawed hand deeper into my body. The pain consumed me, it rattled my head and I let go of myself. I pulled back into myself, and felt nothing anymore. I was numb. Ken's hair blew gently as Jonathan's hand tore free from me. He rose off me and into the air. His body dropped down on the other side of Ken's. There was no longer a head attached to it.

The door to the room crashed open. Growls and snarls surrounded me. Hellhound bodies flew over my head, each one torn to shreds. Some were decapitated. Others were simply split in two. I wasn't going to die like this, and neither was Ken if I could help it. I tried to reach my hand out to him, but something picked him up.

Cool, wet hands slid under my body. I was lifted into the air gently. I looked and saw Makonnen, the large bouncer from The Raven, holding Ken's body. Something dark was smeared all over his body. It was blood.

"I am here, *bella*, you are safe. I will never let anything happen to you again," Giovanni whispered gently into my ear. My eyes were too heavy to keep open.

Giovanni carried me out of Ken's bedroom. We stepped into the hall on the upper level of Ken's townhouse. He carried me towards the stairs. As he held me, we walked past Ken's spare bedroom. Giovanni tried to turn my body so I couldn't look in, but he was not quick enough. What I saw made what was left of my stomach turn. Pallo was naked and spread eagle on the bed while Talia rode him. She cried his name out. He reached up to caress her neck, then I saw no more.

As Giovanni carried me, Talia's cries for Pallo stopped abruptly.

"Get Pallo," Giovanni said to someone behind us. I didn't want any more blood shed, unless of course it was Talia's. No matter what Pallo did to me, I would never want him injured. Caleb had been enough of a loss for me--I couldn't handle another. I tried to free myself from Giovanni's arms, but he held me effortlessly.

"Do not be afraid. I will not harm you." He whisked me downstairs and out of Ken's apartment. Cramps seized my body. My stomach burned and the pain threatened to overtake me.

"We've got to get her to a hospital," a familiar voice said. I had known others were with him, but I didn't know who or how many.

"Yes," Giovanni said.

Chapter 20

I was lucid enough to know that Giovanni did take me to the hospital. We just sort of appeared there. I should have been absolutely terrified that Giovanni was anywhere near me. I knew deep in my heart that he could be the ultimate evil when provoked. With all of the medication they were giving me through the IV, I had trouble staying awake long enough to worry about Giovanni's intentions.

The nurses sucked their breath in when they peeled the blood-soaked nightgown from my body. I caught sight of a pair of dark black eyes staring at me--Giovanni. He held my hand. His hand was cold, yet comforting. I wanted to let myself rest, but I felt his pull on me. He shared his power with me to help me hold on. I knew that without his help, the wounds Jonathan had inflicted would kill me. Even being a faerie had its limits.

Nurses shouted that everyone except family had to get out. Somehow, Giovanni convinced them to let him stay. I could make out talk of possible surgery, and it being too bad to repair. Horrific pain seized hold of my body, and I screamed out. A tall female doctor came forward with a shot of something.

"This will help her rest," she said to Giovanni. He let go of my hand and stepped out of the tiny curtained emergency room.

"Did you see the guy who came in with her?" I heard a nurse

speaking softly to her coworker.

"Yeah, he's pretty bad," a tiny voice replied.

"She's worse," the first nurse said.

My eyes closed.

I woke to find Makonnen sitting at the end of the bed with his head back in a chair, resting. I lay there frozen for a minute, trying to get my bearings. I looked up to see a white canopy above me. I lay on a large four poster bed. The room I was in was large, and I couldn't be sure, but it looked like the walls were blood red. I really hoped it was just a good painting technique. I didn't think the hospital had taken to making their rooms feel like a demonic palace, so it was safe to assume I wasn't there anymore.

I grabbed my stomach. It was whole, no chunk of it missing. I reached around and touched my back. It was fine, too. I wore a red satin short nightie. I pulled it up. Someone had put me into tiny matching underpants. I'd worry about that later. I ran my fingers over my smooth stomach and smiled. I wasn't dead or seriously mangled, only a small pinkish white scar remained. I let myself relax and look around.

To my left was a door, and to my right was a set of Queen Anne chairs that were blood red. I saw a pattern here. The room smelled of freshly cut flowers. At least four dozen red roses sat on the mantle of a large stone fireplace.

Makonnen stirred in the chair and was suddenly next to me. "You okay? Jonathan really did a number on you. Thank the demons that you're not human, you'd be dead." His low voice startled me.

He stood and walked over to the side of the bed.

"Can I get you anything? Giovanni would have my head on a platter if I didn't take good care of you."

I reached my hand out to touch his. "No, I'm fine...."

Before I could finish the sentence, a vision struck me. It was of Makonnen holding Ken in his arms. I saw Giovanni walking out, carrying me ahead of them. Then, to my surprise, Caradoc and James appeared in the room. I hadn't known they were there. I watched as Makonnen handed Ken's body over to Caradoc, then headed out the door. He followed behind us. It was like my spirit floated high in the air above Makonnen, watching as a spectator at a sporting event would. I watched him stop and turn into Ken's spare bedroom.

The temperature in the room rose dramatically, and I saw

Talia's naked body riding Pallo. I could see her ghastly white hands feeling his chest as she moved her body on him. I watched the replay of him reaching his hand up to caress her neck. Pallo lifted Talia's naked body with just one hand, gripping her throat. His face held none of the beauty that it had before. Now, it was twisted and hideous. Demonic was the best way to explain it. He smiled up at Talia, showing his fangs. In one quick motion, he threw her body across the room, but still clutched her throat in his hand.

Makonnen's eyes looked upon the crumpled, bloody body of Talia. I could feel his terror. He rushed towards Pallo. James appeared next to him, and the two of them tackled Pallo to the ground.

I dropped Makonnen's hand immediately. He stood there, looking down at me. I know that he relived the event with me. A wave of nausea washed over me and I bent over the bed and vomited until I passed out again.

I woke to Giovanni sitting on the edge of the bed. I sat up and moved away from him. His dark gaze fell upon me. He lifted his hand out to touch me and before I could even think, I gasped.

"Do I terrify you still?" It took all he had to keep his composure and I knew it.

I nodded. He laughed. I couldn't read him. I didn't know what he thought.

"You saved my life." The words slid out of my mouth.

"Yes, it was an old debt that has now been repaid," Giovanni said. His long hair hung close to my hand. His hair looked too soft and shiny to be real. I had to fight the urge to reach out and touch it. I didn't want to give him the wrong idea. I didn't know if he could possibly think less of me, since I was all over him on the dance floor, but I thought it best not to push it.

The right corner of his soft, rose-colored lips curled into a smile. "My, you certainly have changed."

I got to my feet slowly. I had no idea how long I had been in his home, but I was positive the sun had risen already today. "I thought vampires slept during the daylight? I thought you tucked yourself away in a coffin all day?"

A laugh roared from his belly and his eyes twinkled. "You've watched one too many movies. I have slept next to you in this very bed for the last four nights. I didn't go to a small coffin and hide away." He let himself smile, and his face lit up.

I had been so lost in his dashing good looks that the fact that I had been here four nights had almost passed me by. "Four nights? We slept in the same bed?" My stomach knotted up on me instantly.

"Do not fear, *bella*, I was a perfect gentleman. I have waited hundreds of years to have you with me again. I would never of dream of spoiling it." He reached his hand out to touch my leg, and I didn't back away this time.

"Patient? That's not a word I would use to describe you, Giovanni." A familiar voice boomed through the room. Sharon entered the red bedroom.

"Sharon, you two know each other?"

"Hey, babe! Nice outfit!" She smiled with that same old best friend kind of grin. "Yeah, I've known Giovanni all of my life. He and my father go way back. He's an all right guy, once you get past that tall, dark, and pissed off exterior." She strolled closer to me. She was dressed in a pair of jeans and a yellow short sleeved shirt. Her long hair was smooth and black, and she had let it fall to her shoulders today.

Giovanni's hand still rested on my leg. I didn't want to push it off, but I didn't feel comfortable with it there either.

"I should really be getting home." I slid my leg away from him and stood. "Thank you for everything."

Sharon sighed. She was used to dealing with me, and knew what a pain I could be. "You aren't going back to your apartment. It was ransacked by the hellhounds. Apparently, the crazy redhead went looking for you there first."

I couldn't hide the shock on my face. My apartment wasn't much, but it was home to me. The thought of them hiding out in my apartment waiting for me sent chills up my spine. Had Ken experienced that, too?

"Is Ken...?" I couldn't bring myself to say the words.

"Ken's doing okay. He's drugged up, and in good hands."

Relief washed over me, followed quickly by dread. Where was I going to go now? I couldn't go to Sharon's place. She was in between leases, and stayed with her brother and his wife. I couldn't go to Ken's--it was probably in worse shape than mine.

Giovanni's voice broke in before I freaked out. "You are most welcome to stay here, Gwyneth."

I wondered where "here" really was. I could have been in another country. I didn't know what to do. I did know that he had saved my life, and even stayed with me at the hospital. I needed to trust someone. Could I trust him?

"I guess I can hang out here with the Count for a little while," I said. Part of me wanted to go out to the farmhouse, but I didn't relish the idea of being alone.

"Ouch, that hurt!" Giovanni smiled. He led me to the far wall and pulled the red drape back, exposing a large wooden door. I turned and looked at him, not sure what to do.

"It's the lavatory, it will not bite you." Giovanni grinned.

"Well, file that under the ever dwindling column of things-that-won't-bite-while-here." I opened the door and headed in. I could hear his laughter behind me as I closed the door.

Easing myself out of the red nightgown, I glanced in the mirror. I looked tired. I looked drained. I had been to hell and back in a few short days, and it showed.

The bath water was smooth and refreshing. I could feel the tension in my shoulders easing as I lounged. My mind drifted. It wandered to the events of the last week. I didn't like thinking about how seriously screwed up my life was, so I quit. I got myself all cleaned up and cracked the door open, just a bit. The room was empty and my bags were lying on the huge four post bed. I wrapped the towel around me and headed out to get dressed.

"Gwyneth." The sound of Pallo's voice made me stop in my tracks. I turned around slowly, and saw him standing in the room. I still couldn't get used to how quick vampires could move. I took a step back, refusing to take my eyes off of him.

He moved towards me. I backed up and bumped into the dresser.

"Stay away from me!"

"Gwyneth," he said my name sweetly, softly.

"Don't do that."

"What did I do?"

I pushed my body back against the dresser to keep from running wildly at him and clawing his brown eyes out.

"Don't say my name all sweet, you fucking bastard!" My voice was strong. I was proud of myself for maintaining my composure.

"Please quiet down. I promised Giovanni that I would let the two of you have time together."

"You made a deal with Giovanni? I thought you guys hated each other?" I was intrigued, but worried that I'd forget I hated him now.

"He saved your life, and now he is a guest in my home. I will show him the respect he deserves," Pallo said, taking the smallest of steps toward me.

I glanced around the bedroom. This was his. I'd been in this two-timing loser's bedroom for the last four nights. How the hell many bedrooms did he have? I guess you walk around and think about sex twenty-four hours a day for, like, two hundred years, you make sure you're always prepared for it.

"I liked your taste in wall colors better before you became a monster. Yellow was a much better choice." I made sure to emphasize the word monster. Every bit of my body wanted to hit him, over and over again. He had said such ugly things about me. More importantly, he had fooled me into thinking he really did love me. He headed across the room towards me.

"Stay the hell away from me. I'll get my stuff and go to a hotel."

"Gwyneth, you are being unreasonable."

I couldn't believe the nerve of this guy. He thought I was being unreasonable.

"I didn't turn on you. I didn't fuck somebody else in the room next to you."

He cut me off. "No, you are correct. As I remember it, you did it in the same room as me as you pinned me to the floor to be sure I did not miss the show." He lifted his pale hand and touched his chin. "Ah, yes, I believe you did. Or do you forget your precious little Caleb so soon?"

He had me there. "Christ, Pallo, it was a lust spell! I will not stand here and justify my actions to you. Besides, as I remember it, Caleb wasn't a crazed lunatic who was about to have you killed." I lost my cool fast. "You mean nothing to me, get away from me. I can't even stand to look at you. And, don't you ever say Caleb's name, ever! You will never be close to the man he was."

"I have not been a man for over two hundred years. My quest for your hand saw to that."

Oh, how rich! He was going to twist this around and blame me for everything. I'm not without my faults, but this was not all my doing. "Fuck you, Pallo!"

"Please, lower your voice. I gave my word that I would not see you until tomorrow. If Giovanni finds me here, our agreement is over." There was something in his voice I had never heard before. It was fear.

"You're afraid of Giovanni, aren't you?" The look in his eyes

told me I was right. "Maybe you should pretend to care about
him, sleep with him, or, excuse me, 'fuck him' as you like to call
it, then bash him across the face ... oh ... and then go get fucked
by some psycho bitch from hell. Yeah, that ought to do it." I
could feel my anger rising. It brought my power to the surface.

"That is not what happened, Gwyneth. Talia would have
destroyed us all if I had not tricked her. I could not single-
handedly take on her entire pack of hounds. I am sorry, and I do
love...." Pallo was almost touching me now.

I wanted to lash out at him with my power. "You called me
whore--a *donnaccia*, struck me down, and left me to die by
Jonathan's hands. If that's how you love people, I don't want
any part of it." I pushed at him slightly with my power.

Pallo's shirt blew back against his body, and his pants clung to
him as my power pushed at him. He stood his ground. He
brought his own power to the surface and pushed against mine.

"Gwyneth, I tried to warn you of what I was going to do. I tried
to reach you."

I let more of my energy seep out. "All I felt around you was a
wall. You were blocking me from sensing anything from you."

"I blocked Talia from sensing my lies. She would have ripped
your throat out, right before my eyes, if she knew how I felt for
you."

"Well, thank goodness you beat her at her own game!"

Pallo seemed shocked. "You saw that?"

I pushed more energy at him. "I guess I should feel lucky that
you didn't do that to me after I rode you. Although, that might
have been less painful than telling me that you loved me only
later to find out you lied, and were only using me." I thrust as
much power as I could muster at him. He staggered backwards,
but didn't fall.

"Do not say such things. You know in your heart that is not
true."

"No, Pallo, you're the liar. I hate you." I meant every word of
it.

That last comment managed to do what my power had failed
to. It made him fall to his knees. His broad shoulders slumped
forward. His head drooped down.

"Pallo!" His name came from the doorway. I turned and saw
Giovanni standing there, glaring at Pallo. He looked so
intimidating in his black shirt, jeans, and boots. I really needed to
convince these guys to incorporate some color into their

wardrobes.

Pallo glanced up at him. "It does not matter anymore." His voice was weak.

Giovanni appeared in front of Pallo. I never even saw him move. He turned and looked at me. "*Bella*, is it you who did this?" he asked, referring to Pallo being on the floor.

I smiled and batted my navy blue eyes at him.

His head tipped back, laughed and came to me. He picked my hands up into his. I didn't fight him. "You never cease to amaze me." He pressed his lips to my hands. This felt familiar, but not necessarily safe. Out of the corner of my eye, I could see Pallo watching us.

"I have lived many years, few things surprise me--yet, you always do." My hands were still near his lips. I could feel Pallo's penetrating gaze. I hurt him and I liked it. I moved my body closer to Giovanni's. He was not as massive as Pallo, but every bit as spectacular to look at. I was so amazed at how creamy his skin was. For a vampire as old as I believed him to be, he held his color well. My body, still wrapped in a towel, brushed his. He tensed up. I looked up at him, searching his dark black eyes. I wanted to remember him. I wanted to know why I had chosen Pallo over him. I wanted to know what had drawn me to him in the first place. Was it his beauty, charm, grace? Or was I a horrible person who only went with men for money and power? I looked into his face. It was so familiar, yet so foreign to me. I tugged my hand free from his lips and touched his face. His mouth turned quickly, kissing at the palm of my hand. I could feel his pull on me. He used vampire tricks and I didn't like it.

"Don't," I said to him. He stopped. Even without his pull, I could tell that I knew him well. I knew that when he smiled he got a crease in his forehead. I knew that he had a tiny birthmark on the back of his right leg, right before his butt. I knew that he enjoyed listening to classical music, and spinning me round and round until I was too dizzy to see straight. I had no idea how I knew all of these things about him, but I did, and I knew something else. I knew that he loved me. But, he also felt dangerous, he felt wrong.

Giovanni pulled me close to him. "Shall I send Pallo away?"

I glanced at Pallo, who still sat on the floor. He looked beaten, broken. I remembered him standing in Ken's house, saying how he had only used me for a "fuck." I remembered how much my face hurt when he hit me, how used I felt. He had managed to make me feel like what he accused me of being--he made me feel like a whore.

"No," I said.

Pallo looked up at me with hope in his eyes.

"No, don't send him away, make him stay and watch. *I have seen him bleed, shall we see if he weeps?*" I loved spinning and twisting his words back at him.

Giovanni pulled me to him and put his hands on my towel near my breasts. "Are you sure?"

I thought about seeing Talia's naked body moving up and down on his. I glared at Pallo. My face was hard and cold. I pulled on Giovanni's wrists and my towel dropped to the floor, moving into him. I pulled his shirt over his head. His long, silky hair spilled down his back. I touched his chest, and traced my fingers over tiny scars that covered his perfect body.

"What happened?"

He pulled my hand away from them. "They are not important."

I let my finger slid over his silver nipple ring. It was a tiny hoop, a perfect accent to his creamy tan coloring. My fingers kept coming back to the tiny scars on his chest. I let my hand slide over them again. It was odd how his scars lined up exactly with my fingers. I pulled my fingernails down them, following the path they took. I stared up into his dark eyes. Had I done this to him? Had I clawed his perfect skin with my hands?

Giovanni seemed to read my every thought. He lifted my hand from his chest and brought it to his mouth. He pulled me closer to him as he sucked on my long fingers. I drew in my breath. I wanted to be near him. I wanted to please him. I lost my free will.

"Gwyneth!" Pallo's voice hit me hard.

It was Giovanni who turned first. He threw his hand out. A slash appeared on Pallo's face. I didn't understand how Giovanni had done that, and I didn't want to see an instant replay. I grabbed his outstretched hand and pulled it to me.

"No," I said gently. "Let me be the one to punish him."

A tiny crease appeared on his forehead. "*Bella*, he is my creature. I will have control of him."

His creature? I didn't understand what that meant, but I wasn't going to let Pallo be physically hurt again if I could help it. "You would deny me my revenge?" I had no idea why I said this, but some part of me knew him, and that part was in the driver's seat now.

Giovanni laughed. "Oh, how you have changed. I like the new you. Yes, I like it very much." He slid his free hand around my back, and caressed me. "However, I am his sire, so I will do with him as I see fit."

I tensed up. Giovanni had made Pallo a vampire? Oh, my God. It *was* my fault that Pallo was a monster now. Hadn't he told me that he sought my hand in marriage from Giovanni? His love for me had led him straight to the Devil's doorstep.

"What's wrong?" Giovanni asked. "Tell me what troubles you."

"Why? Why did you do that?"

"I'm afraid that you'll have to be more specific, *bella*."

I looked at Pallo on the floor and then to Giovanni's face. "If you really loved me, than why is it you turned Pallo into one of the undead--a vampire?"

Giovanni stood very still. "I was not aware that you could remember so much about your past." I actually thought I saw a bead of sweat forming on his brow. I didn't think that it was even possible for vampires to sweat.

"I can't remember much, but I put two and two together and came up with that."

"I am so happy for you." As he said it, I could sense the lie.

"Thank you, but you still didn't answer my question."

He nodded slowly. "Ah, yes, Pallo. The reason I gave him the gift of immortality was for you, *cara mia*. I knew that you had forever, and I didn't want your precious little lover to die of old age, while you remained youthful." I heard him talking, but the stench of his lies overwhelmed. "I truly thought that you would be pleased to have him back as one of my children. You had spent a century in awe of my powers, so I passed them onto your little Pallo."

"What will you do with him?"

"I will punish him accordingly. I granted him too much freedom when I allowed him to come here years ago. I would have never allowed him to leave me if the King himself hadn't sent for him personally. Who am I to go against the King's orders?"

Pallo laughed under his breath. Giovanni's hand rose and another slash appeared across Pallo's chest. I sucked in my breath and closed my eyes slightly. Think, Gwen, think! I knew that somewhere, deep inside, I had the answer I needed. I went with what my gut told me to do.

"Would you do something for me?" I asked him, tugging on the top of his pants. Great, my gut reaction was to get frisky with him.

He let out a small moan. "I would do anything you ask, *bella*, anything."

I slid my hand down the front of his jeans. "Free Pallo." I had no idea why those words came out of my mouth. I didn't understand what they meant. Pallo already looked free to me.

Giovanni appeared stunned, but Pallo looked mortified.

"Free Pallo?" he asked sliding his hand around to play with my butt. "Why do you care if he is free from me or not?"

"I don't know." I told him the truth.

"Why do you not wish to be free of me instead? Why him?" Giovanni asked, lifting me up into his arms. I straddled his waist. My body pressed against his open jeans.

"You'll kill Pallo. I see it in your eyes when you look at him. I don't see that when you look at me."

He kissed me softly. "You are wise beyond your years."

"So I've been told," I said, returning his kiss.

"Why should I let him live? He has betrayed you."

Betrayal. When I heard the word come out of Giovanni's mouth, a shudder passed through my body. I associated betrayal more with Giovanni than Pallo, and I had no idea why.

Giovanni stood, holding my naked body to him. He kissed me again. "For allowing me to be this near to you, I give you my word that when I leave you this evening, Pallo is free of me."

"But I didn't hear you promise not to kill him." I didn't know why I had to call him on that. I trusted gut instinct well enough to heed its warning.

"*Bella*, you beat me at my own game. I am impressed. You never used to be this good."

I tugged on his lip with my teeth. He sighed.

"Very well, I give you my word that neither I, nor anyone who represents me--," his eyes rolled slightly then met mine, "--will ever kill Pallo."

"And?" I bit at his chin.

"And I shall not cause him any serious harm either."

"That a boy," I said, smiling at him while I ran my fingers over his bare skin.

"I have one condition of my own," Giovanni said to me in hushed tone. "I ask that you refrain from seeing him after tonight."

My mind raced. Could I really go the rest of my life and never see Pallo again? I thought about his words to Talia, the memory of him terrorizing me in the hallway. I pictured him cramming his fingers in Sandra again, I saw Talia riding him. "It's a deal."

"Why do you want him to live so badly?"

Giovanni was right to question me. Pallo was public enemy number one as far as I was concerned. I didn't like the idea of being used.

"I want him to live with the memory of this forever."

"And what memory would that be?"

"Me being the whore he made me into," I said, soft enough to sound sultry, but loud enough for Pallo not to miss a word of it.

Giovanni pulled my body close to his, and pressed his clothed erection against me. His lust spilled out and into me. My mind switched gears in order to really play the part. I pulled Giovanni's face down and put it between my breasts. I leaned my head back and let my neck stretch out before his eyes. This, I began to understand, was the biggest turn-on for a vampire ever.

Giovanni slid his free hand up my side, over my breast, and to my neck. He ran his smooth cold hands over it, rubbing it, caressing it. His power surrounded me. It was different than Pallo's, it was more threatening. Putting my arms around him, I clutched him tight, pressing my breast in his face the entire time. He let go of me briefly, before touching my hips. He pressed his lips to my neck, and I felt pressure on my neck. He was biting me. The pressure grew more intense as he sucked on me.

"Giovanni." I wanted to let him know he hurt me. I wanted to tell him to slow down, but no words came from my mouth.

"You're hurting her!" Pallo's voice pushed in, invading the moment.

Giovanni stopped and let go of me. His dark black gaze bore through me, and his eyebrow rose slightly. He asked me without asking me. A hot tear ran down my face. He turned and thrust his hand out at Pallo, ripping his shoulder wide open.

"NO!" I screamed out as blood ran down Pallo's arm. "You promised me."

Giovanni held me to him. "I promised not to cause him any serious harm. He is a vampire, he will heal."

Was he really such a monster? Was that why I ran from him? Did he drive me into Pallo's arms? I shook my head slightly, trying to remember. Nothing came to me. My neck throbbed, and I felt a little sick to my stomach. I was sure that it was from blood loss.

"Get out, Giovanni! I've had enough liars in my bed to last me a lifetime." I couldn't believe my own ears. I had just ordered a five-hundred-year-old vampire out of the room, and called him a liar. He spun around and looked at me. He flashed his fangs at me. I didn't budge. "Get out now!"

"He must leave as well! You swore to never see him again," he said, pointing at Pallo.

"As I recall, oh master of the twisted word, you yourself said that I was not to see him after tonight. The night is not over yet, is it? Besides, it would serve you right if I did. You seem to find the arrangement flexible." I had him and he knew it. He threw Pallo a look of disgust and stormed out of the room.

Pallo crawled on the floor towards me. I glared at him. "You're a free man now, Pallo, go enjoy yourself!"

He stood slowly and put his finger to my neck where Giovanni had bitten me. "You did this to free me?" His voice was so low, so quiet.

"Go!"

"I can fix this. I can beg for this to be undone. You should not have aligned yourself with him, he is a monster."

That made me laugh. "Oh, yeah, you're an expert on those aren't you?"

My words hit him hard, and he backed up a bit from me. "I cannot allow this to be. I will go and speak with him."

"Why in hell would you want to grovel at his feet? Go be a man, be free of him. You're free of me. Are you happy you got what you wanted?"

"No."

"Are you telling me that you didn't want your freedom?"

"I did, but not at this price."

"What price is that?"

He was a beaten man, his words fell flat. "You."

Chapter 21

I gathered up my stuff and repacked my bags. Two bags still lay on the floor. When I bent down to pick them up, everything slid out of my arms.

"Would you like some help?"

I looked up. James stood in the doorway, smiling at me. He had on his usual black tee shirt and jeans. I smiled. He was a sight for sore eyes.

"Yeah."

He came over and picked up all the bags. I tried to take one from him, but he wouldn't let me. I got the door for him and we headed down the hall and upstairs. He stopped on the steps before we got to the door.

"Let me take some of those," I said, turning back to take a few bags from him.

He looked at the door. "That's not the problem."

It must be daytime. I had lost all sense of time in Pallo's little basement. I had just assumed, because James was up, that it was night. He'd known I would be leaving, and he'd waited for me. He was a good friend, a true friend, the kind that didn't want sex in return. The kind of friend every girl needed.

"I'll get them from here," I said, touching his hand lightly. "Could you call a cab for me?"

He set the bags down on the stairs and reached into his front pocket. He pulled a set of keys out and smiled. "Here, I thought you might need these. I parked the car out front before the sun came up."

I took the keys from him, and gave him a hug. He held me tight and gave a slight squeeze.

"Gwen, stay away from Giovanni, please!"

"Won't he hear you?" I asked in a low voice. I remembered the night that Pallo had overheard me talking to Ken.

"No, he left last night. He is not Pallo's master anymore, so Pallo had the right to revoke his invitation." James said, as if stuff like this was common knowledge to me.

"Is Pallo good to you?"

"Pallo's not just my master, he's my friend, and that's rare, very rare."

"Where is he?" I asked. I would have thought he'd try to talk me into staying. I was a little disappointed that he hadn't come to see me off.

"Gwen, he hasn't lived this long and not learned a thing or two about women."

"What do you mean?"

"He knows that you need to go. He loves you enough to let you do that. If, or when, you're ready, you'll come back. He knows that."

I had to laugh. I couldn't picture myself setting foot near this place ever again. I'd had enough of the melodramatic life that surrounded Pallo. I wanted to return to the way my life had been before him. Simple.

I gave James another hug and watched him walk back downstairs. When the bottom door had shut, I picked up a couple of my bags and headed out into the sun. It hurt my eyes at first. I had to put my hand up to shield myself from it. I'd gotten used to living in the dark, gotten used to Pallo's world. I stopped and looked in front of me at Caleb's red Explorer. I looked down at my hand holding the keys. James had given me Caleb's truck. Why not, he wasn't using it anymore, and I didn't think he'd mind me borrowing it if he were here. I loaded my bags into the back end and fetched the rest from the stairwell.

Chapter 22

I stopped by the hospital to see Ken. When I walked into his room, he was out cold. His eyes were puffy and black. He had an IV running into the back of his right hand. Lying there, he looked so much smaller than he actually was. I sat in the chair next to his bed and reached up to touch his hand. It was so warm. Being around vampires will make you forget how warm something alive feels. I cupped his hand in mine and leaned forward to kiss it. They had the backs of his arms bandaged. Sharon had said that it had taken the doctors seven hours to stitch Ken's body up. I believed it, looking at all of the bandages. He looked more like a burn victim than the victim of a psychotic, dog-breeding vampire.

I wondered how Ken felt about wearing the hospital gown. He couldn't be comfortable letting the nurses see him naked. He loved his body, but it was his body. I slid my hand up and let it rest on his chest. I could feel it rising softly beneath my hand. Closing my eyes, I put my head down on the cold steel bar on the side of the bed. The feel of Ken's breathing was soothing. The tiny pump hooked to the IV made small swooshing sounds.

I thought of the time Ken took me to look at houses. He wanted us to have a home after we got married. He had his heart set on it, and nothing I said or did would change his mind. He surprised me on my lunch hour by taking me to a real estate agency. We met with a tall woman with short blonde hair. Beth had been her name. I had almost forgotten that. She pulled photos up on her computer of various houses that fit Ken's bill. I sat there with my mouth open. I'd pictured us settling down in a small, three-bedroom ranch in a suburb near the city. He had grander things in mind. All of the houses she pulled up had at least six bedrooms in them. Some had four full baths, two had in-ground pools. I just sat there, not knowing what to say.

Beth and Ken went back and forth about each listing. Ken's hand wrapped tightly in mine. I could feel his excitement. My stomach hollowed out. If he wanted a house with six bedrooms, then he wanted a large family. He knew that it would be hard for us to have even one child, let alone a house full. I wanted to run from Beth's office. A wave of nervousness hit me and I stood up. I looked at him and took off running out of the agency.

When I broke through the doors, I bent over and took several deep breaths. Ken came bursting out behind me. He wasn't upset with me for leaving, he was worried about me. He asked me why I left, and I cried. I told him that I couldn't offer him the life he wanted, and that by seeing the houses he picked, I knew that for sure. He held me tight in his arms, and laughed. He didn't expect me to give him a big family. He expected to give that to me. "We will adopt. We will get you as many little ones as you want." He loved me so much. He just wanted to make me happy.

At that moment, I knew that I loved him too. I loved how kind and gentle he was with me, versus the hard-ass he was in the court room. I had thought we would spend the rest of our natural lives together.

I thought about how strong his body was when he had held me, how powerful and sure of himself he was. My body grew warm remembering how he felt near me. My energy, my power spilled out of my hand and onto Ken's chest. I jerked my hand back and stood up. I was horrified that I might have burned him. His body twitched and I screamed and fell backwards over the chair.

My body smacked the cold hard hospital floor with a thud. The door to his room swung open and a male nurse came running in.

"What the...?" he asked, as he stared from Ken's bed to me lying on the floor.

Ken's body twitched harder now. It lifted off the bed involuntarily. The man screamed for help and pushed past me. I pulled myself to my feet, and backed into the corner. The man shouted at me. He wanted to know what had happened. I just stood there looking at him trying to hold Ken's body down. Two more people ran through the door, a man and a woman. The man looked like a doctor. He wore a long white coat with a stethoscope hanging out of his right front breast pocket. They ran to Ken and the woman helped to pin him down. The doctor huddled over Ken's body. He tried to figure out what had happened. He turned to me and was calm.

"When did this start?" His voice was higher than most other men's voices. He was thin and tall. His hair was short and a very plain dull brown.

"I, I touched him and I ... I touched him and he started to...." I couldn't get the words out.

The doctor turned back to Ken, giving the female nurse instructions on what he needed. She ran out of the room. I followed close behind. I had hurt Ken. I had thrust energy into him and it would most likely kill him. I couldn't watch that happen. I couldn't stand by and watch him die because of me. I ran down the hall and found the stairwell. I ran downstairs and out the front lobby. I didn't stop running until I reached the truck. I climbed in, grabbing the keys off the seat. Old habits die hard.

I peeled out of the hospital parking lot. I drove straight through to the farmhouse. I had no idea how fast I had been going, but I knew that it didn't take me long to get there. I pulled onto the stone lane and headed down it. I parked the truck and got out. Finding the key under the loose porch board, I let myself in. I ran to the phone and dialed Sharon's cell phone.

She answered on the third ring. I told her what had just happened to me at the hospital with Ken. She tried her best to calm me down and told me that she'd call me right back. I hung up and stood there, staring at the phone. I guess I expected her to phone me back instantly, I don't know why. My fingers tapped on the top of the white phone, waiting to seize hold of it when it rang. It did.

"Yeah!"

"Gwen, calm down. I called the hospital. The doctor had been trying to find you since you ran off."

"Oh shit, he's dead. Sharon I did it, I killed Ken. Oh my God! I...."

She cut me off. "GWEN! Ken's not dead."

I stopped carrying on like an escaped mental patient and spoke calmly to her. "He's not?"

She laughed at me. "No, Gwen, he's not dead. In fact, it's the opposite. The guy is fine. He's completely healed. There isn't a scratch on him. The doctor tried to find you, to find out how you did it."

Ken was fine? He was healed?

"Thanks, Sharon, thank you so much,"

"No probs, babe. You gonna be all right?"

I thought about all that had happened to me in the last week. I had seen so much violence, death and destruction, but I had also known love from two different people in that short time frame. I was sure that counted for something, didn't it?

"Yeah, Sharon, I'm going to be all right."

I hung up, went out, unloaded my bags from the back of the Explorer, and took them into the house. It got pretty muggy outside and the house stayed pretty cool even though it didn't have central air, but the sweatpants were getting a little hot. I dragged a couple of my bags upstairs and looked for some shorts. I found a pair of white ones. Those would work.

I changed into the white shorts and headed downstairs. I walked to the hall closet and felt along the top shelf. My hand ran across leather and I pulled it down. It was my father's old hunting knife in its black leather case. The knife was about eight inches long, and he used to use it to gut things he killed. I was going to use it to gut something, too. I was going troll hunting. I stuck the knife into the back of my waistband. It stuck tight to me. I hoped that I would be able to get it out in time if I needed it, but I wasn't planning on needing it. I planned on calling on my power and frying those little troll bastards. Just to be on the safe side, I decided to take Caleb's crossbow with me. I grabbed it out of the back of his truck and brought it in the house. I couldn't figure out what to do with it. Common sense prevailed, and I left it lying on the kitchen table.

I stormed out of the house and down the lane. It was a beautiful, late summer day, not a cloud in the sky. The only storm I felt brewing was the one deep inside of me. I headed down to the river, hoping to find trolls there. I wanted them dead. I owed Caleb that much. I owed myself that much.

I reached the bridge in less than ten minutes. Damn, I walked fast. I walked out onto it and looked around. There was nothing there--just me, standing on the bridge, looking like a crazed lunatic. What else was new?

"Come and get me, you bastards! Come on!" I screamed. It echoed off the sides of the hill that the river wound through.

No one came. I walked to the side of the bridge and climbed down the small, rocky walkway to the river's edge. I looked in all directions. I wasn't going to let one of those nasty, stinky things sneak up on me again. This time, I would be ready for them. I would be ... I heard the sound of leaves being crushed. I stopped thinking and started listening. I heard it again. Glancing in that direction, I saw a black blur. It was on the other side of the river, further down than where I was. I took off in a fast run along the side of the river. My feet hit the sandy, rocky ground and I felt myself slipping to the side. I almost twisted my ankle at least three times before I reached the shallow part of the river. It was near the bend and was only ankle deep. I splashed through it. The water turned murky brown everywhere I stepped. I churned the dirt up in it. My socks got soggy. I didn't care. All I cared about was finding that troll and killing it. I hit the other side of the river. That side was not covered in sand and rocks, it was just dirt. The dirt led up to the edge of the woods. I caught sight of the black blur again and kept on going.

I pushed my way into the woods. My shoes made tiny squeaky noises from all of the water in them. I pushed on. I was being driven by hate, by revenge. I looked around for a sign of where the troll had gone. There was no sign of him. The hairs on my arms stood on end. I ducked down just in time. Something large and wet lunged past my head.

I heard snarls as I turned around quickly. There it was. Those nasty teeth and beady, yellow eyes glared at me, wanted to strike out at me. The thing stank more than ever, and I was actually happy to see it. I could taste my hate. I pulled the knife from its sheath, and gripped it tightly. "Come on, come on," I thought to myself. The troll made another lunge at me. I darted out of its pathway. As it fell past me, I slammed the knife down into its back. I struck out against its slimy, seaweed-like covering. It shrieked, and I laughed. God, I really was sick in the head. Guess Talia had rubbed off on me. I hoped that I wouldn't want to start dressing like her, too. I shook my head--no time to get sidetracked.

The troll pulled itself to its feet, slowly. It still cried out. That didn't faze me in the least. What did bother me was that an identical sound answered it? I dove at it, propelling my body against it. We crashed down onto the edge of the river. It tried to lash out at me with its teeth. I moved my arm quickly to avoid a repeat performance. My hand slid over a large rock. I picked it up. Without thought, I raised the rock over my head and smashed it onto the troll's face. It made a horrible noise that should have brought me to my senses. Instead, I raised the rock above my head two more times and smashed it into the troll until I was sure that I'd killed it. I stood up from it slowly, and felt no remorse as I leaned to rinse my hands in the river water.

The cool, fresh water ran red under my touch. I let my head fall slightly. Warmth came from behind me, and I turned slowly. There, standing on the edge of the river, was the man who had saved my life as a child--the faerie man with the long black hair and navy blue eyes. He had watched me kill the troll. I was mortified.

"Kerrigan," the name fell from my lips.

He smiled. His face was soft and his eyes were warm. He wore robes of black and had a sword strapped to his side.

"You know my name."

I almost fell over. I had never, ever heard him speak before. He was always just there, quiet but there. He had a voice that demanded your attention.

"Yes, I…." I looked down at the dead troll. I didn't know what to say to him. He waved his hand in the air and the troll vanished. I just stared at him. I should have felt wrong, or dirty. After all, this was the second thing I'd killed in the last week. "You're King Kerrigan." I always surprised myself with just how stupid I could sound sometimes.

He smiled wider. "I was the King. They have a new ruler now."

I made a small step towards him. "Caleb said you just disappeared. Why?"

"Caleb. You have met Caleb?"

I got the impression that he already knew the answer, but wanted to hear me say it.

"Yes, I knew Caleb."

"Knew him?" he asked coming closer to me.

"He was … murdered." I didn't know why I told him this. I just felt like I needed to share this with him. He glanced at the bloody stone on the ground and nodded.

"I see now. You sound upset. Did Caleb mean much to you?"

I sat on the ground, and had to fight to keep from crying. "Yes, he meant a lot to me. More than I knew, I guess."

Kerrigan came close to me. I could have reached out and touched him, but I didn't. I simply stared up at him. He was a sight to behold. I could definitely tell he was royalty, his posture alone said it all. Gently, he touched the top of my head, and I gave into my tears.

"I lose everyone I love--somehow I manage to lose them all. I have no one ... no family, no one."

"Gwyneth, you do not lose everyone you hold dear to your heart," he said as he bent down beside me. "And you do have family still alive. I can assure you of that."

I stared up into his dark navy eyes. "Do you know my mother?"

He sat beside me on the ground. Even sitting down he was at least a foot taller than me. "I knew your mother well."

Knew? "She's dead?"

He nodded slightly. "She fought hard to bring you back. She wanted you to have another chance at life, because you had been robbed of yours. She knew when she decided to bring you back that it meant she would die. She gave her life force to you so you could live again."

I wasn't sure I followed him correctly. "My mother died willingly to give birth to me? She sacrificed herself for me? Why?"

"You are the balance, Gwyneth," he said, voice low.

The mysterious woman's voice in my dreams came to mind.

"Between dark and light," I said slowly, remembering her words.

He touched my knee hesitantly. "I see that your mother has paid you a visit."

"What? The dreams were real?"

He grinned. "Ah, yes, she is connected to you. She shared her life force with you, and you will be forever linked."

"Will it always be in my dreams only?"

"That, or by transcending the boundaries of time itself," he could tell that he had lost me. "Like a mystical portal."

Pallo's yellow bedroom! Wasn't that a mystical portal to somewhere? He called it a safe haven.

"What'd she look like?" I'd wondered about that for so many years.

"Ah, she was beautiful. She was about your height and had long, flowing blonde hair. Her eyes were green and glorious. Her frame was small, it made me ache to wrap my arms around her and protect her. Faeries revered her as a goddess."

Blonde hair and green eyes never came to mind when I'd pictured her. I frowned.

"What is the matter?"

"I hoped that we looked alike."

He laughed. "No, I am sorry, but you took after your father." He patted my knee gingerly as he told me this. I noticed the way his head tipped back as he laughed. The way his dark, navy eyes squinted slightly as he smiled. How full his lips were, and how long his hair was.

"You … you're my father," I stammered.

"Yes."

I just sat there, letting it all soak in. It made sense, now that I thought about it. He'd always been there for me growing up. He was like my own personal faerie guardian angel--my father.

"I have one question for you."

He looked at me, waiting for me to ask him.

"Why'd you give me away?"

His hand dropped from my knee. "Your mother would not let me raise you. She feared the idea of you being brought up anywhere near the creatures of the night. I could not blame her. That is no place for a child to grow up."

I thought about the stories of me running off with Giovanni. My mother must have known me well, she knew that'd I'd be too tempted in the Dark Realm.

"Lydia loved you too much to risk anything happening to you."

"Lydia? Pallo's Lydia?"

He nodded. "Yes, Pallo's Lydia. Your mother loved Pallo. She thought he would make a wonderful husband for you. She wanted you away from Giovanni. I could not fault her there, either, but choosing a mortal for a husband would have brought you only more pain. That is why I…." He looked at me. I saw the hurt in his eyes. "That is why I promised you to Caleb."

What was he saying--that I was betrothed to Caleb? To them, my past life was an extension of me. They had all lived to tell about it. But to me, it was secondhand information. I might as well have been hearing about a complete stranger.

"You promised me to Caleb, knowing I was in love with Pallo?"

"No, you were betrothed to Caleb from birth. He was born just a few years before you, and it made good sense in the boundaries of the Realm Royalty."

"I'm not following."

He suddenly seemed to take a keen interest in the ground. "Lydia made sure to shelter you from the life of the Realms. Only now do I see the error in that."

"I'm sorry, Kerrigan. I was raised by mortals. I went to school with human children. They don't believe in magical creatures or demons. They couldn't possibly understand the creatures I know. To them, the idea of Heaven and Hell is a hard one to grasp."

"You were raised by people who loved you. I knew that they would. I could sense it when I neared this farmhouse. Pallo was right to pick them. Of course, I had to check up on you from time to time."

Pallo had a hand in all of this? I'd dwell more on that another time.

"Why didn't you tell me that you're my father? Why wait until now?"

"You were not ready to know. Besides, I promised your mother that I would not endanger you, and you knowing who and what I was would have done just that."

I was bursting with questions for him. "Why would I be in danger? You were the King, who would dare defy you?"

"Oh, I forget how young you truly are now. I have many enemies in the supernatural world, and if they ever found out I had a child, they would kill you to prevent you from taking over the throne."

The throne? How could I take over the throne? I didn't even know one existed until about four minutes ago. He had been the King and I was his daughter, what did that make me, an almost princess? I didn't know, it made my head hurt. Thankfully, Kerrigan launched into telling me about my past.

He told me about Sorcha, the current Queen of Nightmares. She'd been appointed to be Queen after he left. The elders had tried to get him to take her as his Queen prior to that, but he refused. He had already fallen in love with my mother, and was desperately trying to keep that a secret. It was forbidden for a King to marry outside of noble blood. The penalty was death, not for the King, but for the one he took to his bed. This didn't apply to all *Si*, only to the King. They hadn't planned to have a child, I just sort of happened. My mother never told anyone who my father was. She would have been killed, as would I. She raised me away from the watchful eye of the faerie elders. My father was never around during my childhood. Sorcha, upset with not being appointed Queen, was at least given the job of lead council to the King. She'd come into the Dark Realm with a child of her own, a boy. Kerrigan was very taken with the small child.

He did his best to juggle both lives. Unable to balance both worlds, he had to stop seeing me altogether. It broke my mother's heart when he did this. She turned her attentions to me. I'd been a handful from the get-go. At an early age, I showed an odd fascination with creatures of the dark. Other sidhe faeries would question this, and my mother would shrug and pretend that she hadn't noticed. She knew the reason why I was drawn to them, it was in my blood. I was born to be their leader someday. Of course, she told no one of this, and had no plans to let me rule the darkness.

Caleb and I knew each other from childhood. He had come around often. We'd been betrothed to one another since my birth. Spending much time together over the course of a hundred years or so had forged a great love between us. Caleb had only one complaint, it was that I was continually being drawn to the darker elements of life. I was fascinated with them. Caleb was kind, and understanding, and never tried to force my hand in marriage. It was on one of my trips to see Caleb that I met Giovanni. He was already two hundred years old when he came into my life. He was one of my father's best weapons. He would unleash Giovanni onto his enemies with such force, that few challenged him. He was everything that I'd always been fascinated with. He was dark, handsome, mysterious and a creature of the night.

I ran away with him, leaving Caleb behind.

Kerrigan was not able to tell me any more details of the time I spent away from the faeries. He only knew that I called upon Sorcha many years later. I wanted to be made mortal. He found out about this and forbid his head counselor from doing this. She went behind his back and did it anyway. I gave her my immortality, my separable soul, and died shortly after that.

Kerrigan found out about my death from my mother. For two hundred years, my father watched her from afar, wanting to go to her, wanting to comfort her. Finally he did. He asked what he could do to make it better for her. Her answer was simple--give her back her daughter. He wanted me back too, but knew that it meant she would die in the process. He left her that night and returned to his castle. He decided that he would rather have my mother back with him the way they had been, if only for a short time, than to see her like this for the rest of eternity.

He stole my separable soul from Sorcha's collection and went to my mother. They made love, and in the process gave her back what she had wanted so desperately, me. He even managed to spend many nights with her before I was born.

One night Sorcha had him followed. The guards reported seeing him with a woman who was with child. When he returned home, they were waiting for him. They wanted to know who she was, and if the child was his. When they finished questioning him, he summoned Pallo and Caleb before him. He told them of a faerie woman they both knew well, Lydia, and how she was about to give birth to a child. If they saw to it that Lydia's child was safe, then they would be rewarded someday. He had only one word of warning for them. "Be wise with the second time, be very wise." Neither one of them questioned him. They did as they were told. They found Lydia and kept her safe until my arrival. Pallo took me and found me a home. The only instructions my mother had for him were that it must be with humans and that I was to be named Gwyneth. All thought that the name was in honor of her dead daughter, all that is, except my father.

The two of them had no idea that I was the same woman they had both loved and lost. They did as they were told. My mother died shortly after that. Sorcha became suspicious of my father, and wanted the baby born to Lydia. He decided it would be best to disappear and let her rule. If she didn't feel threatened then she might stop looking for me. It worked. And that was all he knew about my history.

I hugged Kerrigan tightly, as a rush of emotions overcame me. He sat very still. I don't think he knew how to hug me back. He hadn't hugged someone in twenty-five years.

"I have one question," I said to him, letting go of his neck.

"What would that be?"

"Did you think I would find Caleb and Pallo again?"

"I had hoped you would find Caleb, I did not know how much of your past had returned with you. No one had ever been able to bring a faerie back to life before. We had no way of knowing what would happen. To be completely truthful, I was shocked to see the only difference between then and now is your eyes."

My hand went to my eyes. In the picture that hung in Pallo's hallway my eyes had been painted violet, now they were navy. I really had come back after being dead two hundred years.

Cool.

"Kerrigan, what about Pallo? You said that you hoped I'd find Caleb, but you didn't mention Pallo. Why?"

He looked at me his eyes were serious. "I was King of the dark creatures. I know what they can do. Pallo is one of them now whether he likes it or not."

"But it's because of me that he is. It's my fault, don't punish him for it."

"My dear little child, Pallo would have been dead many, many years ago had it not been for you. Do not feel sorry for him. He lived to see many nights, since his mortal body should have perished."

"I still love him," I said softly.

"What about Caleb?"

"He's gone now, so unless his mother decides to give her life for him I guess I'm screwed."

He laughed. Something I said was really funny to him, I hoped it wasn't the part about Caleb being gone. He stood up and extended his hand to me. This man had given up his kingdom to watch me grow up. What do you say to that?

"You had a birthday last week, did you not?" he asked, placing my arm in the crook of his, walking with me toward the bridge. I hesitated about going beneath it. I'd forgotten all about the other troll after I bumped into him.

"Never fear my creatures when I am near. They will always obey me, always." He sounded sure of himself. Who was I to argue with the King?

We walked under the bridge, and nothing popped out and grabbed us. I had to laugh at myself for becoming that paranoid in a relatively short period of time. He walked me to the other side of it and stopped.

"I shall have to see to giving you your present. I did not come prepared, my apologies. Your little display of vengeance distracted me." He bent down and kissed my forehead. "If you need me, come here and throw a rock into the water. Think of me while you do this, and I will come."

"But...." I wanted to ask him why he didn't just stay with me, or, better yet, take me with him. I had nothing holding me here. He didn't wait for me to ask him. He pulled my arm out of his gently and looked at me.

"You will know my gift to you when you see it. Take good care of it," he said, and vanished.

I swept my hand out, trying to feel him. He was gone--nothing but air remained. I thought about how smart it was to be hanging out under a bridge at nightfall. Turning, I ran back to the house as fast as I could. I got to the front door, threw it open, and ran in. I turned and locked it quickly. I know, I know, what sense does it make to leave the house unlocked the entire time you're gone, only to lock it when you get home? Okay, I'm not perfect, what else is new?

Something touched my back and I screamed.

"Jumpy, aren't we?"

I turned around and found Ken, in one piece. I threw my arms around his neck and gave him a huge kiss on the cheek. I gripped his neck so tightly my feet had come off the floor.

"Remind me to get attacked more often," he said, peeling me off him.

"How'd you know I was here?" I asked him, not really wanting to let go. He looked so good to me. His skin was smooth, tan, and not cut up. I wanted to run my hands all over his body, just to prove to myself that he was all right.

"Sharon told me. I went looking for you and she said you were up here. I hope it's all right that I came up, I just wanted to see you."

"No. I mean ... yes, it's fine, I'm happy you're here. I thought I, I thought I hurt you this morning."

He reached down and pulled his blue shirt over his head, exposing his naked chest to me. He turned around a few times, and put his shirt back on. "See, not a scratch on me. You did this. The doctor described the woman who was with me, and I knew it was you. You healed me." Bending down, he wrapped his arms around me, hugging me close to him.

"I felt you near me at my house. I knew that you covered me with your own body. I heard *everything*." He put a lot of emphasis on the word everything.

I looked up into his brown eyes. "Everything?" I referred to Pallo's harsh statements to me. Ken caught my drift and nodded yes. He held me tight. He whispered how sorry he was above my head. I couldn't for the life of me figure out why he would be sorry that Pallo did that to me, he didn't even like the guy. You would think that he'd be jumping for joy that Pallo did me wrong. He wasn't. Instead, he stood here comforting me.

Glancing down I noticed his bags lying there.

I pulled back from him a bit, and smiled. "Planning on moving in?"

"No, planning on staying with you as long as you need me to."

"What about work?" Ken's career meant everything to him. He had devoted his entire life to his job. One day he hoped to have a seat on the Commission.

"I took a leave of absence. They understood. After all, I was viciously attacked in my own home. They're trying to catch Talia as we speak. As soon as they do, I'll feel better about leaving you alone."

I remembered seeing Pallo tear her throat out. "I don't think we need to worry about her anymore."

"Gwen, it's just like you to blow off something this big," he said, letting go of me.

I really didn't feel like going into the whole long, drawn out ordeal again, so I left it at that. I went out to the kitchen with Ken and looked around. Caleb and I had done some shopping, but most of it had gone bad. I decided pizza would be our best bet. I hoped they delivered out this far.

I called two of the three pizza places listed in the phone book and neither of them would deliver out here. The third time was a charm, they delivered. I ordered a large pepperoni pizza and hung up.

"Twenty minutes."

"I can't believe I let you talk me into eating that crap tonight." He sat down at the table, and I had to laugh. The entire time we were together, we had only ordered one other pizza. He was always eating some tofu thing, or the latest and greatest diet shake. I had no clue why the man was always watching what he ate. He had never had a weight problem. I quit trying to figure him out and he quit trying to get me to join his fat-free crusade.

We sat and talked about the events that had taken place since I first went down to Necro World. I, of course, left out the part about sleeping with Caleb and Pallo. Oh, and I left out running into my real father. So, I guess you could say I left out pretty much everything that had happened since he sent me down there.

I didn't see the point of hurting him. Caleb was gone, so why bring it up? I was pretty sure he knew that I had slept with Pallo. He had heard Pallo telling Talia that he fucked me. I think the cat was out of the bag there, why beat it to death? As for meeting my father, I didn't want to endanger him. I wasn't sure what would come of him knowing this about me, and didn't want to find out.

Ken told me how, when he got home from work, hellhounds were all over in his house. He shot two, but was outnumbered. He told me that Talia was the one who beat him first, and that she'd handed the whip over to Jonathan. I had the funny feeling he left out some information, but I was in no position to point fingers. He asked me about how he got to the hospital. When I told him that Giovanni and the other vampires had taken us there, he flipped out. He couldn't believe that Pallo had me call him. I tried to explain that I had never actually dialed a number to get him, he just sort of appeared. I didn't go into any details about the price I paid for freeing Pallo from Giovanni.

Ken told me that Rick's memorial service would be held in a week. Rick was cremated, for obvious reasons, and his wife wanted to wait until her oldest son could make it in. I shot Ken a look. Was Justin like the other two? The fact that Rick's twin boys had murdered him was something that I was sure I'd never get over. Ken assured me that Rick's oldest son was on the level, and in no way connected to Talia. Apparently, Jonathan and Jacob had been out of control since birth, and Rick had tried everything in his power to control them. Ken wasn't sure how they had met Talia but he guessed that the underground club scene had something to do with it.

The doorbell rang. I grabbed my purse on the way to the door. I opened the door. Mitchell Smart stood there holding a pizza.

"Mitchell? You deliver pizzas too?" I was surprised to know he was now old enough to be driving.

God, I was getting old.

Ken walked up behind me. Mitchell gave him a dirty look. "So, Gwen, how are you and your *husband* doing?"

I was happy that he'd dropped the whole Gweny Wheny thing, but mortified that he had brought up my "husband." When Caleb and I had seen him I'd foolishly said Caleb was my husband. It had just popped out. After talking to Kerrigan I can understand why. Caleb at one time was to be my husband. Ken coughed. I just stood there looking at Mitchell, speechless.

Ken pushed in front of me. "Hi, yeah her husband is out of town on business, I'm the lover, here ya go, bye now," he said, handing him the money and shutting the door.

"Ken!" I knew he had it in him to be a prick, but slamming the door in a teenager's face was uncalled for. I was about to give him a lecture on not being an idiot when the doorbell rang again. Ken grabbed the door handle and swung the door open.

"Keep the chan--" he stopped in mid-sentence.

"Looks like I got home just in time." A sexy, familiar voice said. My heart leapt, and I couldn't believe my ears.

I pulled Ken back and out of the way. There stood Caleb, wearing a black robe with a red scarf tied around his waist. His hair was pulled back into a long braid. He looked marvelous--he looked alive! I pushed the screen door open and hit him with it on accident. I threw my whole body onto him. He was real, he was alive! I kissed his cheeks, his lips, eyes, nose, whatever I could get my lips on. He held me up and laughed.

"Caleb, you're...." I wanted to say alive, but he cut me off.

"Home--that's right, I'm home," he announced loudly. He turned, and I saw Mitchell slowly getting into his tiny red hatchback. He looked at us like we were a daytime soap. In truth, he wasn't too far off base. *As the Faerie Finds a Mate*, it could be a hit.

I stared into Caleb's dark green eyes and wanted to make absolutely sure it was him. He let them shift and glow. I squealed with delight. It was him! When he put me down, I took a good look at his outfit. The black robes looked very much like the ones I had seen my father wear all the time.

"Kerrigan," I whispered softly.

Caleb nodded and smiled. "I guess you were right about seeing him."

I stared at the gift my father had gotten me, Caleb. He'd saved his life and had known he was still alive when we were talking at the river. He'd heard me say how much he meant to me, and he made sure that he found his way back to me. No present had ever been better.

Ken coughed again. I turned and looked at him. I was at a loss for words. Thankfully, Caleb took over. "Hi, I'm Caleb, the umm, husband. And you are?"

Ken narrowed his eyes. I didn't want him to hate Caleb. I wanted him to be as happy as I was to see him. I pulled Caleb by his arm into the house, but had to push Ken backwards to get in. He did some sort of macho, "this is my turf thing." Whatever it was, I didn't have time for it. I pulled Caleb past him into the living room, jumping up and down, squealing with delight.

Caleb had to bear hug me to get me to quit. I stopped, and he put me down, running his hand over my lower stomach. It was flat and smooth. He looked disappointed. A typical male would have been relieved that he didn't get someone knocked up. Caleb wasn't typical.

I put my hand on his and smiled. It was so good to see him. I didn't want to spoil it with sour moods. As if on cue, Ken poked his head around the corner. He saw Caleb with his hand on my abdomen and looked at me shocked.

"Gwen, you didn't. You're not, you can't be."

I took Caleb's hand off me slowly and wrapped my fingers in his. "I did, and I'm not. But I did."

Ken stormed away. The front door slammed shut. I didn't want him out there wandering around, but I didn't want to leave Caleb. I looked at Caleb for help.

"I'm going to go change. I noticed my truck out front. Are my bags still in the back?" he asked.

"Yeah, sorry about taking it, but I didn't think you were going to be ba--I didn't think you'd mind." I had no intention of saying I thought he was dead so I drove his truck around.

He kissed me on the lips gently, and sent a rush of blood to my head. "Whatever I have is yours, always and forever."

Chapter 23

I watched Caleb head out the door and followed behind him. He went to the back of his truck--I went to find Ken. I called his name a few times before he answered me. He was back behind the house, in one of the three barns. He had parked his black Lexus in it. He kicked the tires over and over again. I walked up to him, and he stopped.

"Gwen, what the hell are you doing? What the hell's gotten into you? You're sleeping with half the damn city now." He bit his lip to keep from saying more.

The time had come. I had to tell him about my past life sometime, better now than never. We climbed into his car and sat. He rolled the window down and I began at the only place I could, the night he sent me to Pallo's. This time around, I left nothing out. I told him about the way I felt around them. I told him about sleeping with them. I told him about meeting my real father, about being promised to Caleb. And, I told him about making the deal with Giovanni to free Pallo. He sat very still and looked out the window.

What he said next surprised me. "Marry me, Gwen."

I looked at him like he was on crack. "Ken, have you listened to a word I've said? I'm in love with two other people."

"Yeah, I heard you, but I also heard you say you loved me too. Now, the way I see it, if you marry me, it solves your problem with them, doesn't it?"

I let out a long sigh. "I'm not going to marry any of you. Okay?"

"Gwen, I refuse to accept this. Screw fate, or destiny, or whatever. I didn't get a shot at you two hundred or three hundred years ago. They did, and they blew it. I won't accept the fact that I'm out of the race. I love you too much to do that."

"Christ, Ken. I'm so screwed up, what the hell do you want with me? You make me sound like a trophy to be won. I'm far from a trophy. Whoever I end up with has their work cut out for them, and at least ten years worth of trips to the therapist with me."

I wanted to try to help him see that he needed to move on, but part of me was being selfish, part of me wanted all of them. That would never happen and I knew it. I did manage to convince him to try to be civil to Caleb. He reluctantly agreed, and we made our way back into the house.

Caleb was in the kitchen setting the table when we walked in. He had on a white tee shirt and a pair of blue jeans. He was barefoot, and looked like himself again. We all gathered around the table and ate. No one really spoke. Ken kept shooting mean looks at Caleb, and Caleb kept pretending that Ken was insignificant. I'd had enough of their crap and headed upstairs to get ready for bed.

Chapter 24

The morning had gone by quietly without any major arguments between Caleb and Ken. That was a relief. I was tired of conflict. I wanted to have everyone hold hands and sing happy songs together. That, I knew, would never happen. When I had gotten up this morning, I found them both asleep on my bedroom floor. It was hardwood and couldn't possibly have been comfortable.

I sent a very stubborn Ken to town to with a list. If I was going to have guests for a while, I needed to have a stocked kitchen. It took me almost an hour of nagging to get Ken to go. He didn't want to leave Caleb alone with me. His car was barely out of the driveway when Caleb came running to me and picked me up. He spun me round and round. It felt so good to be in his arms.

He set me down gently and held me close. "So, tell me what happened while I was gone."

I got a sinking, uneasy feeling. I didn't want to tell him that I'd slept with Pallo. I wasn't sorry that I did, I just didn't want to hurt him. I managed to dodge the subject by kissing him. Our tongues caressed one another. He moaned slightly. I laughed and pulled away from him slowly.

"I'm so happy to see you. You have no idea how worried I was that you would be with...." He stopped there. I knew that he was going to say Pallo. He didn't have to tell me. I couldn't tell him how Pallo had betrayed me. Doing so would mean admitting that I'd made love to him.

"This lifetime is different, Caleb. I can't explain it, but it's different."

He looked at me, suspicious. "Are you telling me that you can remember...?" He didn't know what to call it. Hell, I didn't know what to call it.

"No, just a few things here and there. But I remember how I felt about you."

"And what's changed now?"

"This time around, I made the decision to be with you. No one promised me to you. It was my choice."

He let out a deep breath, pulled me close to him and held me tight. Propping his chin on top of my head, he wrapped his arms around me snugly. I pushed off his chest slightly, and took his hand in mine as I led him into the house. We made it as far as the living room before we were tearing at each other's clothes. I was on the floor with only my bra on, kissing Caleb, when I heard a car pulling up the stone driveway.

"Ken," I said, as I pushed Caleb off me and got to my feet. I scrambled around the living room to find the rest of my clothes.

"Can't you just ask him to leave?"

"Caleb!"

"Sorry." He looked so sweet and innocent, sitting on the floor with his long blond hair spilling down his bare chest. I was happy he still had his jeans on, because he was making no attempt to hide the fact that we had just been making out. I shot him a nasty look, and he jumped to his feet. "Okay, okay."

I ran and opened the door for Ken. He had his arms full of grocery bags. He smiled when I met him. We worked quietly in the kitchen together, making dinner. Attempts at small talk were made while we sat around the table eating. We finally decided on watching some television before we went to bed. That, thankfully, didn't require anyone to feel the need to make conversation. After two hours of wrestling, which both Ken and Caleb seemed all too willing to endure, was under our belt, I called it a night. I headed quietly upstairs to take a bath and go to bed.

I soaked in the tub for almost an hour. I had to add hot water to it twice, just to keep it warm enough to stand. I needed to relax. I decided it best to get out before I fell asleep and drowned. That would be my luck. I survive being attacked by trolls and hellhounds, but drown in a bathtub full of water. Yep, I wasn't taking any chances.

When I walked into my bedroom, I found Caleb standing there. His shirt was off and his jeans were unbuttoned. Ken came walking in behind me, carrying some extra blankets.

"What are you guys doing?" I watched Caleb pull his jeans off and throw them aside. He was nude, and didn't seem to notice or care. He walked over and climbed into my bed. Ken put the extra blankets on the floor and stripped down to his boxers. He walked over and climbed into my bed too. I just stood there. My bed at the farmhouse was only a queen size bed, and having two grown men in it filled it up.

I walked over and grabbed a long tee shirt out of my dresser and a pair of panties. Turning on my heels, I walked out of the room, and headed down the hall to the master bedroom. It was plain, with light tan wallpaper with little brown flowers on it. There were two old oak dressers in the room. The room had two closets, which was nice, but the best part of it was it had a king-sized bed in it. The large oak bed had a white and brown quilt on it. My mother had made it one summer while I was home from college. I pulled the cover back and climbed in.

My head had barely hit the pillow when Ken and Caleb came walking in. Caleb was still nude, and Ken was in his boxers. I gave them a dirty look. I didn't want to play choose one tonight.

I was tired.

"What do you two want?"

Caleb spoke first. "We've decided not to leave you alone." He looked at Ken. "We couldn't come to an agreement on who would stay with you, so here we are."

"Oh, now I get it. You're naked to try to deter Ken from wanting to sleep in the same bed as you." Ken was homophobic and I think Caleb had picked up on that. I got the feeling that the thought of being with other men didn't appeal to Caleb, but didn't repulse him either.

Caleb smiled. I was right--I knew it! "Shut off the lights." I couldn't believe I was okay with this. I knew that I should have sent them away, but I didn't want to. I wanted them both here with me. I wanted them wrapped around me, holding me tight all night.

"Come on," I said, pulling the covers back. Ken and Caleb looked at each other. I guess they'd expected me to fight with them over this. Hell, they probably had hoped I would pick who would get to join me. I bet they were shocked I had let them both in. Caleb slid into bed next to me on my left, and Ken laid on my right. Neither one touched me. They both turned their bodies away from me and lay very still. I could sense their anger for one another growing. They really had hoped I would end it.

"I can't do this," I said. It wasn't much, but it was all I could offer. Putting my hands up, I touched both of their bare shoulders. They were hot. They were upset. I concentrated on calming them down. I let my power flow up from deep inside of me. Caleb reacted to it first. I knew he would, it was the faerie in him. He turned his head slightly and looked at my hand, then my face. Ken turned next. I watched them both. Caleb's green eyes kept pulling me back. I knew at that moment that if I was forced to choose between the two, I would pick Caleb. I was drawn to him on every level, not just sexually. I was happy they weren't asking me to pick, at least not outright.

Not yet, anyway.

They both turned their bodies to me. I looked into Caleb's dark green eyes. I squeezed his arm slightly, and turned away from him to face Ken. Ken smiled, his brown eyes lit up. He thought that by me choosing to face him, my decision had been made. He won. Caleb knew better. He snuggled his naked body against the back of mine, spooning me, sliding his arm around my waist. I pulled Ken near me, our faces almost touching. I closed my eyes. It felt so good to be held by two people who love you. The only thing missing was Pallo. I couldn't believe I thought about him at a time like this. He'd betrayed me, and then lied about it to my face. Anger took hold of me and between that and the three of us huddled together the temperature rose. It became so hot and sticky in the bed that I couldn't breathe. I thought I was going to pass out when something broke through my anger. It was Caleb.

I tried to draw my power back into myself. I concentrated on pulling it inward. I visualized a tunnel and in it, a glowing and green light that receded into me, in my mind. Through the glowing purple and green light a figure came towards me. As it neared, I recognized the long, wavy, hair and strong body. Pallo! He was working out in his home gym. He had on a loose pair of dark gray pants and was barefoot. His muscles rippled as he took varied steps, twisting and turning his body slowly. He was doing some sort of martial arts. Sweat glistened from his white, pale body. I swept down next to him. My presence blew his hair back slightly. He stopped moving and turned to see what was near him. I let my hand run along his hard arms. He saw nothing, but felt much. Tipping his head back, he eyes his closed.

I thought about how much I cared about him, how much I loved him, how much what he had done had hurt me. His words beat in my ear like a drum. "I did not make love to that whore, I fucked her." Each time I heard that, I pulled my projected presence back from him. I rushed over the glowing purple and green light like it was a playground slide. I came crashing through the tunnel and into my body. Hands were running all over me. I didn't know whose they were. Two cupped my breasts, one touched my waist, and one was down the front of my panties caressing me gently. I arched my back. Caleb's naked body was still wrapped around mine. Ken's body was pressed against me from the front. He, too, was naked now. I reached down and cupped them both in my hands. They let out small moans. What should have been an awkward moment between three people felt beautiful--it felt right, natural.

Ken slid his thick fingers between my legs, working one into me gently. I was moist and ready. I reached around to Caleb's ass and pulled him towards me. He spread my cheeks tenderly, and rubbed the head of his cock against my backside. He nibbled at my neck, sending shivers down my spine, and caused even more moisture to collect in the apex of my thighs.

"Tell me to stop," Caleb whispered softly.

Ken began rubbing my clit with his thumb as he continued to work his finger in and out of me. His mouth captured mine and our tongues clashed, fighting for supremacy. The battle waged on as Caleb rocked against my ass, his erection rubbing hard against my cheeks. My inner thighs tightened as an orgasm tore through me. I moaned, and swayed against Caleb. No matter which way I moved, there was some form of stimulation, some form satisfaction.

"Uhh…," I panted, as Ken released his hold on my mouth. Our eyes met and my heart thumped madly in my chest. I reached down, took hold of him, stroking gently, moving up and down his shaft slowly.

"Gwen," he whispered, as his eyes fluttered. He moved his hand from my drenched folds, skimming it over my stomach until he found my breasts. Bending down, he captured one in his mouth and sucked.

"Ohh … uhh." I couldn't have formed a sentence if I tried. I felt so wanton, so free, so loved.

Caleb pushed on my shoulders, signaling for me to lean forward. With Ken still attached to my breast, I could only go so far. It was enough. He eased the head of his shaft into my quim. Extending the walls of it, he caused an involuntary spasm to seize hold of my channel.

"Caleb … mmm," I murmured, rocking my hips back towards him, taking him deeper within me. I moaned. Ken released my breast and stared up at me, a flash of jealously filtered through his eyes. I stroked him harder, faster, and moved to kiss him. My hand slid up and down on Ken, mirroring Caleb's thrusts. It was Ken's turn to moan.

Caleb went still, and pulled out slowly. I tried to hold onto him, but he withdrew himself from me.

"You didn't finish." I sat up with him. Ken followed too.

Caleb sat on his knees on the end of the bed. He was hard and glistening from my wetness. Our gazes locked and he knew that I wanted only him. I could see it in his eyes. Crawling to him on all fours, I took him into my mouth, savoring the taste of my own cream. I worked my mouth over him, taking him deep to the back of my throat. As I pulled off it, I nibbled on him, before taking him again.

"Mmm, Gwen … baby, you have to pace yourself." Caleb's voice was raspy. "We have eternity."

Ken moved in behind me, lifted my hips, and pressed gently against my slit. When he pushed in, I cried out with Caleb still in my mouth. The added sensation made Caleb moan, and throb in my mouth. I moved my head up and down on Caleb's cock as Ken pushed himself in and out of me slowly. Someone began making primitive animal sounds--it was me.

Caleb moved his fingers into my hair as I sucked him feverishly. He tasted salty, yet sweet. I never thought I'd want to spend hours sucking off a man before, but Caleb had made me crave it--crave him. He was an addiction.

Ken pulled out of me, so slowly. I grabbed at his leg. The feeling of Caleb tightening in my mouth took my attention from Ken. He pulled my hair back, gently bringing my head with it. Ken rammed into me, sending me spiraling to a zenith. My orgasm showed no mercy as it took control of my core, fisting Ken, making him come as well. He held tight to me, grunting as he released himself in me.

When Ken pulled out of me, I crawled up and put my body in front of Caleb's. He hadn't yet finished, and I wanted to please him most of all. I ran my fingers over his chest and down the front of torso. He drew in a sharp breath when I grabbed hold of his cock, meeting his gaze head on.

Ken reached around to my breasts, pressed his body against mine, and whispered, "I love you." He pulled away from me, and I felt the weight of his body leave the bed.

Stroking Caleb lazily, my eyes began to burn, to change. They got so warm beneath my eyelids that I thought they might burst into flames. I looked up into Caleb's eyes they were glowing green. I touched mine, and stared at him, wide eyed.

"Yes, yours are, too," he said softly, pulling me close to him.

"Why?"

"Because, you're ready."

Puzzled, I searched his face for answers.

Leaning forward, he kissed me gently. "Your body's ready to create life, Gwen. Your womb's ripe, and primed to accept me."

I froze. Ken had just finished in me. Did that mean? "But, Ken just…."

He shook his head slightly. "Ken loves you, you love him, but he's not a match for you."

"How do you know?"

"Your eyes changed after he was done, when you came to me, ready for me to enter you and fill you with my seed."

Caleb was right. My eyes had changed after Ken had gone. I guess it was good to have your own built-in warning flag for pregnancy, but I wasn't so sure about this. Hesitantly, I touched his hard chest with my hand. He grabbed my wrist and laid me on my back, while he planted tiny kisses all over my chest. I wanted more from him. I tried to coax him on, but he didn't waver.

He planted a chaste kiss on the top of my head. "Gwen, I've wanted to have this, more than you'll ever know, for over four hundred years. I've dreamed about seeing my child grow in you, but I can feel your love for Pallo, and I can't handle it. I love you too much to start a family that I've wanted for centuries, only to be forced to watch you go back to him."

"That will never happen!"

He put his finger to my lip. "Don't make promises that you can't keep."

I tried to protest. "But, you don't understand…."

"No, Gwen, you don't understand. The odds of a faerie finding a perfect match are stacked against us. Hell, the odds of finding a match, even one that's not a faerie, aren't ones you'd bet on. That's how our numbers stay in check. We're immortal, and if we had children all the time we'd overpopulate the world."

I thought about what he had just said. "It's possible to find a non-faerie match, too?" Then it was clear. Yes, it was. Pallo had been the father of my child, and he'd been mortal. Was it possible that I'd been lucky enough to find two perfect soul mates? Was Pallo the one from the past, and was Caleb the present? Did that mean that Pallo could still be a match as well? I remembered my eyes burning warmly in the yellow room with Pallo. Oh, God, he could.

I had so many questions for Caleb. Asking him would mean revealing that I'd been with Pallo while he was gone. I didn't feel like tackling that just yet.

I kissed his lips to mine, and he held me to him. Our naked bodies huddled together on the bed. The moment was right to continue, but the reality of what I'd just done sank in. I'd just had sex with two men at one time. A week ago, I hadn't been having sex with anyone, let alone two at one time. Sickened by my own lack of control, I pushed away from Caleb and ran to the bathroom. I crashed onto the floor in front of the toilet and vomited. I was ashamed of myself, I'd become what Pallo had accused me of being--a whore.

I flushed away the contents of my stomach, and turned to draw a bath. I adjusted the water to get just the right temperature, hot, and sat of the edge of the tub, listening to it fill. The light flicked on, and I knew that Caleb was there.

"Are you all right?" He'd put his jeans on. He walked towards me, then stopped. His gaze fell onto my neck. Giovanni's bite mark was no doubt bruised now. I lifted my hand to try to cover my neck. Caleb motioned me closer. I stood up, the cool bathroom floor felt good on my hot, bare feet. Walking over to the medicine cabinet, I pulled out the toothpaste and my toothbrush.

I saw Caleb's reflection in the mirror. He stood behind me, staring at my neck. Apparently, the bruising was worse from the backside, because his eyes grew wide.

"Gwen?" In that one word he asked so many questions.

I brushed my teeth frantically, like I needed to get every tooth at least six times. I mumbled that it was nothing through a mouthful of toothpaste. He wasn't buying it. He was definitely not in the "mood" anymore. His eyes shifted back to just green. I finished brushing my teeth and turned to shut the bath water off. He caught hold of my arms.

"Its nothing, really, I'm fine." I tried to convince him as well as me. I don't think it worked. I attempted to free myself from him, but he squeezed me tighter. "Caleb, you're hurting me."

"Looks like somebody already did that. What the hell happened while I was gone?" He held to me tight. I saw something in his face I'd never seen before, rage.

"Can I please get in the tub?"

Caleb let go of my arms. I walked around him and got in the tub. I was careful to avoid looking at him. I didn't want to see the anger in his face. He turned and stormed out, slamming the door behind him. I was thankful. I didn't want to talk about what had happened since he disappeared.

What was I supposed to say, "After you left, my dead mother whisked Pallo and I off to a romantic location. Once there, I found out about having lived before, freaked out, and ran straight into the arms of a homicidal maniac, Talia. She tried to have her pets rip me to shreds. I ended up leaving there a murderer. But hey, after we got home, I went out partying and managed to squeeze in a little bit of orgasmic dancing and neck-nibbling with an old boyfriend on the dance floor. Gee, wait, it only gets better. I left there and made love to Pallo. Turns out, he was just fucking me though, so don't sweat that one. I was lucky enough to bump into the crazy lady one more time before returning to Pallo's, where I willingly let Giovanni bite me again. That's how I got the bruises. But hey, Pallo's free, right? Oh, I even managed to bump into my long lost father, the King. At least something good came out of it. Right?"

Yeah, somehow I don't think he'd really want to know what went on. Rather than focus on it all, I opted to get dressed.

Chapter 25

I walked into the kitchen and saw breakfast sitting on the table. Caleb was the only one there. I hadn't passed Ken on the way down. I wondered where he was. Caleb turned and looked at me. He answered before I could even ask.

"Ken left a few minutes ago," he said dryly.

I pulled a chair out to sit down. "He left? Why?"

Caleb sat in the end chair and put his elbows on the table, propping his chin up with his large hands. He looked so stunning in the light from the rising sun. It came in the kitchen door window and illuminated him.

"He said he had to think about some things. Can you blame him?" His tone was different, annoyed. He stared at me, and there was no love in his eyes. I picked up one of the pancakes, and put it on my plate. I tried to ignore him staring at me. His energy prickled up my arm, as he used his power on me.

"What?" I asked, still concentrating hard on my food.

"Ken told me everything."

I stopped chewing and tried to swallow. You never really know how dry a pancake can seem until you are in a stressful situation. I picked up a glass of water from the table, and tried to help it slide down. Finally, I looked at Caleb. His normally soft face was drawn and tight.

"What do you want me to say? What will make it all right?"

He sighed as he tipped his head slightly. "I want you to deny it. I want you to tell me that Ken's a liar."

The prickling on my arm increased. I wanted to reach down and scratch it, I didn't. I looked into Caleb's dark, forest green eyes. Ken wouldn't lie to him. Ken had many faults, but lying wasn't one of them. I learned that after meeting Talia, he'd been telling me the truth all along. He didn't know her and he couldn't help himself. No, I knew that Ken had told Caleb the absolute truth. What I didn't know was how much Ken let him in on, everything or just part of it?

"Ken's not a liar." I fixed my gaze on my glass of water. I couldn't look at Caleb, I couldn't see the hurt and anger in his eyes.

Caleb slammed his fist down onto the table and water leapt out of my glass. I jumped slightly. Caleb rose to his feet. He kicked the chair back against the refrigerator and stormed into the hallway.

"Caleb," I said softly. He stopped, but didn't turn around. "Caleb, please." He stood very still. "I'm sorry."

Bending his head down, he took a deep breath, before headed upstairs. I wasn't sure what he'd done. I had a feeling he'd packed his bags to leave. I'd managed to be fooled by Pallo, left by Ken, and now Caleb. If I blinked, someone else would be gone too. With the way I'd been behaving, I wished I could get away from myself.

I headed towards the stairs, and heard his footsteps coming down them. Caleb had on his boots and a black tee shirt. He had something in his hand--his crossbow. I grabbed the railing.

"Caleb?" I put my hand up to try to slow him down. He moved quickly, just missing knocking me backwards. "Caleb, what are you doing?"

He stood before the door, his back to me. "I'm going to kill him," he said and pulled the door open.

I couldn't get myself to let go of the railing. He was going to kill him? Oh my God, he was going to kill Pallo! I bolted out of the door and found him getting into his truck.

"Caleb … no!" I screamed, running to block him from closing the truck door.

"Don't try to protect him." He tried to ease me out of the doorway. I didn't budge. I would not let the two of them kill each other. Caleb's power flowed like needles over my arms. I tried to rub it away, it did no good.

"No, stay, we can fix this, please, I know we can. Caleb."

Suddenly, wind rushed at me, lifting my hair, pushing Caleb's power away, and enveloping me. Caleb stopped trying to push me away from the vehicle, and started trying to pull me into it.

"No!" He lifted his hand towards me, the wind lashed out at

Mandy M. Roth

him. His arm ripped open.

"*Bella!*" the wind whispered to me. My feet rose from the ground, higher and higher. I tipped my head back. Something tugged on my waist. I looked down. Caleb had wrapped his arms around me tightly. He shouted at me, but I couldn't hear what he was saying.

"Come, *bella*," the wind spoke to me again, so soft, so smooth, so Giovanni's voice. Giovanni!

Snapping my head up, I looked around. I was levitating in the air, three feet off the ground. Caleb fought to keep hold of me, yelling at me to fight it. I did the only thing I could think to do. I screamed.

The wind that had felt so gentle yanked at my hair and my arms. I tried to reach my hands down to grab Caleb, but the pressure was too strong. Something yanked my body up. I kept screaming. My waist slid up and out of Caleb's arms. He tried to hold on to my legs, but it was no use. He would have to let me go or risk tearing me in half. He let go. My body lifted higher into the air. Air wrapped itself around me tighter and tighter, making breathing difficult. I closed my eyes.

Something struck me from behind, crashing onto my back, sending me flying toward the ground. Caleb, with cat-like reflexes, broke my fall. I landed on him, and whatever hit me landed on me. The wind stopped. I no longer heard Giovanni's call to me.

Whatever hit me lifted itself slowly off my back. I rolled over. Caleb and I looked up. We spoke at the same time.

"Kerrigan?"

We were lying on our backs in the grass, staring up at Kerrigan. He was in his normal black dress robes. He had a red sash tied around his waist, similar to the one Caleb had come home wearing. His hair was loose and hung down to his waist, and he looked a little out of breath. Good to know, I was beginning to think he was a superhero.

He reached out and pulled us to our feet.

"My King, thank you, we are honored that you assisted us," Caleb said, bending down on one knee. I looked at him like he was nuts, then faced Kerrigan. He nodded and winked at me. I shrugged and bent down next to Caleb.

"Thanks, oh honorable one, who is the King … yeah, thanks," I muttered.

Hey! It's not like I was used to worshipping someone other

than rock stars and the inventor of chocolate.

Caleb snickered and covered his mouth. I laughed and fell back onto the ground. It felt good to smile and be happy.

Kerrigan coughed. I stopped laughing and let Caleb pull me to my feet. "Come, I need to pay my head counselor a visit," Kerrigan said, walking down the lane.

I looked at Caleb, he looked at Kerrigan. Fabulous, none us knew what was going on. "My King, surely you can't mean you are going back to the Dark Realm now, after all of these years?"

"Stop, Caleb. You have known me all of your life, please call me Kerrigan. As for the Court, it appears that my presence there is much needed. Would you agree?"

Caleb nodded and we followed him. Midway down the lane he veered off the path and into the woods. We headed down the slope towards the river. If Caleb hadn't held tight to my arm, I would have tumbled all the way down the thing. I watched Kerrigan walk right out and onto the river. He walked on it, not in it. I looked at Caleb. He smiled and followed after him, holding tight to my hand. I stepped onto the river. It seemed to be made of glass. My feet stayed completely dry. I concentrated so hard on my feet that when a rush of air passed me I looked up to see us standing in a dark cavern. I could tell that we were no longer standing near the river, at least as I knew it. I watched Caleb and my father duck down to avoid hitting their heads on the top of the cave. I didn't have that problem. I could stand on my tiptoes and touch nothing.

I followed behind them, still holding Caleb's hand. The cave was damp and smelled musty. I used my free hand to steady myself. Slime stuck to my fingers, and I yanked my hand away. I let out a small gasp. It echoed in the cave. Caleb turned around and looked at me as I tried to get the slimy goop off of my hand. He smiled and took my hand and wiped it on his shirt. He bent down and kissed my cheek. I immediately looked to my father. He was still walking ahead of us, but he had his head turned towards us, he smiled. Sex was not shameful in the faerie community. I'd never learned their ways. I wasn't really one of them. I'd never been raised with them. I felt like I should hide my feelings for Caleb in front of my father, but he seemed pleased.

"Caleb, when you were with me you never mentioned if the two of you received the gift I sent," Kerrigan said. He tried to speak softly because his voice was so low it would have shaken our eardrums if he used his normal voice.

Caleb looked at me, and I shrugged. "I'm sorry, Your Maj--Kerrigan, I'm not sure what gift you mean."

"The fruit, of course," Kerrigan said.

Caleb and I both stopped walking. He'd been the one who put the platter of fruit in the garden. When I had awakened after being bitten by the troll, I'd eaten one of the pears. It had contained a lust spell. Did my father put that on the fruit? I looked up at him walking. His broad shoulders were hunched to avoid hitting his head. His long hair hung down his back. Could he really have done that? He was King of the Underworld, King of the Dark Realm. I was surprised he was as nice as he was. Did I really know anything about him?

"Why the hell did you put a spell on it?" I didn't hide the fact that I was mad.

Caleb clutched my hand. He leaned over and whispered something about him being the king. I didn't care who the hell he was, he had no business in my love life.

Kerrigan turned around slowly, looking very intimidating, and arched an eyebrow. "And if I did?"

I walked up to him and put my finger in his chest. "It's none of your business who I choose to share my bed with, are we clear?" I wasn't really asking, I demanded.

Caleb pulled me back towards him. "I'm sorry, Kerrigan. What she means to say is thank you for trusting that we were meant to be together again. She was brought up by humans, she doesn't know any better."

I turned and glared at him. How dare he try and speak for me? How dare he think he could smooth this over with a little butt kissing? His eyes pleaded with me. He begged me to let it go. I ignored him. "Well, I think the good King here is well aware of the fact that I was not raised by faeries, and I think he is well aware of the fact that I am not happy with him right now!"

Kerrigan smiled. "Caleb, I do not envy you. No, I do not." He laughed so hard as he said it that I thought he might cry. He turned the corner and I saw the exit.

Caleb grabbed my arm and pulled me close. "Please, Gwen, he's powerful. He could kill you without even laying a finger on you. Please, don't make him angry."

I had to smile. "When you said Ken told you everything, what did you mean?" I asked, as we walked out of the cave behind Kerrigan.

Caleb gave me a look that said he didn't want to be talking about this right now. Oh well, he was going to have to. "He told me about the hellhounds, and Giovanni." He looked down. "He told me about you freeing Pallo."

So, Ken didn't mention that I had slept with Pallo, or that I had found out who my real father was. I smiled. Caleb had no idea that Kerrigan was my father. God, he probably thought I was the stupidest girl in the world to speak to a King that way. Ha! I loved it!

"What part of what happened to you was amusing?"

"No, it's not that. It's just that…." I began to tell him that Kerrigan was my father, when Kerrigan called to us.

We had walked out into an open, grassy field. The right side of it was lined with brush and trees. Kerrigan walked up to a massive mound of ivy and reached out his hand. It separated into two equal halves. It was beautiful. I followed the two of them in. We stepped through and into a large city. It looked like every other city I had ever seen, right up until I turned and saw the people walking around here. Well, I think the term 'people' would apply. Many faeries walked about. Most had on long robes, similar to the one that my father wore. The colors varied, but it was clear that black was favored. Almost everyone was armed in some fashion, with swords, guns, knives. It didn't seem to bother anyone. They walked about on the sidewalks like it was perfectly normal to be armed and, I presumed, dangerous.

A nagging feeling began in my gut. I couldn't quite identify what, but I knew something wasn't right. I looked at Caleb. His tall, slender, beautiful profile confirmed that he was fine. I looked to my father, who walked just a few paces ahead of us-- he, too, looked fine. My thoughts went to Ken. Had he made it home okay? I let this play about in my mind, then let it go. No, I knew in my heart that he was fine, too. It hit me then. Pallo! Something was wrong with Pallo. Giovanni was behind it, I knew it. I stepped up my pace. I needed to get back home quickly.

We walked down the center of the street. This place was dimly lit. It was a cross between night and day, it was dusk. I wondered if it was always this way here. After all, the Dark Realm was called the Darkness. As we walked, I looked down between the tall buildings, and the alleys were full of strange looking creatures. One had at least fifty eyeballs plastered all over its purplish head. I think it looked at me, too, although I couldn't be sure. I think it looked at everyone. A man walked a ghoul. He had it on a chain--that was something you didn't see everyday. I had always wondered where creatures from nightmares lived. I knew that only a few lived among the humans. They feared the creatures too much and were not tolerant of them. Many of the creatures from the Darkness court were harmless. Some were a little dangerous, and others were downright lethal.

I could see a large building up ahead of us. It looked like a cross between a stone castle and a church. I highly doubted anyone in here sought religion. As we came closer to it, I saw the stained glass windows didn't hold images of the Christian church. They held images of the creatures of the night--sinister things that no one ever wants to think exist. One picture was of a werewolf in mid-transformation. My body had chills running through it. Was I really part of this world? How could my father be King? He seemed so nice.

I watched him start upstairs to the large, gray, church-like building. Two goblins stood guard at the door. One was about a foot taller than the other. It had a snout that looked similar to an alligator and the rest of its face looked like it was a boar. Tusks poked from the edges of its mouth. Its skin was pasty gray. It was hideously wonderful, in its long red robe with a gold sash. The other goblin looked a little less overwhelming. It, too, was a grayish color, but lacked the tusks. Its nose was nonexistent, only two large openings were on its face. That made it appear more pig-like than the other. He looked at us as we approached.

"Halt!" he shouted. I had to laugh. "No one may enter without an appointment."

The Queen of the Dark had appointments? Did she have a secretary, too? He looked at my father, then at Caleb, and a look of shock came over his eyes.

"My Lords," he hissed.

Lords? Whoa, did I travel in good company or what? He moved and opened the large black wood door for us.

"Thank you, Deaglan." Kerrigan said. The goblin dropped to his knees before my father's feet. My father reached his hand down and told Deaglan to rise. He did.

I just stood there, watching the entire thing in awe.

"Where is she?" my father asked Deaglan.

He looked at him with wide eyes. "She is in her chamber, she is…." He fell silent.

My father smiled. "She is entertaining, isn't she?"

Deaglan nodded and avoided looking my father in the eye. I wasn't sure what he meant by entertaining, but I assumed that it was not good. Caleb walked out and stood near my father.

"I will get her," he said, and walked towards an enormously wide staircase. The stairs were covered in red carpet, the stone beneath was painted black. I looked around. We were standing in a huge room, which for the most part was bare. A few paintings hung on the black walls. They looked to be of past Kings and Queens. I looked at them. One thing they all had in common was that in each picture, one person looked like me. No, not exactly like me, but close. I could tell I was related to them in some fashion. The long hair that curled on the ends, the shimmering skin, a mix between bronze and cream, and the dark navy blue eyes. I knew none of the faces.

"Caleb, you go and change. She will not be pleased to see you in those," he said, pointing to Caleb's jeans. "I will go and get her. Gwyneth, you stay here. Deaglan will look after you," Kerrigan said, and walked briskly upstairs.

Caleb turned and looked in my direction. "Deaglan, let nothing happen to her, understand me?"

"Yes, my Lord, I will look after the lady."

Caleb took off down a long hall to our right and disappeared. Deaglan turned and looked at me. He looked as though he were seeing a ghost. I'd been getting that a lot, so I had become immune to it.

"Pardon me, miss," he said softly, with only a slight lisp.

I looked at him, eyes wide. "Yes?"

"Is it really you, Miss Gwyneth?" he asked, coming closer to me. He lifted his hand out to touch my face. He had a thumb and that was all. Where the other four fingers would have been was one fused-together lump. I stood still, and tried my best not to jerk away as he touched me. I assumed he would feel like a pig. I was wrong, he felt like a frog. His skin was cool, clammy, and smooth.

His huge yellow eyes lit up. "It is you, Miss Gwyneth, it is! But how?"

"I'm sorry, Deaglan, I can't explain it."

He nodded and stopped touching my cheek. I wondered if he had known me well before. I thought about asking him, but it seemed a bit insulting to not remember if you knew someone or not. I stood there with him a few minutes, then someone called my name. It sounded like Pallo.

Pallo? What could he be doing here? I knew the guy was a Master Vampire, but he didn't seem the type to hang out in dark, creepy places like this. He called me again. This time he sounded like he asked for my help. I had been right. There had been something wrong with him. I looked at Deaglan. If he heard this, he wasn't letting on. He just stood there staring at me. I heard it again.

I turned around and stopped to listen. Nothing. I closed my eyes. Was I imagining him? I hated him, right? Why would I imagine hearing his voice call to me? I thought about him--his big brown eyes, his wonderful, pale skin, and how broad his shoulders were. I thought about his touch--how loving and gentle it had been before he turned on me. I tried to pull an image of him in my head. I kept seeing him against a stone wall. He wasn't wearing a shirt, but what else was new? I blew my energy at him. He didn't move. I let my mind focus and pull back from him a little. He wasn't standing against the wall. He was chained to it!

Chapter 26

Deaglan yelled for me to return. I ignored him. I tried to reach Pallo with my thoughts. I tried to make him hear me, but could get nothing. I ran my hand over the wall where I sensed him. I could see through it now. Pallo's slumped body hung on the wall on the other side of the room. I pushed on the wall. It was solid. Still, I felt his presence near me. He was behind that wall, I was sure of it. I stood before it and drew upon my power with all of my might. My fingers prickled, and the sensation of heat rose slowly up my arms. Placing the palms of my hands on the stone wall, I released my power. The wall disappeared. I ran into the room and saw Pallo's body chained to the wall.

"Pallo!"

He didn't move. I lifted his hair from his face. There was no sign of life in him. I pulled on the chains binding him, but they didn't move. I yanked on them until my fingers bled. My blood made the iron slippery, it was hopeless. I turned to run to get Caleb's help, but the spot were I had entered was closed. I was drained, I could not open it again this soon. I looked back at

Pallo. I lifted his face in my hands and cupped his chin.

"Don't you dare die on me! If you do, I swear that I'll kill you!" Hey, when you're under pressure, you say stupid things.

I held his chin tight, leaned up and gave him a kiss on the lips. They were ice cold and blue. He was dead--deader than his usual. I let his chin slide slowly out of my hand, and accidentally smeared blood all over his chin.

"Blood," I said aloud.

I took my fingers and pushed them into his cold mouth, it was hard to pry open, but I did. I put them in as far as I could get them. Pallo had once told me that he only needed a small amount of my blood to sustain him. I planned on giving him a hell of a lot more than that. I took my fingers out of his mouth, and put the palm of my hand near the pin in the chain holding one of his arms to the wall. I pulled my palm across it slowly, firmly. My skin ripped open. Gasping, I pulled my hand back and looked at it.

Yep, I had torn it open.

Blood came pouring out of it. I cupped my hand, letting the blood collect, and pulled Pallo's mouth open. I poured my blood into his mouth and concentrated on thinking about how much I cared for him. The fact that he had betrayed me was pushed into the far recesses of my mind. I let him see how I had viewed our night of lovemaking, how I had savored every moment, even if he didn't.

A memory flooded into my head. It was of the two of us. We were making love in the same yellow bedroom, but this was not recent, this was long ago. We were sitting up on the bed facing each other. I had my legs wrapped around his waist. He kissed my breasts with sweet, soft kisses. I tipped my head back. I could feel him inside of me, as I watched the memory in my head. My eyes burned. I saw in my head that they were ablaze with lavender. He and I had been a match. He was human, but it didn't matter, he was a match, a soul mate. I felt him coming in me as I watched it. I knew that he'd just planted his seed in me. I knew that I was with his child in the memory. I knew then as well, but I didn't tell him. I wanted to surprise him. He would be so happy to be a father. I knew that I needed to get away from Giovanni first, and I knew just who I had to see about that. The memory pulled away from me. Something moved by my hand.

I opened my eyes and looked at Pallo. His color was back, as much as it ever would be. He licked my hand and placed tiny kisses on it. The wound closed. He looked at me with eyes of brown that stole my heart. I touched his face lightly, and he kissed my hand.

"The baby was mine," he said softly.

Had he shared my vision with me? "Pallo, I wanted to surprise you, I…." I couldn't remember any more than that.

"No, it is not your fault. I just never knew if it was mine or if it was…." He didn't say a name.

"Caleb's." I didn't know what else to say. I couldn't be held responsible for decisions I made in another lifetime, and Pallo knew that. I had to focus on the now, and that meant freeing him.

I reached up to pull on his chain again. Something growled behind me and Pallo yelled my name. I jumped to the side so I stood directly in front of his body. A hellhound crashed into the stone wall, right where I had been standing. There was another growl from behind me. The one on the floor stood up. I kicked it hard, and it flipped over and whimpered. I turned around quickly and crouched down, putting my hands into the air. A flash of dark brown and then its belly flew at me. I pushed up under it and propelled it up and over me. It just missed hitting Pallo by about two inches. Its back claw caught the back of my shoulder and tore it open. I winced, but didn't stop turning in a crouched down position. I was sick of these little bastard mutant-puppies. I was tired of taking their shit. Another one came at me, but it was too late. It knocked me to the ground. I kept my legs tucked tightly against my chest and thrust them out. It flew off me. Putting my hands on the ground above my head, I pushed up quickly--being a cheerleader in high school will keep you limber. I was silently thanking my adoptive mother for insisting I take gymnastics as a child, and for pushing me to be peppy.

I turned and looked at Pallo, who seemed very impressed. Walking over to him, I tried to loosen his chains some more. My face was so close to his, I could feel his breath on my skin. It smelled sweet and wonderful. I couldn't resist the temptation to kiss him. I stood on my tiptoes and placed a tiny kiss on his lips. He pulled his head back from me fast. I spun around in time to throw my leg up, extending my foot sideways. The chunky sole of my brown sandal hit a hellhound, half in human form, right in the chest. It staggered backwards, taking me with it. I fell to the floor, my ankle twisted and popped. I screamed out in pain. Pallo yelled for me and pulled at his chains. I tried to turn to stand, but a sharp pain went through my leg. It was the same damn ankle the troll had gotten. If this kept up, I'd need a cane.

Pallo screamed at me to move. I couldn't. Something hard and sharp kicked me dead in the center of my back.

"You just keep coming back. You are like a stray dog. Once it gets a taste of something good to eat, it keeps returning."

I turned my head to see the source of the voice. I saw a head of blonde hair that was sleek, straight, and long. It was attached to a tall woman who was at least six foot three inches tall. She wore a long, see-through black dress that had black beadwork on it. It would have looked elegant if it wasn't sheer. Her sleeves were long and hung almost to the ground. I could make out black spiked heels under her gown. I thought that's what she'd hit me with until I saw her raise her hand and send power flying out at me. In an instant, I felt like I'd been kicked in the side--again. It sent me sliding across the floor, crying out.

I didn't know who she was, but it was pretty obvious she knew me, and she didn't like me one bit. She put her hand out again. I braced myself for it, but it didn't come. Instead, it was Pallo who cried out.

I would not let him take her force.

"Bitch!" I called out.

She turned and looked at me, her dark green eyes ablaze. "I have searched for you for many years. I didn't believe the rumors, but I see now that they were true." Her face was soft, yet her voice was hard. She was a stunningly beautiful woman on the outside. I got the feeling she was anything but that on the inside.

Gee, wonder what gave me that idea?

She made no attempt to move any closer to me. She raised her hand towards the wall and it opened. Giovanni walked through it, dressed all in black. He walked up to her and put his arm around her waist. She let him pull her close, their faces met, and they kissed each other with a hot passion. Pulling away slowly, he stepped back.

"I think the child is afraid of us, Giovanni," she said, looking at me. "She was not too afraid of me to come seeking mortality so she could marry the mortal man she loved."

She was the Queen, Sorcha. At least I finally knew who I was dealing with. It didn't really help me any, it only confirmed the fact that I was screwed. I looked at Pallo. Kerrigan had told me that Sorcha had gone behind his back and granted my wish. Pallo had never mentioned this to me, so I assumed he'd just

Mandy M. Roth

heard it for the first time. He looked at me with questioning eyes. I nodded "'yes." He closed his eyes as if in pain.

"You have no right to be here. Your immortality belongs to me, and I will have it back." She turned and looked at Giovanni. "Would you like to do the honors? You did enjoy them so the last time, did you not?"

The last time? I remembered the vision of me being chained to a wall surrounded by vampires. I couldn't make out the face of the one with the long hair, the one in charge. It had been him. He'd been the one to organize the feeding. I scrambled back on the floor, determined to put as much distance between us as possible. I came to Pallo's feet and could go no further. I glanced up at him, chained to the wall. The same wall I'd been chained to in my memory. I pushed myself up and got to my knees.

Giovanni walked towards me. "It hardly seems as fun, now that she's no longer mortal."

How could he be helping her? He saved my life. He promised me. A thought came to my head.

"Giovanni," I said softly. He stared at me with black eyes. They were haunting yet alluring. "Giovanni, you made me a promise." I motioned to Pallo.

Sorcha stepped forward. "What is the whore going on about now?"

"She is correct, my Queen, I did make her a promise." He gave me a wry smile. "I promised that Pallo would not be killed."

The Queen threw her head back, sending blonde hair flying all around her as she laughed. "Oh, Giovanni, I warned you not to touch her. I told you that something was different about her, something powerful lurked beneath the surface." She turned and looked at me. "You are quite a piece of work. You managed to save a life before it was in jeopardy." She looked at Giovanni again. "Kill her, have all the fun you want with her. I know you and so many others enjoyed her the last time around. It's a shame I found about it all after the fact."

Pallo snarled. I looked up at him. His face had changed, twisted. He looked demonic again--evil. His black eyes were fixed firmly on Giovanni. I could sense how badly he wanted to kill him.

Reaching my hand up, I touched Pallo's leg gently. I used his leg to help me stand. I hobbled on my left foot, trying to avoid bearing weight on the right one. I looked at him. He looked like a monster. The Pallo I had known was not there, he was hidden beneath the surface. I could sense him there. I leaned forward and put my lips on his cheek. He snarled and turned his face quickly. At first, I thought he'd rip my head off with his mouth, then I realized he was going to kiss me. I put my mouth on his. His fangs pressed against my lips. I put my hand around to the back of his head and pushed my mouth onto his harder. I felt his face softening. I looked at him. He was back.

"As entertaining as this is, I am done toying with you." Sorcha tossed her hand in the air. "Giovanni, kill her!"

Giovanni whipped his head around and stared at Sorcha. I couldn't read his face. "My Queen, you said...."

"I know what I said. Now kill her!"

"But, you said that I was to scare her away from here--I agreed to do it because you promised no harm would come to her...you swore."

Sorcha threw her hand at him and sent him flying backwards. I felt a little bad for the guy. He stuck up for me, but let's face it, he deserved that. Sorcha walked towards me.

"Mother!" Caleb shouted, appearing in the room. I didn't see him come in and I didn't care how he got there. All I cared about was the fact that he just called that bitch Mom.

"Caleb," she said and walked to him. "Oh, my precious Caleb. I have missed you so." She turned and looked at me. "It is because of her that you left. It is because of her that you have not returned here in over two hundred years." She lashed her power out at me. I fell back into Pallo's body hard, and slid to the floor.

Caleb made a move to come to me. She lashed out at him and knocked him to his knees. He looked up at her stunned. "Mother, why do you hate Gwen so much?"

"She was and will always be a whore. She was not faithful to you. You loved her and she hurt you. Getting pregnant by a human boy." She looked at Pallo and laughed. "Or should I say, what used to be a human boy. She was to marry you, yet she fucked so many other men. I have never in my life met anyone...."

"Quite like yourself," Caleb said, standing up slowly.

Sorcha walked to him and put her hand on his face. "My son, I am a Queen. I cannot control my desires. A hundred men could not satisfy me. It has always been the way." She stroked his cheek. He fought not to pull away. Did he really hate his own mother that much? "She is not of Noble blood. She is just a common faerie whore."

"Mother! I love her, and I won't allow you to speak of her this way."

She laughed from the gut now. She carried a tone of pure evil, and it left me shuddering. "She does not love you my son, she loves that beast behind her." She pointed at Pallo.

I could have denied that I had feelings for Pallo. I could have looked into Caleb's eyes of green, and swore that I would only ever love him, but I couldn't bring myself to do this. It would be a lie.

"I know," Caleb said softly. "But Mother, she loves me as well. I know this."

Sorcha glared at me and lashed out again. I screamed out in pain as what felt like a lead weight crashed into my head. My ears were ringing for a minute. I had to blink to be able to focus. "Whores are not for loving, Caleb, they are for fucking. This seems to escape you."

"Yeah, so I've heard," I said, dryly. I couldn't help but look up at Pallo chained to the wall when I said this.

"Silence!" Sorcha screamed at me. Another blast of her power hit me in the back of the head again. The pain was so great I could not even scream out. I just lay there, letting my eyes roll back in my head. My jaw had tightened and I opened my mouth involuntarily. I could feel Sorcha's power building up around me. Pallo's rage spilled over my body. He hated her, and she fed off that hate. I tried to reach out to him, but my hands went to my head instead. I clutched it, hoping to ease the pressure. Sorcha's sinister laugh filled the room again.

"Mother, no!" Caleb ran to my side and lifted my head slowly into his lap. His power encompassed me. He protected me from his own mother. She had already struck him down once. Helping me could cost him his life. He held me gently in his hands. He bent down over me, kissing my head. I could no longer see Sorcha behind him, which was fine by me. He looked down at me and closed his eyes. He exhaled slowly. He held my hand tightly and spoke to her again. "If you kill her, you will destroy the one chance I have at happiness. You will kill my chance at having a child of my own."

"What is this?"

"She responded to me. We are a match," he said, holding my hand.

"This was not always so. What has changed?"

He shook his head. "I don't know, Mother. I just know that I love her, and that together we could produce a child."

"You are a fool, Caleb. You have fallen for a whore. The elders will never allow her to sit next to you on the throne. You are a Prince. You must mate with someone of royal blood. She is just a nobody little whore, she is…."

"She is my daughter." Kerrigan's loud voice filled the room. "And I am sure that the elders will find that to be acceptable."

"Daddy!" I cried out his name as if I were a child. I was so happy to hear him I didn't care how ridiculous I sounded.

Caleb and Pallo looked down at me. They were both wearing the same look of shock on their faces. I tried to smile, but my head hurt too much.

"No! You are not to be here, you left! I thought you had died," Sorcha said.

"No, you hoped I had died, Sorcha. Let us not pretend. You have no love for me."

"That is not true, I have much lo … I have much lo--" God, she couldn't even get the words out. She must really hate my father. "Kerrigan, you cannot be serious about the girl being yours. I didn't think you could father children."

Caleb's body tightened. I tried to imagine what it must have been like, growing up with a sociopath for a mother. I couldn't. My human mother, the one who raised me, had been kind, she'd been wonderful.

"I have always been able to sire children. I was just extremely careful with whom I chose to do so. I took you as my head counselor because of my fondness for your son. Caleb will make a good King someday, I have always known this. You were part of the package. I had to take you to get him," he said. She gasped. She really did think highly of herself. "I am still the King here, and I will not tolerate you harming my daughter. Leave her be or I will destroy you."

"I am ruler now. You have no power here, Kerrigan. You cannot walk in after almost thirty years and reclaim your throne. It will not be that easy!" she screamed at my father.

"Really?" he asked, and looked hard at her. Her green eyes grew wide as she gripped her throat. He choked her without even touching her. She pulled at her beautiful white neck, eyes widened in terror, and looked to Caleb.

"Kerrigan, please," Caleb said softly.

Kerrigan stopped choking her and looked at Caleb. "I allow her to live because of your love for my daughter and my fondness for you. That is the only reason."

Caleb nodded. He wasn't going to press the issue with him. My father turned his attention to Pallo.

"You, Pallo…do you love my daughter as well?"

Pallo's face turned up. "Yes." I would have thought he would've had more to offer on the matter.

"Is it true that you were to be father to my grandchild?" Kerrigan sized Pallo up, with an intimidating look on his face.

Pallo fought back tears. "Yes, but they…."

My father raised his hand in the air, motioning for Pallo not to speak. He didn't want to hear that his own pregnant daughter had been killed. He didn't want to hear all the gory details of me being tortured and fed to crazy vampires. He walked towards me. Caleb slid aside for him. He bent down and kissed my head. The pain stopped instantly. My vision cleared. He'd taken my pain away, just as he'd done for me when I was hit by the drunk driver as a child. He really was going to be a father to me this time around, and he had proven it by taking a twenty-five year hiatus to oversee my needs. I couldn't stop my tears from flowing.

"Do not cry, my little princess. Do not cry. I will not allow anything to happen to you again. I have two able and willing protectors for you now, as well," he said, looking at Caleb and Pallo.

Kerrigan looked at Pallo's chains. They broke loose. He fell from the wall and almost on top of me. He looked at me and smiled. Caleb looked down at me as well.

"I should have known you two were related, you have his stubborn streak," Caleb said, and looked up at my father. My father smiled at him.

"Do I have your word that the two of you will keep her safe? That you will protect her with your own lives, if need be?"

Caleb spoke first. "I would have given my life for her, even without her being your daughter. I love her."

"Yes, as would I," Pallo said.

"Then go! I have work to attend to here." He looked to Sorcha, who backed into the corner.

"Are you going to kill her?" Caleb asked quietly. I could see the pain in his eyes. Sorcha was an evil woman, but she was still his mother.

My father reached out and touched Caleb, laughing softly. "No, I think I shall rather enjoy her having to squirm at my side for all eternity."

Caleb smiled and nodded at him, the tension eased from his body. He bent down and scooped me up in his arms. Pallo walked close by our side. I turned and looked in the corner of the room where Giovanni had been. There was nothing.

"Giovanni?" I asked, scanning the room for him.

"He disappeared before Caleb came in," Pallo said. "He knew that if Caleb was to see him, he would surely die."

Caleb nodded. "Yeah, I went looking for him earlier. I had every intention of killing him."

Caleb hadn't been going to kill Pallo, after all. He'd been going after Giovanni. I wasn't sure how I felt about that. "I thought you were going after Pallo."

Caleb laughed. "Now I understand why you were fighting with me."

We all laughed as we walked out.

Epilogue

I did try to return to my apartment. It was destroyed. I had to give it up. It was for the best, though. I've been staying at the farmhouse until I can find a new place in the city. It was hard, at first, commuting back and forth for work. Ken solved my problem by suggesting I try telecommunication. It worked out great--except for the fact neither Caleb nor Pallo knew anything about computers or fax machines, so getting their help hooking stuff up was out of the question. Things are different with Ken and me now. He distanced himself from me. He's dating someone else now. I think her name is Beth. She was the realtor that had helped Ken and I house hunt. She seems nice. I have to admit that I'm a little jealous of her. I still love Ken.

Caleb moved into the farmhouse with me. We are getting along well. He's quite the little handyman. He has made it his mission to fix the place up. It's funny to think about having a Prince working on your plumbing, but he seems to be enjoying himself. He cut his hours back, now he only hunts things down a few days a week. While he's gone, he makes someone stay with me. Usually it's either James or Caradoc. They like to come up and spend time with me. We rent movies and hang out. They are like two of my girlfriends now. I rarely see Pallo. He stays away from me as much as he can. I'm okay with that right now. I don't trust my feelings for him--hell, I'm not even sure if I trust him.

I haven't heard anything of Giovanni's whereabouts as of yet. I know that I haven't seen the last of him. I'm not sure how I feel about that. Part of me cared for him once, and I don't know if he destroyed that or not.

As for my father, he has regained his throne. I had no doubt that he would. He's managed to force Sorcha to stand by his side. That's the best revenge a person could ask for. He has kept a tight lid on the fact that I'm his daughter. I think he fears for my life. Too many people would like to have a shot at the throne. Killing me would increase their chances of getting it. My father feels more secure knowing Caleb is with me. He keeps hinting that he would like a grandchild. I keep telling him that we are nowhere near that stage of the game yet.

I went on birth control. I had to see a *Si* doctor for it. Caleb was disappointed at first, but he's getting used to the idea of spending adult time together first. He keeps asking me how I feel about Pallo, and I keep telling him that I don't know. He is a good man, he loves me, and I know that I love him. I hope that is enough.

The End

Printed in the United States
34287LVS00002B/67-537